ALSO BY SCOTT TUROW

FICTION

Reversible Errors (2002)

Personal Injuries (1999)

The Laws of Our Fathers (1996)

Pleading Guilty (1993)

The Burden of Proof (1990)

Presumed Innocent (1987)

NONFICTION

*Ultimate Punishment:
A Lawyer's Reflections on Dealing with the Death Penalty* (2003)

One L (1977)

★ORDINARY HEROES★

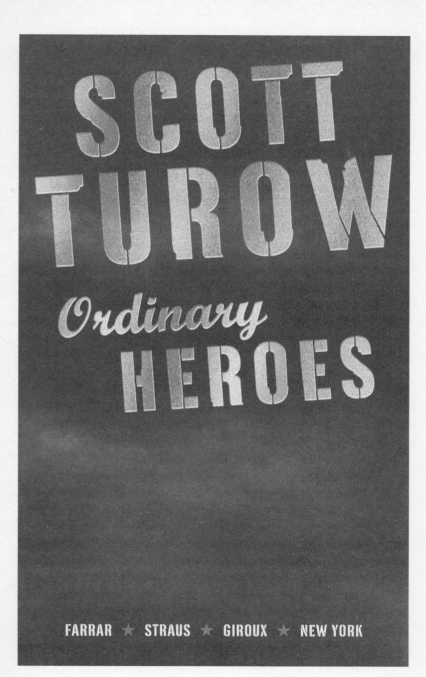

SCOTT TUROW

Ordinary HEROES

FARRAR ★ STRAUS ★ GIROUX ★ NEW YORK

Farrar, Straus and Giroux
19 Union Square West, New York 10003

Copyright © 2005 by Scott Turow
Printed in the United States of America

ISBN -10: 0-7394-6968-1
ISBN -13: 978-0-7394-6968-2

Designed by Abby Kagan

In memory of my father

I.

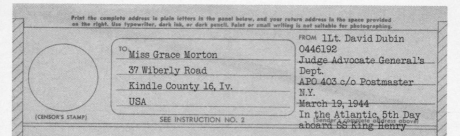

Print the complete address in plain letters in the panel below, and your return address in the space provided
on the right. Use typewriter, dark ink, or dark pencil. Faint or small writing is not suitable for photographing.

TO
Miss Grace Morton

37 Wiberly Road

Kindle County 16, Iv.

USA

FROM 1Lt. David Dubin
0446192
Judge Advocate General's
Dept.
APO 403 c/o Postmaster
N.Y.
March 19, 1944
In the Atlantic, 5th Day
aboard SS King Henry
(Sender's complete address above)

(CENSOR'S STAMP)   SEE INSTRUCTION NO. 2

Dearest Grace--

My sickness is over, and I love you and miss you more than ever! Yesterday I got up feeling fine and ran to breakfast and I have been well ever since. I am beginning to know the routine aboard this commandeered cruise ship, where much of the civilian staff remains on duty--including Indian wallahs who serve the officers in our staterooms. We also have a wonderful band that three or four times a day strikes up sentimental classical numbers in the old first-class dining room, which is still turned out with baubled chandeliers and red velvet drapes. The enlisted men below enjoy many fewer luxuries, but even they know their accommodations are a marked improvement over what they'd get on most of the Navy's old buckets.

With Tchaikovsky on the air, I sometimes forget we are in a war zone and distinctly treacherous waters. Yet with time on my hands, I suppose it's natural that thoughts of what may lie ahead occasionally preoccupy me. During the four days of sickness after we sailed from Boston, I naturally spent long periods on deck. For all the sophistication I like to think I acquired at Easton College and in law school, I am still a Midwestern hick. Until now, I have never been on a body of water broader than the Kindle River, and there have been moments when I've found the vastness of the Atlantic terrifying. Gazing out, I realize how far I have gone from home, how alone I am now, and how immaterial my life is to the oceans, or to most of the people around me.

Of course, with my transfer to the Judge Advocate General's Department, I have much less to fear than when I was training as an infantry officer. The closest I am likely to get to a German is to give advice about his treatment as a POW. I know you and my parents are relieved, as I am, too, but at other moments I feel at sea. (Ho ho!)

I'm not sure why God sets men against each other in war--in fact, I'm no surer than ever that I believe in God. But I know I must do my part. We all must do our parts, you at home and us here. Everything our parents taught us--my parents and your parents, different though they may be--is at stake. I know this war is right. And that is what men--and Americans, especially--do. They fight for what is right in the world, even lay down their lives if that's required. I still feel as I did when I enlisted, that if I did not take up this fight, I would not be a man, as men are. As I must be. There are instants when I

HAVE YOU FILLED IN COMPLETE
ADDRESS AT TOP?

REPLY BY
V····MAIL

HAVE YOU FILLED IN COMPLETE
ADDRESS AT TOP?

POST OFFICE DEPARTMENT PERMIT NO. 1

Print the complete address in plain letters in the panel below, and your return address in the space provided
on the right. Use typewriter, dark ink, or dark pencil. Faint or small writing is not suitable for photographing.

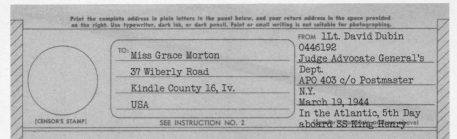

TO: Miss Grace Morton

37 Wiberly Road

Kindle County 16, Iv.

USA

(CENSOR'S STAMP)   SEE INSTRUCTION NO. 2

FROM 1Lt. David Dubin
0446192
Judge Advocate General's
Dept.
APO 403 c/o Postmaster
N.Y.
March 19, 1944
In the Atlantic, 5th Day
aboard SS King Henry

am actually jealous of the soldiers I am traveling with, even when I see them overcome by a sudden vacancy that I know is fear. They are imagining the bullets sizzling at them in their holes, the earthquake and lightning of bombs and artillery. But I envy who they will become in the forge of battle.

I promise you that such insanity passes fleetly and that I'll happily remain a lawyer, not a foot soldier. It is late now and they say there are heavy seas ahead. I should sleep while I can.

Good night, darling. I'll see you in my dreams!

With love forever,

David

★★★

HAVE YOU FILLED IN COMPLETE
ADDRESS AT TOP?

REPLY BY
V---MAIL

HAVE YOU FILLED IN COMPLETE
ADDRESS AT TOP?

POST OFFICE DEPARTMENT PERMIT NO. 1

1. STEWART: ALL PARENTS KEEP SECRETS

All parents keep secrets from their children. My father, it seemed, kept more than most.

The first clue came when Dad passed away in February 2003 at the age of eighty-eight, after sailing into a Bermuda Triangle of illness—heart disease, lung cancer, and emphysema—all more or less attributable to sixty years of cigarettes. Characteristically, my mother refused to leave the burial details to my sister and me and met the funeral director with us. She chose a casket big enough to require a hood ornament, then pondered each word as the mortician read out the proposed death announcement.

"Was David a veteran?" he asked. The undertaker was the cleanest-looking man I'd ever seen, with lacquered nails, shaped eyebrows, and a face so smooth I suspected electrolysis.

"World War II," barked Sarah, who at the age of fifty-two still raced to answer before me.

The funeral director showed us the tiny black rendering of the Stars and Stripes that would appear in the paper beside Dad's name, but my mother was already agitating her thinning gray curls.

"No," she said. "No war. Not for this David Dubin." When she was upset, Mom's English tended to fail her. And my sister and I both knew enough to keep quiet when she was in those moods. The war, except for the bare details of how my father, an American officer, and my mother, an inmate in a German concentration camp, had fallen in love, virtually at first sight, had been an unpleasantness too great for discussion throughout our lives. But I had always assumed the silence was for her sake, not his.

By the end of the mourning visitation, Mom was ready to face sorting through Dad's belongings. Sarah announced she was too pressed to lend a hand and headed back to her accounting practice in Oakland, no doubt relishing the contrast with my unemployment. Mom assigned me to my father's closet on Monday morning, insisting that I consider taking much of his clothing. It was nearly all disastrously out of fashion, and only my mother could envision me, a longtime fatso, ever shrinking enough to squeeze into any of it. I selected a few ties to make her happy and began boxing the rest of his old shirts and suits for donation to the Haven, the Jewish relief agency my mother had helped found decades ago and which she almost single-handedly propelled for nearly twenty years as its Executive Director.

But I was unprepared for the emotion that overtook me. I knew my father as a remote, circumspect man, very orderly in almost everything, brilliant, studious, always civil. He preferred work to social engagements, although he had his own polite charm. Still, his great success came within the mighty fortress of the law. Elsewhere, he was less at ease. He let my mother hold sway at home, making the same weary joke for more than fifty years—he would never, he said, have enough skill as a lawyer to win an argument with Mom.

The Talmud says that a father should draw a son close with one hand and push him away with the other. Dad basically failed on both accounts. I felt a steady interest from him which I took for affection. Compared to many other dads, he was a champ, especially in a generation whose principal ideal of fathering was being a 'good provider.' But he was elusive at the core, almost as if he were wary of letting me know him too well. To the typical challenges I threw out as a kid, he generally responded by retreating, or turning me over to my mother. I have a perpetual memory of the times I was alone with him in the house as a child, infuriated by the silence. Did he know I was there? Or even god-damn care?

Now that Dad was gone, I was intensely aware of everything I'd never settled with him—in many cases, not even started on. Was he sorry I was not a lawyer like he was? What did he make of my daughters? Did he think the world was a good place or bad, and how could he explain the fact that the Trappers, for whom he maintained a resilient passion, had never won the World Series in his lifetime? Children and parents can't get it all sorted out. But it was painful to find that even in death he remained so enigmatic.

And so this business of touching the things my father touched, of smelling his Mennen talcum powder and Canoe aftershave, left me peri-odically swamped by feelings of absence and longing. Handling his per-sonal effects was an intimacy I would never have dared if he were alive. I was in pain but deeply moved every minute and wept freely, burbling in the rear corner of the closet in hopes my mother wouldn't hear me. She herself was yet to shed a tear and undoubtedly thought that kind of iron stoicism was more appropriate to a man of fifty-six.

With the clothing packed, I began looking through the pillar of card-board boxes I'd discovered in a dim corner. There was a remarkable col-lection of things there, many marked by a sentimentality I always thought Dad lacked. He'd kept the schmaltzy valentines Sarah and I had made for him as grade-school art projects, and the Kindle County championship medal he'd won in high school in the backstroke. Dozens of packets of darkening Kodachromes reflected the life of his young family. In the bot-tom box, I found memorabilia of World War II, a sheaf of brittle papers, several red Nazi armbands taken, I imagined, as war trophies, and a curled stack of two-by-two snaps, good little black-and-white photos that must have been shot by someone else since my father was often the sub-ject, looking thin and taciturn. Finally, I came upon a bundle of letters packed in an old candy tin to which a note was tied with a piece of green yarn dulled by time. It was written in a precise hand and dated May 14, 1945.

Dear David,
   I am returning to your family the letters you have sent while you have been overseas. I suppose they may have some

*significance to you in the future. Inasmuch as you are
determined to no longer be a part of my life, I have to accept
that once time passes and my hurt diminishes, they will not mean
anything to me. I'm sure your father has let you know that I
brought your ring back to him last month.*

*For all of this, David, I can't make myself be angry at you for
ending our engagement. When I saw your father, he said that
you were now being court-martialed and actually face prison.
I can hardly believe that about someone like you, but I would
never have believed that you would desert me either. My father
says men are known to go crazy during wartime. But I can't wait
any longer for you to come back to your senses.*

*When I cry at night, David—and I won't pretend for your
sake that I don't—one thing bothers me the most. I spent so
many hours praying to God for Him to deliver you safely; I
begged Him to allow you to live, and if He was especially kind,
to let you come back whole. Now that the fighting there is over,
I cannot believe that my prayers were answered and that I was
too foolish to ask that when you returned, you would be coming
home to me.*

I wish you the best of luck in your present troubles.

Grace

This letter knocked me flat. Court-martialed! The last thing I could
imagine of my tirelessly proper father was being charged with a serious
crime. And a heartbreaker as well. I had never heard a word about any
of these events. But more even than surprise, across the arc of time, like
light emitted by distant stars decades ago, I felt pierced by this woman's
pain. Somehow her incomprehension alloyed itself with my own confusion and disappointment and frustrated love, and instantly inspired a fe-
rocious curiosity to find out what had happened.

Dad's death had come while I was already gasping in one of life's wa-
terfalls. Late the year before, after reaching fifty-five, I had retired early
from the Kindle County *Tribune*, my sole employer as an adult. It was
time. I think I was regarded as an excellent reporter—I had the prizes on

the wall to prove it—but nobody pretended, me least of all, that I had the focus or the way with people to become an editor. By then, I'd been on the courthouse beat for close to two decades. Given the eternal nature of human failings, I felt like a TV critic assigned to watch nothing but reruns. After thirty-three years at the *Trib*, my pension, combined with a generous buyout, was close to my salary, and my collegiate cynicism about capitalism had somehow fed an uncanny knack in the stock market. With our modest tastes, Nona and I wouldn't have to worry about money. While I still had the energy, I wanted to indulge every journalist's fantasy: I was going to write a book.

It did not work out. For one thing, I lacked a subject. Who the hell really cared about the decades-old murder trial of the Chief Deputy Prosecuting Attorney that I'd once thought was such a nifty topic? Instead, three times a day, I found myself staring across the table at Nona, my high-school sweetheart, where it swiftly became apparent that neither of us especially liked what we were seeing. I wish I could cite some melodrama like an affair or death threats to explain what had gone wrong. But the truth is that the handwriting had been on the wall so long, we'd just regarded it as part of the decorating. After thirty years, we had drifted into one of those marriages that never recovered its motive once our daughters were grown. Nine weeks before Dad's passing, Nona and I had separated. We had dinner once each week, where we discussed our business amiably, frustrated one another in the ways we always had, and exhibited no signs of longing or second thoughts. Our daughters were devastated, but I figured we both deserved some credit for having the guts to hope for better at this late date.

Nevertheless, I was already feeling battered before Dad died. By the time we buried him, I was half inclined to jump into the hole beside him. Sooner or later, I knew I'd pick myself up and go on. I'd been offered freelance gigs at two magazines, one local, one national. At five foot nine and 215 pounds, I am not exactly a catch, but the expectations of middle age are much kinder to men than women, and there were already signs that I'd find companionship, if and when I was ready.

For the moment, though, out of work and out of love, I was far more interested in taking stock. My life was like everybody else's. Some things had gone well, some hadn't. But right now I was focused on the failures, and they seemed to have started with my father.

And so that Monday, while my mother thought I was struggling into Dad's trousers, I remained in his closet and read through dozens of his wartime letters, most of them typed Army V-mails, which had been microfilmed overseas and printed out by the post office at home. I stopped only when Mom called from the kitchen, suggesting I take a break. I found her at the oval drop-leaf table, which still bore the marks of the thousands of family meals eaten there during the 1950s.

"Did you know Dad was engaged before he met you?" I asked from the doorway.

She revolved slowly. She had been drinking tea, sipping it through a sugar cube she clenched between her gapped front teeth, a custom still retained from the shtetl. The brown morsel that remained was set on the corner of her saucer.

"Who told you that?"

I described Grace's letter. Proprietary of everything, Mom demanded to see it at once. At the age of eighty, my mother remained a pretty woman, paled by age, but still with even features and skin that was notably unwithered. She was a shrimp—I always held her to blame that I had not ended up as tall as my father—but people seldom saw her that way because of the aggressive force of her intelligence, like someone greeting you in sword and armor. Now, Mom studied Grace Morton's letter with an intensity that seemed as if it could, at any instant, set the page aflame. Her expression, when she put it down, might have shown the faintest influence of a smile.

"Poor girl," she said.

"Did you know about her?"

"'Know'? I suppose. It was long over by the time I met your father, Stewart. This was wartime. Couples were separated for years. Girls met other fellows. Or vice versa. You've heard, no, of Dear John letters?"

"But what about the rest of this? A court-martial? Did you know Dad was court-martialed?"

"Stewart, I was in a concentration camp. I barely spoke English. There had been some legal problem at one point, I think. It was a misunderstanding."

"'Misunderstanding'? This says they wanted to send him to prison."

"Stewart, I met your father, I married your father, I came here with him in 1946. From this you can see that he did not go to prison."

"But why didn't he mention this to me? I covered every major criminal case in Kindle County for twenty years, Mom. I talked to him about half of those trials. Wouldn't you think at some point he'd have let on that he was once a criminal defendant himself?"

"I imagine he was embarrassed, Stewart. A father wants his son's admiration."

For some reason this response was more frustrating than anything yet. If my father was ever concerned about my opinion of him, it had eluded me. Pushed again toward tears, I sputtered out my enduring lament. He was such a goddamn crypt of a human being! How could Dad have lived and died without letting me really know him?

There was never a second in my life when I have doubted my mother's sympathies. I know she wished I'd grown up a bit more like my father, with a better damper on my emotions, but I could see her absorb my feelings in a mom's way, as if soaked up from the root. She emitted a freighted Old World sigh.

"Your father," she said, stopping to pick a speck of sugar off her tongue and to reconsider her words. Then, she granted the only acknowledgment she ever has of what I faced with him. "Stewart," she said, "your father sometimes had a difficult relationship with himself."

I spirited Dad's letters out of the house that day. Even at my age, I found it easier to deceive my mother than to confront her. And I needed time to ponder what was there. Dad had written colorfully about the war. Yet there was an air of unexpressed calamity in his correspondence, like the spooky music that builds in a movie soundtrack before something goes wrong. He maintained a brave front with Grace Morton, but by the time he suddenly broke off their relationship in February 1945, his life as a soldier seemed to have shaken him in a fundamental way, which I instantly connected to his court-martial.

More important, that impression reinforced a lifetime suspicion that had gone unvoiced until now: something had *happened* to my father. In the legal world, if a son is to judge, Dad was widely admired. He was the General Counsel of Moreland Insurance for fifteen years, and was renowned for his steadiness, his quiet polish, and his keen ability in lasering his way through the infinite complications of insurance law. But he had a private life like everybody else, and at home a dour aura of trauma always clung to him. There were the smokes he couldn't give up, and the three fingers of scotch he bolted down each night like medicine, so he could get four or five hours of sleep before he was rocked awake by unwanted dreams. Family members sometimes commented that as a younger man he had been more outspoken. My grandmother's theory, which she rarely kept to herself, was that Gilda, my mother, had largely taken David's tongue by always speaking first and with such authority. But he went through life as if a demon had a hand on his shoulder, holding him back.

Once when I was a boy, he saw me nearly run over as a car screamed around the corner, barely missing me where I was larking with friends on my bike. Dad snatched me up by one arm from the pavement and carried me that way until he could throw me down on our lawn. Even so young, I understood he was angrier about the panic I'd caused him than the danger I'd posed to myself.

Now the chance to learn what had troubled my father became a quest. As a reporter, I was fabled for my relentlessness, the Panting Dog School of Journalism, as I described it, in which I pursued my subjects until they dropped. I obtained a copy of Dad's 201, his Army personnel file, from the National Personnel Records Center in St. Louis, and with that fired off several letters to the Defense Department and the National Archives. By July, the chief clerk for the Army Judiciary in Alexandria, Virginia, confirmed that she had located the record of my father's court-martial. Only after I had paid to have it copied did she write back stating that the documents had now been embargoed as classified, not by the Army, but by, of all agencies, the CIA.

The claim that my father did anything sixty years ago that deserved to be regarded as a national security matter today was clearly preposterous. I unleashed a barrage of red-hot faxes, phone calls, letters, and e-mails to various Washington offices that attracted all the interest of spam. Eventually, my Congressman, Stan Sennett, an old friend, worked out an arrangement in which the government agreed to let me see a few documents from the court-martial, while the CIA reconsidered the file's secret status.

So in August 2003, I traveled to the Washington National Records

Center, in Suitland, Maryland. The structure looks a little like an aircraft carrier in dry dock, a low redbrick block the size of forty football fields. The public areas within are confined to a single corridor whose decor is pure government, the equivalent of sensible shoes: brick walls, ceilings of acoustic tile, and an abundance of fluorescent light. There I was allowed to read—but not to copy—about ten pages that had been withdrawn from the Record of Proceedings compiled in 1945 by the trial judge advocate, the court-martial prosecutor. The sheets had faded to manila and had the texture of wallpaper, but they still glimmered before me like treasure. Finally, I was going to know.

I had told myself I was ready for anything, and what was actually written could hardly have been more matter-of-fact, set out in the deliberately neutral language of the law, further straitjacketed by military terminology. But reading, I felt like I'd been dropped on my head. Four counts had been brought against Dad, the specifications for each charge pointing to the same incident. In October 1944, my father, acting Assistant Staff Judge Advocate of the Third Army, had been directed to investigate allegations by General Roland Teedle of the 18th Armored Division concerning the possible court-martial of Major Robert Martin. Martin was attached to the Special Operations Branch of the Office of Strategic Services, the OSS, the forerunner of the CIA, which had been founded during World War II (accounting, I figured, for why the Agency had stuck its nose in now). Dad was ordered to arrest Major Martin in November 1944. Instead, in April 1945, near Hechingen, Germany, my father had taken custody of Martin, where, according to the specifications, Dad "deliberately allowed Martin to flee, at great prejudice to the security and well-being of the United States." Nor was that just rhetoric. The most serious charge, willful disobedience of a superior officer, was punishable by execution.

A weeklong trial ensued in June 1945. At the start, the count that could have led to a firing squad had been dismissed, but the three charges remaining carried a potential sentence of thirty years. As to them, I found another discolored form labeled JUDGMENT.

The court was opened and the president announced that the accused was guilty of all specifications and charges of Charges II, III, and IV; further that upon secret written ballot, two-thirds of the members present concurring, accused is sentenced to five years' confinement in the United States Penitentiary at Fort Leavenworth at hard labor, and to be dishonorably discharged from the U.S. Army forthwith, notice of his discharge to be posted at the place of his abode.

I read this sheet several times, hoping to make it mean something else. My heart and hands were ice. My father was a felon.

Dad's conviction was quickly affirmed by the Board of Review for the European Theater—the Army equivalent of an appellate court—leaving General Teedle free to carry out the sentence. Instead, in late July 1945, the General revoked the charges he himself had brought. He simply checked off a box on a form without a word of explanation. But it was not a clerical error. The court-martial panel was reconvened by the General's order the next week and issued a one-line finding taking back everything they had done only a month and a half earlier. My father, who had been under house arrest since April, was freed.

The blanks in this tale left me wild with curiosity, feeling like Samson chained blind inside the temple. The Army, the CIA, no one was going to keep me from answering a basic question of heritage: Was I the son of a convict who'd betrayed his country and slipped away on some technicality, or, perhaps, the child of a man who'd endured a primitive injustice which he'd left entombed in the past?

I filled out innumerable government forms and crossed the continent several times as I pieced things together, visiting dozens of document storage sites and military libraries. The most productive trips of all were to Connecticut, where I ultimately acquired the records of Barrington Leach, the lawyer who'd defended my father unsuccessfully at Dad's trial before General Teedle revoked the charges.

Almost as soon as my travels started, I became determined to set down my father's tale. Dad was the only member of the Judge Advocate General's Department court-martialed during World War II, and that was but a small part of what made his experiences distinctive. I toiled happily in the dark corridors of libraries and archives and wrote through half the night. This was going to make not only a book, but *my* book, and a great book, a book which, like the corniest deus ex machina, would elevate my life from the current valley to a peak higher than any I'd achieved before. And then, like the cross-examiners in the criminal courtrooms I had covered for so many years, I made the cardinal mistake, asked one question too many and discovered the single fact, the only conceivable detail, that could scoop me of my father's story.

He had written it himself.

2. DAVID: REGARDING THE CHARGES AGAINST ME

CONFIDENTIAL
ATTORNEY-CLIENT COMMUNICATION

TO: Lieutenant Colonel Barrington Leach, Deputy Associate Judge
Advocate, Headquarters, European Theater of Operations, U.S.
Army (ETOUSA)

FROM: Captain David Dubin

RE: The Charges Against Me

DATE: May 5, 1945

I have decided to follow your suggestion to set down the major details
I recall regarding my investigation of Major Robert Martin of OSS
and the ensuing events which will shortly bring me before this court-
martial. Since I have no desire to discuss this with another soul, including
you as my lawyer, I find writing a more palatable alternative, even while

I admit that my present inclination is not to show you a word of this. I know my silence frustrates you, making you think I lack a full appreciation for my circumstances, but rest assured that the prospect of a firing squad has caught my attention. Yet as a member of the JAG Department who has both prosecuted and defended hundreds of general courts-martial in the year or so I have been overseas, I am fully convinced that I have nothing to say for myself. General Teedle charges that last month in Hechingen I willfully suffered Major Martin to escape from my lawful custody. And that is true. I did. I let Martin go. I intend to plead guilty because I am guilty. The reasons I freed Martin are irrelevant in the eyes of the law and, candidly, my own business. Let me assure you, however, that telling the whole story would not improve my situation one whit.

I may as well start by exp'anding on some of the information I routinely request of my own clients. I am a Midwesterner, born in 1915 in the city of DuSable in Kindle County. Both my parents were immigrants, each hailing from small towns in western Russia. Neither was educated beyond grade school. My father has worked since age fourteen as a cobbler, and owns a small shop a block from the three-flat where they raised my older sister, my younger brother, and me.

I was a good student in high school, and also won the Kindle County championship in the hundred-yard backstroke. This combination led me to receive a full scholarship to Easton College. Easton is only about twenty miles from my parents' apartment, but a world apart, the long-time training ground of the genteel elite of the Tri-Cities. As a man whose parents' greatest dream was for their children to become 'real Americans,' I embraced Easton in every aspect, right down to the raccoon coat, ukulele, and briar pipe. I graduated Phi Beta Kappa, and then entered Easton's esteemed law school. Afterward, I was lucky enough to find work in the legal department of Moreland Insurance. My parents pointed out that I appeared to be the first Jew Moreland had hired outside the mail room, but I'd always endeavored not to look at things that way.

For two years, I tried small personal-injury lawsuits in the Municipal Court, but in September 1942, I enlisted. No one who cared about me approved. Both my parents and my sweetheart, Grace Morton, wanted me to wait out the draft, hoping against hope that I'd be missed, or at least limit my time in the path of danger. But I was no longer willing to put off doing my part.

I had met Grace three years earlier, when I fit her for a pair of pumps in the shoe section of Morton's Department Store, where I'd earned pocket money throughout college and law school. In her round-collared sweaters and tiny pearls and pleated skirts, Grace was the image of the all-American girl. But what most attracted me was not her blonde bob or her demure manner so much as her high-mindedness. She is the best-intentioned soul I have ever met. Grace worked as a schoolteacher in the tough North End and waited several months before letting on that her family owned the department store where I'd first encountered her. When I decided to enter the service, I proposed, so that we could remain together, at least while I was posted Stateside. She instantly agreed, but our marriage plans set off a storm in both families that could be calmed only by postponing the wedding.

After basic training at Fort Riley, I entered Officers Candidate School in the infantry at Fort Benning in Georgia. I was commissioned a Second Lieutenant on April 6, 1943. Two days later, I was transferred forthwith to the Judge Advocate General's Department. I had just turned twenty-eight, making me eligible for JAGD, and some thoughtful superior had put me in for reassignment. In essential Army style, no one asked what I preferred, and I probably don't know the answer to this day. Still ambivalent, I was sent to the stately quadrangle of the University of Michigan Law School to learn about the Articles of War. My graduation in the upper half of my class made my promotion to First Lieutenant automatic.

When I entered the JAG Department, I had requested service in the Pacific, thinking I was more likely to get within the vicinity of active combat, but in August 1943, I was sent to Fort Barkley, Texas, for a period of apprenticeship, so-called applicatory training as the Assistant Judge Advocate at the camp. I spent most of my time explaining legal options to soldiers who'd received Dear Johns from their wives and, as an odd counterpoint, sorting out the many conflicting Dependency Benefit Claims the Army had received from the five women a soldier named Joe Hark had married at his five prior postings, each without benefit of any intervening divorce.

In March 1944, I was at last reassigned overseas, but to the Central Base Station in London, rather than the Pacific. I was fortunate, however, to come under the command of Colonel Halley Maples. He was in his late fifties, and the picture of a lawyer, more than six feet tall, lean, with graying hair and a broad mustache. He seemed to hold a high opinion of me, probably because I, like him, was a graduate of Easton University Law School. Sometime in July, only a few weeks after D-Day, the Colonel was designated as the Staff Judge Advocate for the newly forming Third Army, and I was delighted when he asked me to serve as his acting assistant. I crossed the Channel on August 16, 1944, aboard the USS *Holland*, finally coming within the proximity of war.

The staff judge advocates were part of Patton's rear-echelon headquarters, and we traveled in the General's wake as the Third Army flashed across Europe. It was an advantageous assignment. We did none of the fighting, but time and again entered the French villages and towns jubilantly celebrating their liberation after years of Nazi occupation. From atop the beds of half-ton trucks and armored troop carriers, the infantrymen tossed cigarettes and chocolates to the crowds while the French uncorked bottles of wine hidden from the Germans for years and lavished kisses on us, more, alas, from whiskery old men than willing girls.

In the liberated towns, there was seldom any clear authority, while dozens of French political parties squabbled for power. Locals clustered about the police station and our military headquarters, seeking travel passes or trying to find the sons and fathers who'd been carried off by the Germans. The windows of stores purveying Nazi goods and propaganda were smashed with paving stones, while the cross of Lorraine, symbol of the French resistance, was painted over every swastika that could not be removed. Collaborators were routed out by mobs. In Brou, I saw a barmaid set upon by six or seven youths in resistance armbands who cut off all her hair as punishment for sleeping with Nazis. She endured her shearing with a pliancy that might not have been much different from the way she'd accepted her German suitors. She said nothing, merely wept and sat absolutely still, except for one arm that moved entirely on its own, bucking against her side like the wing of some domesticated fowl engaged in a futile attempt at flight.

Patton was concerned that the chaotic atmosphere would affect our troops and looked to Colonel Maples and his staff to reinforce discipline. I and my counterpart, Anthony Eisley, a squat young captain from Dayton who had practiced law in his father's firm for several years, were assigned to try the large number of general courts-martial which were arising for fairly serious offenses—murder, rape, assault, major thefts, and insubordination—many of these crimes committed against French civilians. In other commands, these cases, especially the defense of the accused, were handled by line officers as an auxiliary duty, but Colonel Maples wanted lawyers trained in the Articles of War dealing with matters that could end in stiff prison sentences or, even, hanging.

The principal impediment in carrying out our assignment was that we had barely set up court when we were on the move again, as Patton's Army rampaged at an unprecedented pace across France. Columns raced through territory even before navigators could post the maps at headquarters. We tried men for their lives in squad tents, with the testimony often inaudible as bombers buzzed overhead and howitzers thundered.

I felt grateful to be at the forefront of history, or at least close to it, and appreciated Colonel Maples as a commander. In the Army officers corps, being built on the double, it was not uncommon, even in the upper ranks, to find commanders who had never so much as fired a rifle in combat, but Maples was not merely a distinguished lawyer who'd risen to the pinnacle of a famous St. Louis firm, but also a veteran of the Great War, which had taken him through many of these towns.

In early September, headquarters moved again to Marson, from La Chaume, bringing us across the Marne. The Colonel asked me to drive with him in search of the field where he had survived the most intense battle he'd fought in. It was a pasture now, but Maples recognized a long stone fence that separated this ground from the neighbor's. He had been a twenty-five-year-old second lieutenant dug into one of the slit trenches that ran across this green land, no more than one hundred yards from the Germans.

There had been more fighting here again lately. In the adjoining woods, artillery rounds had brought down many of the trees, and tank tracks had ripped into the earth. The dead personnel and spent matériel had been cleared away, but there were still several animals, cows and military horses, bloated and reeking and swarming with flies. Yet it was the battles of a quarter century ago which appeared to hold the Colonel. As we walked along the devastated field, he recalled a friend who had popped out to relieve himself and been shot through the head.

"Died like that, with his drawers around his knees, and fell back into the latrine. It was terrible. It was all terrible," he said and looked at me.

Beyond the fence on the neighbor's side, in a narrow culvert, we found a dead German soldier facedown in the water. One hand was on the bank, now withered with a bare leathery husk over what would soon be a skeleton. He was the first dead man I'd seen on a battlefield, and the Colonel studied the corpse for quite some time while I contended with my thumping heart.

"Thank God," he said then.

"Sir?"

"I thank the Lord, David, I shall be too old to come to this place again in war."

Back in the jeep, I asked, "Do you think we might have to fight another World War soon, sir?" Eisley, my courtroom colleague, believed that war with the Soviets was all but inevitable and might begin even before we'd mustered out. The Colonel greeted the idea with exceptional gravity.

"It must not happen, Dubin," he said, as if imparting the most consequential order. "It must not."

By the end of September, Patton's sprint across Europe had come to a virtual stop. Our armored divisions had outraced their supply lines, and the dusty tanks and half-tracks sat immobile awaiting fuel, while the weather turned from bright to gloomy, soon giving way to the wettest fall on record. The front stretched on a static line about ten miles south of the Vosges Mountains. In the interval, infantry replaced the armor and dug themselves into foxholes which, in an echo of the Great War, were only a couple hundred yards from those of the enemy. The Krauts reportedly hurled nighttime taunts. "Babe Ruth is Schwarz-black. Black niggers is at home fucking with your wife." We had plenty of German speakers in our ranks, kids from New York and Cincinnati and Milwaukee, who shouted out their own observations about the puniness of Hitler's balls, hidden under his dress.

The stall allowed the administrative staff, including the judge advocates, to make our first durable headquarters in Nancy early in October. As a student of French in high school, I seemed to have acquired the impression that there was only one city to speak of in that country. But Nancy's center had been erected in the eighteenth century by a king without a country, Stanislas Leszczynski, later to become Duke of Lorraine, with a grandeur and panache equal to my images of Paris. Patton's forward headquarters was in the Palais du Gouverneur, a royal residence at the end of a tree-lined arcade that resembled pictures I'd seen of the Tuileries. Our offices, along with other rear elements, were about a fifteen-minute walk across town, in the Lycée Henri Poincaré, the oldest school in Nancy.

To process the backlog of cases that had collected as we were trying to keep up with Patton, Colonel Maples asked the personnel nabobs in G-1 to appoint two standing courts-martial. They ultimately assigned nine officers to each, allowing the members to attend to other duties on alternate days. Eisley and I, however, were in court seven days a week, ten hours a day. To break the routine we agreed to rotate roles as the prosecuting trial judge advocate, and as counsel for the accused.

The military tribunal was set up in the former party room of the school, where three dormitory dining tables had been pushed together. At the center was the most senior officer serving as president of the court-martial, flanked by four junior officers on either side. At the far left, Eisley or I would sit with our client, and on the opposite end whoever that day was the TJA. In the center of the room, a table of stenographers worked, taking down the testimony, while a single straight-backed chair was reserved for the witness. The president of one panel was Lieutenant Colonel Harry Klike, a bluff little prewar noncom who'd risen through the Quartermaster Corps and was determined to exhibit the cultivation he believed appropriate for an officer and gentleman. Each day's session ended with Klike officiously announcing, "The court-martial stands adjourned until zero eight hundred tomorrow, when we will reconvene to dispense with justice." No one, as I recall, had the heart to correct him.

We proceeded with dispatch and often finished two or even three cases in a day. In need of a break when court adjourned, Eisley and I often strolled down the rue Gambetta to the magnificent Place Stanislas, with its ornate state buildings and elaborate gates tipped in gold. At a café on the square we sipped cognac and eyed the good women of the town, with their wedgies and upswept hairdos. Tony, married but at full liberty three thousand miles away, praised the imagination of French women and their rugged lovemaking style. I listened without comment, while the *patron* tried to shoo the French kids who appeared beside our table with cupped hands, all of them the master of at least one line of English: "Some gum, chum?"

Out on the avenue, long military columns passed, coming from or going to the front. The hardest-hit units on the way back passed with little expression, grimy, embittered hangdog men, on whom the wages of war were posted like a sign. Cordons of ambulances sometimes raced through, carrying the wounded to the local field hospital. But the replacement troops headed for battle made the most unsettling sight. A hush often came over the streets while the soldiers stared down at us from the trucks. In their faces you could see their desperation and anger about the cruel lottery that left us secure and them facing mortal danger. At those moments, I often found myself thinking uneasily about the way the Third Army's successes were described around headquarters using the word 'we.'

Eventually, Tony and I would begin preparing for the coming day. When the crimes involved attacks on local residents we would go out to jointly interview the witnesses. With the benefit of my high-school French, I read well and could understand, but spoke with more difficulty. Nonetheless, I had improved considerably in my two months on the Continent, and allowing for the grace of hand gestures, we could usually make our way through these meetings without a translator.

The MP who drove us most days, Staff Sergeant Gideon Bidwell, was called Biddy, a shortened version of the nickname Iddy Biddy he'd been awarded by the usual boot-camp smart alecks. He was as wide at the shoulder as a bus seat and at least six foot two, with curly black hair and a pink face holding a broad nose and green eyes. Bidwell was highly competent, but in a cheerless way. He was one of those enlisted men who realize that they are the true Army, whose jobs consist of winning the war at the same time that they keep the officers from making fools of themselves. He hauled the gear, and drove the jeep, and turned the map so I had it going in the right direction, but with a sullen air that made him somewhat unapproachable. When he had picked me up in Cherbourg where I landed, I recognized the sounds of Georgia in his speech, after my time at Fort Benning, but in response to my questions, he said only that his folks had left Georgia several years ago. He remained generally closemouthed about himself, not outwardly insubordinate, but with a sour look tending to indicate he didn't care much for anyone. I sensed that sooner or later we were going to clash.

One evening, we stopped at the stockade so I could interview my client for the next day's proceedings. Biddy was with me as we entered the doubled-wire perimeter, where three long lines of pup tents were erected in abnormally tight formation. When my client shuffled out of the guardhouse in his ankle irons and manacles, Biddy buried a heavy groan in his chest.

"Why they always colored?" he asked himself, but loud enough for me to hear. Enough of Georgia seemed to have come North with Bidwell that I preferred not to hear his answer. I gave him a bit of a look, at which he stiffened, but he had the good sense to turn away.

Oddly, Biddy's remark provoked me to ponder his question, albeit from another angle. Given my sympathies for the French families who appeared so often as the victims in our courtrooms, it had not even struck me much at first that many of the soldiers being sentenced to long terms in disciplinary barracks were colored. Yet Biddy was right, at least about the pattern, and the next time I found myself alone with Colonel Maples, I asked why he thought Negroes appeared so frequently among the troops we prosecuted.

"Negroes?" Maples looked at me sharply. "What in the world are you suggesting, Dubin? There are plenty in the stockade who are white." There surely were. Lots of soldiers had ended up in the Army only because a sentencing judge had given them that option rather than prison. Men who were strong-arm robbers and drug fiends at home did not always change their stripes, even on the battlefield. "Do you doubt these boys are guilty?"

In most of the cases I handled, the soldiers were sober by the time I saw them and entered abashed guilty pleas. And the crimes with which they were charged were seldom minor. A few days ago, I had been the prosecutor of a colored soldier who literally knocked the door down at a girl's house, when she refused him; he'd had his way with her only after beating both her parents brutally. It puzzled me that the colored troops had generally maintained such good order in England, but were losing discipline on the Continent.

"They're guilty, sir, no question. But thinking about it, I've found my-self wondering, sir, if we're as understanding of the colored troops."

I did not need to mention any particular incidents, because that week we had evaluated the case of a decorated officer who'd been on the front since D-Day. As he'd watched a line of German prisoners marching past, he'd suddenly raised his carbine and begun shooting, killing three and wounding four others. His sole explanation was, "I didn't like the way they were looking at me." Colonel Maples had decided that we would seek a sentence of only three years.

"These Negro boys aren't in combat, Dubin, not for the most part. We can't treat them as we do the men who've been through that." I could have pointed out that the colored battalions weren't generally given the option, but I felt I had gone far enough. "It's liquor and women, Dubin," the Colonel added. "You're a smart man to stay clear of liquor and women."

I could tell my questions had troubled the Colonel, and I wasn't surprised two days later when he called me into his office. It was the for-mer quarters of the school prefect, a room of tall antique cabinets in mel-low oak.

"Listen, Dubin, I don't know how to say this, so I'll just come out with it. About your remarks to me the other day? You'd best be careful with that sort of thing, man. You don't want people to think you're the wrong kind of Jew. Is that too plain?"

"Of course not." In truth, I received the Colonel's remark with the usual clotted feelings references to my heritage inevitably provoked. My parents were Socialists who disparaged religious practice. Thus for me, the principal meaning of being a Jew was as something people reliably held against me, a barrier to overcome. I had labored my whole life to believe in a land of equals where everyone deserved to be greeted by only one label—American.

The Army did not always appear to see it that way. I was a week into basic training before I found out that the 'H' on my dog tags meant 'Hebrew,' which irritated me no end since the Italians and Irish were not branded with an 'I.' But the armed forces were awash in bias. The en-listed men could not talk to one another without epithets. Spic, Polack, dago, Mick, cracker, hick, Okie, mackerel-snapper. Everybody got it.

Not to mention the coloreds and the Orientals, whom the Army preferred not even to let in. The JAG Department's officers, however, were primarily well-bred Episcopalians and Presbyterians with excellent manners who did not engage in crude insults. Colonel Maples had gone out of his way to make clear he harbored no prejudice, once saying to me that when we got to Berlin, he planned to march up to the Reichstag with the word 'Jude' written on his helmet. But his remark now was a reminder that my colleagues' silence about my ancestry did not mean any of them had forgotten it.

A few days later, the Colonel again asked to see me.

"Perhaps you need a break from these courts-martial day in and day out," he said. "Quite a grind, isn't it?"

Given what the soldiers at the front put up with, I would never have taken the liberty to complain, but the Colonel was right. There was not much about my daily activities that would lift the spirits, sending boys who'd come here to risk their lives for their country to a military prison instead. But the Colonel had a plan to give all of us a breather. Eisley would switch places for a couple of weeks with Major Haggerty, the Deputy Staff Judge Advocate, who had been reviewing convictions and providing legal advice as the law member on one of the panels. As for me, I was to conduct a Rule 35 investigation, looking into the potential court-martial of an officer.

"There's a bit of a problem on the General staff. The Brits have a word: 'kerfuffle.' Lord, I miss the Brits. The way they speak the language! Fellows made me howl several times a day. But that's what there is, a kerfuffle. I assume you've heard of Roland Teedle." General Teedle was a virtual legend, often said to be Patton's favorite among the brigadier generals. His 18th Armored Division had been at the forefront of the charge across France. "Teedle's gotten himself into a state of high dudgeon about some OSS major who's been operating on his flank. How much do you know about the OSS, Dubin?"

Not much more than I'd read in the paper. "Spies and commandos," I said.

"That's about right," said the Colonel. "And certainly true of this particular fellow. Major Robert Martin. Sort of an expatriate. Fought in Spain for the Republicans. Was living in Paris when the Nazis overran it. OSS recruited him, apparently, and he's done quite well. He's been on

the Continent since sometime in 1942. Ran an Operational Group behind German lines—a collection of Allied spies and French resistance
forces who sabotaged Nazi operations. After D-Day, he and his people
were placed under Teedle's command. They derailed supply trains, am-
bushed German scouts, gave the Nazis fits while the 18th was bearing
down on them."

I said that Martin sounded brave.

"Damn brave," said Maples. "No doubt of that. A hero, frankly. He's
won the Distinguished Service Cross. And the Silver Star twice. And
that doesn't count the ribbons de Gaulle has pinned on his chest."

"Jesus," I said before I could think.

The Colonel nodded solemnly during the brief silence, one that often fell among soldiers when they faced the evidence of another man's
courage. We all had the same thought then: Could I do that?

"But you see," the Colonel said, "it's one of those devilish ironies.
Probably what's led to Martin's troubles. He's been a lone wolf too long,
really. He has no fear. Not just of the enemy. But of his own command.
The Army is not a place for individualists." I could tell that the Colonel
had spent time thinking about this case. He smoothed the edges of his
broad mustache before he continued. "I don't have the details. That's
your job. But Teedle claims that Martin's defied his orders. Several times
now. Says Martin is just sitting out in some château leading the life of
Riley and thumbing his nose. Apparently there's a girl involved."

The Colonel paused then, presumably reconsidering his frequent
reminders that women and warriors were a bad mix.

"At any rate," he said, "there's to be a Rule thirty-five investigation.
Follow the manual. Interview Martin. Interview the General. Talk to the
witnesses. Do formal examinations. Prepare a report. And be diplomatic.
Formally, a junior officer shouldn't be interviewing his superiors. I'm trusting you, David, not to ruffle feathers. Remember, you act in my name."

"Yes, sir."

"G-1 is hoping that this Major Martin will see the light when he rec-
ognizes that matters are turning serious. An actual court-martial would
be tragic, frankly. Teedle and this fellow Martin—both are very fine soldiers, Dubin. General Patton hates that kind of catfight. Bring Martin to
his senses, if you can. But watch yourself. Don't forget that at the end of
the day, Roland's the one who's going to have Patton's ear."

The Colonel came around his desk to put a hand on my shoulder, and with it I felt the weight of his avuncular affection for me.

"I thought you'd enjoy this break, David. Get you a little closer to the front. Something's bound to start happening there again any day. I know you'd like that. And there may not be much more chance. Word is that Monty's bet Ike a fiver that the war here will be over before the New Year. Now that would make a fine Christmas present for all of us, wouldn't it?"

He was beaming until something froze his features, the realization, I suspect, that Christmas meant far more to him than to me. But I answered, "Yes, sir," in my most enthusiastic manner and issued a brisk salute before going off to find out whatever I needed to about Major Robert Martin.

3. DAVID: THE GENERAL

The 18th Armored Division had made camp about twenty-five miles north and east of Nancy, not far from Arracourt, where they were enjoying a period of rest and recovery. When Biddy and I showed up at the motor pool for a jeep to proceed to our interview with General Teedle, we were told that because of severe supply discipline with gasoline, we would have to squeeze in four boys from the 134th Infantry who'd missed their convoy. The 134th was relieving troops on the XII Corps front and these soldiers, who'd already seen their share of combat, made glum traveling companions. A private sitting behind me, a boy named Duck from Kentucky, struck up a few verses of "Mairzy Doats," until his buddies finally became spirited about one thing—that Duck should shut the hell up.

The air remained sodden, and approaching the front the bleakness went beyond the weather, clinging to the soldiers trudging down the roads. The signs of the recent battles were all about. The earth was scorched and rutted, and the picturesque French farmhouses, with their thatched roofs that made them look like something out of "Hansel and Gretel," were mostly in ruins. Even the ones that had fared relatively well were usually open to the top, looking like a man without his hat. Timbers lay strewn on the ground and often all that remained of a structure that had been home to a family for decades, even centuries, was the whitewashed chimney or a lone wall. The debris had been bulldozed to the side of the road, but every now and then there were disturbing tokens of the civilian casualties, a decapitated doll, wounded like its human counterparts, or a coat without a sleeve.

Given the conditions of the roads, it took us several hours to reach the 18th. They had spread out across the drier ground on the downslopes of several vast bean and hay fields. Having dealt with the claims for the land our troops trampled in England, I could only imagine the joy of the French farmer who would now get compensation for the use of land on which his crops were already drowned.

The 18th Armored Division had been the heroes of every newsreel we'd seen for months, the troops who'd dashed across France and were going to chase Hitler into some hole in Berlin and shoot a mortar down it for good riddance. There was a bold air here and loud voices after having survived the front. While Patton waited for fuel, ordnance, and rations, he had ordered many of the infantry divisions into intensive training, but for the 18th, with its tanks and mobile artillery, the strict conservation of gasoline left them with little to do each day but clean their weapons and write long letters home.

Crossing the camp with our packs, looking for Teedle's HQ, Biddy and I drew resentful stares. Our uniforms were still fresh, not grease-stained or torn, and our helmets lacked the mottled camouflage nets handed out for combat. Once or twice we passed soldiers who made a chicken squawk behind us, but Biddy's sheer size was enough to stifle most of the insults I was used to hearing tossed down from the troop convoys that passed through Nancy.

Rather than commandeer a house in town for himself, as other generals might have done, Teedle had remained with his men in a large tent that served combat-style as both his billet and headquarters. The heavy blackout flaps had been raised in daytime. Inside, a board floor had been installed in sections, and there were several desks, two of them face-to-face, where a couple of corporals were pounding away at Remingtons. Another, larger desk was unoccupied beside a frame cot which was certainly the General's. Two footlockers were stacked there with a kerosene lamp atop them for nighttime reading.

I approached the first of the two corporals, who was working with a pencil clenched between his teeth, and gave my name and unit. He was a very thin fellow with a wry look and he began to rise. I said, "At ease," but he tossed off a quick salute from his seat.

"Corporal Billy Bonner, Paragraph Trooper in the Armchair Division."

"Oh, isn't that cute?" said the second corporal, without looking up from his work. "Bonner's going back to burlesque when the war is over." Bonner addressed the other corporal as 'Frank,' and told him to shut up. They bickered for a moment.

"Well, then just don't talk to me at *all*," Frank concluded. His voice was high and he gave his head a dramatic toss. I exchanged a look with Biddy, who had remained at the tent opening. No need to ask why that one wasn't in combat.

In frustration, Bonner arose and limped toward Biddy, waving me along. Bonner proved chummy enough that I felt free to ask about his leg. He'd been shot at Anzio, he said, and had opted to become a clerk rather than go home. The reward for his dedication, he said, was working beside Frank. "Welcome to the Army," he added. Listening to him, I remembered a sergeant in basic training who'd warned me not to tell anybody I could type, good advice as Bonner could now attest.

The Corporal had just finished explaining that Teedle was due back momentarily from an inspection of forward installations, when he caught sight of the General and scurried to his desk like a schoolchild.

I snapped to attention as Teedle stormed past us. A private from the Signal Corps was trailing him, hauling the body of a huge radio telephone while Teedle screamed into the handset, alternately venting at the poor fellow at the other end and at the signal man, whenever the sound faded.

"Tell him that I have two battalions down to one ration a day. No, damn it. *Two* battalions, one ration. *One* ration. An army moves on its stomach. Ask him if he's heard that one. If the Nazis kill these boys it's one thing, but I'll be damned before I see their country starve them to death." I'd heard that the frontline troops were often hungry. In the officers' mess in Nancy, food was plentiful—canned goods, pastries with honey, tea, Nescafé. Midday meals were often huge. The meat and poultry, requisitioned from the locals, swam in heavy gravies.

Teedle handed the phone roughly to the signal man and dismissed him, then plunged to his seat, looking unhappily at the papers stacked on his desk. He had yet to remove his helmet. The General barked suddenly at Bonner.

"Are you telling me that Halley Maples sent that pup to deal with Martin?" As far as I had noticed, Teedle hadn't even looked at me.

Bonner turned my way and said with his subversive smile, "The General will see you now."

When I'd first heard Teedle's name, I had expected some round little fellow who'd look at home in a Technicolor musical movie like *The Wizard of Oz*. But the General gave every impression of being a soldier, the kind who would have been happy to be referred to as a rough-and-ready son of a bitch. Teedle was a big red-faced man, with a chest as round as a cock robin's, and tiny pale eyes set off starkly within lids that appeared to have been rubbed raw, probably from exhaustion or perhaps an allergic condition, or even, I suppose, tears.

In front of the General's desk I came to attention again, gave name, rank, and unit, and explained that with his permission, I would like to take a statement from him, in connection with the Rule 35 regarding Martin. Teedle studied me throughout.

"Where'd you go to college, Dubin?"

"Easton."

"Uh-huh. I'm from Kansas. None of those fancy-ass schools in Kansas. How about law school?"

"Easton. If I may, General, I went on scholarship, sir."

"Oh, I see. A smart guy. Is that what you're telling me?"

"Not to suggest that, sir."

"Well, if you gad about telling everybody you meet first thing how bright you are, you're not very smart at all, are you, Lieutenant?"

I didn't answer. He had me pinned and that was the point anyway. Teedle was plainly another of those commanders who wanted his troops to know he was the match of any of them. He took a second to set his helmet on his desk. His hair, what little was left of it, was somewhere between red and blond, and stood up on his head like stray wires. He'd found his canteen and screwed off the cap. Even at a distance of six feet, I could smell the whiskey. He took a good solid slug.

"All right, so what do I need to tell you about Martin?"

"As much as you can, sir."

"Oh, I won't do that. You'll start thinking Martin's a wonderful fellow. You're likely to think he's a wonderful fellow anyway. I'll tell you something right now, Dubin. You're going to like Robert Martin a good deal better than you like me. He's charming, a sweet talker. And brave. Martin may be the bravest son of a bitch in the European theater. You seen combat, Dubin?"

"No, sir. I'd like to."

"Is that so?" He smirked and pointedly lowered his line of sight to the JAG Department insignia on the collar of my tunic. "Well, if you ever find yourself in the middle of a battlefield, Lieutenant, what you'll see around you is a bunch of fellows scared shitless, as they should be, and one or two sons of bitches jumping up and down and acting as if the bullets can't touch them. They get hit sooner or later, believe me, but it takes a hell of a lot longer than you'd think. Martin's one of those. Thinks he's invincible. I don't like that either. A soldier who's not afraid to die is a danger to everybody."

"Is that the problem, sir? The root of it?"

"Hardly. The problem, if you want to call it that, is that the fucking son of a bitch won't follow orders. He's gone off on several operations without my say-so, even though he's supposed to be under my command. Successful operations, too, I don't dispute that, sabotaging train lines, mostly, so those Nazi pricks can't get troops and supplies where we're heading. He's a whiz at that. Every railway worker in France seems to bow at Martin's feet.

"But twice I've sent troops to the wrong position because I didn't know he'd already blown the lines. I've had to hold off artillery because I got late word that Martin and his men turned up in the target area, without any prior communication to me. And I've slowed deployments several times because Martin was off screwing with the Germans, instead of finishing the recons he'd been assigned. And it's not just discipline that concerns me, Lieutenant, although I believe in discipline as much as any other general you've ever met. What makes my hemorrhoids ache is that men were in danger each time, men who didn't need to be killed. Not that day. Not in that place. And I take that personally."

My face must have reflected some doubt about his choice of words.

"You heard me, Lieutenant," he said, and stood behind his desk. "It's personal. I get up every goddamn morning knowing that young men under my command are going to die—even now with nothing special happening, I'm losing thirty men a day, and I'll carry their souls with me as long as I live, Dubin. I mean that. While I last on this globe, there will always be some shadow of grief. I wanted this star so bad I probably would have killed someone to get it, but I didn't realize that the dead stick with generals this way. I grieved for plenty who died under my command at lower ranks, but that burden departed, Dubin, and it doesn't now, and when I've asked others, all they can say is that this is just how it is."

He paused to see how I was taking this. His face, especially his large, lumpy nose, had gained even more color, and he helped himself to another snort from his canteen.

"That, in a few words, is what I don't like about Robert Martin. I've been a soldier my whole life, Dubin, I know how the game is played, and I realize I'd get nowhere with the General staff complaining about Martin's heroics. But I passed the word to OSS that he's outlived his usefulness here. And eventually they agreed. Told me I should order him back to London. And now we get the melodrama. Because Martin won't go.

"The prick won't go. I've given him his orders in writing three times, and he's sitting there like he's on vacation. I've tolerated the bastard when I had to, Dubin, but I've got him dead to rights now, and I'm not taking any more of his crap. All understood? So type that up, just the last part there, and I'll sign it."

"I thought there was something to do with a woman, sir. That's what Colonel Maples indicated."

Teedle laughed suddenly. He was so relentlessly intense that I nearly jumped at the sound. I would have bet the man in front of me laughed at nothing.

"Oh, that," he said. "I'll tell you the truth, Dubin. I don't give a dry turd about the woman. Patton's G-1 cares—they want the same rules for all personnel, naturally. Before D-Day, Martin commanded an

Operational Group here on the Continent—Sidewinder, or some such name. They were spying and making the Nazis' lives difficult with little hit-and-run operations. He must have had thirty men under him, a few Allied spies who'd come ashore like him, but most of his command were members of the French and Belgian underground. The Frenchmen have all run home, the spoils of war and whatnot. I suppose the bastards are going to fight each other about who runs the show here.

"There are still a few odd ducks remaining with Martin, probably because they're not welcome anywhere else. And one of them's a woman, a beautiful little bit from what I hear. He recruited her in Marseilles a few years ago, and she's been beside him, helping with a lot of the ruses OSS is always employing. These OSS women have been damned effective, Dubin. Don't sell them short. You know the fucking Krauts, they think they're gentlemen, so they're never as suspicious of females as they should be. This girl claims to be a nurse sometimes. You can go just about anywhere in a nurse's uniform in the middle of a war.

"Now it's true, she's probably twenty years younger than Martin, and by all accounts he's been giving her the old one-two and maybe he's even in love with her or thinks he is. That's the theory in London, I suspect, about why he won't go back. My theory is that it just jollies him up to grind his finger in my eye.

"But as for the fact that he's stuck on the girl, or fighting beside his bed partner, they may not like that in the General staff, think it's bad for discipline when our troops catch on, but I couldn't care less. Soldiers always want sex. Do you know why?"

Because they were away from women, I answered. Their wives, their girlfriends.

"You think they'd hop their wives the way these boys go diving after these French girls? I don't. They think they're going to die, Dubin. The reasonable ones anyway. That's what I think. And if you get the time in combat you say you'd like, you'll be thinking that way, too. And when you feel death imminent, Dubin, you don't want to be alone. Isolation is the next stage, in the casket. You desire nothing more than contact with life, and life in its purest form. You want sex. And God. These boys want God, too. They want to fuck. And they want to pray. That's what a soldier wishes for when he doesn't wish he was back home. Forgive me for lecturing, but you're new to all of this and you're better off getting used to the truth.

"So I don't care if Martin's fucking this girl, or some calf he encounters on the road. We have a few troops doing that, too, I get the farmers in here complaining. Fuck who you want to as far as I'm concerned. But follow orders. So write up what I need to sign and then tell that son of a bitch to get the hell out of my area or he'll have an escort to the disciplinary barracks. That's all."

Yet again, Teedle lifted the canteen. It was his fifth or sixth drink. He should have been loaded, but his fury burned at such intensity that the liquor was probably vaporized on the way down his throat. I had no idea exactly what to think of General Teedle, especially the eagerness with which he'd invited me to dislike him. He seemed to have been one of those boys picked on all his childhood who grew up determined to be tougher than the bullies, yet who never overcame the hurt of being the odd man out. But his brusque honesty impressed me, especially since it even seemed to go so far as acknowledging his own unhappiness.

After seeing General Teedle, it made more sense not to return to Nancy, but rather to set out for Major Martin, who was nearby. The General directed his G-1 to assist us, and the personnel officer, Lieutenant Colonel Brunson, briefed us further and ordered maps. When we were done, we returned to the motor pool, where the sergeant in charge informed us that they'd dispatched our jeep and couldn't spare another until morning.

Biddy caught on immediately. "Burnin our gas, not theirs," he murmured to me. He was right, of course, but we still weren't going to get a vehicle. Instead we went off separately to seek billeting. The captain of the headquarters company found me a cot in a four-man tent and showed me where dinner would be in the officers' mess, formed from two squad tents. The meal, when it was served, was hot B ration reduced to a greenish mash, but no one around here was complaining, since even headquarters company, which usually wangled the best, was down to only two meals a day. One of my most embarrassing little secrets was that I had found during training that I did not mind field rations, even what came in tins in the B and C: meat and vegetables, meat and beans, meat and spaghetti. The typical lament was that it looked like dog food and tasted like it, too. But much of it struck me as exotic. My parents, for all their lack of formal religious practice, had never brought pork into our home. Pork and beans was not my particular favorite, but I regarded ham as a delicacy, so much so that even Spam was a pleasure.

Afterward, I wandered toward the staging area where the enlisted men were encamped to make sure Bidwell had found a place. There was a virtual tent city there encompassing several battalions. It had its own eye appeal. The ranks of pup tents were in perfect lines stretching out hundreds of yards, with the latrine slit trenches dug at regular intervals, all of it illuminated by the brightness of the fires the cooks were still tending. I walked along, exchanging salutes with the enlisted men who took notice of me, trying to find Division Headquarters Company, with whom Biddy was said to be quartered.

Now and then, when I asked directions, I'd also see if I could swap novels with some of the men. I had stuffed books in every pocket of my fatigues before we left Nancy, eager for new reading material. I sometimes felt I had read every novel in the city. I had been holding on to two of the most popular titles, *Lost Horizon* and *Sanctuary*, by William Faulkner, the latter much in demand because of Popeye's foul activities with a corncob. My hope was for more Faulkner, which I was lucky enough to find in the hands of a redheaded private from Texas. I also got a novel by James Gould Cozzens in exchange for *The Last Citadel*.

It would be hard to say how important the few minutes I spent reading each night were to me. Thoughts of my parents, of my brother and sister, or of Grace were fraught with emotion. I could not surrender to the comfort of imagining myself among them again, to the security of the life I had left, because I knew I could go mad with yearning and with regret that I'd been so determined to do my duty. But the chance to feel myself in another locale, neither here nor home, if only for a few minutes, was a special reprieve, an essential sign that life would again have the richness and nuance it holds in times of peace.

I never found Bidwell. But after I made my last literary trade, I bumped into Billy Bonner. He'd been tippling and was holding a cognac bottle, most of the contents gone now.

"Trying to become acquainted with native customs, First Lieutenant," Bonner said. "French might be onto something with this stuff." He hefted the bottle and missed his mouth at first. Half the off-duty soldiers I encountered in France were pie-eyed, fueled by stores of wine and newer treats like Pernod and Benedictine they'd never seen in the States. Not that the officers were any better. Those of us at headquarters were still receiving the garrison ration of liquor every month, and even officers in foxholes were supposed to get a quart of scotch, a pint of gin, two bottles of champagne, and a bottle of brandy, although it was rarely delivered, given the strains on the supply chain. I traded away most of what arrived. Even at Easton College, where Prohibition had made drinking an adventure, I tended to abstain, never caring much for liquor's loose feeling.

"You seem fairly deep into your exploration of local culture, Bonner."

"Yes, sir. Just so long as I can roll out in the morning."

Bonner saw the pocket book in my hand and we exchanged thoughts about novels for a moment. I promised to trade him *Light in August* on our next visit. I had turned away when Bonner said clearly behind me, "They've got you investigating the wrong one, Lieutenant."

I revolved to stare at him.

"Teedle and Martin?" he said. "You're investigating the wrong one. At least, as I see it. You oughta ask around."

"Then I'll start by asking you, Corporal. Tell me what that remark means."

Bonner peered at length into the mouth of the bottle, as if the answer were in there.

"It probably means I've had too much of this," he said after quite some time. He gave me that thin, conspiratorial smile and without waiting for a response slipped off into the dark camp.

II.

4. STEWART: MY FATHER'S LAWYER

According to the Record of Proceedings of my father's court-martial, a high-ranking JAG Department lawyer from Eisenhower's headquarters, Barrington Leach, had been Dad's attorney. His name rang a bell, and a search online reminded me why. In 1950, Leach took a leave from the prominent Hartford law firm in which he was a partner to become Chief Counsel to Senator Estes Kefauver in his investigation of organized crime. The televised Kefauver Hearings introduced many Americans to the Mafia and, not coincidentally, to the privilege against self-incrimination. From then on "taking the Fifth" inevitably brought to mind the line of dark gentlemen in expensive suits who answered every question by reciting their rights from index cards adhering to their palms. It was Leach, most often, who was up there making them sweat.

After returning to Connecticut, Leach in time became a judge, eventually rising to the Connecticut Supreme Court. His name actually turns up in a few news accounts in the Johnson era as a potential candidate for the U.S. Supreme Court.

I had started researching Leach during the months I was stalemated by the government in my efforts to pry loose the court-martial file. (I finally got it in June 2004, but only because I could demonstrate by then that I knew virtually all the information contained there.) I had assumed that Leach, an experienced trial lawyer in 1945 and thus quite a bit older than Dad, had to be dead, and I only hoped that his family had kept his papers. In late October 2003, I called the Connecticut Supreme Court to locate Leach's next of kin.

"Did he die?" the clerk asked me. He turned from the phone, inquiring of a colleague with alarm, "Did Justice Leach die?" I could hear the question ping-ponging across the room, until the clerk came back on the line. "No, sir. Happy to say Justice Leach is still with us." He declined to provide an address or phone, but promised to forward any mail. Within a week, I had received a response, with a return address at the Northumberland Manor Assisted-Care Facility in West Hartford, written in a craggy hand that brought to mind that enduring children's toy, the Etch A Sketch.

> *I surely recall representing your father. David Dubin's court-martial remains one of the most perplexing matters of my life as a lawyer, and I am willing to discuss it with you. In answer to your inquiry, I have retained some materials relating to the case that you would probably wish to have. As you can see, writing letters is a particular burden at this stage of my life. We could converse by telephone, if need be, but, if I may be so bold, I suggest that, if possible, you pay me a visit.*
>
> *While I am happy to provide you with my recollections and these papers, doing so is a bit sticky legally, inasmuch as your father was my client. You would set an old man's mind at ease if, when you came, you brought a letter from all your father's legal heirs—your mother, if she remains alive, and any siblings you have—stating that each of you relinquishes any objections related to what I share. I'd suggest you contact the lawyer who is handling the estate to help you. I will be happy to speak with him, if he likes.*
>
> *Without being alarmist, I call your attention to the fact that I am ninety-six years old and that I no longer purchase green bananas. I look forward to meeting you soon.*
>
> *With all good wishes,*
> *Barrington V.S. Leach*

Watching me dash around the country, passing hours in dank library basements and talking about opposition from the CIA, the members of my family were convinced that my elevator had stopped between floors. Nona regarded it as conclusive proof that she'd gotten out at the right time, while my daughters offered a succinct explanation to anyone who asked: "Dad's on crack."

My mother said the least, but might have been the most unhappy. Mom remained as fiercely possessive of Dad in death as she had always been. She had picked his suit and tie each day and had remained his principal counselor on the wary maneuverings of the commercial world, where he was often led astray by his native inclination to see almost every issue as a question of principle. But in my house, each of us depended on Mom's vitality and shrewdness, regarding it as a fact-established that my mother, as a camp survivor, had an extra measure of whatever living required. She took it as my single greatest fault that I had not been smart enough to marry someone like her.

In light of all of that, it was predictable that she wouldn't like me claiming a piece of my father on my own. There were no tirades, just occasional remarks indicating that she found it distasteful that I was making Dad's Army secrets a professional project. To her it was as if I were beating drums with bones I'd uncovered in the graveyard. And it was worse than cruel irony that I was digging into a period whose anguish they'd spent a lifetime trying to inter.

Which made Leach's letter a problem. My sister would do what Mom said. But it would take some talking to get my mother to sign off. I strategized for at least a week. Then one morning when I stopped in, as I did most days, I sat her down at the kitchen table, where important family discussions always have occurred, and made my pitch. She listened avidly, her small black eyes intent, and asked for a day or two to think. I left with hope.

But walking in a week later, I knew from my first breath that I was doomed. She'd baked. Rugelach, an all-time favorite, sat on the kitchen table. She might as well have used the pastries as blocks to spell out COM-FORT FOOD. Being who I am, I ate, and being who she is, she waited until I was in the initial stage of near delirium before she started.

"Stewart," she said, "about this lawyer and his papers. Stewart, I have thought very hard. I tell you, with all my heart, I believe your father *alav hashalom*, would be moved to tears to know that you have made this effort to understand his life. And the one question I have asked myself for the last few days is whether that might have made him reconsider. Because I agree with what you said when Daddy died, Stewart, that he must have made a choice not to discuss this with his family. But in the end, you are asking me to set aside my loyalty to him. It is not for me to imagine new decisions for your father now, Stewart. He is entitled to my support in his judgments about what he wanted to say about his own life."

I whined, of course. I was his kid, I said. I was entitled to know. That remark provoked her.

"Stewart, where is it written that a parent is required to become your journalistic subject? Is giving life to a child, Stewart, like running for public office, where every piece of dirty linen is open to inspection? Is it not a parent's right to be understood on his own terms? Do you pretend that your daughters know every seamy detail of your youth?"

That was a low blow, but effective. I took a second.

"Mom, don't you want to know the story?"

"Stewart, I know the only story that matters, and I knew it from the moment I fell in love with your father in the concentration camp. David Dubin was kind. He was intelligent, educated. Jewish. I could tell at once he was a loyal person, a person of values. What more could matter to me, or to you? Then. Or now?"

Naturally, I phoned my sister. Mom could dress this up however she liked, I said, claiming she was bound by Dad's wishes, but it was really about her. And being in control.

"God, Stewie, why do you always make her the bad guy? So what if it's about her? She lived with the man for fifty-eight years. Now you come along to tell her that her husband was a convict? Of course she doesn't care to hear the details. Leave her alone. If you have to do this, do it when she's gone."

I reminded Sarah that Leach was ninety-six. "Look," I offered, "I swear I won't tell her anything I find out."

"Oh, Stew," my sister said, tart as always, "when was the last time you kept a secret? Haven't you figured out yet what you liked about being a reporter? I'll sign whatever you like after she's gone. But I don't want to hear another word about this now. Maybe you should spend some time asking yourself why you're hyperventilating to learn all this."

I already had. Every day and every night. But the simplest answer to Sarah was probably the best: he was my father. We can all dream up the hero we want to be when we're adolescents and spend our adult years trying to live out the ideal, but sooner or later we each realize that our options are limited by the raw materials, that dose of DNA we get and the imprinting of early childhood. As a young man, I did not see myself in Dad. Now when I go through the many photos I have assembled from his youth, there are moments when I cannot tell whether the fellow standing there is he or I. That body, which years ago stopped belonging to either of us, was fundamentally one: the same corrupted posture, sagging somehow from a point between the shoulder blades, the same dark-complected look like a warm tan, the same uncertain approach to the camera, unsure how much to surrender. I have his nose, they say, and at moments, his haunted eyes. From Dad I got my taste for salty things, and my acceptance of the Trappers' losses as a piece of fate.

In my research, I discovered many unacknowledged debts I owed my father. Scouring his letters, and later, what he had written for Leach, I was struck that my old man could turn a phrase. My father spent two hours every night reading any novel he could get his hands on, a habit so unvarying that he actually wore two rawhide stripes into the leather ottoman where he perched his feet. Yet it had never clicked that Dad was probably the source of my own interest in writing, even though I'd always been heartened by his quiet pride in my bylines. Now, looking back, I realized that he must have intervened to get my mother to quit her pestering about law school.

Yet it was not the things I liked about myself that fed my hunger to find out what he'd done wrong. In the end, I fear it was probably more of the affliction that had made me a happy observer in criminal courtrooms for decades: I wanted to know Dad's failings, so I'd feel better about my own.

And given what happened next, you might say that self-acceptance is not all that it's cracked up to be. But I have always been a slave to impulse, and slow to face the fact. When I look in the mirror, I see a trim guy, inconveniently burdened with a few dozen pounds that belong to someone else. That's because the thinner fellow, with his good intentions, generally holds the rudder on my soul. On a perpetual diet, I'm the guy at the restaurant who orders the little salad that comes topped with a tiny pellet of poached salmon—before I eat the French fries off everybody else's plates. My eternal undoing arrives in these instants when my appetites are more than I can handle. My saddest turn as a courthouse reporter came in the early '90s as I was walking past the jury room and, with no planning whatsoever, pressed my ear to the door, hoping for a scoop on an important verdict. When a bailiff caught me, I was suspended from the paper for thirty days and, far worse, showered doubt on every honest success before and after. It's a lifetime pattern. I resist. I struggle. But I also succumb.

Which in this case means that when I wrote back to Barrington Leach, I not only set a date to visit, but formally released him from any legal responsibility for what he might reveal. How? I simply stated that my mother had died a few years ago and that I was an only child. Just like the crooks I covered for twenty years, I told myself that nobody would ever know.

5. DAVID: MAJOR ROBERT MARTIN

With the Third Army in France

Dearest Grace,

I have been sent to the front (where all remains quiet, so
please don't worry) to do a little investigation, involving
Army politics among the brass. Since I have been able to borrow
a typewriter, I wanted to say hello and tell you I think of you
always.

Yesterday was really a banner day, as I received four
airmails and a V-mail from you. I've brought all of them with
me to read a second (and third!) time. In your V-mail, dearest,
you tell me of your cold--please take care of yourself. If you
don't feel well, stay home from school. I don't want anything
happening to you--you mean too much to me, and we have too much
living together in the near future for you to take any chances.

Tonight, my bed will be a cot in a tent, a reminder of how
embarrassingly good life is in Nancy. Eisley and I have found

new quarters with Madame Vaillot, whose husband has been
carted off by the Germans to God knows where. She greets us
each morning at 6:30 a.m. with strong coffee and our laundry,
for which she refuses to take any money. She says in cultivated
French, "We are repaid enough by your keeping the Germans out
and protecting us." So what can we say? Our room is nice, but
cold with the constant rains, and fuel is in short enough
supply that we start a fire only if we are going to be awake
in the room for a while, which we seldom are.

I've been thinking about the nest egg I'll have when the day
comes that I get back. With allowances, I should be making
around $350 per month when my promotion comes through
(November 1, they swear). I'm going to send $300 a month to Mom,
by way of a Class E allotment, to put into my savings account.
(Please tell my dad to make sure Mom uses a few bucks to buy a
new frock or something as a birthday gift from me. They won't
do it unless you insist on my behalf.) There will be $300
mustering-out pay plus the insurance policy of $250 I have, and
fifteen or twenty war bonds. All in all, I'm thinking you're right
and that I should open my own law office. There may even be
enough left over to buy a jalopy. I wouldn't mind getting a
little joy out of this money. Other boys have done more to earn
it, but it's not a picnic being away from all of you. I still keep
my house key in my wallet. Call it loony if you like, but several
times a day, I'll reach to my back pocket and feel its impression
against the leather, and know that I have a place to return to.

Well, I'm getting maudlin, so I'll stop.

Love forever,

David

Lieutenant Colonel Brunson, General Teedle's personnel officer, had
said that Martin and the remainder of his Operational Group were
quartered at the country estate of the Comtesse de Lemolland, west
and south of Bezange-la-Petite, near the skirmishing edge of the front.
Brunson couldn't explain how Martin had arranged such a scenic billet,
but it was clear that many of Teedle's officers, camped in tents on wet
ground, had taken notice.

It was nearly noon the next day before the 18th Division's motor pool surrendered a jeep to us, and I thought for a second that Bidwell was going to get into a fistfight with the private filling the tank, who might as well have been using an eyedropper.

"That ain't but a third of the gas we come with," Biddy told him.

"Sarge," the boy said, "this here's my orders. And you'd do better to look close at that map than keep your eye on me. Krauts are two miles from where you're headed. One wrong turn, Sarge, and your war might end early."

As we drove north into the hills, the sun arrived like a blast of horns, lighting up the isolated groves of trees in full fall color. This was rolling country, principally open fields, resembling southern Wisconsin, where my parents sometimes took us for long Sunday drives in my Uncle Manny's borrowed Model A when I was a boy. After a day together, Bidwell had become more approachable and we laughed about the private who'd parceled out gasoline as if he expected us not to come back. Half an hour later, when we heard the echo of mortars and the pecking of rifle fire from the east, we grew a trifle more serious.

I asked Biddy if this was the closest he'd been to the front. A sardonic snort escaped him.

"D-Day," he said. "That count, Lieutenant? D plus one, actually. Landed my whole MP company on Omaha. Needed us to take custody of the POWs, but we had to scrap our way up that beach like everybody else."

"D-Day! My God, I bet this duty seems boring after that."

He found the idea amusing.

"Hell no, Lieutenant. That was the like of somethin I don't never wanna see again. Truth to tell, I didn't care much for it when they made me an MP. Basic, I put in for an engineering company, truck mechanic. I been fixing cars at home a couple years since I left high school, figured it'd only make sense. But this here is the Army. My orders come through sayin 'Provost Marshal Section,' I had to ask what all that was, and cussed when they told me. I don't hold nothin 'gainst po-licemen, Lieutenant, but it ain't what I ever had a mind to do. Turns out, though, it got its good side. Generally speaking, MPs don't get there till the shooting's over and Mama's little boy here, he promised her he's gonna do his best not to get hisself killed. You can keep combat, Lieutenant. All I care for is take a few pictures and go home."

Like half the soldiers I knew, who remained part tourist, Bidwell always had a camera in his hand. Given his size, he looked almost dainty when he put it to his eye. Most troops took photos of the wreckage of war and of their buddies, but Biddy seemed more studious about it and, typical of his solitary ways, would go off at moments and fix on particular objects and scenes that didn't appear to hold much interest. Driving yesterday, we fell in with the convoy from the 134th and came to a halt when they did, so we could empty our bladders in a roadside ditch. The drivers were Negro troops, as was often the case, and six or seven of them had gathered for a little society, since the white boys as a rule would have nothing to do with them. From behind one of the trucks, Biddy snapped several photos of the colored men carrying on with one another over their cigarettes. It had disturbed me that he hadn't bothered to get their permission.

Recollected, the incident brought Biddy's Georgia roots to mind and I asked when his people had left there and where they'd ended up. He seemed to have no interest in answering. That was this man's army. From boot camp on there were guys who showed you photos of their ma and pa and sweethearts and told you every imaginable detail about them, right down to dress size, and others who wanted to keep home as far from this mess as possible. I was in the latter group anyway, but I prodded a bit now, because I wanted to be sure before criticizing Bidwell's manner with the coloreds that he'd actually had the chance to learn the difference between North and South.

"Daddy, he was a tenant farmer down there. His people been workin that patch, only God Hisself knows how long, hundred years, two hundred years, but it just didn't make no sense to him, when times got so bad. In 1935 he picked us all up and moved us North. He was thinkin to find somethin in a factory, I guess."

"Yes, but where did you settle, Bidwell?"

He smiled for a second while he looked over the road.

"Ever hear of Kindle County?"

I actually cried out. "Dear God, Biddy! You must have heard me talk to Eisley a dozen times about home. Why didn't you say anything? I'm half a world away and it turns out I'm touring around with a neighbor."

" 'Cause of just that, Lieutenant. Wasn't much way you and me was neighbors."

"Don't be so sure, Biddy. I don't come from the high and mighty. My father's a shoemaker." I rarely shared this detail, fearing it might undermine me, both among fellow officers and the troops, and as I'd anticipated, I could see I'd caught Bidwell by surprise. "Pop's been at that trade since he was a boy, right after he landed in the U.S. An uncle took him in and taught him. I grew up in a three-flat on Deering Road. The folks are still there. What about you?"

Biddy shook his head as if he didn't know.

"We was all over," he said. "You know how that goes when a man's scratchin for work. Come the end of the month, sometimes Dad and the landlord wudn't seein eye to eye. I must have been near to eighteen 'fore I stopped in askin why we didn't move in daytime like other folks." He smiled at the memory, but his green eyes drifted over to see what I made of that. As the son of a cobbler, though, I knew a lot about hard times. In the Depression, Pa had plenty of work because people wanted to make their shoes last. But many of them couldn't come up with the six bits once their footwear was mended. Some pairs left on credit, if Pa knew who he was talking to, even when it was all but certain he'd never get paid. But he'd let a man walk out barefoot rather than get cheated.

After hearing the gunfire, we stopped several times to check directions with the locals. In the end, a farmer on a horse trotted ahead of us and pointed out the Comtesse's narrow drive, which we might well have missed amid the heavy brush. The Lemolland property was bounded by an old stone fence, topped in the French way in red roofing tiles, but the gate was open and we headed up an incline beside the vineyards, where several workers were tilling among the stubby twists of the grapevines. The plants, hanging on long wire supports, looked to have been recently harvested.

At the top, we found a square formation of joined sand-colored buildings. I thought of a fort, but I suppose the arrangement was a small replica of a feudal manor. Each wing was several stories high, sporting long red jalousies folded back beside the deep windows and topped with a steep mansard roof. Huge wooden doors were thrown open on an arch that passed through the building facing us, and we drove into a vast cobblestone courtyard. At the far end stood the house. It incorporated a round tower that had to date from the Middle Ages, giving the residence the look of a little castle.

An unshaved worker with a hoe watched us warily as we stopped. Visible behind a corner of the Comtesse's château were a ramshackle chicken coop and a pasture, where two cows swished their tails.

At the house, I pulled several times on a bell rope until the door was parted by a large dark man, with the stub of a cigarette in the corner of his mouth and one eye closed to the smoke. He was a Gypsy, with a potato face and women's-length hair tied behind him. In French, I asked for Major Martin. The Gypsy took a second surveying our uniforms, then motioned us in and bellowed up a staircase at his right.

"Ro-bert," he called, giving the name the French pronunciation, without a 't.' "Un moment," he told us, then disappeared out the door we'd entered.

Biddy and I remained in the entry for several minutes. The old house had stone walls of monumental thickness. It was dark and still, except for the bright kitchen which lay ahead of us at the end of a hall. From there, I could hear voices and a pump handle squealing, and smell pleasant aromas—burning wood and something cooking. Standing here, I was reminded of waiting in the foyer of Grace's great stone house, when I would pick her up for the evening. They were excruciating moments for me, especially when her father was around, since he was convinced I was a fortune hunter. For my part, the distaste was mutual. Privately, I realized that Horace Morton would never accept my good intentions regarding his daughter, because he himself wouldn't have pursued any girl without first knowing all about her bank account.

With great pounding, a middle-sized man in a khaki Army officer's shirt bounded down the heavy stairs. He wore no tie or insignia but there was a trench knife on his belt, in addition to a bayonet in its scabbard. This, without question, was Major Martin.

Biddy and I saluted. Smiling, he tapped his forehead, but only to be polite.

"We don't do that around here," he said. The Operational Groups, as I was to learn, proceeded with a minimum of military formalities. There was a "leader" from whom all took direction, but the OGs included not only members of the armed forces of several nations, but civilians in the underground who had no duty to adhere to Army rules.

"Where from?" Martin asked, when I gave him my name. I repeated that I was with Staff Judge Advocate, Third Army, which brought a laugh. "No, I can see that wreath on your lapel, son. Where in the States? Where's the home this war has taken you away from?"

When I told him Kindle County, he brightened. "Oh, that's a swell place. I've had some swell times there." He shared a few memories of a Negro speakeasy in the North End, then asked about my education and my family. These were not the kind of questions a superior officer usually bothered with on first meeting, and I enjoyed his attention. He made similar inquiries of Biddy, who predictably retreated rather than offer much of a response.

Martin was no more than five foot ten, but remarkable to behold, dark haired, strong jawed, and vibrating with physical energy. Much like Grace, he had the all-American looks, with tidy, balanced features, that I, with my long nose and eyes shadowed in their sallow orbits, always envied. A single black curl fell across the center of Robert Martin's forehead, and even racing down the stairs he made an impression of unusual agility. Despite addressing me as "son," he did not look to be much more than forty.

He interrupted when I tried to explain my mission here.

"Oh, I've heard about that," he said with a brief smile, waving us behind him down the hall. When we entered the kitchen, a young woman was over the sink washing her hair beneath the cast-iron pump. She was small and striking, dressed in surplus camouflage fatigues far too large for her, and she glanced my way immediately to size me up. She had a tiny, almost childlike face, but it held an older, ruthlessly cool aspect. I could see at once that this was the woman who was the problem.

Finding herself unimpressed, she went back to wringing out her short wavy tresses over the copper basin. At the same time, she spoke to Martin. "*Qui sont-ils?*" Who are they?

Martin answered her in French. "The Lieutenant is sent by Teedle."

"*Merde*," she replied. "Tell them to go away." She reached beside her and lit a cigarette.

"By and by," he answered. He waited until she was done frisking a towel through her hair, then made introductions in English. She was Gita Lodz, a member of OG Stemwinder and the FTP, Francs-Tireurs et Partisans, one of the largest resistance organizations, union-oriented and supposedly red. When Martin gave Mademoiselle Lodz our names, she offered a smile as purely formal as a curtsy.

"*Enchanté*," I answered, thinking that this might clue them that I had understood their conversation, but I saw no sign that either took it as more than a tourist courtesy.

"Excuse, pliss," Gita Lodz said in English, "I go." She had a heavy Slavic accent, undetectable to my ear when she had spoken French. Hastily she recovered her cigarette from the sink edge as she left.

A meal of some kind was under way and a servant in an apron was stirring a huge iron pot on the black stove. The kitchen, like the rest of the house, was rustic but the room was large and light. Copper pans with burned bottoms were suspended from the exposed timbers of the ceiling, and blue delft plates decorated the walls, a sure sign that this place had so far escaped the war.

"You've arranged charming quarters, Major," I said.

"Quite," he said. "Stemwinder is on R and R with the war at a standstill. Here it seems far away." He swept his arm grandly. "The Comtesse de Lemolland is a magnificent patriot and a great friend to our OG."

The house, he said, had been the country home of the Comtesse's family, bankers from Nancy, since the time of Napoleon. She had maintained it even after marrying the Comte de Lemolland after the First War, when her principal residence became a château in the Côtes-du-Nord. This property had not suffered as badly under the Germans as many others. Periodically, SS would take over the house as a resort for officers, and a German garrison would come each fall to confiscate crops and wine. Nonetheless, with the Comtesse's return, the vineyard and farm were already returning to life. The Comtesse herself, Martin confided, was not doing as well. Her son, Gilles, a member of another resistance group, Forces Françaises de l'Intérieur, FFI, had been confirmed captured and burned alive by the Nazis earlier this month. The old woman had largely kept to herself since then.

"Nonetheless," said Martin, "she would never forgive me if an American officer visited her home and I did not allow her to say a word of welcome. You will enjoy meeting her. She is a remarkable and gallant woman." Preparing to summon the Comtesse, Martin caught sight of Mademoiselle Lodz peeking into the kitchen, probably to see if we had yet been dispatched. She was now in country attire, a blouse with ruffled sleeves and a flowered dress with a bib and flouncy skirt.

"*Va leur parler*"—Talk to them—he told her, gesturing her in. To us he said, "If you chaps will excuse me just one minute, Gita will keep you company." He admonished her in a low voice as he breezed out, "*Sois plaisante.*"

Biddy had retreated to a corner, leaving me to face Gita Lodz in silence. She was narrow as a deer, and in that fashion, pleasingly formed, but with a second chance to observe her, I had decided it would be a stretch to call her beautiful. Dry, her hair proved to be a brass-colored blonde. Her nose was broad and her teeth were small and crooked. Given the darkness of her eyes, her complexion was oddly pale. But she had what the Hollywood tattlers liked to call "it," an undefined magnetism which began with a defiant confidence about herself, palpable even from across the room.

I attempted small talk.

"May I be so bold as to ask about your name, Mademoiselle Lodz? Do you hail from that Polish city? From Lodz?" I said this in very correct French, which drew a pulled-down mouth from her, a seeming acknowledgment that she had not given me that much credit. But she replied in the same language, clearly delighted not to struggle with English.

"I am Polish, yes, but not from Lodz. It is no one's name really. I am a bastard." She made that declaration with utter equanimity, but her small black eyes never left me. I always thought I'd learned a good poker face watching Westerns, but I feared at once that I'd reacted to her frankness, and I was grateful she went on. "My mother was Lodzka," she said—'Wodjka,' as she pronounced it—"from her first husband. She had not seen him in years, but it was convenient, naturally, for me to share her name. The French, of course, can only speak French. So it is easier here to be simply Lodz. And your name?" she asked. "How would it be spelled?"

"Doo-ban?" she said once I had recited the letters. I said it again, and she tried a second time. "Doo-bean?"

I shrugged, accepting that as close enough.

"But what kind of name is that? Not French, no?"

I answered simply, "American."

"Yes, but Americans, all of them come from Europe. Where in Europe was Doo-bean?"

I told her Russia, but she took my answer with mild suspicion.

"In what part?" she asked.

I named the village where both my parents had been born.

"Near Pinsk?" she said. "But your name does not sound Russian."

"It was Dubinsky, back then," I said after a second, still not acknowledging everything I might have. However, I had won a brief smile.

"Like 'Lodzka,'" she said. A second passed then, as we both seemed to ponder how to go forward, having found an inch of common ground. I finally asked where she was from in Poland, if not Lodz.

"Eh," she said. "Pilzkoba. A town. You put a thumbtack in a map and it is gone. *Que des crétins*," she added bitterly. All idiots. "I ran from there in 1940. After the Germans killed my mother."

I offered my condolences, but she shrugged them off.

"In Europe now we all have these stories. But I could not stay. I hated the Germans, naturally. And also the Poles, because they hated me. Bastards are not favorites in small Polish towns, Doo-bean. So I left. You see?"

"Yes," I said. In English, I quoted Exodus. "'I have been a stranger in a strange land.'"

She lit up. The phrase delighted her. "*Parfait!*" she declared and haltingly repeated as much as she could.

Martin reappeared just then and swept behind her.

"Ah, but no stranger to me," he said, and with his arms around her waist swung her off the floor. Once she was down she pried his hands apart to escape.

"I am enjoying this conversation," she told him in French.

"So you like this American?" Martin asked her.

"I like Americans," she answered. "That must be what interested me in you. *Pas mal*," she added—Not bad—a reference to my looks, then winked at me with Martin behind her. She clearly had no wish to let him know I understood.

"You think he has silk stockings and chocolate bars?" asked Martin.

"*Merde*. You are always jealous."

"Not without reason," he answered.

"Yes, but without right."

"Eh," he responded. It was banter. Both were grinning. He faced me and said that the Comtesse would be down momentarily.

With Martin's reappearance, I had taken a notebook from my fatigues and asked the Major if we might use the interval before the Comtesse's arrival to discuss my mission here. I presented him with an order from Patton's adjutant authorizing the Rule 35 investigation, but Martin did not read more than the first lines.

"Teedle," he said then, as if it were the most tiresome word in any language. "What does he say? No, don't bother. Mark it as true, whatever he says. All true. 'Insubordinate.' 'Mutinous.' Whatever the hell he wants to call it. Write down in your little book: Guilty as hell. The Army still doesn't know what to do with me." He laughed, just as he had when he recollected the Negro speakeasy.

I followed him across the kitchen. "I wouldn't make light of this, Major. Teedle has laid serious charges, sir." I explained his rights to Martin—he could give a statement himself or direct me to other witnesses. If he preferred to speak to a superior officer, he was entitled to do so. And certainly he could hear a specification of what had been said against him.

"If you must," he answered. He picked at a plate of grapes.

"General Teedle alleges that you've been ordered to disband your Operational Group and return to London. He says you've refused."

"'Refused'? What rubbish. I'm here under the command of OSS London, and London has directed me to continue as before. Gita and I and the others are going to finish our business in France, then continue on to Germany. I have built networks there, too, Dubin. We will see this to an end. Teedle can be damned with his nonsense about refusing orders."

"This is a misunderstanding, then?"

"If you wish to call it that."

I was somewhat relieved to find the matter could be settled quickly. I asked Martin to see his orders from OSS, which brought an indulgent smile.

"You don't know much about OSS, do you, Dubin?" In fact, I had tried to learn as much as I could, but except for an old propaganda piece in *Stars and Stripes* and what I gleaned at the 18th Division from Martin's sanitized 201 file, I was largely in the dark. "An OSS officer carries no written orders," he told me. "The Nazis have said forthrightly that they'll shoot any OSS member they capture. Teedle knows this. But mine are orders nonetheless."

"Well, if I may, sir, who gave those orders?"

"My operational officer in London. I was ordered back to see him the last week in September, as a matter of fact."

"And his name, if you please?"

Again, Martin smiled as he would with a boy.

"Dubin, OSS has strict rules of secrecy. It is not a normal military organization. Only London can reveal the information you're asking for. But feel free to check with them. They will confirm everything."

I frowned.

"Oh, pshaw, Dubin. You doubt me? Look around here. We live in the open in the French countryside, fed and housed by a noted French resister. If London didn't want this, don't you think they could inform the local networks, the Free French, with whom they've worked hand in glove for years now? Do you think the Comtesse would defy them? I am here only with the leave of OSS."

He was making some sense, but I knew I could not conclude this investigation merely by inference. However, I had lost Martin's attention. On the threshold was an older woman, very erect, very slim, very drawn. Her graying hair was swept back smoothly and she wore a simple dress, sashed at the waist, and no jewelry besides a cameo that hung between her collarbones. Biddy and I were introduced to the Comtesse de Lemolland. I bowed briefly, accepting her hand.

She addressed us in English.

"I owe to all Americans my deepest gratitude for your courage in behalf of my country."

"I am only a lawyer, Comtesse. Your thanks go to the likes of Major Martin, not to me."

Martin interjected, "The Comtesse herself is a great heroine."

"Not at all true," she answered.

"May I tell the story then, Comtesse, and allow Lieutenant Dubin to judge for himself?"

Leaning against a large cutting block in the center of the kitchen, Martin played raconteur, a role that clearly pleased him. He explained that when the Nazis arrived in 1940, they had commandeered the Comte de Lemolland's ancestral house in the Côtes-du-Nord, where the Comtesse, a widow of three years, had been residing. The Germans turned the château into a communications node. The Comtesse was forced to live as a guest in her own home, confined to an apartment of several rooms. Because the Germans adored rank, they accorded her some dignity, but they partied with prostitutes and nailed maps to the wainscoting in the parlor and abused her servants. Twice maids were raped.

One of the Comtesse's house staff was a member of the underground, and it was she who secretly introduced Agnès de Lemolland to Martin. The Comtesse agreed to the installation in her salon of a listening device, an induction microphone no larger than a button, which was attached by a filament to a tiny earphone that ran to her sitting room. There the Comtesse listened to the daily flow of information through the communications center downstairs, reporting what she'd overheard. When the plans were laid for D-Day, the Comtesse understood that it was from this very center that German reinforcements would be routed to Normandy. With no request from Martin, she designated her own house for bombing once the invasion began, fleeing with her servants only minutes before the first strike.

"Major Martin is quite correct in his assessment," I told the Comtesse. I bowed again, but felt pained to realize that this frail old woman had done far more to win the war than I ever would.

"I am no one," she said simply, "but if you insist that I am as important as all that, Lieutenant, I must take advantage and insist that you and your companion honor me by joining us at supper." Without awaiting a reply, she instructed Sophie, the servant who was at the stove, to set two more plates.

I went looking for Bidwell, whom I found outside, leaning on the jeep and shooting pictures. In the bright daylight, looking back at the Comtesse's little castle, I felt as if I'd just left an amusement park.

"Quite a bunch, aren't they?" I asked. They were all captivating, the gallant Comtesse, and fierce little Mademoiselle Lodz, and of course Martin. "I think the Major is the first actual war hero I've met," I said.

From Biddy I received one of his sour looks, a step from insubordination.

"No disrespect, Lieutenant, but ain't no way rightly to tell where all the malarkey ends in there, sir. Only it's plenty of it, this country boy knows that." He closed the snaps on the leather camera case. "Food smells just fine, though," he said and headed inside.

6. PRINCIPLES

Supper at the Comtesse de Lemolland's was an idyll. In an alcove beside the kitchen, we ate at a long table of heavily varnished wood, enjoying a savory stew. It might have been veal, although there was not much meat among the root vegetables that were the main ingredients. Nevertheless, the usual French hand with food prevailed and the victuals were far tastier, if less plentiful, than even the very good rations we had at HQ. Some of my appreciation for the meal might have been due to the Comtesse's wine, newly pressed, which was poured freely. But in time I realized that the principal charm was that at the Comtesse de Lemolland's I had left the military. A civil—and civilian—atmosphere prevailed. I sat next to the old woman while she shared reflections in English on the history of the region. When we started, Biddy lingered, uncertain if he was invading the officers' mess, but Martin waved him to a chair. Sophie, who had cooked, joined us, too. The Gypsy I had seen, called Antonio, was at the far end of the table speaking in French with Peter Bettjer, a ruddy blond Belgian, who was the Operational Group's communications expert.

Last to sit was Mademoiselle Lodz, who took the empty chair on my right. Midway through the meal, I felt the weight of her gaze. She was studying me unapologetically.

"I am reflecting about you, Doo-bean," she told me in French. It was clear already that she was never going to pronounce my name any other way.

"I am delighted to know I concern you at all. What exactly is it you are thinking, Mademoiselle?"

"If you are indeed Dubinsky from Pinsk"—she puckered her lips, then stared straight at me—"*vous êtes juif.*"

So that was it. In the little fantasia of the Comtesse's home, I felt especially scalded, which my face apparently betrayed.

"This is nothing to be ashamed of," she said in French. "In my town there were many Jews. I knew them well."

"I am hardly ashamed," I said quickly.

"There are many Jewish soldiers in the American Army?"

"Some."

"And they stay among the other troops?"

"Of course. We are one nation."

"But the dark ones I see—they drive and move the equipment. The Jews do not have separate battalions like the Negroes?"

"No. It is entirely different. The blacks were slaves to some of the Americans' grandfathers, who, regrettably, have not allowed the past to die."

"And these Jew soldiers. They look like you? You have no sidelocks. Are there *tsitsis* beneath your garments?"

"I am not a Jew in that way."

"In my town they had only one way, Dubin. *Red Yiddish?*" she asked. That made the third language in which she had addressed me, and her smile revealed a dark space between her front teeth.

"*Ayn bisel. Yich red besser am franzosich.*" My grandparents who had followed my father to the United States spoke Yiddish, but my mother and father used only English in the presence of their children, unwilling to risk hindering our development as Americans. My Yiddish was not even close to my French, as I had just told her.

"*Ach mir,*" she answered, "*ayn bisel.*" With me, too, a little bit.

Martin, across the table, asked her in French, "What language is that?"

"We are speaking Jewish, Robert."

"Jewish? I thought you disliked the Jews."

She looked at him sharply. "Wrong. Stupidly wrong. This is because you will never listen to anything I say about my home. My only friends as a child were Jewish. They alone would allow me in their houses. Why would I dislike them?"

"But they spurned you."

"For a bride, Robert. It is their way."

He turned away to ask Sophie for the bread, while Mademoiselle Lodz was left to explain.

"*C'est une histoire compliquée,*" she told me. It's a long story. "My mother, Dubin, wanted me to find a Jew to be my husband. She said, 'They are seldom drunks and rarely beat their wives.'" Mademoiselle Lodz's mother had clearly never met Julius Klein, who lived on the third floor above us when I was a child and whose wife and children often ran for their lives while his drunken rages shook the entire building. "But no Jew, of course, would marry me."

"You are a Catholic?"

"Only to a Jew. I have never set foot inside a church."

"So you felt, as the Major put it, spurned?"

She wagged her head from side to side, as if weighing the idea for the first time only now.

"The Poles were far worse. Those who regarded themselves as respectable would not even speak to my mother—including her own family. So we lived happily among the Jews. And if I'd had a Jewish husband, I would have been on the trucks beside him. For me, in the end, it was a piece of good fortune."

"The trucks?"

"*Vous m'étonnez!* You do not know of this? In my town, every Jew is gone. The Nazis took them away. They are in the ghetto in Lublin, held like livestock inside fences. This has happened everywhere. France, too. In Vichy, Pétain rounded up the Jews even before the Germans asked. As a Jewish soldier, you, especially, should be here fighting Hitler."

When I enlisted, my first choice was to battle Tojo and the sinister Japanese who had launched their sneak attack on Pearl Harbor. As for Hitler, I knew about his ruthless war against the Jews in Germany, smashing Jewish businesses and confiscating Jewish homes, and felt a stake in bringing him down, but it was not the same as the sense of direct attack I'd experienced from the Japanese bombs on American soil.

I was disinclined to try to explain any of this to Mademoiselle Lodz. Instead, I gave my attention to Martin, who was across the table regaling Bidwell with tales of the Operational Group during the years before the invasion. To introduce Antonio and Bettjer, Martin was detailing their most entertaining success against the Nazis, which had come in a small town to the west. There vintners sold *vin ordinaire* by hauling it through the streets in a hogshead mounted on two wheels, from which the villagers would fill their carafes through a bunghole in the bottom. Together Antonio and Bettjer had inserted a wooden partition in one of these casks, leaving wine in the lower portion. In the upper half, Bettjer had crawled between the staves. Looking out a tiny spy hole, he radioed information to Martin on the whereabouts of a German Panzer division moving through the town, while Antonio rolled the barrel down the street so their wireless was immune to the German direction-finding trucks that crawled around the area in search of resistance transmitters.

"It was all brilliant," said Martin, "except that poor Peter literally got drunk on the fumes. When we opened the cask, he had passed out cold."

Around the table, there was a hail of laughter and several jokes about Bettjer and alcohol, to which he'd clearly become more accustomed. Right now he was bright red with drink. I had been more careful with the wine, but the same could not be said of most of the others and the level of hilarity had increased as Martin went on recounting their adventures.

"You appear, Major, to have been destined for this life," I said to him eventually.

"Oh, hardly," he answered. "I was organizing for the International Transport Workers around Paris, when the Nazis decided to go marching. I had no desire to return to war, Dubin. I'd had more than enough of it in Spain. I'd led other Americans in the Abraham Lincoln Brigade, then became a commando when the foreign troops were sent home. It was all quite dismal, to be frank. I had no desire to see more friends and comrades tortured and killed by Fascists. After Paris fell, I moved back to Madrid, where I was a transportation official with an oil company. Spain was a neutral country, and with a Spanish passport I could go anywhere, even Germany, which is why the OSS approached me. Originally, I thought I was to be a mere conduit for information. But one thing led to another. I had no interest in joining the Army, yet I could not refuse when they asked me to lead the OG."

Yesterday, at the 18th, I had reviewed a clip from *Stars and Stripes* in Martin's file, detailing how the Operational Groups had been formed. Colonel Donovan, the founder of the Office of Strategic Services, had corralled swashbucklers from everywhere, Russian émigrés, Spanish Civil War veterans like Martin, and a number of Italian speakers from New York, Boston, and Chicago. All of them had been trained at the Congressional Country Club outside D.C., where they had done conditioning runs on the famous golf course and received instruction in the black arts of silent assassination, demolition, secret radio broadcast, judo, cryptography, lock picking, safecracking, and installing listening devices. Martin's efficiency reports from that period were often marked out, but made clear he had been a star, except with Morse code, where he never succeeded in getting above twelve words a minute.

Following his training, according to Lieutenant Colonel Brunson, Teedle's G-1 who'd briefed me, Martin and two comrades, as well as eight supply chutes carrying radios, weapons, and necessities like currency, were dropped over France by a low-flying bomber in October 1942. Each man had a fake ID, a work card, and a cyanide capsule. Somehow, the Nazis had seen the drop. The Englishman with them was shot, while Martin and a French sergeant, who I believed was the Gypsy Antonio now at the end of the table, spent two days in the woods barely avoiding the Germans.

Over time, however, the OG was established. Because of his union activities before the war, Martin was able to build an active network among the rail workers, many of whom he had known for years. Together they sabotaged 370 trains in the succeeding months, destroying railheads and tracks, setting locomotives afire, igniting fuel dumps, and attacking German convoys on the run. After D-Day, as the Third Army advanced north, Stemwinder monitored German troop movements and brought down bridges along the Loire. In the file, there were several laudatory communications from grateful commanders. Leaving aside Teedle.

"And before Spain?" I said to him. "May I ask what you asked me, Major? Where is the home war has taken you from?"

He laughed, but the wine gave him a wistful look.

"Good for you, Dubin. That's the sixty-four-dollar question. But I left all that behind long ago." His smile had faded, when he added, "The answer is as lost to history as the ruins of ancient Greece."

After coffee—Nescafé, about which the Comtesse permitted herself one rueful remark over the lost pleasures of former days—I asked Martin to help me find evidence that would show that OSS had directed him to remain here. Very drunk now, he took a second to marshal himself, and in his confused expression I could see he was peeved by my determination. But in the end he laughed and patted my back.

"What a serious fellow you are, Dubin. Yes, of course."

The first thought was to show me the shortwave radio through which they received London's orders, but I needed something better than that. Martin frowned again at my doggedness but put the question in French to his Stemwinder colleagues who remained at the table.

"*Londres?*" asked Bettjer. "*Les documents des cons, non?*"

Martin laughed. "How wonderful. Yes." The papers of the idiots' referred to the Finance Officers in OSS, who were the same relentless penny-pinchers in that outfit they were everywhere else, demanding that Martin keep exact accounts of the funds advanced for the Operational Group. If I had not been in the Army, I might not have believed that Martin's orders to mount commando attacks were never reduced to writing, but that nickels and dimes required precise records. Mademoiselle Lodz said she kept the papers with the radio, and I followed her outside to find them. At 3:00 p.m. the daylight was still bright, and leaving the dim house, especially after the wine, I needed to shield my eyes.

"*Cela vous dérange si je fume?*" she asked. Does it bother you if I smoke? It was a meaningless courtesy since she already had the flame of her lighter, an American Zippo, to the tip. She had not lit up at the table in deference to the Comtesse, who did not approve of women with cigarettes. Otherwise, Mademoiselle Lodz had barely been without a Lucky Strike between her fingers. I took smoking as the source of her appealing cough-drop voice, like June Allyson's. I declined when she offered me one, telling her I'd never picked up the habit.

"The C rations are terrible," she said. "But the cigarettes? This is the best thing the American Army brought with them." She actually hugged her green pack of Luckys to her breast. "In Vichy, the women were banned from buying cigarettes altogether. Martin says that is why I had no choice but to join the resistance." She laughed at herself.

At supper, Martin had recounted several of Gita's adventures. On D-Day, for example, she had calmly turned the road signs at an intersection ninety degrees and stood there long enough to direct an entire Nazi tank battalion south rather than west. Later that afternoon, according to Martin, they had destroyed a large part of the same unit, when Gita and he herded dozens of sheep onto a bridgehead the Nazis were hoping to cross. While the German soldiers were shooing the livestock, Antonio slipped beneath the bridge and set detonators and dynamite, which they blew when the tanks moved forward.

"Martin's stories of your exploits are remarkable."

She smiled. "And even better if they were true."

I lost a step, which evoked another spirited laugh from her.

"Those of us with Martin," she told me, "have watched our lives grow larger when he describes our activities. But he is so good at it, we all believe him. That is Martin's way. At times, there's not a person here who knows whether he's speaking the truth. I am not even certain that his name is Martin. With the OSS, they all take noms de guerre. But it does not matter. Who are we, Dubin, but the stories we tell about ourselves, particularly if we accept them? My mother said that always."

I had never heard anyone declare such a notion aloud, that we somehow had the power to make ourselves up on the go. Yet it was an idea that attracted me, and I reflected a moment, trying to determine whether life allowed that kind of latitude and how far it might extend.

"Without disrespect to your mother, Mademoiselle, it is better, is it not, if those stories are also true?"

"But who is to tell the truth, Doo-bean? In my town, they said my mother was a tramp. She was a seamstress, but she had lovers among the well-to-do, and took their money. In her view, she was a nonconformist, an artiste at heart. She chose to believe that, and I did as well."

"I am sure that is so," I said, deferring to the reflective softness that had come over Mademoiselle Lodz as she spoke about her mother. "Her loss must have been terrible for you," I said quietly.

"Quite terrible. She remains with me every moment. If not for those assassins, she would have lived to be one hundred. In my family, all the women do. My mother said that was our problem, she and I. There is too much life in us. It makes us wild in youth. And for her that made enduring burdens." She smiled sadly as she touched her own blouse.

"And when she died and you ran from Poland, where did you go first?"

"I landed in Marseilles. I was seventeen. I envisioned myself as the new Bernhardt. Bold, eh? I could barely speak a word of French. I did what needed doing. My mother had taught me to sew, and I found a job mending sheets in a hospital laundry. Soon I was promoted and allowed to empty bedpans." Again, she permitted a husky laugh about herself. "I found my way. Come," she said, "I will show you the items you wish to see."

Walking briskly, she reached the cowshed at the far end of the courtyard, which, like all the connected buildings, had been built of thick stones clad in a coating of cement and sand. On the second floor were quarters for a staff. Judging from the line of curtained windows that surrounded us, the Comtesse once must have employed dozens more workers than now.

Inside the old barn, the air was dense with the ripe smells of animals and moldy hay. Entering a cow stall, Mademoiselle Lodz took hold of a weathered milking stool. With a screwdriver, she removed a metal plate from the bottom of the seat, revealing the radio and its battery.

"Peter says only a few years ago the radios were enormous. Ten, twelve kilos. But now." She withdrew the sleek transmitter and placed it in my hand. It was about six inches long and did not weigh even a pound. Before D-Day, she said, their orders came over the BBC in code with the 9:00 p.m. news. These days, messages were relayed back and forth once a week, when an OSS plane carrying a radio relay to London passed overhead. I nodded, but it was the papers that interested me and I mentioned them again.

"Voilà." Mademoiselle Lodz drew a wad from inside the stool. Included was the yellow duplicate of Standard Form 1012a, Martin's travel voucher, signed and stamped by the paymaster at Central Base Station in London, and containing the details of Martin's trip there and back between September 26 and 30. There were also receipts for two meals Martin had consumed on the way, and French war scrip. Martin's itinerary was exactly as he claimed: OSS had redispatched him here a little more than three weeks ago. When I asked to take the papers, Mademoiselle Lodz was reluctant, but I promised to have them back within a week. In return, she wanted to know what this was all about. I gave her the bare details of Teedle's complaint.

"London just sent Martin back," she said. "You can see yourself." The records didn't seem to leave much doubt of that. All in all, it had the look of a typical Army SNAFU. "Teedle would be eager to believe the worst," she said. "*Bon sang.* Teedle, Martin—that is a bad match. They have been unpleasant with each other from the start."

"Teedle is the superior."

"*Il a une dent contre lui.*" He has a grudge against him. "It is true Martin does not like to receive orders in the field," she said. "He prefers to reach concord with his commanders. Teedle wants only to be obeyed."

"There must be order in war. A chain of command."

"In war, order is no more than a good intention. Order is for generals. Not soldiers. *Tu te mets le doigt dans l'oeil.*" You are putting your finger in your eye, meaning I was fooling myself.

"I am a lawyer, nonetheless. I must defend the rules."

"Lawyers are functionaries. Little men. Are you a little man, Dubin? It does not seem so."

"I don't regard the law as little rules. I regard it as an attempt to impart reason and dignity to life."

"Justice imparts reason and dignity, Dubin. Not rules. Little rules and large wrongs are a bad mix. I don't know your rules. But I know what is wrong. As does Martin. The Nazis are wrong. Fight them. That is the only rule that should matter. Not whether Martin does Teedle's bidding."

"You argue well," I said to her. "If Martin has need of a lawyer, he should consider you."

At the idea, she laughed loudly, until giving way to a hacking smoker's cough. I was impressed by Mademoiselle Lodz's raucousness, which seemed bold compared to Grace, who literally raised her hand to her mouth when she was amused. We had reached the sun again. Mademoiselle Lodz flattened her small hand above her eyes as she regarded me.

"You interest me, Doo-bean."

"I am flattered, Mademoiselle. Is that because I am a lawyer, or an American, or a Jew?"

"*Ça ne rime à rien.*" That doesn't rhyme with anything, meaning there was no point. "Who you are, you are, no?"

"I suppose. And who, Mademoiselle Lodz, may I ask, are you?"

"Who do you take me for, Dubin?"

"You seem to be a soldier and a philosopher."

She laughed robustly again. "No," she said, "I am too young to be a philosopher. I spout, but you should pay no attention. Besides, I don't trust intellectuals. They place too much faith in ideas."

"I am probably guilty of that."

"It seems so."

"But principles matter, do they not?"

"*Mais oui.* But do they come before anything else?"

"I hope so. Certainly that is desirable, is it not, to care first about principles?"

"*C'est impossible,*" she said.

I expressed my doubts, and she told me I was being naïve.

"Perhaps," I said, "but if I was being a lawyer—or a philosopher—I would tell you that a convincing argument requires proof."

"'Proof'?" She smirked. "Proving is too easy."

"How so?"

"Eh, Doo-bean. You are an innocent at heart. I will show you, if I must. *Un moment.*" She disappeared into the barn again, but promptly called out, "Come."

I stepped back into the humid scents and darkness. At first, I saw no one.

"Here," she said behind me. When I turned, Gita Lodz had lifted her skirt to her waist, revealing her slim legs and her undergarment, a kind of cotton bloomer. It fit snugly, revealing her narrow shape and, with another instant's attention, the indentation of her female cleft and the shadow of the dark triangle around it.

"Is it principle you feel first, Dubin?"

I had long recognized that the hardest part of life in a war zone was that there was so often no routine, no order, nothing to count on. Every moment was a novelty. But this display exceeded even the limited boundaries that remained. I was literally struck dumb.

"*Touché,*" I finally said, the only word I could think of, which brought another outburst of laughter while she smothered down her skirt. By pure chance, I had come off as a wit.

"We are primitive, Dubin. If we are not to be, then we require one another's assistance. But first know who we are."

I gave a simple nod. Satisfied she had made a potent demonstration, Mademoiselle Lodz strolled from the cowshed, looking back from the sunlight with a clever smile. I waited in the shadows. She would treat this as a prank, but free to watch from the darkness, I had a sudden vision of Gita Lodz and the riot of feeling that underlay her boldness. Her upbringing in scorn had left her with no choice but to defy convention, yet despite her confident airs and the stories she wished to believe, I sensed, almost palpably, that her personality was erected on a foundation of anger, and beneath that, pain. When I stepped back into the sun, some sadness must have clung to the way I looked at her, which I could tell was entirely unexpected. As we considered each other something fell away, and she turned heel immediately, headed toward the house.

I caught up, but we trudged back in silence. It was she who spoke finally, as we approached the little castle.

"Have I offended you, Dubin?"

"Of course not. I challenged you. You responded. Convincingly."

"But you are shocked."

"Pay no attention. I am easily shocked, Mademoiselle Lodz."

"Good for you," she said. "In France, no one will admit to being bourgeois."

I laughed. "In America, it is the universal aspiration. But I still must respect proprieties. I am sent to inquire of a man. The law might question my impartiality if I was interested instead in looking at his woman in her dainties."

"Not his woman. I am not with Martin in that way, Dubin. That is done between us. Long ago."

I thought of Martin embracing her in the kitchen.

"I have heard many refer to you as his woman."

"That is convenient for both of us. There are soldiers everywhere, Dubin. It is better to be known as spoken for. Do not be repelled for Martin's sake. Only your own." She gave me that sly smile. "À la *prochaine,*" she said—Until next time—and breezed through the door, restored to her former self.

Biddy was waiting there. We needed to be back at the 18th before dark, but I was still reverberating like a struck bell. It had been months since I'd had anything to do with a woman, except with the clinical neutrality of a lawyer interviewing witnesses, and I had forgotten the pull that seemed to emanate from every cell. I had been resolutely faithful to Grace, even in the brothel atmosphere of London, where the joke went that every girl's knickers had the same flaw: one Yank and they were off. There I had known what to expect. Sex was everywhere—you could hear the moans when you passed a supposedly unoccupied air raid shelter, or walked in the dark through Hyde Park. The U.S. soldiers, with their Arrid and Odo·Ro·No, seemed rich and well-groomed compared to the poor beaten-down Brits, who had a single uniform and their noisy hobnailed boots. Now both Biddy and I were looking at the doorway through which Gita had gone.

"You have a girl at home, Biddy?" I asked.

"Nope. Had one, but let her get away. Joyce Washington. Courted with her all through high school. Was het up to marry, too. She got herself a job typing at the First National Bank. And there was some fella there, Lieutenant, I guess he just swept her off her feet. And her with my ring on her finger. She come to tell me and I said to her, 'How can you do this, go off with another man when you promised yourself to me?' And you know what she says? She says, 'Gideon, he's got a Hudson.' Can you imagine? I honestly got to say, Lieutenant, I really don't think it was the letdown that bothered me so much as wondering how in all get-out I could have been fool enough to love a woman like that." He fixed on the distance while the pain swamped him again, then shook it off.

"I done all right with those English girls," he said, "but I can't make head or tail of these Frenchies. All that ooh-la-la junk may go in Paris, but out this way, these are just country gals, Lieutenant, and it ain't no different than in Georgia, mamas tell them all their lives to keep their legs crossed till the day they say 'I do,' war or no war. What about you, Lieutenant? You been makin any time?" Unconsciously perhaps, his eyes diverted toward the doorway.

"I have a fiancée back home, Biddy." We both knew this was not a direct response. Eisley, with a wife in Ohio, could explain in utter seriousness how all formalities, especially marriage vows, were suspended during times of war. But I left it at that.

Martin had stepped out of the house, still flushed from the wine and smiling hugely. I took it that he'd had a word with Gita and had come outside to say goodbye to us.

"So I hear we actually found your precious papers. I could tell you came here with the wrong impression. Mark my words, Dubin, Teedle is trying to stir things up. He's giving orders where he has no call to."

"Mademoiselle Lodz says he has a grudge against you."

"That would be one way to put it." His blue eyes went for a moment to the horizon, the first occasion when I had seen him measure his words. "Look, Dubin, sooner or later you're going to figure out what this is all about. You don't need my *j'accuse.*"

"If you'd rather I not share your response with General Teedle—"

"Oh, I don't care a fig about Teedle. Look, Dubin, it's this simple. He thinks I'm a Communist. Because I fought in Spain. After the Axis, the Soviets are next. I'm the new enemy. Or so he believes."

"Are you?"

"An enemy of the United States? I should say not."

"A Communist, sir."

"I've been fighting too long, Dubin, to call myself anything. I believe in power for the powerless, food for the hungry, shelter for the homeless. Does that make me a revolutionary? Here, Dubin, it all comes down to this. The man is wasting your time and he knows it. I intend to fulfill my mission. And I won't allow Teedle to get in my way, or bog me down with Army folderol. I can melt into this landscape, or that of any other place from here to Berlin, if I choose."

He gave me a pointed look. I was startled by the openness with which he discussed insubordination, but there was no chance for rejoinder, because both of us were drawn to the buzz of planes overhead. Martin was immediately on alert, like a pointer in the field, squinting to search the sky. But the aircraft were ours.

"B-26s, I reckon," he said then. "They're going to take advantage of the break in the weather to bomb."

Just as he predicted, the heavy sounds echoed a few minutes later. At first, the distant bombardment was like oil popping in a skillet, but as the squadrons kept passing overhead, the noise came closer. A barrier of smoke and dust arose and drifted back to us, damming the light and ghosting over the Comtesse's fields, carrying along the odor of gunpowder. We could hear German antiaircraft fire. No more than a mile ahead, we saw a plane burst into flame and parachutes bloom in the sky.

A number of the farmworkers as well as Antonio had joined us on the cobbles as spectators. Martin asked the Gypsy about the position of the 26th Infantry to be certain they would be able to reach the downed fliers. While this discussion was under way, another squadron passed, flying lower. We had been trading around a pair of field glasses that someone had brought from the house and when I took my turn, I could see the bomb bays open beneath the planes. I had just remarked on this to Martin, when an explosion shook the air around us, and a column of fire rose on the next hill.

"Lord," said Martin. "We'll be lucky if they don't drop on us as well." He looked up one more time, then dashed into the little castle, yelling first to Gita, then everyone else. He emerged in seconds behind the Comtesse and her servants. In both English and French, he commanded everyone into the old stone cellar beneath the house. He stood at the door, shooing all of us down, ordering us to be quick. The workers came running out of the fields, some still in waders they had been wearing in the flooded lower grounds. I was already in the earthen-floored cellar when another detonation reverberated, closer than the first. I looked to the entrance to see about Martin, but he appeared in a moment, slamming the door behind him and thumping down the stairs. The cellar was no more than six feet high and there was now no light. I'd seen Biddy hunched in the corner, next to the shelves of jarred fruits and an adjoining wall racked with dusty bottles of wine. There must have been twenty people huddled in the dark. The air quickly grew close. There were the usual jokes. One of the women said, "Keep your hands to yourself," and a man responded, "You, as well." In a far corner, a cat was meowing.

"*D'ici peu, on va se sentir tous comme des cons,*" someone remarked across the room. In a moment we will feel like fools. He had barely spoken, when the atmosphere was rent by the fabulous concussion of an explosion directly overhead.

The Germans still had 280mm railway artillery pieces in the Vosges elevated over Nancy, and once or twice a day the cry of incoming fire would ring out and everyone in the court-martial session would scramble into the cellar of the Lycée, waiting for the big boom of the shells. But that was no preparation for being bombed. The air seemed to slam shut on me, then opened briefly only to pound me again, while the earth literally jostled beneath our feet. I felt the shock across my entire body—even my cheeks and eyeballs were compressed. And the sound was worse. I had never understood until that moment that noise alone, even when you knew its source, could be loud enough to inspire panic. My ears went numb, then revived, throbbing.

In the instant afterward, I assumed the house had been struck and would collapse on us, but there was no sign of that. Instead there was light now. Eventually I realized that the wooden door of the cellar had been blown off. Martin went out first and in time called down that it was safe to emerge. Coming up into the daylight, I noticed that my boots were soaked with wine.

The crater of the bomb, the depth and the size of a small pond, had disturbed earth all the way to the house, but the actual point of impact seemed to have been about 150 yards away in the pasture. Everyone who had been in the cellar radiated off to inspect the damage. It was quickly determined there were no human casualties, although a number of those who had been near the cellar walls had been struck by falling bottles and several had been cut, including Biddy, who had pulled a shard the size of an arrowhead out of his arm.

Around the farm, the Comtesse's chicks and her one cow were nowhere to be found, and a horse was dead, keeled over like a life-size toy with his lips raveled back fearfully over his huge teeth. The family dog had literally been blown to bits. His leather collar was about a hundred yards from the house. I suspected that the blast that blew off the cellar door had been the end of the hound, who had probably been cowering there.

As for the little castle, the damage was moderate. All the rear windows had been blown out, and their shutters were gone. A piece of the roof had been ripped off like the corner of a sheet of paper. Inside, I saw that much of the crockery had shattered. For the Comtesse de Lemolland, this proved too much. She had withstood the death of a spouse and a son with dignity, and the destruction of her husband's château, but the loss of an old delft plate that her mother had hung on the wall sixty years ago somehow exceeded her meager abilities to carry on. She was on the wooden floor of the kitchen, her skirt billowed about her, while she gathered the chalky pieces in her hands and wailed in complete abandon. Gita held one shoulder to comfort her.

I fled outside, where Martin still searched the sky with the field glasses to be sure we were safe.

"Did they lose their coordinates?" I asked.

"Perhaps," said Martin, then erupted in a sharp laugh. "Perhaps not." He lowered the binoculars to look at me. "I rather suspect, Dubin, we've all had a greeting card from General Teedle."

III.

7. STEWART: BEAR LEACH

Northumberland Manor occupied a large campus in West Hartford, a collection of white clapboard buildings containing various facilities for the elderly, everything from independent housing to hospice, and the several other stages in between as decline rolls downhill to death. Arriving early, I awaited Justice Barrington Leach, my father's long-ago lawyer, in the front room of the Manor's nursing home. With its wall-to-wall robin's-egg carpeting and nice Ethan Allen furnishings, the place presented itself as far superior to the usual holding tank for the barely living.

Given everything it had taken to get to Leach, including passing myself off as a lately orphaned only child, I sat there with high expectations. Leach, after all, was a longtime legal hotshot, whose skills had somehow allowed him to erase his trial loss and persuade General Teedle to revoke my father's conviction and prison sentence. Thus, I couldn't help being disappointed when a nurse's aide pushed the old man into the room. Overall, Justice Leach gave the physical impression of a fallen leaf crisped down to its veins. His spotty bald head listed, barely rising above the back of his wheelchair, and the hose from an oxygen tank was holstered in his nose. He had been so whittled by age that his sturdy Donegal tweed suit, perhaps older than I am, was puddled around him, and his skin had begun to acquire a whitish translucence which signaled that even the wrapper was giving out.

Yet none of that mattered once he started talking. Leach's voice wobbled, just like his long hands on which the fingers were knobbed from arthritis, but his mind moved along quickly. He remained fully connected to this world. To say Barrington Leach still took great joy in life would be not only hackneyed, but probably inaccurate. The Justice's wife and his only child, a daughter, were both dead of breast cancer. His three adult grandkids lived in California, where they had been raised, and he had resisted their heartsore efforts to move him from Hartford. As a result he was largely alone here, and he suffered from Parkinson's, among several other ailments. I doubt he found life either comfortable or amusing most of the time.

But none of this inhibited his intense curiosity about human beings. He was a gentle wit, and full of a generous acceptance for people's foibles as well as reverent wonder at our triumphs. I come easily to envy, but with Barrington Leach, when I mused, as I always did, about why I couldn't be more like him, it was with pure admiration. He was inspiring.

My first order of business with Leach was to set the record straight, not about my mother and sister, naturally, but rather about what to call me. He had written to me as "Mr. Dubin," but in 1970, I had reverted to the name my grandfather had brought from Russia and have been known as Stewart Dubinsky throughout my adult life. The story of that change, too involved to repeat here now, made a fairly poignant introduction to my relations with my father. Leach asked several searching questions before going on to inquiries about my work, my parents, and the course of my father's life. He was so precise, and cautious in a way, that I feared at first that he knew I'd lied about Mom, but it turned out he had something else in mind.

"You know, Stewart, I think you mean to honor your father's memory, but I would be remiss if I didn't issue a caveat. If you go forward, you could very well discover things that a loyal son might not enjoy finding out. I've always believed there is great wisdom in the saying that one must be careful what to wish for."

I assured him I had reflected about this. After hanging around court-rooms for a couple of decades, I knew that the odds were that my father had been convicted of a serious crime for a reason.

"Well, that's a good start," Leach said. "But the particulars are al-ways worse than the general idea. And that assumes you even have a general idea. You may find, Stewart, you've been running headlong with blinders."

I told him I was resolute. Whatever happened, I wanted to know.

"Well, that's one problem," said Leach.

"What are the others, Justice?"

"'Bear' is fine." I was never sure if the nickname had to do with his physique as a young man—he was anything but bearlike now—or, more likely, was merely a convenient shortening of his given name, adopted in an era when being 'Bare' would have been too risqué. "I confess that I've spent quite a bit of time, Stewart, since you contacted me, wonder-ing what call I have to tell you any of this. I feel a good deal of fondness for David, even today. He was a fine young man, articulate, thoughtful. And it was his wish not to speak about this with anyone, a wish he ap-parently maintained throughout his life. Furthermore, wholly aside from personal loyalties, I was his attorney, bound by law to keep his secrets.

"On the other hand, I have things of your father's, Stewart, a docu-ment of his, as I've mentioned, that belongs to you as his heir. I have no right to withhold it from you, and therefore, as to the matters disclosed there, I believe I am free to speak. That, at any rate, will be my defense when the disbarment proceedings begin." He had a prominent cataract in one eye, large enough to be clearly visible, but it could not obscure the light that always arose there with a joke. "But you and I must reach an understanding to start. I can't go beyond the compass of what's writ-ten. You'll find me able to answer most of your questions, but not all. Understood?"

I readily agreed. We both took a breath then before I asked what seemed like the logical first question, how Leach had been assigned my father's case.

"It was roundabout," he answered. "Throughout the war, I had been in the sanctuary of Eisenhower's headquarters, first in Bushy Park outside London, and then later in 1944 at Versailles. These days, I'd be referred to as a 'policy maker.' I had been the District Attorney here in Hartford and certainly knew my way around a courtroom, but my exposure to court-martials was limited to reviewing a few trial records that came up to Eisenhower for final decision, hanging cases most of them. However, your father's commanding officer, Halley Maples, knew my older brother at Princeton, and Maples made a personal appeal to my superiors to appoint me as defense counsel. I had very little choice, not that I ever regretted it, although your father as a client came with his share of challenges." That remark was punctuated with a craggy laugh.

At ninety-six, Bear Leach had been what we call an old man for a long time, at least twenty years, and he had grown practiced with some of the privileges and demands of age. He had been asked about his memories of one thing or another so often that, as I sometimes joked with him, his memoirs were essentially composed in his head. He spoke in flowing paragraphs. As we grew friendlier over the next several months, I brought him a tape recorder in the hope he would use it to preserve prominent stories of his life. But he was too humble to think he'd been much more than a minor figure, and the project didn't interest him. He was, as he always said, a trial lawyer. He preferred a live audience, which I was only too happy to provide.

"It was late April 1945 when I first came to Regensburg, Germany, to meet your father. Officers facing court-martial were traditionally held under house arrest pending trial, and your father was in the Regensburg Castle, where the Third Army was now permanently headquartered. This was a massive *Schloss* occupied for centuries by the Thurn und Taxis family, a palace as Americans think of palaces, occupying several city blocks. Its interior was somewhat baroque, with pillars of colored marble, Roman arches with lovely inlaid mosaics, and classical statuary. I walked nearly twenty minutes through the castle before getting to your father, who was restricted to a suite the size of this sitting room, perhaps larger, and full of marvelous antiques. In this splendor your father was going to remain jailed until the Army got around to shooting him. If you have a taste for irony, you can't do better than the United States military, let me tell you that." Leach smiled then in his way, a gesture restricted by age and disease, so that his jaw slid to the side.

"Your father was an impeccable man, nearly six feet as I recall, and the very image of an officer and a gentleman. He had a perfectly trimmed line mustache above his lip, like the film star William Powell, whom he resembled. From my initial sight of him, the notion that David Dubin had actually engaged in any willful disobedience of his orders, as was charged, seemed preposterous. But establishing that proved one of the most difficult propositions of my career."

"Because?"

"Because the man insisted on pleading guilty. Nothing unusual in that, of course. There are persons charged with crimes who understand they've done wrong. But your father would not explain anything beyond that. Any questions about the events leading up to his apparent decision to re-lease Major Martin were met only with his declaration that it served no point to elaborate. He was very courteous about it, but absolutely adamant. It was a bit like representing Bartleby the Scrivener, except your father said solely 'I am guilty,' rather than 'I would prefer not to,' in response to any request for more information. I was forced to investigate the matter entirely without his cooperation. I learned quite a bit about your father's wartime experiences, but next to nothing about what had gone on between Martin and him.

"Eventually, I had an inspiration and suggested to your father that if what had transpired was so difficult to speak about, he at least ought to make an effort to write it all down, while matters were fresh. If he chose not to show the resulting document to me, so be it, but in the event he changed his mind, I would have a convenient means of briefing myself. He did not warm to the proposal when I made it, but, of course, he had little to do with his days. He enjoyed reading—he soon had me bringing him novels by the armful—but I took it that he, like many other soldiers, had been an inveterate writer of letters and that that outlet was no longer very rewarding for him. As I recollect, he had disappointed his fiancée, and had then horrified his family with the news of his current predica-ment. Apparently, producing a written account of what had led to these charges provided an agreeable substitute, and after his initial reluc-tance, he took up the task with ardor. Whenever I visited him in quarters he was chopping away on a little Remington typewriting machine which sat on a Louis XIV desk, yet another priceless antique, that wobbled with his pounding. About a month along, during a visit, I pointed to the sheaf of pages stacked at his elbow. It was over an inch by now.

"'That's getting to be quite a magnum opus,' I said. 'Are you considering showing any of it to me?' I had been waiting for him to reveal the material in his own time, but with the hearing coming closer, I was concerned that I wouldn't be able to assimilate what clearly was turning into an imposing volume, especially if it opened up new avenues for investigation.

"'Some days I think yes, Colonel,' he said to me, 'and some days I think no.'

"'And why "no"?'

"'I don't believe it's going to help me.'

"'Because I'd think poorly of you? Or accept your judgment of your guilt? You know well enough, Dubin, that nothing would prevent me from making a defense for you.'

"'I do. Reading this, Colonel, might satisfy your curiosity. And it will prove I'm right to plead guilty. But it won't change the result. Or make things any easier for you. More the opposite.'

"In weaker moments, I sometimes considered sneaking in and stealing the pages, but he was right that it was his ship to sink. But I kept after him about letting me see it. Each time he seemed to give full consideration to my points, and then, after due reflection, rejected them. And so we went to trial. David tendered a plea of guilty at the start. The trial judge advocate, the prosecutor, had agreed to drop the most serious charge in exchange, but he still went on to prove his case, which was commonplace in serious court-martials. This, of course, was a decided contrast to the usual criminal matter, where a guilty plea avoids a trial, and I couldn't quite accommodate myself to the difference. I cross-examined with a fury, because none of the accounts were consistent in any way with a soldier who would willfully abandon his duties. Very often, I retired for the night, thinking how well I had done, only to recall that my client had already conceded the validity of the charges.

"The *Manual for Courts-Martial* at that time—and now, for all I know—gave the accused the right to make an uncross-examined statement to the panel, immediately preceding closing arguments. The night before the hearing came to an end, I made my last effort to get your father to share his written account, urging him to consider submitting his memoir, or portions of it, to the court. My heart leaped when he came to the proceedings the next morning with what I judged to be the manuscript under his arm in two portfolios, but he kept them to himself. He made a brief statement to the court, saying simply that in releasing Martin he had meant no harm to the United States, whose service remained the greatest honor of his life. Only when the evidence was closed did he turn the folders over to me. It was meant as a generosity on his part, I think, to repay me for my efforts on his behalf, so that I could accept the result with peace of mind. He told me to read it all, if that was what I liked, and when I was done to return it to him. He said forthrightly that he was then going to set fire to the whole thing.

"Even at that stage, I remained hopeful that I'd find something recorded there that I might use to reopen the case. The court was recessed on Sunday. I spent the whole day reading, morning to night, and finished only instants before I arrived for court at eight a.m. on Monday."

"And what did it say?" I was like a child listening to campfire tales, who wanted only to know what children always do: the end of the story.

Bear gave a dry laugh in response.

"Well, Stewart, there aren't many tales worth telling that can be boiled down to a sentence or two, are there?"

"But did you use it?"

"Most assuredly not."

"Because?"

"Because your father was right. He was a good lawyer. A very good lawyer. And his judgment was correct. If the court-martial members knew the whole tale, it would only have made matters worse. Possibly far worse."

"How so?"

"There were many complications," he said, "many concerns. As I say, I was fond of your father. That's not just prattle. But a trial lawyer learns to be cold-blooded about the facts. And I looked at this as trial lawyers do, the best case that could be made and the worst, and I realized that nothing good was going to come from revealing this to the court. Your father's cause, in fact, could have been gravely prejudiced."

"You're not being very specific, Justice. What was so bad?"

Bear Leach, not often short of words, took a second to fiddle with his vintage necktie, swinging like a pendant from the collar of his old shirt, which, these days, gapped a good two inches from his wattled neck.

"When I read your father's account, I realized he had been the beneficiary of an assumption that the trial judge advocate might well regard as ill founded, once the underlying facts were better known."

I tumbled my hand forward. "You're being delicate, Justice."

"Well, it requires delicacy, Stewart, no doubt of that. I'm speaking to a son about his father."

"So you warned me. I want to know."

Leach went through the extended effort it required to reposition the oxygen in his nose.

"Stewart, your father was charged with willfully suffering a prisoner to escape. The evidence, in sum, was that Robert Martin had last been seen by several troops of the 406th Armored Cavalry in your father's custody. Your father admitted he had allowed Martin to go, freed him from his manacles and leg irons and saw him out of the bivouac. The escape charge took it for granted that Martin had fled from there. But what your father had written suggested a far more disturbing possibility, one whose likelihood was enhanced, at least in my mind, by your father's rigorous silence."

"What possibility?"

"Now, Stewart, let me caution that this was merely a thought."

"Please, Bear. What possibility?"

Leach finally brought himself to a small nod.

"That your father," he said, "had murdered Robert Martin."

8. DAVID: TEEDLE'S SECRETS

By the time Biddy and I had returned to the 18th from the Comtesse de Lemolland's, we found no one in General Teedle's tent. The MP outside said that both orderlies were off duty, and Teedle was surveying battalions. With time, I wandered down to the enlisted men's area again. The bombing at the Comtesse's had revived my curiosity about Billy Bonner's remark that I was investigating the wrong man.

The skies had closed in once more, leaving no chance for further air traffic. Freed from blackout restrictions, the men had built fires and were enjoying themselves amid the usual barroom atmosphere. Somebody had run Armed Forces Radio through a loudspeaker. Harry James was on *Command Performance*, and I stopped to listen as he blew his way majestically through "Cherry." It suddenly hit me how much I missed music, for which I'd once felt a yearning as keen as hunger. These days, that longing was dampened under piles of law books and by the frantic concentration required for seven-day weeks in court. Closing my eyes, for just one second, I caught the sure feel of Grace's waist beneath my hand while we were dancing.

I ran across Biddy unexpectedly. He was standing back with his camera, taking snaps of four men playing cards by lantern in a mess tent. They'd come inside to keep the invasion currency they were gambling with, French francs that had been printed in the U.S., from blowing off in the wind. Each man was straddling an empty cartridge case, while they used a crate emptied of bazooka rounds for a table.

"Jesus God almighty," one said. "Play a fucking card, won't you, Mickey. You're gonna be dead this time next month, and still wondering what you should have led for trump."

"Mortenson, don't talk like that."

"You think the Krauts are listenin?"

"No, but it's kind of like you're putting the evil eye on me."

"Oh, shut your damn swill hole, Krautbait, will you, and play a card."

"Don't be a sorehead, Witkins."

"Yeah, take a bite of this."

"Several soldiers in line in front of me for that pleasure."

"Fuckin Mickey still ain't recovered from striking out with that Frenchy. Only because half the platoon had some ass with her and she still wouldn't come across for him."

"Half the platoon are doggone liars. That girl was a nice girl. I just wanted to buy her a Coke."

"Coke ain't what you wanted her to swallow."

"Geez, Mort, what kind of pervert are you?"

"Listen, kiddo, these French girls use their mouths."

"Not on me. That's strictly perverted."

"Would youse guys shut the fuck up. It's gonna be fuckin reveille by the time this slowpoke plays a card."

I enjoyed Tony Eisley, but there was none of this raw camaraderie among JAG Department officers. Not that I shared in it here. Twenty-nine was old to most of these boys, and the presence of an officer was unsettling, even resented. My visits to the enlisted men's quarters reminded me of coming home to DuSable from Easton, when neighbors asked about the "college man" in a tone that was not altogether admiring. I was going to make money, they thought. I was going to move away from there, and them. In the enlisted ranks these days, there were a fair number of college boys because early this year Congress had put an end to the Army Specialized Training Program that had sent recruits to college

classes full-time. On the other end, a few enlisted men from the premo-
bilization Army had been commissioned. For the most part, though, you
might as well have put up signs over the enlisted men's and the officers'
sides of camp that said POOR and RICH. I had not figured out yet why the
Army thought discipline or any other military purpose was advanced by
these disparities. Yet I knew, much as I had in basic, that here I was
among the real soldiers. The generals' names might be remembered by
historians, but it was these men who would fight the true war.

Emerging from the tent, I wandered for some time before I caught
sight of Billy Bonner around a fire with several other soldiers, each of
them holding a dark bottle of wine. Bonner clearly regarded me as the
law and stopped with his arm in midair, causing two or three of his buddies to turn away, until I said, "At ease."

We strolled off a few paces and I explained to Bonner that Teedle appeared to be gone.

"Oh, he'll be back. General likes his nights in his own tent." One of
Bonner's smart-aleck looks accompanied the remark.

"Bonner, you don't seem to hold the General in high esteem."

"No, sir," he said. "He's as good a brass hat as this Army's got."

"But?"

Bonner shook his head and rolled his lips into his mouth, but I was
persistent tonight. After quite a bit of cajoling, he finally motioned me
farther from his companions.

"You didn't hear this here," said Bonner. He lifted the wine bottle
again to stick his courage. "The bastard's a nelly."

"I'm sorry?"

"Teedle's a fruit, damn it."

"In what way?"

"In *that* way. Jesus, Lieutenant, don't you know what a queer is?"

"Good Lord, Bonner." I told him that if he wasn't potted, I'd have
had the MPs take him off.

"Just remember you said that, Lieutenant. That's the reason no one
does anything about him."

"About what?"

"I already told you. The man's a homo. You know, the General, he's
got his billet right there in his tent. Makes like it's so he can work around
the clock. But that's not why. Damn bugger gets himself rip-roaring—

worse than normal—and then sends Frank for this enlisted man or that. Always some boy who looks like he rolled out from under a hay bale, too, strapping kids from the country, blond-haired. I'm dismissed when they get there. Now and then, I come back in the morning, those poor boys are still around. Some, God save them, they're sleeping like lambs. But there must have been a few to put up a fight, 'cause the General, he's had some damage on him, a shiner once that wouldn't go away for a week. I'll tell you, Lieutenant, I've been there, and two or three of those boys come out—there isn't a thing those Krauts could do to them that would be worse. His own damn CO. You can just see how bewildered these kids are. They don't know nothin anymore."

I wasn't sure I'd ever heard a more revolting story.

"Why, the bloody bastard," I said. "And haven't you brought this to the attention of an officer?"

"Well, I'm talking to you, Lieutenant. General Patton hasn't come by to chew the cud lately. But who's to say I didn't make this up? None of these boys care to discuss it, not the ones who like it, and especially not the ones who don't. I thought that the fellow who socked the General in the eye, soldier named Lang, I figured he might have a word to say, but his sergeant wouldn't even hear about it. Wasn't getting his private in a swearing match with that star, not about something like this, not in this man's Army. But maybe you fellas can loosen tongues. I don't know boo about Captain Martin," Bonner said. "But I'd say if Teedle wants a court-martial so bad, get started with him."

At 0730, when I came by, General Teedle was in his tent, speaking with his G-3 Major Michaels. As the operations officer, Michaels would not have had much to do lately, but today he had laid out several large battle maps on the General's desk. This was work, planning combat movements moment by moment, sequence by sequence, in which I'd excelled in infantry officer training at Fort Benning. At this stage, before the bullets flew, it was an exercise of pure intellect, a cross between chess and playing with tin soldiers, but the deadly reality of these decisions was manifest in the intensity of both men. Seeing them, it was obvious that new stores of fuel and ammo were finally on the way. The 18th's R & R was going to end shortly.

As I waited between the tent flaps, I found myself turning over Bonner's accusation while I scrutinized Teedle, with his cock-robin posture and his rosy drunkard's hue. The very notion of the General's conduct had wrenched me awake several times during the night. Eventually, I'd settled back to the practical problem of what to do. Because I liked Billy Bonner, I'd taken him at his word. But God only knew all the reasons he might be lying. Finally, near 4:00 in the morning, I resolved that I would simply wait for a private moment with Colonel Maples and pass the word to him. Sometimes the Army's long chain of command was not all bad. If a problem was big enough, you could hand it to somebody else.

Even so, I had no confidence that I wouldn't break into a visible sweat when Teedle was finally ready to see me. I was only grateful that Bonner was not yet on duty so I wasn't obliged to meet his eye.

"So how was Charming Bob?" Teedle asked me, when I saluted before his desk. "Charming, eh? Did he entertain you like visiting royalty?"

"More or less."

"Have his girlfriend flirt with you, too? She's as clever as Martin, you know. She's batted her eyes at several folks I've sent down there. Anything that works, with those two." Bonner's remarks had been enough that my mind hadn't worked its way back very often to Gita Lodz. Nonetheless, Teedle had his intended effect of deflating me a bit, by revealing that I was not the first of his emissaries on whom Mademoiselle Lodz had settled her candid look and told them, one way or the other, how interesting they were. On the other hand, I was hardly surprised that a woman who'd raise her skirt for a debater's point wasn't shy around other men. For whatever reason, though, I felt some need to stick up for her.

"I wouldn't say she batted her eyes, General."

"That surprises me, Dubin, handsome young fellow like you." He gave me a wry look, chin lowered. Under the circumstances, Teedle's assessment nearly made me jump.

"I'm engaged, sir," I finally blurted.

"Good for you," he said, then asked what Martin had to say for himself. I had wondered how I was going to question General Teedle about Martin's claims—I had no right to demand answers from a general. But Teedle was far too voluble for that to prove a problem.

"That's horse hockey," he responded, when I explained that Martin said OSS had returned him from London late last month with directions to proceed into Germany. Showing Teedle Martin's papers stopped the General cold.

"I'll be a son of a bitch," he said, as he looked them over. "First I heard of this, I admit. All I know is that two weeks ago OSS told me I was finally free to send him packing. I'd asked several times before. I can't tell you why they changed their minds."

"General, the only way to resolve this is to get written confirmation from OSS about whether they have or haven't given Martin other orders."

"Written?" Teedle frumped around in his chair. "Christ, so that's the game! What an operator this prick is. The Army has never been any match for a good operator, Dubin, and Martin's one of the best. OSS isn't going to put anything on paper about Special Operations and send it near the front. Soldiers are taken prisoner, Dubin, but spies are shot. Martin knows all that. Messages from OSS are coded radio transmissions and 'DAR.'" Destroy after reading. The General thought for a moment. "All right. I'll take care of this."

He made a note. It would have been better practice for Colonel Maples or me to communicate with OSS, rather than Teedle, the complainant, but the General didn't seem in any mood to hear about further legal technicalities.

"What else?" said Teedle. "Let's hear all Martin's folderol now, so I can deal with it at once. I'm sure he had a few choice words for me."

I described the bombing. Teedle, to his credit, asked first about casualties.

"I'd heard something about that," Teedle said then. "General Roy from 19th TAC sent a signal yesterday evening. Says he had a squadron that lost its bearings and might have dropped on our troops. He was damn apologetic. If I'd known it was Martin, I'd have sent back a thank-you note."

"Yes, sir, well, I was there, too."

Teedle shot me a look riddled with irony. I could not have understood much about being a general, this look said, if I expected him to be concerned about that. He called out to Frank to have his staff JAG expedite the Comtesse's damage claims.

"So now what mud was Martin slinging? That I have control of the Army Air Corps and arranged to bomb him?"

"He allowed how it was possible."

Teedle answered with a crude laugh. "There are plenty at my rank, Dubin, who wouldn't bother with a Rule Thirty-five investigation when they had an insubordinate officer. They'd send Martin out personally to scout a hilltop guarded by a full German company and never lose a wink. But if that was my idea, I wouldn't have bothered going to HQ, would I?"

"Quite right, sir."

"Oh, don't give me that 'quite right' horseshit. If you don't believe me, say so."

"I think you're making sense, General." I did, too, but Teedle seemed far too complex to expect all his actions to line up with reason. Having a minute to think, I didn't understand why General Roy had apologized to Teedle. The 26th Infantry, not Teedle's unit, was under Roy's bombs. Unless Roy forgot they had changed positions. Which was possible, too.

"Any other calumnies Martin spread to which you'd like a response?"

"May I speak freely, sir?"

"You just accused me of trying to bomb one of my officers. I think you're doing a pretty fair job of it already, Dubin, but help yourself."

I knew better than to debate Teedle by pointing out what had been said previously and by whom. He was amusing himself with the verbal fencing, knowing he had rank on his side. For all his bluster, though, I didn't have the sense that Teedle was baiting me to be cruel, so much as test me. He was an unusual man. Forthright. Opinionated. Harsh. It did not stretch credulity, watching his mobile face, the way he veered between imperiousness and collegiality, and the frankness with which he dared you to dislike him, to think that Teedle's peculiarities extended to far darker realms, as Bonner maintained. But not necessarily to cruelty. Cruelty was a part of human nature, I suspect he would say. We were all mean. But he was no meaner than most.

"Sir, he says your desire to get rid of him is all about the fact that you think he's a Communist."

When he heard that, Teedle put his feet up on his footlocker beside him, while he smiled and stroked his chin. It was the first time I'd seen him pause to reflect, much as Martin had shied away from the same subject. All the while, he tossed his head and the little bit of red steel wool on top of it, with what appeared to be admiration. He could never anticipate Martin. That seemed to be the meaning.

"Well, first of all, Dubin, I don't *think* Martin's a Communist. I *know* he's a Communist. He was a party member in Paris when he went off to fight in Spain. That's one of the reasons OSS wanted him in the first place. Because of his influence with the Communist unions.

"But put that aside. I'm not charging the man with disagreeable politics. I'm charging him with insubordination and endangering other troops. Even in Russia, despite calling me Comrade General, if I told him to get on his knees and kiss my ass, it's same as here, he'd have to do it."

Until that remark, I'd almost put Bonner out of my mind.

"Now whether his political background is the reason OSS agreed with me that it's time to send Martin elsewhere, nobody's said that, but frankly it's a pretty fair guess, and it makes sense. *Stars and Stripes* and the newsreels don't tell you everything our precious Russian allies are up to, Dubin. Do you know anything about what happened in Poland in August?"

I hadn't heard much and Teedle enjoyed filling me in. With the Soviet Army on their border, thousands of Polish patriots in Warsaw had risen up against the Nazis. Many on our side, Teedle said, believed that Stalin had encouraged the Home Army to think that the Soviets would storm into Poland and join them in expelling the Nazis. But the Russians held their ground. In fact, Stalin wouldn't even allow the Allies to assist the Poles by dropping arms and supplies. Instead the Home Army was crushed. Thousands were executed, shot on the spot or locked in buildings which were then set ablaze, while the Nazis leveled Warsaw's city center.

"And why, you might ask," said Teedle, "why would the Soviets do that? Why would the Russians not help the Polish resistance, since it could very well diminish their own losses in retaking Poland? Any ideas?"

Nothing came to me.

"Because, Dubin, a patriot who resists Nazi occupation is just as likely to resist the Soviets. Stalin got the Nazis to do his dirty work in Poland. At that point the Supreme Command, Roosevelt, Churchill, they all knew with absolute certainty what we are in for. Stalin might as well have let his air force put it in skywriting. They aim to conquer and occupy eastern Europe. They want to substitute Soviet rule for Nazi rule. And you're damn right, we don't need anybody operating in advance of our troops who might take the Soviets' side. Martin has many friends in the ranks of the Soviet Army. He fought for at least three different Soviet generals in Spain. And I'll wager a good sum that he'll give their orders a lot more heed than he's given mine. So yes, the fact that he's a Communist, that concerns me. It concerns me a good deal. Especially since he won't follow fucking orders. But if he weren't insubordinate, I wouldn't care if he went to sleep each night in red pajamas."

The General leaned forward with his fists on his desk. "Now, man to man, Dubin, tell me the truth, does that bother you? Because listening, I thought this asshole's complaint that I'm after him because of what he thinks about political matters—I had the impression that cut some ice with you."

I took my time, but I knew I wasn't going to back down from General Teedle. It wasn't required.

"General, there are a lot of Socialists who are loyal to the United States. And hate Stalin." Two of them happened to live in an apartment in Kindle County and had raised me. I didn't say that, as usual. Who I was and where I came from was my own secret. But Teedle was perspicacious enough to sense I spoke from experience.

"And are you one of them, Dubin? Is that what you're saying? Are you a loyal American Socialist?"

"I'm a loyal American, sir. I don't agree with the Socialists all the way. My problem with Socialists, sir, is that I've met quite a few who don't strike me as idealists. They hate the rich, because they envy them." Of course, socialism and how to react to it were topics of unending contemplation for me throughout high school and college. Easton had brought me into contact with many of the people my parents reviled, and Grace herself might belong in that category, even though she largely shunned her family's privileges. Between the two of us, one of our enduring discussions was about whether we were Socialists. There was so much that went wrong in the world that came down to being poor. But I never felt comfortable with the socialist morality of my parents, by which they were entitled to want more, while the rich were obliged to want less.

"Interesting, Dubin, very interesting." I had no doubt Teedle meant that. He flipped a pencil in the air and caught it. "You and I are polar opposites here. What I have against the Commies is what you seem to want more of. I dislike them, Dubin, because they're fools. *Fools*. Hapless idealists who want to believe that humans are inclined to share and think first about others, when that's never going to be the case. Never.

"And because they don't see us as we are, Dubin, don't see how brutal and selfish we are, because of that, Dubin, they think we can do without God. That's why I truly dislike them. Because they believe mankind can be good without His assistance. And once we go down that road, Dubin, we're lost. Utterly lost. Because we need God, Dubin. Every man out here needs God. And not to save his soul or keep him safe, Dubin, none of that guff. Do you know why we need God, why we must have Him, Dubin? Do you?"

"No, sir," I said. I was no surer of God than of socialism, but it was one of those moments when Teedle was on the boil again, full of a locomotive fury that forbade me to get in his way.

"Well, I'll tell you, Dubin. Why we need God. Why I need God. To forgive us," he said then, and with the words his anger almost instantly subsided to sadness. His tiny eyes were liquid and morose, and any doubts I'd had about Bonner vanished. "Because when this is over, this war, that's what we'll need, all of us who have done what war requires and, worse, what war permits, that's what we'll need, in order to be able to live the rest of our lives."

Teedle went for his canteen for the first time since I'd been there. When he lowered it, he dragged the back of his hand along his lips like a tough in a beer hall, but his little birdie eyes rimmed in pink remained on me, full of his sorry knowledge of the excesses of war and the bleak mystery of a God who, before forgiving, allowed those things to occur in the first place.

9. FURTHER ORDERS

In the two weeks following our return to Nancy, it became clear that the pace of the war was again quickening. Stores of gasoline had finally been received. Other field supplies—tents, blankets, jackets, two-burner stoves—remained short, but the General staff had swapped ten thousand gallons of no. 10 motor oil with the Seventh Army for an equal amount of diesel fuel, and it was a good bet that Patton's push into Germany would start whenever it arrived.

Yet even with the changed atmosphere, life in Nancy still seemed as relaxed as a summer resort, compared to my three days near the front. As Colonel Maples had anticipated, I had relished the excitement, and even felt some awkward satisfaction about surviving a bombing, never mind that it had been inflicted by our own forces. On the whole, my encounters with Teedle and Martin and Gita Lodz were probably the first moments since I had enlisted that fulfilled some of my hopes.

On November 3 an orderly appeared in court to tell me that Colonel Maples wanted me when we finished for the day. As soon as Klike promised to dispense with justice, I went upstairs, where the Colonel showed me documents that had been pouched from the 18th Armored Division. Teedle had ordered me to deliver them to Robert Martin.

```
            HEADQUARTERS, 18TH ARMORED DIVISION
                    APO 403, U.S. ARMY

                      E X T R A C T

    1. Major Robert P. Martin, 04264192, is relieved of duty with
    this Division at once and assigned to Central Base Station,
    London, England. WP w/o delay reporting upon arrival to CO
    thereat for duty. Govt. T is authorized. EDCMR: 1 November 1944
    BY ORDER OF BRIGADIER GENERAL TEEDLE

    Official:
                                            James Camello
                                              Major AC
                                           Ass't Adjutant


    cc:
    Colonel Bryant Winters
    U.S. Army
    68 Brook Street
    London
```

Except for the designation of a carbon copy to Colonel Winters, who I inferred was Martin's OSS commander, the order didn't differ noticeably from prior ones I'd seen. Attached, however, were travel documents identical to those Gita had produced on my visit to the Comtesse's. They, too, were issued by Central Base in London and directed Martin to return to England forthwith, even enclosing $20 in Army scrip for a per diem. Teedle had answered Martin in kind. Since OSS would not issue direct written orders to an operative, the travel authorization was the best proof that its commanders backed Teedle.

"Well, that explains it," Colonel Maples said, once I'd reminded him that I'd needed something from OSS to deal with Martin's claims that he had other orders. "When he rang, General Teedle passed a comment about you. I think he finds you a bit precise for his taste."

"I thought that's what lawyers are, Colonel. Precise."

"Teedle regards it as an impediment." Seated behind a large oak desk as substantial as a half-track, Maples was smiling, touching his mustache as he often did for comfort. "Not all that different, by the way, from my clients in private practice, who gritted their teeth before talking to their lawyer. For some it was akin to the discomfort of going off to Sunday prayers."

"I'm not trying to be difficult, Colonel, but when I think this over I still can't make top or bottom of it. Why would a decorated officer suddenly defy his commanders? The girl is rather emphatic that her romance with Martin is over."

"Perhaps Martin has had enough of war. He wouldn't be the first. But ours is not to reason why, David. I told you, Rollie Teedle is not an enemy you need. Get out there and finish this off. Teedle wants Martin packing and on to London before you leave."

"Yes, sir." Maples' renewed warning about Teedle banished any lingering thought of reporting Billy Bonner's accusations. I'd hesitated when I'd briefed the Colonel on my return, realizing once I was in his office that Maples would regard the charge as patent lunacy and be displeased with me for pulling the pin on this kind of hand grenade, then lobbing it on his desk. The truth was that in the presence of the Colonel, a person of gentle but unrelenting propriety, I had no idea even how to relate what Bonner had said.

With Teedle's order in hand, Biddy and I had no trouble securing a jeep and left not long after sunrise on November 4, headed again toward Bezange-la-Petite. There was now heavy traffic on the small roads with lines of trucks and armor moving out. We made slow progress and finally came to a complete halt behind a tank battalion stalled on its way north. The 761st was all colored, except for some of the officers. They were the first Negroes I had seen in combat, and they looked as apprehensive as everybody else did making the journey to the front.

After half an hour, I took the jeep and went to see about the holdup, which proved to be three convoys crossing paths. Two MPs had arrived on motorcycles and stood at the crossroads directing traffic, just like cops at the busy hours on the streets of Center City back home.

When I returned, Biddy and a colored soldier were having words. Biddy was shaking a finger and telling the soldier, another sergeant, not to talk to him. The fellow threw a hand in Biddy's direction and walked away as I came up.

"What was that about?"

"Just some boy from Georgia causing a ruckus. Said he was from that town where I growed up." Biddy was still following the man with his eyes.

"Was he?"

"Mighta been. But I didn't need no strolls down memory lane, Lieutenant." The brooding air that overtook Biddy when he was dealing with the colored was evident. Whatever my reluctance about pulling rank, or disturbing our increasing amity, I felt I had no choice about speaking up.

"A colored man's as good as anybody else, Gideon." This was my parents' perpetual lesson. Once the goyim got done with the Negroes, we all knew who'd be next. "I had several colored friends in high school, men I played music with and studied with, as fine and smart as anyone I know. I realize you come from Georgia, Biddy. I can't change the way you think, but I don't want to see it or hear it. Clear?"

Gideon's green eyes remained on me for some time, but he seemed more startled than defiant.

"Yes, sir," he said eventually.

Ahead, the tanks were finally moving.

When we pulled into the courtyard in front of the little castle, Gita Lodz was there, just stepping out of the Comtesse's charcoal-burning Citroën, where Antonio was at the wheel. She was dressed like a city lady, in a plaid skirt, with her wavy bronze hair pulled straight in a bun.

"Doo-bean!" she cried, and greeted me in French. "So you return." She approached beaming and kissed me on each cheek. We were already old friends. I remarked that she did not appear to be dressed for combat. "For spying," she answered. "We have been to look in on some people in Strasbourg. Martin will need them soon. Antonio has fetched us from the train."

Strasbourg was nearly seventy miles away, far behind the German lines.

"My Lord! You just went?"

"*Pourquoi pas?* Our documents say we are from Arracourt, going to see Robert's *grandmère* who is near death. The Nazis are oxen. A snake with proper papers could board the train. This has been our life for years, Dubin."

Behind her, the Comtesse's house was under repair in the wake of the bombing. Heavy tarpaulins hung over many of the broken windows, although in the few instances where the shutters remained they had simply been closed. Either way, it would make for a cold winter. There had been talk after the blast that by December the Comtesse would have to abandon the house for the servants' quarters across the courtyard, which were undamaged.

On the other side of the vehicle, Martin had arisen. Until now, I had been too intent on Gita to notice. He was dressed in a suit and a fedora, looking proper and bourgeois. I saluted, which drew a faint smile, as he wandered up with far less enthusiasm than Gita had shown.

"Back so soon, Dubin?"

I reminded him of my promise to return his documents. "And I've brought you a few new ones."

He read for a while, nodding. "Very good," he said. He handed the orders back, with a bright grin. "I guess I've won this round."

"Sir?"

"Proves the point, doesn't it? Teedle has given up his claim to be my commanding officer. I'm under OSS direction. And London has ordered me to proceed here. That's my duty. All cleared up, I'd say."

"Major, these documents require you to travel to London at once."

"Yes, and I've done so and London sent me back. You're holding the proof of that in your other hand. Am I to be court-martialed because I have already carried out my orders?"

Martin gave another glowing smile, as if this weren't flimflam. On the other hand, there wasn't much here to prove him wrong. Nothing showed OSS's involvement or that some obliging paymaster hadn't simply sent the travel papers at Teedle's request, a prospect I hadn't considered until now.

"Major, I mean no disrespect, but even if there's a mistake, had you asked OSS to contact Third Army G-1 or Colonel Maples, this could have been resolved instantly."

"Well, it *is* a mistake, Dubin, quite clearly, because I received the go-ahead by radio yesterday on an operation that's been planned for months.

And inasmuch as the one thing Teedle and I now agree upon is that I take my commands from OSS, I will carry out those orders. I'll deal with your papers straightaway when we return."

I asked the nature of this new operation, but Martin gave a strict shake of his head.

"I'm hardly at liberty to discuss that, Dubin. The other members of Stemwinder don't even have the details yet. We work strictly on a need-to-know basis. Capture is always a risk in this line of work, Dubin. And what difference would that make?"

"I'm just looking for a way to confirm your position, Major."

Standing by and listening, Gita suddenly interjected, *"Laisse-le venir."* Martin drew back. What Gita had said was, Let him come.

"Très dangereux, non?" he responded.

"Demande-lui." Ask him. Martin reflected, then took on a look of revelation.

"My God, she's right. What a marvel you are, Gita, you never cease to amaze." He swung an arm around her waist and planted a paternal kiss atop her head. "You want evidence of my orders from OSS? Come watch me follow them. You say I get to present any proof I wish to your investigation, don't I?"

"Yes, sir." Those were surely the rules.

"Then this is it. Patton's going to be on the move again momentarily, and this operation is an essential prelude. You're more than welcome to observe, Lieutenant, to see once and for all that I'm under OSS direction and not sitting out here on Roman holiday, or whatever else it is that Teedle imagines. It will put an end to all questions. If you choose not to come, there's no more I can do."

I had no idea, of course, what I was being asked to say yes to. Except that I'd heard the word 'dangerous.' It was a dare, actually, the man of action's challenge to the deskbound bureaucrat, and Martin was probably betting I would never accept. But his logic was impeccable. If I refused, I'd have denied him the opportunity to offer the only evidence he had. In fact, reading the rules, I might even have been derelict. I told him I would have to consult Maples.

"As you wish. But we start this afternoon, Dubin. You'll have to be there and back before three."

That was impossible, especially with the movements on the roadways that could sidetrack us for hours. Martin, still with his hand on Gita's back, turned away, and she gave me a quick private frown before heading off beside him. I was being just the man of small points she'd ridiculed last week. Worse, I felt like a coward.

"I'll go," I told Martin.

Martin didn't flinch when he revolved my way, even though I'd probably called his bluff.

"Bravo, Dubin. I'll brief you shortly. Glad to have you," he said, and continued toward the house with his arm still around Gita's waist.

I found Bidwell with the Gypsy, Antonio, and several of the farmworkers, showing off the photos he had taken during our last visit. They were little two-by-twos and he was complaining about the supplies he'd had to work with.

"Can't get no bigger film. Damn lucky for what I have. Wanted my folks to send some six-twenty but they-all is hoarding silver on the home front."

Small or not, the images were striking. After the bombing, Biddy had shot through a broken window into the darkness of the house. Within, you could detect the form of a tall chifforobe, while the glass reflected uprooted trees outside leaned together like a tepee and, farther in the background, Antonio, with his long hair and dark intense eyes aimed right at the camera. Biddy had taken another photo inside the bomb crater looking up at two of the dead animals. There were also several pictures he'd snapped on our way here last time of haystacks being gathered in the open fields.

"Put me in mind of those paintings in the Museum of Art," he said. "You seen them?" I had. Famous Impressionist works in vivid hues, but the artist's name eluded me. "Same idea," Biddy said, "but in black and white. You think that's okay?"

They were beautiful photos. I asked what could be wrong.

"I don't know," he said. "Seems like if you make a picture you oughta rightly be thinkin about life, not other pictures. But I got those paintings in my head."

"Did you study art, Biddy?"

"Aw, hell, Lieutenant, my daddy, he'd probably just keeled over dead if I'd a tole him I was going to art school. I just liked them paintings, seein what happened to our world when it went flat. I was over there whenever I could. A lot of that, the stuff folks are doin these days especially, they really talk to me, you know?"

My mother was always hauling me down to the museum, hoping something would rub off, but the truth was I couldn't make heads or tails of the works that excited Biddy.

"I think I'm too practical-minded for modern art, Gideon. Art and opera. My mother loves that, too. But I like your photographs."

He shook his head. "You see things through that lens, Lieutenant, you can't catch with your eye. And I like how I feel when I'm lookin, with that contraption between me and everything else. Here in this mess and able to stand back like that, I'm a million miles away sometimes." He looked at me. "I don't know what the hell I'm talkin about, you know."

"You're making plenty of sense, Biddy. Don't sell yourself short. Maybe you should think about art school."

"Maybe I should. We-all gotta live through this first."

That was the reminder I needed. I told him about my conversation with Martin. As his expression darkened, I could see he was resisting the impulse to stab me.

"No disrespect, Lieutenant, but what the heck is it you call yourself doin?"

I tried to explain the logic of the rules that required me to follow where Martin led.

"This here," said Biddy, "is how the law sure enough don't make sense. Figures Martin'd use it against you. Ain't no tellin what kinda trouble a huckster like that is gonna get us into, Lieutenant."

"This is my frolic and detour, Biddy. You're not required."

"Hell, I'm not. You think they send an MP sergeant out here with you, Lieutenant, just to drive? Ain't no way I can let you go do this whatever on your lonesome. Only I'd think a growed man would have the sense to ask what he was doin 'fore he said yes." Biddy had never been this direct with me, but after the scolding I'd given him on the way here, he apparently felt inclined to speak his mind. And there was no question of his loyalty. Still shaking his head, he walked beside me toward the little castle to see what was in store for us.

* * *

By 3:30, we had moved out. In a time of short provisions, Martin was remarkably well supplied. He may have been the scourge of General
Teedle, but in these parts he was widely respected, and the Quartermaster
with the Yankee Division had given the Major whatever he needed for
this venture more than a month ago. Biddy and I had our choice of combat and cargo packs, cartridge belts and M1A1 carbines. I hadn't fired a
weapon since training camp, and I spent some time handling the rifle to
bring back the feel of it. We had come with our own raincoats, which we
folded behind us over our belts, following the example of the rest of our
party, which consisted of Gita, Martin, Antonio, and two locals, Christian and Henri. They were frumpy-looking farmers, a father and son,
both shaped like figs. They trudged along in silence at Martin's side, acting as guides, with American rifles over their shoulders. Beside me, Gita
was in farm overalls, but wore a surplus Army helmet with the liner tightened to the maximum so it fit her.

"Do you like battle, Mademoiselle Lodz?"

"No one should like battle, Dubin. It is much too frightening. But
Martin's style is most successful when not a gun is fired. You will see."

"But it remains strange to me to think of a woman in combat."

She laughed, but not in good humor. "Ça, c'est le comble!" That's the
last straw. "Men think only they can fight. With guns? With planes?
With artillery. Who is not strong enough to pull a trigger, Dubin, or
throw a grenade?"

"Yes, but a man who does not fight is called a coward. No one expects
this of you. Quite the contrary. Do you think fighting is as much in a
woman's nature as a man's?"

"Knowing what is right is in the nature of everyone. I allow, Dubin, that
I do not enjoy killing. But many men feel as I do, and fight nonetheless."

Martin had turned back to us with a finger to his lips, inasmuch as we
were leaving the Comtesse's lands. I still had little idea where we were
headed. Martin would brief us only when we'd made camp for the night.
For the time being, he wanted to use the weakening daylight to move
ahead. We proceeded due north, across adjoining farms. Knowing the
fence lines and the old paths, Henri led us along at a good pace. The
rains held off while we hiked, but the ground everywhere was soft and in
the lowlands we splashed through standing water, soaking my wool
trousers and the socks inside my shoepacs.

As darkness encroached, I was certain we were behind Nazi lines. Martin, Biddy, and I were in uniform and stood at least a chance, if captured, of being taken prisoner, rather than executed. The Frenchmen with us were all but certain to be shot on the spot. But there was no sign of Germans. In these parts, the locals were firmly committed to the Free French, and Martin regarded his intelligence on enemy positions as virtually faultless. Nonetheless, whenever possible, we remained on the other side of the shallow hills, so we were not visible from the road, and ducked into the trees if we were near a wooded draw. When there was no choice but to cross an open field, we ambled along in pairs, as if we were hikers.

At one point, as we stopped briefly to refill our canteens in a spring, Martin came back to check on me. Gita and Antonio were on lookout at the perimeter, apparently enough security for a quiet conversation.

"Holding up?"

I was hardly laboring with a full pack. I had a bedroll, a canteen, a bayonet, and ammunition, but I hadn't been out on maneuvers since basic and Martin was right to suspect I was tired. I told him I was fine.

"Nothing like this in the past, I assume?" he asked.

"I was trained as an infantry officer, but aside from exercises, no."

"You'll have an exciting time. You'll be thanking Gita for suggesting this." He waited. "She seems to have taken a shine to you."

"Has she? I'm honored. She is very charming." Then as the only avenue to approach the lingering question, I added, "You have a charming woman."

"Oh, yes," he said, "very charming. Only I doubt that Gita would agree."

"That she's charming?"

"That she is my woman. Candidly, I wonder if Gita would ever choose but one man. Besides," he said, "she is much too young for me." He had raised his eyes to her up on the hill, where the wind tossed around the kinks of dark gold hair that escaped her helmet. "I have only one thing I want for her, really. Most of all, Dubin, I would like to see her safe. That would be my last wish. Were I permitted one. I owe her that." Catching Martin's eye as we were looking her way, Gita knotted her small face in an open frown.

"There, you see. She is always displeased with me." His glance fell to the ground. "Does she speak ill of me?"

I didn't understand the crosscurrents here, only that they were treacherous.

"On the contrary," I answered. "She is your admirer."

"Surely not always. She calls me a liar to my face."

"Does she?" I felt certain that Martin knew exactly what Gita had said to me the last time I was here. "It is the nature of this life, Dubin. Somewhere, buried in the recesses of memory, is the person I was before I was Robert Martin." He pronounced his full name as if it were French: Ro-*bear* Mar-*tan*. "But I was trained to tell every tale but his. And it suits me well, Dubin. No soul in war is the same as she or he was before. You'll learn that soon enough."

He took a tiny humpbacked metal cricket from his pocket and gave its twanging steel tongue two clicks, calling an end to our respite. Scampering down from the prominence, Gita fell in at the head of our column but shortly worked her way back to me, as we were weaving through a small woods. She had heard her name and wanted to know what Martin had said. I tried to satisfy her with the most neutral remark I remembered.

"He told me he hopes you are safe. When the war ends."

"He lies. As always. That is not what he hopes. He would much prefer we die side by side in battle. *Tellement romantique.*"

Long ago I'd learned not to be the messenger in couples' disagreements, a lesson originally taken from childhood. The more I heard from both Gita and Martin, the less sure I was of the dimensions of their relationship. Nor did it seem that it was very clear to either of them. I was better off with another subject and asked her about Bettjer, the radioman, whose absence I had noticed.

"Peter? Peter is no good anymore. For some, bravery is like blood. There is only so much in your body. He was very courageous, very bold, but with a month to sit and think about all he has survived, every fear he did not feel before has rolled down on him like a boulder off a mountain. He will drink three bottles of cognac in the day we are gone. *Ainsi va la guerre,*" she added in a tragic tone. So goes war.

This discussion of Bettjer and his anxieties somehow became a gateway to my own worries. I had felt my nervousness growing as we tromped along. Now, with the description of Bettjer as unmanned by fear, I was attacked full-on by shrieking doubts. Apparently, I did a poor job of concealing them.

"This is bad talk," said Gita. "I should have told you something else. Martin will watch out for you. He watches for all of us. And there is no need for you to be in the midst of things when the operation starts."

"If I can be helpful, I would like to take part. I'd feel as if I were a child, merely watching from safety."

"That is for Martin to say. But if so, you will do well, Dubin. You are a man of principles, no? Principles are the main ingredient of courage. A man with principles can get the better of fear."

"I thought you doubted the existence of principles."

"*Touché*," she answered, and gave me a fleet impish smile. "I do not doubt the power of principles, Dubin. I say only that it is an illusion that they are the first thing in life. It is an illusion we all crave—better principles than the abyss—but an illusion nevertheless. Therefore, one must be careful about what he deems issues of principle. I despise petty principles, obstinate principles that declare right and wrong on matters of little actual consequence. But there are large principles, grand principles most men share, Dubin, and you have them, as well." She showed a tidy smile, and actually patted my hand in reassurance.

Ahead, Martin had halted at the edge of another open field. He clicked the cricket again as a signal for silence, and Gita dispensed a quick wave before moving toward her assigned place at the head of the line. Antonio fell in behind me. We both watched her dash away, her legs tossed outward with unexpected girlishness, as she drew abreast of Martin. She was extraordinary. No doubt about that.

"What is she to him?" I asked Antonio suddenly.

He gave a rattling laugh and shook his long hair, as if I had asked an eternal question.

"I think she is his glory," he answered. "I think when he looks at her he remembers what he once believed."

10. LA SALINE ROYALE

November 5, 1944

Dearest Grace—

Tomorrow I will see my first action. It is too complicated to explain why (and the censors would black it out anyway). But please focus on the word "see." I am going only as an observer, for one day, and by the time you receive this, I will be back and safe and will have written you to say so. I'll mail both letters together, so you never have occasion for concern. I feel as I have always imagined I would in this circumstance, as if my skin might not contain me, and thus I doubt I'll sleep. But for better or worse, I remain eager.

We start very early in the morning, so I will close now. Just to let you know how much I love you and am always thinking of you.

David

✳ ✳ ✳

November 7, 1944

Dear Grace—
 Back at HQ and safe. I am much too disappointed in myself
to say more. Will write further later in the week.

David

L a Saline Royale, the royal saltworks, had been opened in 1779 to put an end to fractious competition between bishops and lords for control of what was then a precious commodity. The King declared himself the owner of all the salt in France and auctioned it to European merchants from open-air barns here in Marsal, where the prized granules were mined.

After invading France, the Nazis had commandeered the saltworks, whose long radiating shafts made it ideal as a munitions dump, eventually becoming the largest in the Lorraine. The works had been built like a fortress, surrounded by both twenty-foot walls of limestone and brick, meant to repel thieves, and the river Seille, which formed a virtual moat at the northern border. With the armaments, mostly large-caliber artillery shells, stored more than six hundred feet under the earth, they were invulnerable to air attack, and a German garrison was stationed in the former mine offices as further protection.

Martin and his OG had been dispatched to this vicinity in early September to destroy the dump, but the operation had been put on hold when the pace of combat slackened. Now, Martin said, London wanted the mission completed. The Germans had fortified their stores in the interval, making La Saline Royale an even more inviting target.

We were gathered probably a mile from the saltworks, inside a small shepherd's hut in the field of a farmer who was a member of a local resisters' unit, or *réseau*. Sitting on the dirt floor, the six of us listened as Martin illustrated the operation's plan beside a Coleman lantern. From his field jacket, Martin had removed a pack of playing cards, peeling a backing off of each one and laying them out in rows, until they formed a map of the saltworks and the surrounding area. Biddy and I grinned at each other. The OSS's ingenuity was equal to its legend.

There were two breaches, Martin said, in the saltworks' fortifications. The only formal approach was from the north to the massive iron front gates, behind which the German troops waited. On the west, the walls parted a few meters where a railroad siding ran down into the mine. Laid for the shipment of salt, the tracks continued to be used to deliver and remove armaments, and emerged on an angled trestle over the Seille, meeting the railhead on the western bank.

A ground assault against the railroad gate also appeared unpromising. Fording the Seille without bridge work was nigh impossible. 'Seille' means 'pail,' the name drawn from the depth of the narrow gray river below its steep banks. Even in a season of record floods, the waters remained a good ten feet under the stone retaining walls, which were overgrown with moss and creepers. Worse, where the tracks passed through the mine wall, crews manned two MG42 high-caliber machine guns. Nonetheless, Martin laid his pencil tip there on the map and said this opening would be the point of attack for our party of seven.

"*Merde*," said Henri.

"*Tu perds la tête*," said Christian to Martin jovially. You've lost your mind.

"There is a way," said Martin, and in the sallow lantern light, looked about the circle like a schoolmarm to see if anyone who did not know the plan could guess.

"By train," I answered.

"Bravo, Dubin."

My clue was Martin's background. Members of his former union, the International Transport Workers, were so thoroughly committed to resistance that before D-Day the Germans had been required to take over the French railroads, importing nearly 50,000 rail men from Germany. As the Allies advanced, however, most of these civilian crews had been shipped home, or had simply deserted. While the rail yards remained heavily patrolled, the Nazis had had no choice but again to let Frenchmen run the trains in the corner of France the Germans controlled.

This evening, mechanics at the yard in Dieuze, a few miles farther east, would conclude that the arriving locomotive on a Nazi supply train needed repairs. It would be steered toward the mechanical facility at the distant side of the yard, and would slowly roll right through. A mile farther on, Antonio would board, replacing the engineer and the rest of the crew, and steam off toward the dump. In the morning, after the operation, the local *réseau* would tie up the crew members, leaving them in the bushes along the right-of-way, where, upon discovery, they would claim to have been set upon by dozens of saboteurs many hours before.

Martin expected no trouble with any of that. If there were to be problems, they were more likely to come at La Saline Royale. If the Germans here realized what was happening, they would blow or blockade the trestle leading to the mine, so stealth was essential. There were two guards at a switching point, set up roughly a mile and a half from where we were now, to keep unauthorized traffic off the spur. They had to be quietly subdued. After that, a distraction on the other side of the works would obscure the sounds of the approaching locomotive. That was Henri and Christian's task.

"Ever seen one of these?" Around the circle Martin handed an object about the size of an apple, Army green, with yellow stenciling that said T13. From the ring on top, I could tell it was a hand grenade, but twice as big as any other I'd seen.

"It's called a Beano. I have damn few left, too. Like a grenade but with one great advantage. Blows on impact. No one kicks this out of the way or throws it in the river. And if you have to hold on to it after you pull the ring, you can. I wouldn't walk around with it in my pocket, mind you, but I've carried one along for several minutes."

The Beano—actually two of them—were for Christian and Henri. We would all initially approach from the south, ascending the hills behind the saltworks, with Christian and Henri then fanning off toward the front gates. They had grenade-launcher attachments for their M1s, which, even firing something the size of the Beano, would have a range of one hundred yards. Their target was the gasoline tanks that serviced the garrison. If the fuel ignited, all troops would rush out there to extinguish the flames burning perilously close to the wooden entrance to the shafts and the tons of munitions below. But even if the father and son missed, the Germans could be expected to rouse off-duty troops to begin combing the overlooking hills. In the meantime, the locomotive would speed across the trestle, crash the railroad crossing gate, and hurtle down into the mine. There was a chance that the impact of the locomotive with the train cars loaded with shells might detonate them, but rather than count on that, Martin was packing a satchel charge whose fuse he would light before jumping from the train.

The explosion inside the mine would act more or less like a pipe bomb, with the shafts channeling the huge force of the blast from either end. If we made it back over and down the hill from which we'd come, we would escape unharmed. Martin didn't address his own safety, but I couldn't see how he'd get away, since he had to remain on the locomotive to steer it over the trestle. As for Biddy and me, Martin planned for us to wait on the hillside. We would have a clear view of his activities, but would need only a few seconds to get back over the top and down.

"But be alert for Krauts," Martin told us. "They may be out by then, looking for the saboteurs who fired the grenades."

We would start again at 5:00 a.m. That left about six hours to sleep, but I was much too excited to try.

Ready to turn in, Gita came to check on me. She remained concerned that she had told me too much with her stories about Bettjer.

"I am fine," I told her. "I am sure that before I sleep, I will think of those I have left at home and feel bad about that, as soldiers do. But I am pleased finally to know a little of what soldiers feel."

"I have that luck," she said. "No home." She dug a stick into the ground and pondered it. "Robert does not like talk of home," she said quietly. "He says it is not good for soldiers. But it would be unnatural to forget, no?"

"Of course," I said.

She did not look up, but smiled wistfully as she turned over clods.

"Did I tell you, Dubin, that my mother was killed for harboring Jews?"

"Certainly not. You have not mentioned she was a hero."

"No," Gita answered decisively. "She was no heroine. She did it for money. She hated the Nazis, naturally. She worried constantly that they would send me to Germany to be made German as had been done with dozens of the Polish children in my town. But a man, Szymon Goldstein, came to her when the Nazis began rounding up the Jews and deporting them to Lublin. Goldstein ran a tannery and had been rich before the war. And was once my mother's lover, as well. Their affair had ended badly, as my mother's affairs tended to do. They were gruff with each other, but she was the only Pole he knew who might be daring enough to take his money. It was a huge sum. And even so, Dubin, I was very much against this. But my mother always refused to do what other people considered wise.

"So in the middle of the night, Goldstein and his wife and his four children stole into our tiny house and lived in our little root cellar. For the month it lasted, it made for a strange household—my mother under the same roof with Madame Goldstein, who despised her, these six people whose noises we always heard from below like mice in the walls. Then they were betrayed. The Nazis found another Jew who had been hiding in the woods. To save himself, he told them about Goldstein. The SS came into the house and found my mother and all the Goldsteins and shot them. I was out trying to find coal that day. When I came back the bodies were piled in front of the door, as a warning to anyone who might do the same.

"I have always thought, if only I had come back in time I could have saved them. But I have no idea how. Naturally enough, people say I am lucky not to have died with them, yet how can one remember such a thing with any feeling of good fortune?" She had been driving the stick into the ground all the time she told this story. "So what do you think, Dubin?"

"I think it is a terrible story. It makes me very sad for you."

"Yes." She said nothing for a moment, then finally cast her stick aside. "So tonight we both think of home before we are soldiers." She grasped my hand for a second, before moving off to her bedroll.

I was grateful to hear Gita's story, a powerful reminder of why we were fighting, but it had not brought me any closer to sleep. Instead, I watched Martin pack the satchel charges. He had a bottle of brandy, which he offered to me, and I took a long pull in the hope that it would make me weary. Martin was clearly going to finish off the rest himself. That did not strike me as wise, but his hands were still nimble assembling the charge. It was essentially dynamite, sixteen square blocks of TNT fixed in sawdust, each weighing more than a pound. Martin would strap them around a blasting cap, but first he had to prepare the fuse. He stood outside, lighting and relighting varying lengths, recording how fast they were consumed. He planned to hang the satchel charges in the windows of the locomotive cab, so that the explosions had the maximum effect, but timing was essential. If the charges went too quickly, they'd drop the locomotive into the Seille; too late and the Germans might have time to extinguish the flame. I held the ends of the lines for him, watching the flame sparkle toward me. Nine feet, six inches, is what he ultimately figured. It would give him about four minutes to escape. When he was done, at last, he carefully slid the charges into a green canvas sack.

"Time to turn in," he told me. He clapped me on the shoulder. "Exciting, eh?"

"Major," I said, "I'd like to do more than watch."

"You're here as an observer, Dubin."

"Frankly, sir, if something goes wrong, I don't think the Germans will care why we're here. We might as well take part."

"We'll see. Sleep now." He smiled. "You can carry the satchel in the morning. Damn heavy, too."

Biddy had brought a pup tent for the two of us. There was a strange domestic order in that. I thought of myself as tidy, but Bidwell was downright precise: boots, weapon, pack, in perfect rank. As a boy who'd grown up sleeping with my brother in the kitchen in my parents' small apartment, I sometimes thought I'd feel more at home in the closeness of enlisted quarters. Crossing the ocean, while the officers lived in style in our staterooms, the enlisted men below slept in shifts on rows of canvas bunks suspended between the posts every two feet like shelving. Their deck was tight as a hive, which made the perpetual good cheer of the troops there more remarkable—and enviable.

I crept in now and found paper and a pencil in my field jacket and stood outside to write quick letters to Grace and my parents by firelight. There was almost no chance the mail would be delivered if something went wrong, but it was a ritual I felt obliged to carry out. With that done, I crawled into the tent. Quiet as I'd been, I'd apparently roused Bidwell.

"Permission to speak, sir?" Biddy rarely invoked these formalities. "Lieutenant," he said, "you got me wrong today. And it's been weighin on my mind. About that Negro soldier I didn't talk to? I don't feel no better than him, Lieutenant. Not one bit. He knew my momma and daddy and there was some ruction at home I didn't want to hear tell about. But it wasn't 'cause I looked down at him for being colored. I swear."

There'd been too many incidents, but this was hardly the time for a debating society.

"I'm glad to hear that, Biddy."

"Yes, sir."

We said no more then.

11. ACTION

I awoke from a dream of music. Biddy was up already, organizing his pack, and we took down the tent together.

"I dreamed I was playing the clarinet, Biddy."

"Was that your thing, that old licorice stick?"

"It was. Not much of an embouchure left now. I thought I was Benny Goodman, Gideon. I just couldn't find anybody to agree."

He laughed and we talked about music. I asked which musicians he liked.

"Duke," he said. "Pretty niftic."

"I'll say."

"Did you have a group, Lieutenant?"

Here in the hills of Lorraine, about to take my first intentional risks since going to war, I felt the embrace of the summer nights when we played on Mo Freeman's front stoop. The neighbors had been less than enthusiastic when we were freshmen, but by the time we reached our senior year we used to draw a little crowd.

"Killer-diller," I said, repeating the compliment we once gave one another on our improvisations. "Haven't played like that in years."

"What happened to you-all?"

"Oh, the world began to get in the way. I went off to Easton College. Mo deserved the scholarship more than me, but he was colored. He ended up okay, though. I saw him before I left. You know, that little tour we all made of the folks we wanted to remember us if anything happened? He went to medical school at the U. Two coloreds in his class, but he was past the rough part. He's done by now. He was laughing because the draft board didn't know what to do with him. They weren't going to take a colored doctor. If he's over here, it's as a damn private in the Negro troops. And that's not right, Biddy."

"No, sir, it ain't, it surely ain't." I had a hard time believing I'd made a convert overnight, but he sounded sincere.

Antonio had been gone for more than two hours now. The remaining six of us moved out a little after 5:30 a.m., careful as we climbed into the first hills. At one point when we stopped, Henri pointed to a stork's nest, the size of a harvest basket, on the roof of a farmhouse beside a small lake.

Halfway up the hill behind the saltworks, we parted with Henri and Christian. Each of us took turns wishing them well.

"*Merde*," answered Henri. I don't believe I'd heard another word from him in twelve hours. In the dark, they would assume positions on an adjoining hill to the north. The Germans walked the walled perimeter of the works in daylight, but at night, they relied on sentries posted in towers. If Henri and Christian were quiet, they could pitch down their grenades and be gone almost instantly. The wall would end up protecting them from the German forces, who would be a long time getting outside.

To signal Henri and Christian to fire, Martin would blow the locomotive whistle once, indicating that the guards at the switch had been dispatched. The Germans were unlikely to make much of the sound coming from the main line, but one minute later, the grenades would explode among the salt barns.

Without his guides, Martin touched a button on the tunic he wore beneath his field jacket and a compass popped open on his chest, mounted upside down so he could read the phosphorescent dial. Until now I'd been so absorbed with my own apprehensions that I had largely forgotten why I'd come. But witnessing the elaborateness of the plans, the ingenious OSS gizmos with which Martin had been supplied, and the extensive cooperation from local elements, it was beyond doubt that Martin was acting under OSS command. Whether it was political prejudice or egotism or simply miscommunication amid the smoke of war, Teedle was plainly wrong.

The separation from Henri and Christian had brought a new gravity to both Martin and Gita, who led us in heavy silence as we ascended. Every now and then Martin took a strip of cloth from his sack and tied it to the bough of a buckthorn or other small tree, marking the way back. I wasn't certain if the sky was brightening a trace, with perhaps an hour to dawn, or if my eyes had adjusted to the dark, but smoky puffs of fog were visible beneath the cloud cover. When we made the crest, Martin reached out to take the satchel charge from Bidwell. I'd labored with it, and Biddy had grabbed it from me, toting it along as if it were no heavier than a lunch bucket.

"Gentlemen," said Martin, "here we part. I suggest you continue down perhaps a hundred yards. You'll be able to see our activities clearly. Again, eye out for Krauts."

"And if we wish to help?" I asked.

Martin shrugged, as if it were no matter to him. "I'm sure Gita could use a hand in Bettjer's place."

I looked at Biddy. He had a straightforward analysis. "Seems to me we're a helluva lot better off, Lieutenant, stayin with folks who know what all they're doin."

I could see Martin had anticipated these responses, not because there was anything special about Biddy, or me, but because there wasn't. It was a tribute to our soldiers, most of whom would have made the same choice.

Before saying goodbye, Martin loosened the chinstrap on my helmet.

"You don't want that around your neck when the dump goes, Dubin. It could garotte you. Follow Gita," he said. "She'll give you directions."

Our role was to cover Martin. We edged our way down the hill behind him. At the foot, we were on the plain beside the Seille, still a quarter mile south and east of the switching point. The train tracks lay before us, and we dashed across one at a time, plunging into the heavy growth on the riverbank. Gita followed Martin, and I followed her; Biddy was at my back. It was slow going. Martin pulled aside the branches as if parting a heavy curtain, but there were still thorns that grabbed my clothes and clawed my face, and I stumbled several times on the soft ground. We crept along this way for half an hour until Martin suddenly stopped, one hand aloft.

He had caught sight ahead of the two Germans guarding the switch. They were kids, of course. They sat on two ammunition crates, using a third as a table while they played cards, betting cigarettes and cursing fate with each hand. They were in full uniform, wearing their Dutch-boy helmets. Their rifles were slung across their backs and would be inaccessible just long enough to make it easy to overtake them, four soldiers on two. With hand signals, Martin drew a plan in the air. He was going to continue until he was behind the two sentries. When he erupted from the bushes, ordering them to surrender, the three of us would rush forward to surround them.

Martin had gone about ten paces, mincing through the underbrush, when he again stilled. The soldiers remained occupied with their game, but after another second, I heard what Martin had: the rising clatter of the locomotive.

The two Germans noticed the racket down the track at the same time, both standing and swinging their rifles into their hands. I would have thought they'd have an established drill with passing trains, but they had been taken by surprise and they shouted at each other while they tried to decide what to do. One galloped down the track, coming within a few feet of our hiding place in the brush as he raced toward the sound of the engine, which remained around the bend of the hill. The other watched over his shoulder as he wandered toward his radio. He was headed directly to the spot where Martin was hidden in the greenery along the bank.

Martin killed him quickly. He was as expert as his stories suggested. As soon as the soldier turned again to check on his comrade, Martin slipped from the bushes, loping in a peculiar side-to-side crouch, meant either to cushion his footfalls or to make him less visible if his sound was detected. When he neared the boy, he tossed a pebble to draw the soldier's attention forward. The German had raised his rifle in that direction when Martin caught him from behind, circling a length of wire around his windpipe. He snatched it taut, dumped the soldier on his seat, and braced his knee in the boy's back as he finished him. The only sound throughout was of the boy's heavy boots thumping on the ground, hardened by the native salt deposits.

I had watched the mangled, eviscerated, and limbless men who came off the Red Cross vehicles in Nancy, and I'd encountered corpses now and then, as on the day with Colonel Maples, but I'd seen a man die only once before, when I'd been sent as the departmental representative to a hanging. I had looked away immediately when I heard the trap sprung. But now the moment of death struck me as far more ordinary than I might have thought. Life was headed toward this instant and we all knew it, no matter how much we willed ourselves to forget. Wiping the wire on his gloves before returning it to the side pocket of his combat jacket, Robert Martin was the master of that knowledge. He appeared entirely unaltered by what he'd done.

Instead, he waved us forward, while he went flying down the track toward the locomotive. By the time we arrived, the other German soldier was on the ground with his face covered in blood. Antonio had stopped the engine on the young soldier's orders, then smashed the boy across the cheek with a wrench as soon as he tried to mount the ladder to the cab. He was moaning now, a low guttural sound from deep within his body. From the looks of it, I wasn't sure he was going to live, but Martin stuffed a handful of leaves into the long gash that was once the boy's mouth, and bound him with the laces of the low rawhide boots he'd worn under gaiters.

Then we stood in silence beside the enormous steam-driven machine that Antonio and the *réseau* had stolen. It was the height of at least four men and probably one hundred feet long, with six sets of steel wheels polished by the tracks, and a black boiler right behind its front light. Unlike American trains, the turbine was exposed. But there was little time to admire it. Martin's gesture set Gita running, and Biddy and I sprinted behind her. When I looked back, Antonio and Martin were leaning together to free the switch.

We retraced our path, running back along the riverbank as fast as the undergrowth would allow. A hundred yards on, behind a bend in the wall, we crossed the track again and headed up the hill, climbing on all fours to a path that rose steeply along the ridgeline.

Three or four minutes after leaving Martin, we heard the long lowing of the locomotive whistle. The train was on its way. I counted to sixty as we ran, and the detonations of Henri and Christian's grenades followed precisely. We were close enough to the saltworks to hear the cries of

alarm go up in the German garrison—shouting and a siren pealing—
and to see color against the low clouds. We continued upward until we
could look down on the works and the trestle, two hundred yards from
the railroad gate Martin was preparing to attack. Only one of the machine guns looked to be manned. Inside the high walls, the red flames
were partially visible, and in that light, we could see the anthill swirl of
soldiers pouring in that direction.

The locomotive lumbered around the bend then, moving at no more
than ten miles an hour as it rocked on the old rail bed. The three machine-
gun crewmen had turned to watch the fire, but the train sounds caught
the attention of one of them. He stepped toward the trestle with his
hands on his waist, an idle spectator for a lingering second, and then,
with no transition, an image of urgent action waving wildly to his comrades, having suddenly recognized that the grenades and the locomotive
bearing down on them were part of the same attack.

Watching from above, I briefly panicked when I realized what would
happen if the gunners were smart enough to begin firing at the trestle.
Delivering nine hundred rounds a minute, the MG42s probably could
have damaged the ties enough to derail the train, maybe even to send
it into the Seille. But they'd clearly given that alternative no forethought
and prepared to take out their attackers more directly. One soldier stead-
ied the MG42 on its tripod, while the gunner put on his helmet and the
third crewman strung out the ammunition belt. Beside us, Gita raised
her M1 and whipped her chin to indicate Biddy and I should move
apart. Before the Germans could fire, we began shooting down at them.
We did not have the range at first, and the gunners suddenly swung
the MG42 in our direction. As the long muzzle crossed my plane of vision my entire body squeezed in fear and I started firing frantically, until
one of our bullets, maybe even mine, took down the gunner. With that,
the other two retreated inside the walls, dragging the fallen man behind
them.

When I lowered the carbine, I found my heart banging furiously and
my lungs out of breath. I was at war. In war. The momentousness of it
rang through me, but already, with just this instant to reflect, I felt the
first whisper of disappointment. Below, the locomotive went down the
trestle like a waddling hen, the burning fuse of the satchel charge now
visible in the cab window.

I caught sight of Martin then, rolling along the right-of-way between the river and the high wall of the saltworks. As the engine rumbled past him, he sprang back to his feet and sprinted down the track, taking advantage of the cover provided by the huge iron machine. Once he was beyond the curve of the wall, he swung his rucksack around him and removed two lengths of rope, both secured to grappling hooks, which he dug into the crotches of two small trees. Bracing himself that way, he backed to the edge of the river, and then, without hesitation, skidded down the concrete retaining wall on the bank, disappearing into the water.

Suddenly, a gun barked on my left. I flinched before I heard Biddy crying out. He was shooting, and Gita immediately joined him. A gunner had returned to the other MG42. I fired, too, the jolting rifle once escaping my shoulder and recoiling painfully against my cheek, but in a moment the man was back inside the walls. One of the Germans had closed the low iron gate, but it was thin and presented no obstruction to the locomotive that crashed through it, headed for its descent into the mine. With a little shout, Gita signaled us to run.

Once we were beyond the crest, Gita dropped to her knees and threw herself down the hill in a ball. I fell where she had started but ended up spinning sideways into a tree stump. Biddy came somersaulting by, bumping along like a boulder. I dashed several feet, then tripped and accomplished what I had meant to, rolling on my side down the hill, landing painfully and bouncing forward.

In the midst of that, I heard an enormous echo of screaming metal piped out of the tunnel and knew the locomotive had barreled into the loaded flatcars. In the reality of physicists, there were actually two detonations, the satchel charges and then the ordnance, but my experience was of a single sensational roar that brought full daylight and fireside heat and bore me aloft. I was flying through the air for a full second, then landed hard. Looking up, I saw giant pillars of flame beyond the hilltop, and nearby a corkscrew of smoking black iron, a piece of the locomotive, that had knifed straight into the earth, as if it were an arrow. My knee, inexplicably, was throbbing.

"Cover up," Biddy yelled. My helmet had been blown off. I saw it back up the incline, but a fountain of dirt and stone and hot metal began showering around me. Debris fell for more than a minute, tree boughs and shell pieces that plummeted through the air with a sound like a wolf whistle, and a pelting downpour of river water and the heavy mud of the bank. At the end came a twinkling of sawdust and the tatters of leaves. I had crawled halfway to my helmet when there was a second explosion that blew me back down to where I had been at first. The concussion was less violent, but the flames reached higher into the sky and the hot remains of what had been destroyed rained down even longer.

I still had my hands over my head when Gita slapped my bottom. I jumped instantly and found her laughing. "*Allons-y!*" She took off down the hillside. Biddy was already in motion and I sprinted behind them. He moved well for a man his size, but lacked endurance. I had retained some of the lung strength of a swimmer and eventually pulled past him, but I was no match for Gita, who flew along like a fox past the strips of cloth Martin had tied, stopping only when we reached the edge of the last open farm field we'd crossed this morning. At the margin of a small woods, Gita scouted for signs of the Germans, but we all knew that the blast that had roared out of the tunnel, as from a dragon's mouth, had to have devastated the garrison. Biddy arrived and laid his hands on his thighs, panting.

"What about Martin?" I asked her, when she signaled we were secure.

"We never worry about Martin," she said.

"Because he is safe?"

"Because it could drive one to lunacy. *Regarde.*" Across the field, Henri and Christian were ambling toward us, both so thoroughly relieved of their prior grimness that I failed to recognize them at first. They had ditched their rifles to appear more innocuous, and approached in their muddy boots and soaked overalls, smiling broadly. Henri, it turned out, lacked most of his upper teeth. They hugged Gita first, then both embraced Biddy and me. Henri virtually wrested me from my feet, and isolated within his powerful grasp and his warm husky scent, I felt the first stirrings of pride at the magnitude of our achievement and my own small role in it.

"We showed them," Henri said in French. The way back to the shepherd's hut was safe, he said. There they had built a fire and filled a cistern with water from a nearby spring, and we all sat on the ground, drinking and warming ourselves, while we waited for Antonio and

Martin. As we recounted the operation in a jumble of conversation, every spark of shared memory seemed to make each of us hilarious, but there was truly only one joke: we were alive.

When I was warmer, I hiked up my woolen pants leg to see what I had done to my knee. There was a gash, only an inch wide but deep, a smile amid a large purple welt. I had no clue how it had happened. Prodding the edges of the wound, I could feel nothing inside.

"For this a Purple Heart?" Gita asked Biddy in English, when she saw me toying with the injury. I had found my first-aid kit in my field-jacket pocket and Gita helped me wash the cut with a little of the gauze in there. Across the cut, she dumped a dusting of sulfa powder out of a packet, then skillfully fashioned a bandage from the remaining gauze. Wrapping my knee, she told me that it would be a week or so before I danced in the Follies again.

"Your nursing skills are impressive, Mademoiselle Lodz. How were you trained?"

"In Marseilles, in the hospital, I watched and learned."

"Is that what drew you to the hospital, a vocation for nursing?"

"Far from it. I wanted to steal opium." She smiled regally. More than anything, Gita Lodz enjoyed being shocking, and in me, she had easy prey.

"You were a drug fiend?"

"A bit. To dull the pain. Principally, I sold to opium dens. War is very hard on those people, Dubin. I survived on their desperation—until I met Robert. But I am a good nurse. I have what is required, a strong stomach and a soft heart. Even someone whom I would despise were he in good health moves me as an invalid."

"A bit of a paradox, is it not? To be a soldier and a nurse?"

Her small shoulders turned indifferently.

"I told you, Dubin, I do not fight to kill. Or conquer."

"So why, then?"

She pulled my pants leg down to my boot and smoothed it there. Then she sat back on her haunches.

"I will tell you how it has been with me, Dubin. I have fought because the Nazis are wrong and we are right and the Nazis must lose. But I also fight death. I see it in the barrel of every gun, in the figure of every Boche, and when they are defeated, I think each time: Today I may live.

Tu comprends?" She finished off by giving her full brows a comic wiggle, but her coffee eyes had been lethally intent. I knew she thought she had told me something remarkable, but I did not really grasp it. Right now I felt the thrill of surviving in all my limbs, as if I'd acquired the strength of ten.

"I fear I am too dense to fully understand, Mademoiselle."

"No, Dubin, it does not mean you are slow-witted." She stood with a sealed smile. "It means you are lucky."

The plan called for us to remain in the shepherd's hut until we had all reassembled and the local *réseau* could assure safe passage. Christian wandered down to the farmhouse to see if there had been any warnings.

"All quiet," he said. Word was that Patton's Army was advancing. The Germans had more pressing business than to hunt a few stray commandos on friendly ground.

Antonio arrived about half an hour later and the same circle of embraces was repeated, despite the fact that his face and uniform were pasted with mud.

"*Nom de nom,*" he said. "What an explosion! I was more than a kilometer away and it drove me into the riverbank so deep I thought I would suffocate. When I looked up there was not a tree standing for five hundred meters from the tunnel."

His account of the blast made me more concerned about Martin, but Gita refused to worry. Just as she said, an hour and a half along, Martin appeared. His pack and helmet were gone and the knee was torn out of his trousers. He was entirely soaked, but cheerful. Whistling, he came sauntering across the field.

When OSS had originally planned the operation in the fall, their engineers had calculated that Martin would survive the explosion by jumping from the trestle into the Seille and swimming away in a sprint. Knowing the timing, he would dive for the bottom just in advance of the blast, where the waters' depths would protect him from the plummeting debris.

But that scheme had been drawn up before the record rains of the autumn. The Seille, normally a slow-moving canal, was ten feet over its usual level and now a rushing river. That was why Martin had secured the ropes, so that he could use them to keep the current from carrying him back toward the tunnel. The theory was no match for reality when the shafts blew.

"Damn stupid," he said. "Lucky I didn't rip my arms off." With the explosion, the ropes tore through his hands, burning both palms despite his gloves, and lifting Martin from the water. He plunged back down farther on, but he was too dazed to get a footing or a handhold and was driven by the current at least a hundred yards until he was stopped by a dam of mud and rock that the explosion had dropped into the Seille almost directly opposite the point of attack. Swimming to the west bank, he crawled in a rush up the hill, expecting to be fired on any second, but from the top, he saw no soldiers moving amid the lingering smoke. The garrison appeared to have been wiped out to a man.

"What a beautiful locomotive," said Martin as we went over the events yet again. "Hochdruck by Henschel." In the midst of his recollection, his gaiety and wonder swiftly passed. "It was bad business about those boys," he said abruptly. No one added more about those deaths.

After walking through another field, we arrived at the road, where an old farmer rolled up on a horse-drawn flatbed loaded with newly harvested grapes. With their dusty skins, they looked like high clouds in a darkening sky. Martin instructed us to wade in and work our way down to the wagon bed to hide. Biddy and I went first. I could feel the grapes burst under my weight and their juice soaking my uniform. I positioned myself on my side to protect my knee, then heard Gita's rasp as she swam down through the bunches. Suddenly she was on top of me, her leg over mine, her face and torso some short distance away, the crushed fruit leaking out between us, but she made no effort to move, nor did I, and we remained that way all the time it took the wagon to clop back to the Comtesse de Lemolland's.

12. CELEBRATION

At the Comtesse de Lemolland's there was a celebration. The explosion had resounded even here and the giant flames, phosphorescent orange, shot a mile into the sky. In the house, the sole question was whether we had survived. The Comtesse would not consider the possibility that we had not, and once the lighting fixtures had stopped rocking, she ordered preparations for *une grande fête*. By the time we arrived, several dozen local residents, all with resistance affiliations, had gathered in the courtyard. It was the liberation scenes all over again—embraces, shouting, bottles of wine and cognac for each hand. A whole lamb was being roasted over an outdoor pit beside the stables. The seven of us—Biddy, Henri, Christian, Antonio, Gita, Martin, and I—stood shoulder to shoulder amid the grapes, waving our fists, praising France and America, to unending laughter and applause. It was 3:00 p.m. and Biddy and I might have reached HQ by nightfall, but I gave no thought to that. With my arm around Gita's slim waist, the other hand mounted on Biddy's wide shoulder, I felt an exhilaration and freedom that were new in my life.

The smell of the cooking meat woke an enormous hunger, but I desired even more to shed my uniform, mud-slimed, grape-stained, bloodied in spots, not to mention sopped and chafing. Gita sent the drunken Bettjer to fetch dry fatigues for both Biddy and me, and we changed in a room in the farmhands' bunkhouse over the barn. My knee was growing stiff, but in my present mood even the discomfort seemed a pleasant souvenir.

"Oh, now look at this," said Bidwell. His pants stopped midway down his shin. I offered to swap, but mine were the same length and Biddy was just as happy to be silly. The Frenchmen were delighted when he appeared in his 'culottes.'

I had never been one to enjoy parties, but it seemed that I hadn't ever before had so much to celebrate. When the rain began again the crowd moved inside, where I drank and repeated the story of the attack for little knots of Frenchmen who gathered around. Almost all of them had assisted somehow over the months the operation had been planned, surveillance agents who fished the Seille to reconnoiter the dump, or silent sentries who'd kept watch once we'd slipped behind the German lines. The size of the explosion was remarked on again and again, tangible proof of the risk and of the triumph.

Eventually, the talk turned to other developments in the war. Patton's principal force was said to be moving against Metz. Many of the French were convinced that the fight would end soon, that in a matter of months *la vie normale* would resume and the Americans would be returning to the States. In response to questions about my home, I pulled my Kodaks from my wallet and set them on the long planked dining table where I had taken a seat, a bit woozy from the cognac I'd been sipping. The little snaps were all somewhat disfigured from the impression of my house key that I kept beside them, but that did not seem to deter my audience, who made laudatory remarks as they examined the photos of my parents, sister, and baby brother, and of Grace.

I became aware of Gita leaning over my shoulder. She was dressed again as a civilian, in a simple blouse and skirt. She lifted Grace's photo from the table with her customary boldness. Everyone else had treated the pictures as if they were sacred relics that could not even be touched.

"Ta soeur?" Your sister?

"Ma fiancée."

She gave me a direct look, finally a pursed grin. *"Mes félicitations,"* she said and turned away.

A few minutes later, as I was about to replace the snapshots, Biddy plopped beside me, and asked to see them. Slowed by drink, he took a long time with each.

"Not your quality," I told him, "but it helps me remember their faces. You have Kodaks of your family, Biddy?"

He gave his head a solemn shake.

"Now, how could that be," I asked, "a picture-taker like you?"

"Just reckon it's better that way, Lieutenant. I got 'em here and here." He touched his heart, his head. Our exchange in English had isolated us from the Frenchmen. Gideon gathered the pictures up tenderly and handed them to me.

"You come from a big family, Biddy?"

"Not compared to some. Me, Momma, Daddy, two brothers."

"Brothers in the service?"

"No, sir. The older one, he's *too* old, and my middle brother, he just never got called."

"Volunteered for the Navy?" I knew several fellows who put in for the Navy and still hadn't gone in when I did.

"Nope. Just somethin 'bout him the draft board didn't never take to."

"Four-F?"

"Nothing wrong with his body, not so they ever said." He shrugged, as baffled as the rest of us over the Army's eternal unreason.

I asked if he heard from them.

"My momma. You know how moms are. I must get four letters from her every week. My middle brother, he ain't much for writing, same as my dad. But Daddy, he sends me stuff, you know, magazine clippings and whatnot. It's hard on all of 'em my bein here. My folks got into a big tussle before I went into the service, and they ain't quite set that right yet. You know how families go."

"That I do. My folks still haven't forgiven me about this girl I'm going to marry."

"Now how's that, Lieutenant? She looks like a million bucks."

"And smarter and nicer than she looks. But Grace's family is Episcopalian and I'm Jewish, Biddy." I paused to wonder if I'd said that as frankly since I'd entered the service. "That difference didn't sit well in either house."

At the news of my proposal, Horace Morton had exploded. Grace related only that he had denounced me as 'conniving,' but I'm sure 'Jew' had been the next word. Grace's mother, however, took my side, and in time the two women wore down Mr. Morton. Soon I was allowed to enter the great stone house to ask for his daughter's hand. Along the way, to help subdue the histrionics there, I had volunteered to become an Episcopalian so Grace could marry at her church.

Because of my parents' hostility to religious practice, I had convinced myself that this last detail would not greatly concern them. I knew that my mother did not favor my romance with someone so different, but I had dismissed that view as Old World. As I later learned, my father had persuaded Ma not to say more by pointing out that people as highly placed as the Mortons would never let their only daughter marry so far below her class. Now, when I told them about my proposal and my prospective conversion, my mother probably felt she'd been double-crossed. In any event, she stood straight up from the kitchen table, making no effort to contain herself.

"This is madness, Duvid," she said, pointedly using the Yiddish version of my name, as my parents sometimes did. "You think some priest can wave a magic wand and go poo, poo, poo so that instead of a chicken you are now a duck? To people like this, you will always be a shabby Jew and nothing else."

In answer, I described the church service Grace and her mother had envisioned, believing it evidenced their acceptance of me. My mother responded by sobbing.

"I don't go to a synagogue," she cried. "I should go kneel in a church so my son can forget where he comes from? Feh," she said. "Sooner dead. Not for all the gold in Fort Knox. If this is how you marry, you marry without me."

"She means it, Duvid," my father said, then added, "Me, too."

I hesitated even to tell Grace for days, because she would have no way to break this to her mother. Mrs. Morton had taken the side of love, but its culmination in her mind required an organ and afternoon light through the rose window in the nave. With little time to negotiate, we debated eloping, but I simply could not go off to war so deeply at odds with my family. Not quite knowing how it had happened, I shipped out for basic training with Grace still my fiancée, rather than my wife.

I told Biddy the story in shorter strokes, but drunk as he was, it seemed to move him.

"Ain't that terrible, Lieutenant, when folks get goin on like that? Someday people's just gonna be people." He looked pitiably confused and morose, his face contorted as he kept going "Mmm, mmm, mmm" in disapproval. I ended up putting my hand on his shoulder in consolation, and struck by that, Biddy smiled, eyeing me for some time.

"You are all right, Lieutenant. You gotta get outta your head and into the world, but you are definitely all right."

"Thank you, Biddy. You're okay yourself. And we were definitely in the world today."

"Yes, sir. We sure enough were. I ain't never gone see nothin like that again. This bird Martin, Lieutenant. Could be I had him wrong. I think he may be all right, too."

I knew the image of Martin dropping so gracefully into the quick waters of the Seille despite the many perils would retain a hallmarked spot in my memory.

Some of the Frenchmen were circulating now with dinner, which had been set out on a buffet in the kitchen, and I could not wait to eat. Even after the relative grandeur of my meals in Nancy, the lamb was a spectacular treat, even more so to the locals after years of wartime privations. The animal, I was told, had been hidden from the Germans. It had been slaughtered out of season, old enough to be closer to mutton, one farmer said, but still remarkably tasty as far as I was concerned.

Martin eventually arrived at the center of the kitchen by the huge iron stove and called for silence. He praised our success and the courage of everyone present and thanked the gallant Comtesse yet again for her bravery and magnificent hospitality throughout the weeks they had waited.

"I raise my glass last to those of you who were with me. To do what we do and live, one must be lucky. You were all my luck today."

There was applause, shouted congratulations, to which Gita's voice was eventually added from the back of the room.

"I am always your luck," she called. "It's boring. Every time, the same thing. Martin fights, I save him. Martin fights, I save him."

This was comedy, and her parody of the shrewish country wife evoked drunken laughter. Inspired by her audience's enthusiasm, Gita mounted a chair to continue, very much the girl who had seen herself as the new Bernhardt. Now she engaged in a dramatic retelling of the story of Martin's capture by the Gestapo early in 1943. The Nazis had not recognized him as an American. Suspecting instead that Martin was a Frenchman connected with the underground, they imprisoned him in the local village hall, while they investigated. Knowing there was little time, Gita stuffed her skirt with straw and arrived in the receiving area of the hôtel de ville, demanding to see the German commandant. At the sight of him, she dissolved in tears, decrying the son of a bitch who had left her with child and now was going to prison without marrying her. After twenty minutes of her ranting, the commandant was ready to teach Martin a lesson, and sent four storm troopers to bring him in chains to the local cathedral where the marriage could be performed. It never was, of course. The four soldiers escorting Martin and Gita were set upon by two dozen *maquisards*, resistance guerrillas, who quickly freed them both.

"I curse the fate that intervened," cried Martin in French, raising his glass to her. "I will marry you now."

"Too late," she cried, and on her chair, turned away, her nose in the air, an arm extended to hold him at bay. "Your horse has eaten *le bébé*."

Their tableau was received with more resounding laughter and clapping. A moment later, as the first of the crowd began departing, Martin took the chair beside me. I had barely left my seat. The cognac had me whirling.

"You did well today, Dubin."

I told him sincerely that I hadn't done much more than fire my M1 a few times, but he reminded me that we had all been in harm's way when the machine gun had swung toward us. He stopped then to ponder the circle of brandy in his glass.

"That was unfortunate with those young soldiers. I don't mind killing a man with a gun pointed at me, but I took no pleasure in that." I, on the other hand, had still given no thought to those deaths. I was aloft on the triumph and my reception as a hero. I was surely different, I thought, surely a different man.

"When I was their age," he said of the two Germans, "I'd have thought they had met a good end. Foolish, eh? But as a young man, I woke up many days feeling it would be my last. Gita and I have this in common, by the way. I recognized the same fatalism when I met her. The bargain that I struck with myself to forestall these thoughts was that I would die for glory. So that at the moment that the bullet entered my brain, I could tell myself I had made this a better world. I was looking for a valiant fight for years until I found it in Spain. But it turns out I'm a coward, Dubin. I am still alive, and now an old warhorse."

"You are the furthest thing from a coward I have ever met, Major."

He made a face. "I tell myself each time I will not fear death, but of course I do. And I wonder what all of this has been for."

"Surely, Major, you believe in this war."

"In its ends? Without question. But I have been making war now for a decade, Dubin, give or take a few years off. I have fought for good causes. Important causes. But I mourn every man I've killed, Dubin. And not merely for the best reason, because killing is so terrible, but because there really is no point to so many of these deaths. This boy today? I killed him to save all of us at the moment. But I don't fool myself that it was indispensable, let alone the dozens, probably hundreds, we left dead or maimed in that garrison. We make war on Hitler. As we must. But millions get in the way and die for the Führer. What do you think? How many men do we truly need to kill to win this war? Ten? Surely no more than one hundred. And millions upon millions will die instead."

The tragedy of war, I said.

"Yes, but it's a tragedy for each of us, Dubin. Every moment of terror is a month of nightmares later in life. And every killing like today's is a mile farther from ever feeling joy again. You think when you start, 'I know who I am. At the core, I am inviolate. Permanent.' You are not. I did not know that war could be so terrible, that it would crowd out everything else in a life. But it does, I fear, Dubin."

I was startled by this speech, given my own buoyancy. But Martin was not the first man I'd met to find gloom in alcohol. To comfort him, I repeated the prediction I'd heard tonight that we were going to make short work of the Germans, and Martin answered with a philosophical shrug. I asked what he would do then.

"Wait for the next war, I suppose," he answered. "I don't think I'm good for much else, that's what I'm saying, unless I spare the world the trouble and put an end to myself. I really can't envision life in peacetime anymore. I talk about a good hotel room and a good woman, but what is that? And I am not so different, Dubin. Soon everyone will be driven into this lockstep. War and making more war."

"So you think we will fight the Russians, Major?"

"I think we will fight. Don't you see what's happening, Dubin? No one has choices any longer. Not here and not at home. I always thought that the march of history was forward, less suffering and greater freedom for mankind, the chains of need and tyranny breaking apart. But it's not what meets my eye when I look to the future. It's just one group of the damned making war on the other. And liberty suffering."

"You're in the Army, Major. This has never been freedom's Valhalla."

"Yes, that's the argument. But look at what's happened on the home front. I get letters, I read the papers. War has consumed every liberty. There's propaganda in the magazines and on the movie screens. Ration books and save your tin cans. Sing the songs and spout the line. There's no freedom left anywhere. With one more war, Dubin, civil society will never recover. The war profiteers, the militarists, the fearmongers—they'll be running things permanently. Mark my words. Mankind is falling into a long dark tunnel. It's the new Middle Ages, Dubin. That's the bit that breaks my heart. I thought fascism was the plague. But war is. *War* is." He looked into his glass again.

As he spoke, Teedle came to mind. I wondered if Martin and he had had this argument face-to-face. Or simply suspected as much of one another. They both saw the world headed to hell in a handbasket. I gave them credit for worrying, each of them. For most of the men out here, me included, the only real concern was going home.

"May I assume I am quit of your charges?" Martin asked then.

I told him I'd certainly recommend that, but that the safest course, given the orders he'd received, would be for him to return to Nancy with me in the morning to sort it out. He thought it through, but finally nodded.

"I'll spend a few hours," he said, "but I have to get on now to the next assignment." That would be the operation in Germany he'd mentioned when I first arrived here, the one for which he'd been called back to London. "I think it will be the most important work I've done, Dubin. There's no counting the lives we may save." He lifted his eyes toward the bright light of that prospect, then asked when I wanted to start in the morning. Dawn, I said, would be best, given how long we'd been away.

That reminded me that I needed to retrieve my uniform. I stood hesitantly, my knee quite stiff, to seek Gita. She had been outside saying adieu to the locals. I met her in the parlor, where Bidwell had crawled up on one of the Comtesse's elegant red velvet divans and was fast asleep beneath a lace shawl from the back of the couch.

"Leave him," she said.

"I shall, but I can't take him back to headquarters in culottes."

Gita consulted Sophie, the maid who had washed our uniforms and left them to dry over the same fire, now banked, where the lamb was roasted. As we headed out, Gita threw her arm through mine companionably as I limped along between the puddles etched in the candlelight from the house. The rain had been heavy for a while but had ceased, although the eaves and trees still dripped. The Comtesse's other guests had gone down the road in a pack and their drunken uproar carried back to us in the dank night.

I told her about my conversation with Martin. "Is he normally so dour?"

"Afterward? Afterward, always. Have you known gamblers, Dubin? I have often thought that if there were not war, Martin would probably be standing at a gaming table. Many gamblers have moods like this. They exult in the game, in betting everything, but their spirit flags once they win. *Voilà la raison*. Martin speaks the truth when he says he is miserable without war. That was the case when I met him."

"In Marseilles?"

"Yes. I sold him opium, when he visited from Spain." I managed not to miss a step. I seemed to have prepared myself for anything from her. "He smoked too much of it, but he recovered a few months later once he agreed to go to the States to train as a commando."

"His new wager?" I thought of the way Martin had raised his eyes at the thought of his next assignment in Germany.

"Precisely," Gita answered.

The uniforms were by the barn entrance, now imbued with an intense smoky aroma, but dry. She helped me fold them and I placed them under the arm she had been holding.

"Martin says his remorse is over no longer being who he was," I told her.

"Does he?" She was struck by that. She squinted into the darkness.

"Well, who is? Am I who I was when I ran to Marseilles at the age of seventeen? Still," she said, "it is true he suffers."

From what she'd told me, I said, it seemed as if Martin had suffered always.

"*D'accord*. But there are degrees, no? Now at night, he sleeps in torment. He sees the dead. But that is probably not the worst of it. There is no principle in war, Dubin. And Martin has been at war so long, there is no principle in him. I was not sure he recognized this."

"Ah, that word again," I said. We were standing in the open doorway of the barn, where the dust and animal smells breathed onto us in the wind. Her heavy brows narrowed as she sought my meaning.

"Principles," I said.

She grinned, delighted to have been caught again. "And here we debated," she added.

"You most effectively," I answered.

"Yes, I showed you my principles." She laughed, we both did, but a silence fell between us, and with it came a lingering turning moment, while Gita's quick eyes, small and dark and sometimes greedy, searched me out. She spoke far more quietly. "Shall I show you my principles again, Doo-bean?"

The hunger I felt for this woman had been no secret from me. Amid the peak emotions of the day, the increasing physical contact between us had seemed natural, even needed, and the direction we were headed seemed plain. But I had been equally certain that reason would intervene and find a stopping point. Now, I realized there would be none. I felt a blink of terror, but I had learned today how to overcome that, and I also had the tide of alcohol to carry me. Yet drink was not the key. Gita was simply part of this, this place, these adventures. I answered her question with a single word.

"Please," I said. And with that she took her thin skirt in her fingertips and eased it upward bit by bit, until she stood as she had stood two weeks ago, delicately revealed. Then she was in my arms. With her presence came three fleeting impressions: of how small and light she was, of the stale odor of tobacco that penetrated her fingertips and hair, and of the almost infinite nature of my longing.

For a second, I thought it would happen there in the barn, among the animals, a literal roll in the hay, but she drew me to the narrow stairs and we crept up together to the tiny room where Biddy and I had changed. Her blouse was open, one shallow breast exposed. She stepped quickly out of her bloomers, and with no hesitation placed one hand on my belt and lowered my fly, taking hold of me with a nurse's proficiency. We staggered toward the bunk and then we were together, a sudden, jolting, desperate coupling, but that seemed to be the need for both of us, to arrive at once at that instant of possession and declaration. My knee throbbed throughout, which seemed appropriate somehow.

Afterward, she rested on my chest. I lay on the striped ticking of the unmade bunk, my pants still around my ankles, breathing in the odor of the mildewed mattress and the barnyard smells of manure and poultry feathers rising up from below while I assessed who I really was.

So, I thought. So. There had been something brutal in this act, not between Gita and me, but in the fact it had happened. The thought of Grace had arrived by now to grip me with despair. It was not merely that I had given no consideration to her. It was as if she had never existed. Was Gita right? No principle in war and thus no principle in those who fight it? It was the day, I thought, the day. I conveniently imagined that Grace would understand if she knew the entire tale, although I harbored no illusion I would ever tell her.

Gita brought her small face to mine and whispered. We could hear the snores of the farmhands sleeping on the other side of the thin wooden partitions that passed for walls.

"À *quoi penses-tu*, Doo-bean?" What are you thinking?

"Many things. Mostly of myself."

"Tell me some."

"You can imagine. There is a woman at home."

"You are here, Dubin."

For the moment that would have to be answer enough.

"And I wonder, too, about you," I said.

"*Vas-y*. What do you wonder?"

"I wonder if I have met another woman like you."

"Does that mean you have met such men?"

I laughed aloud and she clapped her small hand over my mouth.

"That is your only question?" she asked.

"Hardly."

"*Continue*."

"The truth?"

"*Bien sûr.*"

"I wonder if you sleep with all the men you fight with."

"Does this matter to you, Dubin?"

"I suppose it must, since I ask."

"I am not in love with you. Do not worry, Dubin. You have no responsibilities. Nor do I."

"And Martin? What truly goes on between Martin and you? You are like an old married couple."

"I have told you, Dubin. I owe much to Robert. But we are not a couple."

"Would he say the same thing?"

"Say? Who can ever tell what Martin might say? But he knows the truth. We each do as we please."

I did not quite understand, but made a face at what I took to be the meaning.

"You do not approve?" she asked.

"I have told you before. I am bourgeois."

"Forgive me, but that cannot be my concern."

"But Martin is mine. And you intend to stay with Martin."

"I am not with him now, Dubin. I am with you."

"But I will go and you will stay with Martin. Yes?"

"For now. For now, I stay with Martin. He says he dreads the day I go. But I stay with Martin to fight, Dubin. Will the Americans allow me to join their Army?"

"I doubt it."

She sat up and looked down at me. Even in the dark, I could see she was narrow and lovely. I ran my hand from her shoulder to her waist, which did nothing to diminish the intensity with which she watched me.

"How many women, Dubin. For you? Many?"

I was shy of this subject, not the doing, but the talking. At twenty-nine, my sexual history remained abbreviated. Some love for sale, some drunken grappling. It was best summarized by the phrase a college friend had applied to himself that fit me equally: I had never gotten laid with my shoes off. Tonight was another example.

"Not so many," I said.

"No? You forgive me, but I think not. Not from the act, Dubin, but from how you are now. And how is it with this woman of yours at home?"

I recoiled at that, then realized the question was not all that different from the ones I'd been asking her.

"It has not occurred, as yet."

"Truly?"

"She is my fiancée, not my wife."

"This was her choice?"

It was mutual, I supposed. Not that there had ever been much discussion. Grace and I had the same assumptions, that there was special meaning in the union of man and woman.

"I worship Grace," I said to Gita. That was the perfect word. 'Worship.' It had not dawned on me until this moment that I could not say in the same way that I craved her.

"She should have insisted, Dubin. She had no idea what she was sending you to."

I could see that much myself.

Gita went down to the barn to attend to herself. A pump handle squealed. Most single men I knew talked a tough game about the women they slept with. But my experience had always been the opposite. In the wake of sex, I inevitably felt a bounty of tenderness, even when I paid a local lunatic called Mary Quick Legs $4 for my first encounter. Now that Gita had left my side, I longed to have her back there. I lay there wondering if I had ever known people like Martin and Gita who had so quickly altered my understanding of myself.

Her small tread squeaked up the stairs and she crept in, standing near the bunk. Seeing her dressed, I reached down and drew up my trousers.

"I must go, Dubin," she whispered. "They will be looking for me shortly. Au revoir." She peered at me, albeit with some softness. "Doobean, I believe we shall have other moments together."

"Do you?" I had no idea if I wanted that, but I told her that I would probably return one more time to give Martin the final papers on my investigation.

"Well, then," she answered. She hesitated but bent and pressed her lips to mine lightly. It was more of a concession than an embrace. She said au revoir again.

I had been so raddled by emotion all day that I would have thought my nerves would be too unsettled for sleep, but as with every other expectation of late, I was wrong. I had purposely not drawn the wooden shutters outside and woke at 7:30, as I intended, with the livid sunrise firing through the clouds. Coming to, I recognized my knee as the discomfort, which, like a leash, had seemed to drag me up from sleep periodically throughout the night. The leg was swollen and stiff and I eased myself up slowly, then put on my uniform, refastening the insignia. As I went back toward the house to rouse Bidwell and to see about Martin, I could hear mortars pounding. The 26th Infantry Division, as it turned out, was about to seize Bezange-la-Petite. I was standing there, trying to make out the direction of the booming guns, when Bettjer, still with a cognac bottle in his hand, stumbled into the courtyard.

I asked if he knew where Bidwell was. Peter answered in perfect English.

"Inside. Just now awake. The rest are gone for several hours."

"Who?"

"Martin. Antonio. The girl. Packed and gone for good. They have left me behind. After all of that, they have left me behind."

"Gone?"

"They went in darkness. Hours ago. They tried to creep away, but the Comtesse wept terribly. You must have slept soundly not to hear her."

"Gone?" I said again.

Bettjer, the very image of a sot, whiskered and disheveled in his brown Belgian uniform with half a shirttail out, lifted his bottle to me. He had fallen during the night and bloodied his nose and now when he smiled, I could see he had lost half a tooth as well, from that stumble or from one before. Still, he was having a fine time at my expense.

"I see," he said. "I see."

"What do you see, Peter?"

"Why, they have left you behind, too."

IV.

13. SWIMMING

My father had learned to swim as a child in Lake Ellyn, a man-made lake that was actually a large retaining pond in the South End, dug to keep the Kindle River from overflowing its banks in wet seasons. His parents apparently liked the water, too, because there are many photos of the whole family in the ridiculously full bathing costumes of that era, cavorting at the lake, or in the Garfield Baths, a giant teeming indoor swimming pool which was a favorite diversion for Kindle County's working families until the baths' role as a polio breeding ground led them to be closed in the 1950s.

Watching my father swim was always mesmerizing to me. His grace in the water, and the carefree way he splashed around, was inconsistent with the guy who existed on dry land. And so was the physique revealed in his bathing suit. He was a fair-sized person, five foot eleven, and while not exactly Charles Atlas, pretty muscular. Whenever I saw the solid body concealed beneath the shirt and tie he wore until he went to bed each night, I was amazed. So this was who was here. I felt simultaneously reassured and baffled.

Eventually, when I was around fourteen, my father, never much for boasting, admitted in response to my questions that he had been the Tri-Cities high-school champion in the hundred-yard backstroke. Even then, I was hungry for any morsel about who he was, and so one day when my duties on *The Argonaut*, the high-school paper, required me to visit the U High Athletic Association, I decided to look in the archives to see if I could find my father's name.

I did. Sort of. The backstroke champion of 1933 had been called not 'David Dubin,' but 'David Dubinsky.' I knew, of course, that immigrants of all kinds had Americanized their names. Cohens had become Coles. Wawzenskis had become Walters. But it did not sit well with me that he had made this alteration just before starting on his scholarship at Easton College, that gentile bastion. It was a bitter hypocrisy to disown your past and, worse, a capitulation to the happy American melting pot that had marginalized many citizens, especially those with darker skin, whom it could not fit into the blender. When I discovered that Dad had talked his parents into following this example, so he wouldn't be undermined in his new identity, I couldn't keep myself from confronting him.

He defended himself in his usual fashion, with few words. "It seemed simpler then," he said.

"I am not hiding my heritage," I told my father. "However you felt, I'm not ashamed." This was a fairly cheap shot. In our home, my mother had insisted on Jewish ritual and Jewish education. There was a Sabbath meal on Friday night, Hebrew school, and even a quaint form of kosher in her kitchen, in which *traife* of all kinds, including the ham sandwiches she loved, could be consumed, but only if they were served on paper plates and stored on a single, designated shelf in the Frigidaire. Dad had never seemed adept with any of that, probably because he had absolutely no religious training in his own home, but on the other hand, I never doubted that my mother had his full support. Nonetheless, in my final year of college, in 1970, I did my father one better and legally changed my name back. I have been known as Stewart Dubinsky ever since.

Nature, of course, has this way of getting even. Daughter Number 1, since the age of six, has told me she hates Dubinsky (which first-grade meanies turned into 'Poop-insky') and has vowed to take the last name of whomever she marries, even if it's Bozo A. Clown. And I didn't do my fa-

ther much worse than he'd done his own dad. My grandfather, the cobbler, was in his last years when I made the change, and actually seemed
pleased. But as I labored throughout 2003 to recover what my father had
never seen fit to share, there was always a little sore spot in my heart
whenever I recalled how I had shunned the one thing of my father's
I'd had.

This, then, was the story I told Bear Leach immediately after first meeting him in the front sitting room of Northumberland Manor. Bear extracted the complete tale with adroit questioning and accepted my rueful
second thoughts about the change with a sage smile.

"Well, Stewart," he said, "I sometimes think that's everything that
goes wrong between parents and children. What's rejected. And what's
withheld."

In the latter column I could count my father's manuscript, which I eventually thought to ask Leach about. At that point, I assumed Dad had carried through on his threat to burn it. When I said as much, Leach struggled
to his left and right, muttering until he located a Redweld he'd rested
against the chrome spokes of his wheelchair. Inside the expandable
folder he handed over was at least an inch and a half of jumbled papers,
but thumbing through them I instantly recognized my father's lovely cur-
sive hand on several interlineations. Big goof that I am, I sat there on the
little love seat where I was perched and cried.

I'd read every line by the time I returned home, finishing by spending
three hours in the Tri-Cities Airport after stepping off my plane, unable to
endure even the thirty-minute drive to my town house before reaching
the culmination. I was a sight, I'm sure, an economy-size fiftysomething
guy bawling his eyes out in an empty passenger lounge, while travelers
on the concourse cast worried glances, even while they went on hustling
toward their gates.

The day Bear had given the typescript to me, I eventually asked how
he had ended up with it.

"I have to say, Stewart, that I've always regarded my possession of
this document as the product of ambiguous intentions. As I told you, your
father said he was intent on burning it after my reading, and once I finished, I felt strongly that would be a terrible loss. I held on to the manuscript for that reason, claiming that I needed it in order to clarify little

matters connected to his appeals. Then in late July 1945 your father was released quite unexpectedly and left Regensburg in haste, with other things on his mind. I expected to hear from him about the document eventually, but I never did, not in Europe, and not when we returned to the U.S. I thought of looking him up from time to time over the years, especially as I moved the manuscript from office to office, but I concluded that your father had made a choice he deemed best for all of us, and certainly for himself, that he go on with his life without the complications and memories our renewed contact would raise. The typescript has been in storage at the Connecticut Supreme Court among my papers for several years now, with a note informing my executors to locate David Dubin or his heirs for instructions on what to do with it. I was quite pleased to hear from you, naturally, since it saved my grandchildren from making that hunt."

"But why burn it?" I asked. "Because of this stuff about murdering Martin?"

"Well, of course that was my suspicion, at least at first." Bear stopped then, something clearly nagging him, perhaps a thought about how close he was to the boundaries of what he could properly disclose. "I suppose all I can say for certain, Stewart, is what David told me."

"Which was?"

"Oddly, we never had a direct conversation, your father and I, about what he had written. Even once I'd read it, he was clearly disinclined to discuss the events he'd described, and I understood. The closest we came was a day or two after the sentencing. Your father was going to remain under house arrest during the pendency of his appeal, but he was beginning to accommodate himself to the idea of five years at hard labor. I told him what criminal lawyers always tell their clients in this predicament, that there was going to be another day, a life afterward, and that he might look back on all of this, years from now, with different eyes. And in that connection I brought up the manuscript, which at the moment I'd conveniently left in the safety of my new office in Frankfurt.

"'I think you should save it, Dubin,' I said to him. 'If nothing else, it will be of great interest to your children. Surely, you can't pretend, Dubin, you wrote something like this just for me. And certainly not to reduce it all to ashes.' He pondered that, long enough that I thought I'd struck a chord, but in the end he stiffened his chin and gave his head a

resolute shake. And at that point, Stewart, he gave me the only explanation I ever heard about his determination to destroy what he'd put on
paper.

"'My most desperate hope,' he said, 'is that my children never hear
this story.'"

14. STOP

Dearest Grace—

Sorry for the silence. As you can tell from the news reports,
the troops are on the move again, and the pace of our work has
picked up, too. There are battlefront incidents that by their
nature are often urgent, and we know that the move to a new HQ
may not be far off. Our hope is that it will be in Germany—
better yet, Berlin.

I'm feeling more myself now than when I last wrote. You must
be wondering about those letters I dashed off a couple of
weeks ago, bracketing my little detour into "action." With the
distance of time, I have decided to put the entire experience
behind me. That is what the old soldiers tell you to do: take
the past as gone, and realize the chasm between war and normal
life is wider than the Grand Canyon and not to be crossed.
Darling, believe me, one day when this thing is over, I want you
sitting beside me, so I can stroke your hair while I think over

some of this. But please don't mind if it turns out that there's not much I care to say.

On a happier note, your most recent package, no. 15, arrived today. Only two of the sugar cookies were in pieces and I enjoyed them that way, too, believe me. Even better was the bottle of Arrid you sent, which I know is in short supply and thus made me the envy of many. Because of the lack of fuel, hot water is a rarity, meaning few showers and baths. Let your brother know how much I appreciated the deodorant. Say what you like, but sometimes it _is_ an advantage having your own department store. On that score, I'd like to request a favor. If George sees any film pack, size of 620, I'll take whatever he can find. My sergeant, Biddy, is quite the photographer and is having trouble getting film. He's probably the best fellow I've met in the service and I'd love to help him out.

Winter has come. The weather has gone from dank to bone-chilling. It is still raining, at least in name, but what falls now are icy pellets that sting the skin and freeze solid within hours. I wear my woolen gloves when I am sitting at my desk, although the courtroom has a little heat. The cycles of rain and ice are far worse for the boys in the foxholes. Trench foot has become a plague. Estimates are that a third of the troops are suffering from it, many with cases so severe they have to be hospitalized. Patton has ordered 85,000 extra pairs of socks and is rumored to have lectured troops that in war, foot hygiene is more important than brushing your teeth. Overshoes are coveted. The boys out there continue to amaze me with their courage and determination.

Their hardships are at great remove from me, as I continue with the safe but dreary life of a lawyer in court. I do have one piece of news. My promotion came through yesterday (only four months overdue). I am now Captain Dubin, with the word "acting" removed from my title as Assistant Staff Judge Advocate. I put on my silver bars immediately and walked around all day feeling great satisfaction every time a lieutenant saluted as I passed.

Have a wonderful Thanksgiving, my love. I expect to be with
you, by the fire, this time next year.
    I love you and think of you always,
David

One afternoon in the second week in December a clerk dropped my mail call on my desk, three letters and a card. I was stuffing them inside my tunic, to be savored in privacy later, when the postcard grabbed my attention. On one side was a black-and-white photo of a gabled structure, with narrow variegated spires and two concentric arches over the door. The tiny legend on the reverse identified the building as the synagogue at Arlon, the oldest in Belgium. But I was more astonished by the handwritten note there.

Dubin—
Am sorry we fool you. Robert says was no choice. You is good
fellow. Please not to think bad of me. Perhaps we meet again
when is not war. For Jew is ok to say Joyeux Noël?

                                                              G.

Gita Lodz's handwriting was pointed and not particularly tidy, just as I might have guessed. She had used English, knowing that a message in French might be months getting past the Army censors.

I read the postcard perhaps twenty times in the next day, trying to determine if it had any larger meanings. Why did she bother? Did I actually care? Eventually I began to wonder whether she was truly in Belgium or if this was another ruse, designed by Martin. I asked a postal clerk if he could tell the mailing location of the card, which bore the purple circled stamp of the Army post office. A three-number code at the center was from the First Army Headquarters near Spa, Belgium.

After pondering, I sent a teletype to Teedle's headquarters at the 18th Armored Division, stating that I'd had a communication indicating where Martin might be. By now, the 18th had returned to combat, moving past Metz into Luxembourg where they were skirmishing with the Germans as they fell back toward the heavy concrete fortifications of the Siegfried line, ringing Germany. With the approval of General staff, only days after Martin had disappeared, Teedle had issued an order for Martin's arrest, bringing a formal end to my investigation. Thus relieved, l had been doing my best not to think about either Robert Martin or Gita Lodz, both of whom had misled me to my serious detriment. On my hangdog visit to Teedle the day Martin had decamped, I'd gotten the hiding I expected, but not simply for losing track of the Major. Patton was incensed about the explosions at La Saline Royale, and in Teedle's words, wanted "Martin's balls for Thanksgiving dinner." The raid on the dump had been planned by OSS in the fall, but, as it turned out, no one had given Martin permission to proceed now. Apparently, it was an adventure he just couldn't stand to miss before absconding. Without coordination, it proved a tactical disaster. The Germans' 21st Panzer Division had been spooked by the massive fireball and curtailed its advance on the region near Marsal, unwittingly avoiding three American antitank battalions Patton had had lying in wait.

My message to Teedle brought a quick response. Late the same day, I was hauled out of court for an urgent phone call. Dashing upstairs, I found Billy Bonner on the other end. Teedle was apparently in range of an Antrac phone relay and wanted to talk to me personally. The sound quality on the field telephone was static-scratched and thin, and when Bonner went to get the General, the thunder of artillery resounded down the line.

"I have your goddamn teletype, Dubin," said Teedle without preliminaries, "and it's too fucking lawyerly, as usual. I need some details in order to contact VIII Corps. What kind of communication was it you received?"

"A card, sir."

"A postcard? The son of a bitch sent you a postcard? Who does he think he is, Zorro?"

"It was from the girl, sir."

"His girl?"

"Yes, although I don't think she's really his girl, sir."

"Is that so? Dubin, you're turning out to be more interesting than I imagined. Well, whatever you call her, she's stuck to him like glue, right?"

"Oh, I expect she's with him, sir. I just doubt she'd do anything to jeopardize him. That's why I wasn't sure if I should bother you with this. I realize you've got your hands full, General, but the arrest is under your command."

"You did right, Dubin. And don't worry about us. We're kicking the shit out of these pricks. Not that it wouldn't be going even better if our President stopped mousing around with the Russians. We should be in Saarbrücken, but FDR's afraid if we move into Germany too fast Stalin will go batty." Teedle held up there, clearly reconsidering the wisdom of his remarks over an open telephone line. The heavy guns went off again in a second and the connection was lost.

A few days later, on December 15, I was in the officers' mess at about 7:00 a.m., eating a breakfast of powdered eggs with Tony, when a pimply young orderly, a new recruit who took virtually every development as an occasion for hysteria, flew in to tell me that I was wanted in the signal office. It was Teedle, this time at the other end of a coded teletype writer. Once the signalman indicated I was present, the machine began spitting tape, which the code reader transferred with intense chattering onto the yellow bale in the machine.

"Bastard located," Teedle wrote. "Up near town of Houffalize in the VIII Corps sector. Robin Hood now. Whole merry band with him. Told VIII Corps command was sent by OSS to reconnoiter German positions. Wish you proceed to Houffalize to arrest."

"Me?" I said this to the signalman, who asked if I wanted to transmit that response. I chose something more diplomatic, suggesting the duty might be better suited to the Provost Marshal.

"Negative. You will recognize subject," he wrote back. "Also know entire background. MPs here have combat responsibilities with POWs. We are fighting a war FYI."

I considered my alternatives, but ultimately responded that I understood my orders.

Teedle wrote, "Subject due back in 72 hours. Presently scouting behind enemy lines."

"How likely to return?"

"Very. Left girl behind. Proceed at once. Will notify London of imminent arrest."

I went immediately to Colonel Maples. With Teedle, I had been reluctant to raise technicalities, knowing he would not tolerate them, but there was a fundamental problem. I opened a copy of the *Manual for Courts-Martial* on the Colonel's desk to Rule 20.

20. COURTS-MARTIAL PROCEDURE BEFORE TRIAL—ARREST AND CONFINEMENT—*WHO MAY ORDER: METHOD*—THE FOLLOWING CLASSES OF PERSON SUBJECT TO MILITARY LAW WILL BE PLACED IN ARREST OR CONFINEMENT UNDER ARTICLE OF WAR 69, AS FOLLOWS:

OFFICERS—BY COMMANDING OFFICERS ONLY, IN PERSON, THROUGH OTHER OFFICERS, OR BY ORAL OR WRITTEN ORDERS OR COMMUNICATIONS. THE AUTHORITY TO PLACE SUCH PERSONS IN ARREST OR CONFINEMENT WILL NOT BE DELEGATED.

In other words, Martin could only be arrested by someone directly under Teedle's command, a member of the 18th Armored Division. After some debate at the time the arrest order was issued, our staff had concluded that Teedle, rather than Winters at OSS, remained Martin's commander, because Martin had disobeyed the very order transferring him back. But surely I wasn't under the General. If so, I couldn't arrest Martin without jeopardizing the ensuing court-martial.

Maples pinched his thumb and forefinger through his long mustache, which had gone completely white in the last few months and now resembled a smear of shaving lather. As usual, he remained reluctant to buck Teedle and came up with a lawyerly solution. He would get Third Army G-1 to designate me to the 18th solely for the purpose of carrying out Martin's arrest.

"We'll have to button up the paperwork. But you best get up there, David. Patton won't be amused if Martin slips away again. What a peculiar situation." The Colonel wobbled his hoary head. "Human misconduct, David. There's more imagination and mystery there than in the world of art."

"May I take Bidwell, Colonel?"

"Yes, of course." He sent me off to find a replacement in court for the day.

By noon, Biddy and I had our papers and were once more on the road. It was dank, with fog again gathered like smoke over the hills, and we had full side panels mounted to the canvas top on the jeep. Houffalize barely showed up on the maps, but it was somewhere in the vicinity of Saint-Vith, about 150 miles away. We'd be approaching areas of serious fighting and figured we'd do well to make it there by sunset the next day. Not knowing exactly what we'd encounter, we traveled with full packs and winter overcoats.

As we neared Metz and the territory the Americans had taken in recent weeks, we encountered signs reading ACHTUNG MINEN, left behind by the retreating German Army. I was not sure if these were warnings for their own troops, or a form of psychological warfare. When we made a stop, I checked with units from the Sixth Armored Division, who reported that minesweepers had been over the roads, but otherwise to proceed with care. "You wouldn't be the first guy, Captain, who walked behind a bush to take a leak and got a leg blown off instead," a sergeant told me.

Proceeding north, we passed occasional lines of ambulances heading to the local field hospitals. For lack of Red Cross trucks, jeeps had been commandeered, with the wounded strapped on stretchers over the hoods and backseats. Near 4:30, after we began thinking about putting down someplace for the night, we encountered an MP roadblock. A squint-eyed policeman pushed his head all the way inside our vehicle. I removed our orders from the inside pocket of my overcoat, but the MP didn't bother with them.

"Where does Li'l Abner live?" he asked me.

"Are you sober, soldier?"

"Answer the question, Captain."

"Dogpatch."

"And what's the name of Brooklyn's baseball team?" He was pointing to Biddy at the wheel.

"The Dodgers," he answered grumpily. "And they ain't no kind of a team neither." Amazingly, that response drew a laugh from the MP and immediately solved the problem. All day, the policeman told us, they'd had reports of German impostors in American uniforms who'd crossed our lines to engage in sabotage, cutting phone connections, removing signs, and occasionally pointing our units toward German forces, the same stuff Gita had done to them on D-Day.

"This happens again," the MP said to me, "show them your ID card. Theirs all say 'For Identification Only.'" Our officers' IDs bore a typo, 'Indentification,' quickly noted among the newly commissioned as a token of the value of their promotion. Some stone-headed Kraut had been unable to resist correcting the Americans on their English.

We crossed into the First Army zone and spent the night in Luxembourg City, in a hotel being used as rear-echelon headquarters by elements of the Ninth Armored Division. We had gotten farther than we expected, and it looked as if we would reach Houffalize by the next afternoon. I was awakened at about 5:30 a.m. by heavy shelling to the north. We would be headed straight that way, and I asked the major who'd arranged our billet what was happening.

"No worries. The Germans like to fire their guns while they still have them. They're not going anywhere. Bradley's pulled VIII Corps back for the time being. We're thin up on the front lines, but the Krauts know they'd just be running right into a huge force if they pushed forward. All this banging won't last more than an hour."

On our way out of town a young bazooka man with a strange accent asked if he could hitch a ride to his unit about ten miles north and climbed in back next to our packs. From a small town in Pennsylvania where they still spoke a German dialect, he was an amazingly cheerful kid, utterly indifferent to the war. He sang us several songs he'd learned at home in a strong, if not always perfectly pitched, tenor, and was in the midst of a ballad about a young lass pining for her lover gone to battle, when the jeep suddenly vaulted through the air aboard a tidal wave of sound and dirt. Next thing I knew, I was in a wet ditch at the roadside. When I looked up, there was a smoking pit in the farm field beside me, probably from a heavy mortar. The jeep was several yards ahead, canted at a thirty-degree angle with the front and rear right wheels also in the ditch. The canvas coverings I'd been thrown through flapped uselessly in the wind, while the young Pennsylvania Dutch boy was nearby in the field, still smiling as he got to his feet. I yelled to him to watch for mines, but promptly discovered that the rocket had fallen out of his bazooka and landed in the mud alongside me. I looked at the shell in a little pool of still water, afraid even to touch it for fear it would arm itself. I was edging away when another shell hit about a quarter mile ahead, leaving a crater that had taken out the road from side to side. The Germans had to be closer than anyone figured.

I yelled twice for Bidwell. He turned out to have been thrown only to the vehicle floor, and he poked his head up, none the worse for wear. The jeep was still running, but Biddy looked it over and announced that because of the angle at which the vehicle was pitched, the differential wouldn't let the rear wheels turn. We swore at the thing as if it was a spavined horse, and tried to shoulder it back up to the road, well aware that another shell could land any instant.

A small convoy arrived behind us. The gold-bar lieutenant in charge jumped down from the truck to help, while he sent his sergeant ahead to try to figure how they were going to get past the crater in the road.

"Some hellacious fighting up ahead, Captain," he told me, when I explained where we were headed. "You picked the wrong day for legal work. Looks like Hitler's decided to make his last stand." He suggested we proceed west.

With the help of several of his troops, we got the jeep out of the ditch and fixed a flat on the right rear tire. The bazooka man put his weapon together and climbed onto one of the convoy's trucks, while Biddy and I headed in the direction of Neufchâteau. Two of the canvas panels had torn and flapped as we drove, admitting a frigid breeze.

The sky was too low and bleak for aircraft and thus for bombs, but the pounding of heavy artillery was constant. About an hour later, we reached a crossroads, where the roads wagon-wheeled in all directions, beside signs for Aachen, Luxembourg, Düsseldorf, Neufchâteau, and Reims. Two MPs stood at the center of the intersection, holding up every vehicle. When one reached us, he asked for our papers, which he examined for quite some time.

"If you're headed north, how come you're going west?"

I told him about the shelling.

"Uh-huh," he said. "And how long you been stationed in Nancy?" When I'd answered that, he said, "What's the name of the main square there?"

I answered again, but pulled my ID card from my wallet. "See here." Biddy pointed out the word 'Indentification' but the MP stared as if we'd chosen another language.

"Sergeant, aren't you trying to make sure we're not German impostors?" I asked.

"Captain, all due respect, but I'm trying to make sure you're not a deserter."

"Deserter!" I was offended by the mere notion.

"Believe you me. Yes, sir. If you don't mind my saying so, Captain, those RTC boys," he said, referring to the replacement troops, "they don't know what the fuck to do when the shells start flying. Over in the 28th it seems like half the division has taken off for the rear. I found several hauling along dead bodies, making like they were looking for the medics. Another one told me he was a messenger, only he couldn't recall what he was going to tell anybody. And plenty waving their hankies and giving themselves up to the Krauts with barely a bullet fired. I hear close to ten thousand boys from the 106th surrendered to the Germans already. And not just enlisted men, not by any means. We got plenty of officers running from the bullets today, saying they were going to check with battalion."

"Are we talking about Americans?" I asked. "What in the hell is going on?"

"Heavy woods up north. Apparently the whole fucking SS Sixth Panzer was hidden in the trees. Von Rundstedt busted out of there with tanks and artillery, going through our lines like grease through a goose. The VIII Corps is getting a pretty good pasting right now. I'm hearing a lot of crazy stuff. Some guys are claiming there are German tanks fifty miles west of here already. We had an antiaircraft battalion in retreat come through twenty minutes ago, and some of the enlisted guys were saying rumor is their orders are to fall all the way back and defend Paris. I'll tell you one thing, Captain, this fucking war ain't over yet."

We turned north from there, but within half an hour, as the MP had warned, the road was choked with trucks and armored vehicles streaming south in full retreat. Many of these units were in complete disarray, separated from command and driving on only to find safety. We came upon an armored battalion stopped on the side of the road, completely out of gas. A young boy, a buck private, was sitting on a wheel well, crying with abandon, wailing and looking around as if he expected someone else to tell him how to stop. Every minute or so, another soldier gave him a few pats on the shoulder. A sergeant explained that the boy's best buddy had been blown to bits not three feet from him this morning.

Back in the jeep, Biddy said, "Sir, this here ain't no time to be arresting somebody, not in the middle of a battlefield."

"We have orders, Biddy." I really didn't know what else to do.

"I'm just saying, sir, gotta have a way to carry out your orders. Better to hold back here for a day or two till the smoke clears. Wherever the hell Martin was, Captain, he's gotta be on the move now, probably comin right this way."

He was making sense. We headed west again, where we were stopped twice more by MP patrols pushing back deserters. Near dark, we finally arrived in Neufchâteau. It was a postcard of a town, with a crush of pretty, narrow buildings and steep streets of cobblestone, but there was an air of chaos. We reported to the rear-echelon headquarters for VIII Corps, in the columned Palais de Justice, where they were receiving grim reports from forward command in Bastogne. Men seemed to be rushing in and out of every office, shouting information that someone else immediately screamed was wrong. Several regiments had given up under white flags, while many other units were unaccounted for. Whenever I could get someone's brief attention, his eyes seemed to wander to the windows, expecting to see the German Panzers out there any second. Clerks were in the halls boxing papers, separating what needed to be carried along so the remainder could be burned at the inception of the retreat.

After a long wait in the signal office, I finally got a young corpsman to send a wired message to General Teedle, giving our current position and asking for further direction. Then I conducted a reconnaissance for a billet. I was directed to officers' quarters that had been set up two blocks away in the city hall. As I passed down the corridors, looking for an empty bunk, I encountered little knots of off-duty officers, huddled and often passing around whiskey as they talked in suppressed murmurs. No one seemed able to accept what was happening. There hadn't been a day since I'd landed in Europe that the Germans had made progress across a broad front. A fellow who claimed to have seen the latest maps said we'd been suckered too far east, that the Nazis were about to split the Twelfth Army group, dividing the First Army from the Third, and the Ninth from the other two, with pincer actions to follow on the northern and southern flanks. No one knew the limits of today's German advance, but it was clear they had the upper hand, and several of these officers remarked about earlier reports of Nazi movements that General Bradley had ignored. Every face reflected the same thoughts: We were not going home soon. We were not going to win the war by Christmas, or New Year's, or even Valentine's Day. When I bedded down, I finally asked myself the question that nobody would utter: Were we going to win the war at all?

We were, I thought then. We had to. We had to win this war. I would give my life in order to stop Hitler. And I knew, despite whatever panic gripped the replacement troops who'd deserted on the front, that most of the seasoned officers sleeping in this building felt the same way. I turned off the light and realized only then that I'd forgotten to eat. There was a K ration in my pack, but I was too tired and disappointed to bother.

Light across my eyes woke me a few hours later. My first thought was another explosion, and as I gathered myself I couldn't understand how I had missed the sound. Instead, I found the young corporal from the Signal Corps who'd taken my message to Teedle holding the flashlight against his face so I could recognize him. My watch said 2:10 a.m. He whispered to avoid waking the other five officers snoring around me in the old office, and led me into the hall, still in my briefs.

"Captain, this signal just came through, sir, labeled 'Immediate Attention.'" I could see from the boy's face he had read the telegram in the envelope and thought immediate attention was warranted. It was from Teedle, and had arrived in code, the boy said, requiring deciphering by the cryptographers.

Classified Information/Top Secret/Destroy After Reading
    OSS states man you seek Soviet spy STOP Arrest top
priority STOP Further instruction by radio 0600 STOP

15. JUMP

Teedle never got through on December 17. Many of the Allied communications centers around Saint-Vith had been cut off by the Germans. Although we were south of there, the remaining lines and relays were dedicated to signal traffic more important than the fate of one man, even a spy, and I spent approximately forty hours on a bench in the VIII Corps signal office, waiting to hear from the General.

In Neufchâteau, like many other places, the Signal Corps had established its headquarters in the dusty offices of the PTT—Postes, Télégraphes et Téléphones—which was housed in a narrow pinkish building on a corner. Topped by a strange iron cupola, it looked as if it were wearing a helmet. From my seat inside, I could watch the young women, with their bright lipstick and the sleek hairdos required to fit under their headsets, plugging and unplugging the lines in the tall switchboards. American enlisted men strolled back and forth to keep an eye on them, just as the Germans had been doing a few months ago. Every now and then, civilians would enter to mail a letter or package, which the dour clerks accepted with no assurance that the item would ever get through.

The one compensation in my wait was that this was probably the most informative location in Neufchâteau. I asked no questions, but overhearing the messengers and aides who rushed up the stairs made it possible to piece things together. The news was almost completely dismal. Sepp Dietrich's 6th Panzers were rolling steadily in our direction, overrunning the thinly manned VIII Corps positions. Nor was it clear yet if any force could come to their aid, since the 5th Panzer Division was advancing south to hold off Patton.

Listening from my outpost on the bench, it was difficult not to admire the Nazi strategy, however reluctantly. Given the salient Dietrich was cutting, Runstedt's plan seemed aimed at severing the American forces, then crossing the Meuse and driving on toward Antwerp. If the Nazis succeeded, the Allied troops in Holland and northern Belgium would be cut off entirely, without avenue for retreat. Dunkirk would look like a minor setback by comparison. With a third of the Allied forces held hostage, Hitler might be in position to negotiate an armistice. Or, if his madness prevailed, he could destroy them and then turn south, with other forces roaring out of Germany in one last effort to reconquer western Europe. The betting in the signal office was that, insane or not, Hitler would make peace, if only to give himself time to rebuild his military. On the bench, I thought repeatedly about Martin's predictions of war and more war. It was hard to believe a victory that had seemed inevitable could be imperiled in only days. Every few minutes the same simple resolve lit up in me like a flashing sign, as it had since I arrived here. We had to win this war. I had to help.

Now and then, in mild desperation, I would cross the street to the rear headquarters in the Palais de Justice, a vast columned building of orange stone, to see if my orders had been misdirected there. Biddy also visited on occasion, and we walked in circles up and down Neufchâteau's tiny sloping streets, although the cobbles proved icy and treacherous on the steeper grades. It snowed both days, heavy flakes descending from a sky so low it seemed only a few feet over our heads. Hitler had either planned well or been lucky, since the cloud cover made it impossible for us to put planes in the air, unless they wanted to fly right over the barrels of the German antiaircraft guns.

I hesitated at first to share Teedle's highly classified message with Biddy, but decided I had to tell him, so he would understand whatever happened next.

"A spy!" I was ready for Biddy to say he'd always had suspicions about Martin, but he seemed to have the same difficulties I had in accommodating himself to the idea. "Cap, how in the world's that make any sense after what we seen?" I'd pondered that and one of the most disconcerting thoughts to invade me in the last two days was that the operation at La Saline Royale, which we'd so proudly joined, had been undertaken in reality to hinder the U.S. Army for the benefit of the Soviets. Despite Patton's outrage about the timing of the explosions, I couldn't quite make the notion add up, but then again, I realized, that was how spies succeeded, by making themselves appear to be patriots. OSS was bound to have had reasons for its conclusion.

At 4:00 a.m. on December 19, the same corporal, Lightenall, shook me awake on the bench where I'd been sleeping. Teedle had gotten through, once more using the encrypted teletype. I sat down in front of the keyboard myself. I'd had time to learn how to use the machine while I waited.

"Confirm receipt of my signal of 12/16/44."

I did.

"Not even I thought that," Teedle continued. "London insists there is evidence." Without fears of interception, the General proved expansive. I imagined him after a day of battle, his canteen in hand while he shouted at the teletype operator and, in the midst of another sleepless night, diverted himself with one more duel with me. The dialogue was stranger than ever because of the eerie interval before his response emerged with a sudden violent clatter.

In a gauged way, I asked what had been on my mind, whether the operation we'd taken part in at La Saline Royale was somehow in service of Martin's new allegiance.

"No idea. London still talking riddles. Seems our man not working against good guys in current game. Instead, getting ready for next one, moving ahead so he can inform red team re our team's movements, also try to slow them. If our team, red team don't come to blows, red team gets bigger piece of what's been taken when this game ends. Following?"

"Roger."

"London desperate for arrest, but per usual won't put in writing. Prefer not to explain to 535 fans in D.C. how star began playing for other team. Continue proceeding on my order. Our man still believed in VIII Corps sector. Contact General Middleton to make arrest."

I explained the problems with that directive. By now, Middleton had decided to abandon Bastogne as a forward HQ. His artillery, six or seven battalions of 155mm guns and eight-inch howitzers, had already begun a staged withdrawal, but none of them had been able to occupy their pre-pared rearward positions because the Panzer elements were upon them so quickly. They were basically on the run back here. A faster-moving Airborne Division, the 101st, was going to take over and was trucking up from Reims. I told the General it was chancy for any communication to get through. More important, there were legal issues. As I had discussed with Colonel Maples, only someone under Teedle's direct command could arrest Martin. Teedle reacted as I expected.

"Goddamn Army's been fucked up since they put Washington on a horse."

"Rules, General. We would have to free him."

There was a long wait for an answer. I was sure Teedle was contem-plating how he would explain it to both the OSS and Patton, when Martin waltzed off through a legal loophole.

Finally Teedle wrote, "You volunteering to go?"

My fingers faltered on the keys. But I understood the logic. Bidwell and I were the nearest soldiers for 150 miles who were even arguably un-der Teedle's command. I couldn't imagine how two men in a jeep were supposed to move on terrain under assault by Panzer forces, but what I'd been thinking for three days remained close to my heart. I would do what I had to to win this war.

I wrote, "Yes, sir."

"Good," he fired back in a moment.

"Sir, will need better information on our man's whereabouts. Unlikely still at Houffalize." Biddy had told me an astounding story, which he swore he'd heard from the MPs who'd been at Houffalize on December 17. American and German military police had stood back to back at an in-tersection in the town directing traffic, both sides too busy and too lightly armed to bother battling one another. The Americans pointed their forces toward retreat, while the Germans waved on the reconnaissance and mine-clearing crews that were making way for the Panzers only a few miles behind them. By now, Houffalize had fallen.

"London already contacted Supreme Headquarters, which understands utmost priority. Will seek their assistance. Stand by for further orders."

I thought we were done, but a second later the keys flew again.

"How bad up there?"

"Fine here," I typed. "Hell on wheels a few miles forward."

"Tell them, hold on. Cavalry's coming. Will see you at the Siegfried line. Expect that SOB in chains. Out."

It took two more days before further orders came by cable.

```
Confirmed officer you seek commanding battalion NW of
Bastogne STOP Proceed RAF airstrip Virton for transport to
make arrest STOP
```

Late in the day on December 21, Biddy and I drove due south. Snow so solid that it looked like someone emptying a box of baking powder had been coming down all night, letting up only with the arrival of a cold front that felt just like the Canadian Express that bore down on Kindle County in the worst of winter.

The so-called airstrip at Virton proved to be no more than a wide dirt path recently bulldozed through a snowy field, but we found the small ground crew, mostly flight mechanics, expecting us. There were no hangars, because it would have been mad to house airplanes this far east in the face of the offensive, but the Brits had been landing in the dark here for a few days, hauling supplies cadged from Montgomery's forces, which were then trucked to our troops. Our soldiers, once expected to slice through the Germans in no time, were now short of everything, except, ironically, fuel, which had been stockpiled for their lightning advance.

"You the one going to Bastogne, then?" a flight sergeant asked me. "Place is damn near surrounded, you know, sir. Germans battering the hell out of everything. All the big roads go right through there, so Jerry can't go rolling on without taking the town." The Ardennes had provided an excellent hiding place for the Panzers, but one reason Bradley and Middleton had discounted the reports that the German tanks were massing there was because a forest was such an unpromising locale for a tank assault. It was easier to run over men than thousands of trees. Once the

Panzers had crawled from the woods, they still were not able to maneuver freely, because the fall we'd been through had left half the fields swamps. I'd heard often about our tanks sinking. The Panzers were regarded as better machines—our Shermans were so likely to ignite that the troops called them Ronsons—but German treads got stuck in the muck same as American, and the weight of the biggest of Panzers, the King Tigers, would literally bury them in the wet ground. Because the Panzer forces were confined to the existing roads, holding on to the paths and byways for as long as possible was the key to slowing the Germans and allowing the Americans to reassemble for a counteroffensive. Patton reportedly had outflanked the 5th Panzer and was still speeding north to help out.

"Sounds like it's going to be a difficult landing there," I said to the sergeant.

"Landing?" He had a wrench in his hand and was toying with an engine part, but now he turned full around, a craggy English face. "Crikey, mate. Don't you know you're getting dropped?"

"Dropped?"

"Parachute. You know, big bedsheet in the sky?" His smile faltered. "You're a paratrooper, then, sir, ain't you?"

"I'm a lawyer."

"Oh, Lord Jesus."

His reaction said it all. It was so absurd, I laughed out loud. As I left to tell Biddy, I heard the sergeant explaining my situation to his crew. "Poor sod," he said, "thought he was going to Bastogne in the royal carriage."

Biddy couldn't even manage a pained smile.

"Parachute? Shit, Captain, my knees are lard when I get up on the roof of our tenement. I don't know about no parachute. You got any parachute training?"

I'd had none. Yet I had told myself for three days that I would do whatever I had to to win this war. It was a vow I'd taken and now would keep. If Martin was really intent on impeding our troops in Germany, I had to do this.

"Biddy, there's no need for both of us to go."

"Aw, hell, Captain. You know I'm just blabbing. Ain't no way I'm gonna let loose of you now, so let's not bother with that talk."

The plan, as it was explained to us, was essentially an experiment. For the moment, there was no way to resupply the troops in Bastogne. The main road from Neufchâteau had been cut off and in Hitler's weather, flyers could not navigate by sight to make airdrops at heights safe from antiaircraft fire. The RAF pilots had agreed to try one low-altitude night flight, thinking that if it worked, more planes would do the same tomorrow evening. Three pallets of medical supplies were going to be parachuted in with us. If Biddy and I made it, doctors might follow.

There were a couple of hours before the plane was due and in that time we got what would pass for jump instruction: toes down, knees and feet together, eyes straight ahead. We made dozens of efforts to practice rolling as our boots struck the ground. The knee I'd cut when the dump exploded had healed well and had given me no pain for weeks, but now there were little phantom throbs each time we reenacted landing. After the first half hour, it was clear to me that our instructors, with all but one exception, had never jumped themselves. Nonetheless, they made a good case that if the chute released, we didn't have much to do but hang on and try not to break our legs. Real training, which addressed maneuvers in the event the chute ripped or inverted, or the suspension lines or risers snarled, would do us no good anyway from five hundred feet. None of those problems could be fixed before we hit the ground.

"Telling you the truth, Captain, t'ain't the jump what ought to concern you. Hanging like an apple on a tree, if Jerry works out you're there—that's a worry, sir."

The crew packed our chutes for us, then bundled our overcoats and cinched them beneath our val-packs, which would come down behind us with the medical supplies. We donned jumpsuits over our wool outdoor uniforms, and traded our headgear for paratroopers' helmets with their leather chin cups, the better to absorb the shock of the chute opening. Then we waited. Every ten minutes, I wandered outside to pee. My body temperature was about the same as marble. I simply could not imagine the circumstances under which I might be alive in another two hours.

Nearing 8:30, the truck convoys that would carry off the supplies on the arriving aircraft began to form in the field, but there was still no sign of the planes. By 9:00, I began to suspect they would not get here and wondered if I could pretend to be disappointed, when the mere thought flushed me with relief.

And then they came. The initial drone might have been insects if it were another season. The ground crew ignited dozens of Coleman lanterns and ran them out to illuminate the borders of the strip, and the planes came down with barely thirty seconds between them. The convoy crews rushed forward to unload.

The flight sergeant who'd been assisting me helped me into the rest of my parachute gear. First was a Mae West, the life vest required because there was no guarantee we wouldn't settle in a lake or pond, then I stepped into the harness, a web of straps and buckles that were tightened on each side of my crotch.

"Not exactly comfy knickers, but your nuts might still be rattling round once you land, Captain." What I had on already was cumbersome, but it turned out I'd just made a start. Since we could put down on enemy ground, the sergeant inserted a Thompson submachine gun under the waist web, and clipped on two five-pound boxes of machine-gun ammo, then strapped a fight knife on my leg and, for good measure, a small Hawkins mine, looking like a can of paint thinner, against my boot. He turned my woven waist piece into a combat tool belt, hanging off it a trenching shovel and a canteen, my pistol in its holster, a skein of rope, a pair of wire cutters, and a folding knife. An angle-headed flashlight went under a band on my chest. Then, when I thought he was done, he put a reserve chute across my belly. I expected to topple any second. Even Biddy, huge as he was, looked weighed down.

"You're traveling light, mate, 'cause you're first-timers. Paratroops usually carry a Griswold bag under one arm."

Biddy and I were jeeped to our plane, a light bomber called a Hampden. It had two engines, a silvery fuselage, and a low glass nose that made it appear like a flying turtle. We stood with difficulty on the car's hood and with two men steadying us from below climbed a ladder through the bomb bay into the bare sheet-metal belly of the plane.

There was a four-man crew there—pilot, bombardier, gunner, and radioman—but their attitude toward us seemed slightly standoffish, even for Brits. I wondered if the RAF would have been trying this run without Teedle's—or the OSS's—insistence at Supreme Headquarters on the paramount importance of Biddy and me reaching Bastogne. Perhaps, I decided, these four were just exhibiting a natural reluctance to develop attachments to the doomed.

With all the gear on, we could get only the rear edge of our butts onto two fold-down seats bolted to the fuselage, but the radioman harnessed us in with the strapping that had secured the unloaded cargo. The pilot, a Flying Officer, came rear to brief us. We would reach Bastogne in twenty minutes, he said. As soon as the joe hole, the bomb bay in the silver floor in front of us, opened, we should hook our rip cords to the line above and get out on the double. Our drop area was in open fields just west of Bastogne, near a town called Savy. If the Germans figured out we were in the air, the gunner and radioman would put down covering fire with the Vickers machine guns on turrets in the gun wells in front of us. However, the pilot thought the Nazis would never see the chutes in the dark, because the sound of the plane would draw all the fire. He was businesslike but made it plain that if there was a fools' contest here, they were probably the winners. I understood then why we'd received such an unenthusiastic greeting.

Sitting there in the instants before the plane took off, I felt completely detached from myself. I thought I had given up on life, but as soon as the engines triggered, a sharp whinny of protest rose straight out of my heart. This is crazy, I thought. Crazy. Men down there are going to try to kill me, men who have never met me, men I've never tried to harm. Suddenly, I could not remember why that made any sense.

We built speed, enduring that second of weightlessness when we left the ground. I looked to Biddy, but he was staring at the floor, clearly trying to contain himself. As we climbed, I remembered that I'd passed all that time waiting without writing to my family or Grace, but I couldn't think of what I would have said besides 'I love you, and I am going to leave you for the sake of madness.'

As we flew, the interior grew unbearably hot, but I was principally preoccupied with trying to ignore the urgency of my bladder and my bowels. The bombardier came over and crouched beside me. He was a Leading Aircraftsman, the British equivalent of a corporal, a handsome dark-haired kid.

"First jump, then?" He had to repeat himself several times because the throbbing buzz of the engines filled the entire belly of the plane.

I nodded and asked for last-minute pointers.

He smiled. "Keep a tight arsehole."

Almost on cue then, Biddy vomited in front of himself and sat there shaking his head, manifestly ashamed. "It's the heat," I yelled. The interior of the Hampden was like a blast furnace, and fouled with the sickening fumes of the plane's exhaust. I felt woozy myself. The bombardier acted as if he'd seen it all before.

"You'll feel better now," he told Biddy.

When the phone beside the hatch flashed, the bombardier grabbed it, then motioned to fix our chinstraps.

"All right, then," he yelled, "who's first?"

We hadn't discussed this, but Biddy raised a hand weakly, saying he had to get out. He hooked on, then crawled to the edge of the joe hole. The doors fell open slowly, emitting a frozen gale. Some part of my brain was still working, because I realized the plane had been overheated in anticipation of the cold. The bomb bay was not even fully extended when Gideon lowered his head and suddenly disappeared without a backward glance.

After hooking overhead, I tried to stand, but my legs were like water, and it would have been difficult anyway given all the equipment I was wearing and the shimmying of the plane. Like Biddy, I went on all fours, remembering too late to avoid the puddle he had left behind. The instant he was gone, I was at the edge, leaning into the great rush of icy air. My face went numb at once, as I looked down to the vague form of the land moving below in the darkness. In the white leather jump gloves, my hands were clamped to the edge of the bomb bay. The bombardier placed his face right next to mine.

"Captain, I'm afraid you must be going. Otherwise, sir, I'm going to have to put my boot in your bum."

Ma, what am I doing? I thought. What am I doing? And then I thought, I must do this, I must do this, because it is my duty, and if I do not do my duty, my life will be worth nothing.

But still, my body would not surrender to my will. I shouted to the bombardier, "I'll take that kick in the ass."

It was like diving into a pool, the shock of cold, the sudden distance from sound. I did a complete somersault in the air and came upright with my heart pumping nothing but terror, while one thought leaped at me with startling clarity. As my chute snapped open and I was slammed against the sky, a white pain ignited in my arms. I had forgotten to grip the harness, falling with my hands spread before me like a child taking a spill, and I feared for one second that I had dislocated my shoulders. But even that was not enough to distract me. Because in the instant of free fall, I had realized I hadn't really come to find Martin. The form I'd seen as I tore through space was Gita Lodz.

For half the descent there was no sound or sensation except the racing cold. I saw only the earth, black on black, a swimming form without perspective. And then it was as if the night, like the shell of a hatching egg, was suddenly pecked by light. Volleys of antiaircraft fire came from at least three sides and the rockets tore by like massive lethal bugs. Then, without warning, a squeal of red flares brought day to the sky. I caught sight of Biddy's chute, mushroomed below me, and took heart for just a second, knowing I was not alone here, but that was replaced at once by another spasm of terror when I realized that the Germans were firing at us. The AA was still blasting, but smaller rounds also ripped by like shooting stars. In the instantaneous glow, I actually saw one make a hole in the canopy of Biddy's chute, whose descent accelerated. It would be a good thing for him, though, assuming he survived, to get out of the barrage.

Paying my nickel on a Saturday afternoon, I'd heard the shots whanging past Tom Mix in the movie-theater speakers. But the real sound of a round that misses is just a sinister little sizzle and a wake of roiled air, a bee farting as it passes, followed instantaneously by the sharp report of the rifle the bullet came from. The German infantry, thank God, hadn't practiced shooting falling objects. A dozen shots missed by only a few feet. But as the ground came near, my ear was bored by an intense pain.

My next memory is of lying in the snow. Under my nose, Biddy was waving an ammonia ampoule he'd extracted from the first-aid kit on the front of his helmet. I flinched from the driving odor.

"C'mon, Captain. Those 88s will be on us any minute." I continued to lie there while I put things together. Somewhere along, I realized he'd already cut me free of my chute. "You passed out, Cap. Maybe a concussion." He wrestled me to my feet. I reached to grab my pack, which he'd also collected, then stopped dead, astonished by what I felt against the back of a thigh. I retrieved the sensation at once from the remote memories of childhood. I had shit in my pants.

Behind Bidwell I ran in a half crouch through a farm field where the snow was up to our knees until we reached a wooded border. All that worry about parachute training and it turned out we were landing on a pillow. After the flares, we knew American forces would be looking for us, assuming we'd come down in an area they controlled. While Biddy struggled in the dark to read the compass strapped to his arm, I shed my parachute harness and pushed farther into the brush, where I dropped both pairs of trousers. It could not have been more than ten degrees but I still preferred to stand there naked, rather than go on with crap trailing down my legs. I cut my briefs off with the jackknife from my belt, cleaned up as best I could, and hurled away my underwear, which ended up snagged on one of the bushes. Biddy was watching by now, but asked for no explanation.

A recon group arrived five minutes later. We raced with them to gather up the medical bundles before the German artillery turned on us, then clambered into the backs of a pair of two-ton trucks from an ordnance unit that had pulled up. As the vehicles rolled out, Biddy, beside me, reached up to touch my helmet. Removing it, I saw a dent in the steel above my right ear, and a fracture running down two inches to the edge. That was from the round that had knocked me out. I shook my head, as if I could take some meaning from the nearness of the miss, but nothing came to me. There was alive and there was dead. I wasn't dead. Why or how close really meant nothing compared with the elemental fact.

We had ridden half a mile before I picked up on the radio traffic blaring from the cab. Someone had not been found.

"The Brits," Biddy said. "The Hampden went down right after you landed." The Kraut AA had caught it in a direct hit, a giant ball of fire and smoke, he said, but they were east of us by then, over the Germans. I thought about the four men we'd flown with, but I could make no more of their demise than I had of my own survival. Instead I turned to Biddy to complain for a second about the cold.

The soldiers who had collected us were elements of the 110th Infantry Regiment of the 28th Infantry Division who had been cut off in their retreat and ended up here, formed up with the 101st Airborne, which was the principal force defending Bastogne. They drove us back to their command post set up in the hamlet of Savy. The town consisted of a few low buildings constructed of the native gray stone. In the largest of them, a cattle barn, the acting combat team commander, Lieutenant Colonel Hamza Algar, had established his headquarters.

Algar was working at a small desk set in the center of the dirt floor, when we came in to report. The orderlies had done their best to sweep the place clean, but it was still a barn, with stalls on both sides and open beams above, and the residual reek of its former inhabitants. Four staff officers were standing around Algar, as he went over lists and maps beside a lantern. They were in field jackets and gloves, shoulders hunched against the cold. It was better in here, because there was no wind, but there was still no heat.

Algar stood up to return my salute, then offered his hand.

"How much training did you have for that jump, Doc?" he asked me. "That was damn brave. But, Doc, you came to the right place. Unfortunately." This made the third or fourth time since we'd landed that I'd been addressed as 'Doc.' Perhaps it was the concussion, or the numbness of surviving, but I realized only now that this greeting wasn't being offered in the fashion of Bugs Bunny.

"Begging your pardon, Colonel, but I'm afraid you have a misimpression. I'm a lawyer."

Algar was small, five foot six or seven, and perhaps in compensation was plainly attentive to his good looks. He had a narrow split mustache over his upper lip, carefully trimmed even on the battlefield, and his hair was pomaded. But he was clearly bewildered.

"I was told you were dropped with medical supplies. Sulfa. Bandages. Plasma." Algar sat down and turned to his aides. "We get lawyers by parachute," he said. "What about ammunition? Or reinforcements? Jesus Christ." In a second, he got around to asking why I was there. He stared at me even longer than he had when I'd said I wasn't an M.D., once he heard my explanation.

"Martin?" he asked. "Bob Martin? They've sent you to arrest Bob Martin? Don't they know what the hell is going on here? We've got everybody firing a weapon, including the cooks. I have three companies under the command of NCOs. I've got two second lieutenants who between them have a total of one week's experience in Europe. And they want you to arrest one of my best combat officers?"

"Those were my orders, sir."

"Well, I'll give you different orders, Captain. You arrest Major Martin or anybody else who's able-bodied and firing back at the Germans and I won't bother arresting you. I'll shoot you, Captain Dubin, and don't take that for jest."

I looked to the circle of officers for help.

"Three days from now," Algar told me, "four, whatever it takes to deal with the Krauts, we can sort this out. McAuliffe can talk to Teedle. They can take it up with Patton if they like. Or even Eisenhower. They'll hash it out at the top. Right now we're all trying to save this bloody town. And ourselves. Understood?"

I didn't answer. There was a silent moment of standoff, before Algar spoke again.

"Just out of curiosity, Dubin, what is it exactly that Martin's supposed to have done?"

I took a second evaluating what I could say, then asked to speak to him alone. It was too cold for Algar to ask his officers to step outside, but he shooed them to a corner.

"Colonel," I said in a whisper, "there's a question of loyalty."

Algar leaned forward so quickly I thought he meant to hit me.

"Listen, Dubin, Bob Martin has been fighting with the 110th for almost a week now, leading a combat unit, and doing one heck of a job. As a volunteer. He's been through hell, like the rest of us, and he's just taken on another mission that requires more guts than common sense. I'll stake my life on his loyalty."

"Not to the Allies, sir. It's a question of which one."

Algar watched me, once more trying to figure me out. He betrayed his first sign of nervousness, nibbling at the mustache over his lip, but that, it turned out, was only as a means to control his anger.

"Oh, I see," he said, "I see. More red-baiting? Is that it? I've been watching the brass give the cold shoulder to a lot of the French resisters whose politics they don't care for, men and women who risked everything for their country, while half of France was kneeling down in Vichy. Well, I've got no use for that, Dubin. None.

"I'll tell you the truth, Captain. I feel sorry for you. I do. Because that jump took some guts. And it was for a bunch of silly crap. And now you're not just out of the frying pan into the fire, but straight into a volcano. The Germans have us surrounded. We have damn little food, less ammunition, and the only medical supplies I've seen are the ones that fell with you. So I don't know what the hell you're going to do with yourself, but I promise you this—you're not arresting Bob Martin. Ralph," he said, "find Captain Dubin and his sergeant a place to sleep. Gentlemen, that's all I can do for you. Dismissed."

16. NIGHT VISIT

Biddy and I were transported about a mile to the town of Hemroulle and a small stone church that stood amid a clutch of dark farm buildings, where we put up for the night with an infantry unit under Algar's command. I slept on an oak pew, better than the cold floor, but too narrow to be comfortable. Between that and the reverberations of jumping and deflecting bullets, I could not really manage much sleep and I woke easily at the sound of two men, Americans, shouting at each other in the back of the sanctuary. Somebody else hollered to take the row outside. The radiant dial on my watch showed nearly 3:00 a.m. I lay there a second longer determined to sleep, then suddenly recognized both of the quarreling voices.

When I bolted up, Biddy was visible in the light of a candle beside the door, dragging Robert Martin along by the collar of his field jacket, looking like a parent with an unruly boy. I took just an instant longer to convince myself I was awake, then grabbed my tommy gun and rushed back there. Biddy's woven belt was tied around Martin's hands. The Major was furious.

"Why is it when you tell even a good man that he's a policeman, he turns into a thug?" Martin asked as soon as he saw me.

According to Bidwell, Martin had driven up only a moment ago, while Bidwell was on his way back from the outhouse.

"Smiles like he was my auntie come to visit and asks for you," said Biddy. "My orders say arrest him and that's what I done."

I knew Biddy had laid hands on Martin just for the pure pleasure of it, given what we'd been through. Nor did I blame him. But Algar would treat this as mutiny.

"Let him go, Gideon."

He looked at me in his way. "Hell, Captain," he said.

"I know, Biddy. But untie him. We need to get things straightened out first."

One of the men from the platoon sleeping behind us sat up on his pew and called us jerk-offs and told us again to take it outside.

We passed into the church's narrow entry, just beyond the sanctuary. Two candles had been placed in the corners for the benefit of those using the outhouse. As soon as Biddy untied Martin, he banged out the old wooden doors. I assumed he was leaving, but the Major returned in an instant with his steel flask. Apparently he'd lost it after offering it to Bidwell. Martin's knowledge of judo might have given him a fair chance, even against Gideon, but Biddy had fallen on him without warning, while Martin was offering him a drink.

I remained astonished to see Martin. If he knew we were here, he had to know why.

"Come to taunt us, Major?"

"More to pay my respects and clear things up. That is, until I ran into Primo Canera here. I understand it was you two we saw being shot at in the sky last night. What kind of training did you have for that, Dubin?"

I was not sure I wanted to answer, but shook my head a bit.

"Quite heroic," said Martin. "I hope you weren't patterning yourself after me." He found the comment amusing. Martin was dressed as he was at La Saline Royale, in a field jacket and combat fatigues, with a vest full of equipment. He was dirty and unshaved and rubbing at one of his wrists, which must have been a little sore after his tussle with Gideon. Every now and then he reached down to swipe off more of the snow that had collected on his trousers when Bidwell had pinned him out on the church steps.

"I don't fancy myself a hero, Major. It's not a label I deserve. Or that I'd exult in."

"Is that a personal remark, Dubin?"

It was, but I wouldn't admit it. "I admire what you've done, Major."

"Is that why you've come to arrest me?" He said he'd heard about my orders from Ralph Gallagher, Algar's Exec. I still had a copy of Teedle's written directive in the inside pocket of my tunic, now wrinkled and still moist with my sweat. Unfolding it, Martin walked closer to one of the candles to read, his shadow looming enormously behind him. Biddy was crouched down along the paneled wall opposite. His hand was on his tommy gun and his eyes never left Martin.

"Seems like everybody's quite vexed with me, Dubin," said Martin as he handed the paper back. "Including you."

"You lied to me, Major. And stole away in the dead of night."

"I told you I was about to depart on a mission, Dubin, when you arrived that day at the Comtesse's."

"You were referring to blowing the dump at La Saline Royale."

"Was I? Your misunderstanding. I'm sorry. Have you spoken yet to OSS? What is it they've told you about my current orders?" I realized then that was why Martin had come around. He wanted to know what OSS surmised about his disappearance—whether they thought he'd gone mad, or had deserted, or if, more critically, they'd figured out that he was working for the Soviets. I was determined to give him no answers to that.

"London has approved your arrest, Major."

"Rubbish. I'd wager a large sum, Dubin, you have not heard that personally from anyone at OSS. They're the ones who sent me this way. Don't you recall? I told you several times I was being dispatched to Germany." To link up with his old network and save lives, he had said. There was no doubt OSS would want German supporters at this stage.

Across the entryway Bidwell's eyes had jumped from Martin to me to be certain I wasn't going to be taken in again, but he had no need for concern. The motto of the law remained with me. *Falsus in uno, falsus in omnibus.* False in one thing, false in all. One lie was enough to deprive any witness of credibility and Martin's fabrications were beyond tolling. Whatever the irony, I reposed considerable faith in Teedle's veracity by now. He was too direct to lie. I simply shook my head at Martin.

"You make it your business to get to London, Dubin, and to speak with Colonel Winters. You'll see I'm telling the truth."

"For your sake, I hope you are, Major. But there is no ambiguity in the orders I have. You are to be arrested. Whenever we can make safe passage to the west, Bidwell and I will escort you back to Third Army Headquarters. As an officer you'll be held under house arrest until your trial."

"'House arrest?'" He chuffed some air after the words. "That sounds like my childhood. And won't Teedle be satisfied?" That thought wilted him. He slumped against the wall across the entryway from Bidwell, and opened up his flask. He offered me a slug, which I declined. I wanted no more of Robert Martin's generosity.

"Do you read Nietzsche, Dubin?" Martin asked after a moment.

"I have."

"Yes, I have, too. General Teedle has read Nietzsche, of that you can be certain. 'Life's school of war: what does not kill me makes me stronger.' It's all rot," he said. "And Teedle is not Superman. Do you know why the General wants the world to think he's a great man of action, with his arms across his chest? Have you seen him strike that pose in the newsreels? The General is a fruit," Martin said. "Have you learned that yet?"

I said nothing.

"I don't mind faggots," said Martin. "There've been several who've done some damn good stuff for me over the years. One of them was a waiter in Paris. Can't imagine what a waiter overhears, Dubin. But he was one of those wispy queers who made no bones about it. The General thinks he's just a man who sleeps with men."

"Are you saying that feeds his grudge against you, Major?"

"Who knows? Probably not. For Teedle it's probably all about me supposedly being a Communist. Have you asked him about that?"

I took a second to consider what I should say. I couldn't entirely surrender my curiosity now that he'd raised the subject.

"Teedle says you were a party member, Major. In Paris."

Rarely given to laughter, Martin managed a short high-pitched cackle. "Well, I've always liked a good party," he said. "And for that I'm to be arrested?"

"You're to be arrested for insubordination, Major. But General Teedle would probably tell you to your face that he suspects that when our armies meet, you'd follow the orders of Russian generals rather than his." Given my experiences with Martin, I wouldn't have placed much faith in his denials. But I was still taken aback when he made none. Instead, he chuckled again.

"You can lay good money on that, Dubin. I'd sooner take directions from a squawking parrot than Teedle. But fortunately I'm here under a fine commander. I have no problems with Algar, you'll notice."

"The Lieutenant Colonel said you were about to undertake some new operation, Major?"

"Indeed. We start about an hour from now." I expected him to invoke the privileges of required secrecy, but apparently the mission was common knowledge. The military situation around Bastogne was even worse than the flight mechanics at Virton had suggested. The Germans had cut the last roads yesterday and fully encircled the area. Now they would tighten their grip until they could blast the American troops into submission. Our position was tenuous, but the men I'd encountered, including those with Algar, and Martin now, remained calm. Patton was on the way, supposedly, but the troops all felt that what they needed was bullets and equipment so they could break out themselves. That was what Martin's operation was about.

On December 19, as the Germans had flanked Bastogne to the south and west, they had cut off an American supply train near Vaux-les-Rosières, blocking the tracks with tanks and leaving the train there, probably waiting to determine if they could make any use of its contents themselves. Along with some of the men from the 110th Regiment whom he'd been commanding for a week now, Martin aimed to reach those railcars full of ammunition. The bet was that when his troops and his three Hellcat tank destroyers cut into the thin German lines, the Nazis would fall back to consolidate their position, thinking this was the spearhead of a concerted American effort to pierce the encirclement. Martin and his men would probably have an unimpeded path to the train. If Martin could get the locomotive moving, they would steam into

Bastogne. If not, they would off-load as much as they could of the 75mm ammunition and the bullets for smaller arms and then dash back before the Germans closed in again.

The only difficult part, Martin thought, might be getting through in the first place.

"The infantry's thin," he said. "We'll go right past them. The Panzer Lehr are roaming out there somewhere, but even McAuliffe thinks it's a solid plan," he said, referring to the commander of the 101st who was directing the defense of Bastogne. "Even if the Lehr show up, we can fall back. And if we make it through, our chances of success are very high."

"Trains and ammunition," I said. "You seem to have a motif, Major."

"Old dog, old tricks," he answered. "It's damn boring to be a specialist. I never wanted to specialize in anything when I was a boy. But then I fell in love with the railroad."

I asked if he was the kind who ran model locomotives around a track decorated with miniature trees and stations.

"Never had patience for that. I was somewhat frenetic as a child. I suppose you can still see that. No, trains for me came at a later point. I left home for a spell when I was seventeen. Hopped a freight car. First taste of freedom I'd had in my life was when that car went hurtling out of Poughkeepsie. I decided at that moment that the railroad was the greatest of mankind's inventions. I loved being around trains. When I went to my mother's people in Paris after I dropped out of college, that was the work I sought. Started as a porter. Ended up as an engineer. The idea that I was a common workingman appalled my father, but it delighted me."

"I don't think I've heard you mention your parents before, Major."

"No accident in that, Dubin." He nipped at his flask again and looked at the candles. "My father's a professor of Romance languages at Vassar College. Met my mother when he was at the Sorbonne. Very distinguished fellow, my father. And the meanest man walking God's green earth. I agree with him about everything. Politics. Music. I don't like his attire, I suppose, I don't like his hats. But it goes to show you beliefs aren't everything. He's a complete son of a bitch."

"Hard on you?"

"Very. And harder on my mother. She couldn't get away by hopping a train. So she blew her head off with his shotgun when I was sixteen."

As the wind came up outside, the wooden doors knocked and the candles guttered, but he didn't take his gaze from the corner. I expressed my sympathies.

"Well," he said. "It was hard, of course. Horrible. But it wasn't a picnic before then. My mother was always in bed, an impossibly beautiful woman, but utterly morose. I can barely remember her features because I rarely saw her anywhere but a dark room." He drank and looked at the wall. "These aren't stories I often tell, Dubin."

I could understand that. But I recognized Martin's instinct always was to master the moment however he could. His charm had been undermined by his lies. So now he would prey on my sympathies. Or parade out Teedle's perversions.

"I think I should come along on this operation with you tonight, Major." I had been considering that for a while. Across the entryway, Biddy could not contain himself.

"Jesus Christ crucified," he moaned. I found a pebble on the floor and tossed it at him, then repeated my request of Martin.

"Afraid I'll run away, Dubin?"

"That would not be without precedent, Major."

"Well, right now you have the Germans to ease your mind. Every road has been cut. And the snow is high. And I've got a team to bring back."

I said I still wanted to come.

"Don't be an ass, Dubin. You won't be there for the mission. You'll be there to keep an eye on me. Which means you'll be a danger to both of us. And damn certain to get in the way."

"We didn't get in the way at the salt mine."

"At the salt mine, Dubin, you stayed in one place. This is a mobile operation. In armored vehicles on which you've never been trained."

"I'll speak to Algar."

"It's not Algar's choice. It's mine. And I don't want you there."

The chance that Algar would overrule Martin was minimal, but given the situation I needed to try. I asked if Martin was willing to drive me back to Algar's headquarters so I could make my case to the Lieutenant Colonel. He wound his head disbelievingly, but smiled brightly at my doggedness, as usual.

"I have to get ready, Dubin, but I'll drop you there. Come along."

I told Biddy to stay and sleep. He seemed unconvinced.

"He's got a tommy gun with him, Sergeant," said Martin. "I think he'll have a fair chance against me." Martin called Gideon "Bruiser" when he gestured goodbye.

As soon as we were under way in his jeep, Martin said, "Aren't you going to ask me about Gita?"

I took a second. "I hope she's well."

"As do I."

"I understand she's near Houffalize."

"You won't find her if you look there, Dubin." Martin turned from the road with a tart, narrow look and we stared at each other. It was the first instant of actual hardness between us, undeflected by irony. He wanted me to ask where she was, and I wouldn't give him the pleasure. Even so, this friction reminded me yet again what a terrible mistake I'd made with her.

"If you have a complaint with me, as far as Mademoiselle Lodz is concerned, Major, feel free to lodge it."

"No complaints," he said quickly. "She wouldn't stand for it. Her life is her own. Always has been and always will be." This was a disciplined answer, like a soldier taking orders. "She's in Luxembourg. At least I hope she is. Roder. Overlooking the German border. We both sent reports to Middleton that the Germans were massing tanks, but nobody wanted to hear that. God bless the United States Army." He tossed his head bitterly, as he pulled the vehicle in front of the barn where Biddy and I had been with Algar a few hours earlier. When Martin's hand came forward, I lifted my own to shake, but instead he pointed at my side.

"I wouldn't mind having use of that tommy gun, Dubin. We don't have anything like that around. It might come in handy and you have my word it will be returned. I'll swap you my M1 for a few hours."

I looked at the submachine gun. I was glad Bidwell wasn't here, so I didn't have to hear the sounds he would make at the idea of giving Martin anything.

"Will you promise to surrender yourself to me, Major, when we're capable of moving out?"

Martin laughed. "Oh, Dubin," he said. In the darkness, he looked out to the snow. "Yes, I'll surrender myself. On the condition that you reach OSS personally before turning me over to Teedle."

We shook on that and I handed him the gun and the one ammo box I had with me.

"You'll have it back in a few hours," Martin promised before he drove off.

He was barely out of sight when the sentry outside the barn told me that Algar had gone up to the staging area to go over the maps one last time with Martin and his team. He said that Martin and Algar had set that meeting only half an hour ago when Martin first stopped here. I stood there in the wind. I would never be sharp enough to deal with Martin. I was not even angry at myself. It was simply the nature of things.

I considered walking back to Hemroulle, but I had a faint hope Algar might return before Martin's team set off. There was a hay locker attached to the barn, a platformed area raised so that the fodder could be tossed in from the back of a cart or truck through an opening outside. The sentry told me troops had slept in there the last two nights. He promised to rouse me as soon as Algar came back.

Only a little hay remained in the height of winter, but its sweet smell lingered. My predecessors had swept up the remnants and mounded them into a couple of beds and I lay down on one and fell soundly asleep. My dreams seemed rough and desperate, the kind that make you cry out in the night, but I stayed for many hours in that world, rather than this besieged circle in Belgium.

My name roused me. Hamza Algar, looking weary and nibbling at his mustache, was a few feet below me in the barn. He shoved my tommy gun across the board floor of the hay locker.

"Martin told his men to make sure this got back to you," he said and turned away. As I crawled out, Algar walked to his desk at the center of the barn. There was daylight visible in the seam between the stone walls and the tin roof of the building. Sitting, Algar rested his face in his hands.

"How did they do?" I asked Algar.

He sighed. "Poorly. The Krauts pinned them down and then blasted the shit out of them at first light. The men who made it back came on foot."

"And Martin?"

"Gone," Algar said.

That was the same word Bettjer had used when I'd awoken at the Comtesse's after we blew the dump. I'd known it would happen. I reviewed in my mind what I'd been through—the terror of the jump, the shot, and the enduring indignity of fouling my trousers—only for Martin to have run from me again. Sisyphus came to mind.

"Any idea where he headed?" I asked.

I received another fixed uncomprehending look from Algar. So far all our conversations had somehow devolved into a competition in provoking speechlessness. The Lieutenant Colonel sighed deeply again.

"Well, if there's anything to your arrest order, Captain, he's probably headed to hell. Captain Dubin, you didn't understand me. Bob Martin is dead."

17. CHAMPS

Since December 16, Robert Martin had been in command of units that had been isolated from the 110th Infantry Regiment during its retreat from Skyline Drive in Luxembourg in the early hours of that day. Regrouping here with the remains of the regiment, Martin's two rifle companies and two towed guns from a tank destroyer battalion had been teamed with a platoon of M18 Hellcats. It was these troops Martin had led toward Vaux-les-Rosières, where the ammunition train was marooned. North and west of the town of Monty, they had crossed our lines and encountered thinly manned German positions, which they quickly pushed through.

Half a mile on, however, they were engaged by the Panzer Lehr, the tank division formed from Nazi training units. Less brazen forces might have fallen back to form a stronger line, as McAuliffe and Algar had anticipated, but the Panzer Lehr prided themselves on backing off from no one and had spread out to take on Martin's team. During the protracted firefight that resulted, Martin and his men moved to the top of a knob, which allowed them to destroy a number of the German tanks. Near daybreak, the Panzer Lehr withdrew. Martin and his unit leaders had gone up to the second floor of a small lodge on the hill to assess whether they still had a chance to reach the ammunition train. From there, they saw what had provoked the Germans' retreat, a battalion of American tanks emerging like specters through the falling snow. Patton had arrived.

Even when the first rocket came screaming toward Martin from a turret of the approaching armor, no one in his command had caught on that the tanks they saw had been captured by the Nazis from the 9th Armored Division. Never mustering a defense, Martin's unit had been left with only isolated survivors. The Major himself had gone down when the initial tank shell flew in the window at which he stood. At least four other shells hit the building, reducing it to a bonfire.

All of this was related to me the morning after we jumped into Savy by a boy named Barnes. He was perhaps five foot two, and slight as a butterfly. His nose was dripping the entire time I spoke to him, and he flinched whenever a shell exploded in the distance. For the moment, the fighting seemed to be a couple of miles off, to the north and east.

"Captain, we was blown to shit, there just ain't no other way to put it. I mean, those was American tanks. How was we supposed to know any different?"

Algar had corralled this boy, and one of the few other survivors of Martin's team, Corporal Dale Edgeworthy, and the two of them sat with Biddy and me, on wooden chairs in a corner of the empty barn.

"Martin got it right at the start of the attack," said Edgeworthy. "That's what came over the radio. We all saw the building go, Captain. It was the only thing standing out there. Sort of looked like when you toss a melon out of a truck and it hits the road. Pieces everywhere. The tech sergeant had command after that. But that couldn't have been more than fifteen minutes. Soon on, Captain, it was just run like hell and scatter, run for your life. There wasn't any choice, sir, but to leave the dead and wounded behind."

Edgeworthy, a tall man close to thirty, began to cry then. He kept saying there wasn't any choice about running.

I was ready to dismiss them, when one more question occurred to me. I told myself not to ask, then did anyway. These men had been with Martin nearly a week.

"What about the woman? I heard there was a woman with Martin originally."

Barnes and Edgeworthy looked at each other.

"I don't know, Captain," said Barnes. "When the offensive started on the sixteenth, we was up near Marnach in Luxembourg. The first night, when Major Martin took over after Colonel Gordon got it, the Major led us around to this farmhouse after dark. There was three people there, this farmer and this round old doll and their daughter. Seemed like they knew Martin, at least I thought so, 'cause the Krauts was a pretty good bet to take that ground, but they was still letting us in, a few soldiers at a time, so we could warm up while we ate our rations. But that was just a couple of hours. The Krauts never stopped fighting that night. They had their tanks painted white to match the snow and bounced them klieg lights off the clouds and they come right up that hill. They've got all that territory now."

"How old was the daughter?"

"Young, I guess." Barnes dragged his sleeve across his nose. "You know, Captain, I'm like any other fella, but I was pretty grateful to be out of the cold, I wasn't gonna give that girl the hairy eyeball. She was small," said Barnes, and smiled for the first time in the half hour we'd been with him. "You know, I'm kind of always watching out for short women. That's about all to tell you. I remember she was the right size."

Once they were gone, Biddy and I waited for Algar to return, shooting the breeze with the troops and officers who passed through the headquarters. The shelling continued in the mid-distance. It had begun at daybreak and started and stopped intermittently. Reports on Patton's progress were mixed. For each man who'd heard the Third Army was gaining, there were two bearing rumors that its divisions were stalled. In the meantime, the shortages of food and ammunition were past critical, not to mention the complete lack of medical items. This was not the moment to get wounded. The 101st's Division Clearing Station, and the eighteen doctors who manned it, had been captured on December 19. Yesterday, American artillery units south of the German troops had tried to cannon in bandages and plasma in howitzer shells, but the firing charge had blown all of it to smithereens. Everybody we encountered thanked us for the medical supplies that had fallen with us.

However, what the men here really craved was a few more degrees on the thermometer. They had stopped referring to the town as Savy. Everyone, officers included, usually called the village 'Save Me,' with salvation from the cold being their chief desire. Tank turrets and gas lines had frozen, and the soldiers routinely found their M1s inoperable until the bolts were freed by beating them with hand grenades. Some of the men who'd started suffering frostbite a couple of days ago claimed that they'd been cold so long that the intense burning sensations had ceased. The troops called themselves 'doggies' and everybody made the same joke: "This doggy can't feel his paws."

Algar came in, stamping the snow off his boots. He asked if I was satisfied after the interviews.

"Not to be grisly or cynical, Colonel, but I'm going to have to view the remains when they're recovered. Martin's been fairly slippery and there are people in London who'll want proof positive. I'd like to be certain myself."

I had irritated Algar again. He told me I'd know better than to say that if I'd ever seen a wooden building hit by four tank rockets. But he promised that as soon as the skies cleared and supplies came, we'd all be back on that hill, not so much for my sake but so that the men who'd died there, including Martin, could receive a proper burial. At his desk, Algar spent a minute shooting fire into the bowl of his pipe.

"And have you had a chance to consider what kind of duty Teedle's orders foresee for you now, Captain?" Algar asked this neutrally, as if it were not a loaded question. Biddy and I had discussed the answer at length this morning once Gideon had walked up here.

"Well, sir, Bidwell and I called a Yellow Cab so we could get back to Nancy, but they say there will be a delay picking us up, so we thought we might be able to serve with you, sir, in the meantime." Biddy had grumped around when I told him we had to volunteer for combat, but by now I understood that for him that was simply a prelude to bravery. He knew the score. If we didn't volunteer, Algar would have to order us into action. And there was no choice, anyway. The town was surrounded. It was a matter of fighting for our own survival.

"I don't suppose you two have any combat experience, Captain."

I said that Bidwell had gone up Omaha Beach. Algar had been there, too.

"That was a bitch," he said to Biddy.

"Hell on earth, sir."

"That's about the size of it. And what about you, Dubin?"

I told him I had only been shot at twice, including last night. "But I was trained as an infantry officer before I went to JAG school, sir."

Algar actually jumped out of his seat.

"A trained infantry officer? Ho my God," he said. He turned to his Exec, Ralph, who'd just arrived. "A trained infantry officer fell out of the sky, Ralph. Christmas has come early."

The 110th Infantry Regiment, what little was left of it, had been aggregated in a combat unit which Algar and his officers had named Team SNAFU. They were now under the 101st Airborne, plugging gaps as General McAuliffe designated, working in coordination with the 502nd Infantry Regiment. I was placed in command of a re-formed rifle company in a re-formed battalion. Given my lack of experience, I would have been challenged as a platoon leader, but on the other hand, G Company, which at full complement would have numbered around 193 troops, was all of 98. I had no lieutenants, just three sergeants, including Biddy, in charge of three platoons, and sparse support personnel.

On the afternoon of December 22, the newly re-formed G Company was assembled at the center of Savy. By daylight, Save Me was no more than it had seemed at night, a cluster of farm buildings composed of small slate-toned stones with thick joints of yellowish mortar. The tin-roofed structures had been added on to over centuries, and the windows and doors were all different sizes and varying heights, making them look as if they'd been thrown onto the buildings.

My first sergeant, named Bill Meadows, functioned for all purposes as my first lieutenant. Meadows greeted me when we met as if we were going out together for a night of drinking.

"Whatta you know, Captain?" He smiled widely and seemed on the verge of delivering a comradely poke in the shoulder. Bill Meadows was a stocky man in his early forties, wearing metal-framed specs. Like every other soldier I had, he was unshaved and his face after nearly a week of fighting was grayed by perspiration, gunpowder, and the airborne debris of shell bursts. "All right, boys," he called out to the troops. "Bend an ear. Captain Dubin's going to give us our orders."

Outmanned and outgunned by virtually everyone, Team SNAFU

had been positioned here on the west of Bastogne because it was the least likely point of attack. Most of the German tanks and artillery remained north and east. Given the difficulties of moving over the snowy hills, particularly with the remaining softness in the bottomlands, the odds were against the Germans mounting a major offensive from this direction. The fact was they didn't have to. Due to the thinness of the western defenses, Team SNAFU had been unable to prevent the Germans from working their way around us, flanking south toward the town, where they were now positioned.

For all of that, no place around Bastogne was secure. There had been a skirmish outside Champs earlier yesterday, when a German grenadier team and one half-track had briefly appeared there. But just as McAuliffe situated Algar to be less in harm's way, so Algar was locating G where we were not as likely to suffer attack. We were assigned to seal off a narrow farm road that came down from the west through Champs and Hemroulle and joined the main byway at Savy. Algar wanted G to go out after dark and dig in, in a wooded draw just north of Champs, on high ground that looked down on the road and the railroad track and a cow path directly to the west. The Germans, in theory, could come from any of those approaches. We were relieving E Company, who had been closer to Hemroulle and were taking a shellacking from German artillery which had gotten a fix on their position. E, which was down to seventy-two men, would serve as Headquarters Company, waiting as reinforcements if there was an assault.

Algar was certain that yesterday's encounter near Champs was a diversionary feint. If the Germans launched a significant western attack, they were far more likely to come at Savy, which was on one of the main roads to Bastogne. It ran north to Longchamps, and was big enough to make it vulnerable to the King Panzers. For that reason, Algar kept what little armor he had with him. Naturally, if the Krauts sent an armored column toward Champs, he would use his tanks and half-tracks and tank destroyers to reinforce us. Our job would be only to hold the road for a short time until the cavalry arrived, but that was a formidable assignment given our lack of ammunition. Algar ordered us not to shoot, even when fired on, unless we could see a human target. I was with Algar when Colonel Hunt, the 502nd's commander, called, and Algar described his intended defense of the Champs road as consisting of "a couple of empty muskets." It was something less than a vote of confidence.

I sent the men to pack up, ordering them to be in formation at 1615. Meadows drew what few rations we were allowed and gathered the maps. At 4:15 p.m., as dark was falling, I walked down the line for inspection, greeted every man by name and checked his equipment. Not one had an overcoat. They were dressed only in field jackets, sometimes more than one. All of them looked dirty, grim, and sleep deprived, but I was already proud to be their CO. They were prepared to fight, and that, I recognized, was what I'd really wanted to know in all my fretting about combat—what was worth fighting for.

The feelings of admiration were far from mutual. Most of the men hated me on sight and were sullen at best when I addressed them. For one thing, I had warmer clothes and a Thompson submachine gun, neither of which I was about to surrender, even after I learned that the undersupplied 101st had been instructed to shoot anyone in an overcoat, on the theory they were German impostors. Envy, however, was not the primary motive for my troops' discontent. They knew they were under the command of a man with no combat experience, and might as well have been led by a crawling infant.

I had little appreciation at that point for what these boys had been through, since nobody ever talked about the beating the 110th had absorbed in the last week. After my time in the VIII Corps signal office, I knew that the LVII Panzer Corps had literally swept the entire 28th Infantry Division, of which the 110th was part, from the map. But positioned with only two of its three battalions along Skyline, the paved highway that paralleled the border between Luxembourg and Germany, the 110th had absorbed the worst of the initial assaults, when the Panzer infantries had crossed the Our River in rubber boats in darkness and overwhelmed them at dawn.

In the desperation of the first hours, with no Americans behind them, the 110th had been ordered not to surrender and had forced the Germans into house-to-house fighting in towns like Clervaux, Consthum, and Holzthum. Most of the men I commanded were alive only because they had run when their lines finally broke, and, given their orders, probably didn't know how to regard their survival. The majority of my troops had been replacements themselves, with less time on the Continent than I'd had, but they all seemed to feel they had unfinished business with the Germans, whatever the perils.

At 1630, Meadows called out, "Drop your cocks and grab your socks, gentlemen, we're heading out." We marched south a few blocks to the crossroads, then turned north and west out of town, proceeding a little more than a mile. Despite the cold, nobody complained, knowing they were warmer than they'd have been traveling in the back of an open truck. Halfway to our position, we passed E Company marching in. A sergeant was in command, because the other officers were dead, and he and I exchanged salutes. The enlisted men were less formal. Some wished us good luck. Several suggested my troops should write their wives and sweethearts now and tell them to forget about having a family. "The only good your nuts will be is for ice cubes." Meadows put an end to the banter. We were on foot because it was imperative to arrive unnoticed. Yesterday's skirmishing had made it clear the Krauts were nearby. The intelligence officers in McAuliffe's G-2 believed the grenadiers were hidden north and west of us in the trees.

When we reached the place the maps called for us to set up, we found a zigzagging network of foxholes already there, each of them set about five yards apart. They had almost certainly been dug in the late summer by the Germans, rearguard units protecting the retreat from Allied forces coming up from the south. After consulting with Meadows, I ordered most of the men to shovel out these holes, rather than digging our own. Each of the three platoons had a Browning water-cooled machine gun, a cumbersome high-caliber piece manned by a three-soldier crew, and I directed the Brownings to be set up on three strongpoints running around the curved edge of the woods. Then I ordered two squads to scout defensive positions at our perimeters, forward and rear. The squad moving back discovered an old pump house, good news since the closed structure would provide a few men at a time some relief from the biting wind.

Shoveling the snow out of the holes revealed the Germans' debris—empty rations and rucksacks, spent ammunition, rusted rifles and canteens. Despite the severe cold, there was a distinct odor. This area had been liberated in mid-September by the V Corps, First Army, and I had no memory of hearing about any major action at Hemroulle. The Nazi company that had preceded us here—probably SS given the difficulty of their assignment—had to engage the Allies and slow them, knowing that there were no reinforcements behind them. Two of the foxholes in the group had been hit by Allied artillery, reducing them to half circles twice the depth of the others. I suspected that what we smelled was the German soldiers who had been in there, literally blown to bits that had moldered through the wet fall and now were sprinkled under several inches of snow.

When we were done digging, we cut boughs from the surrounding fir trees and laid them in each hole to form a base. A few pine branches were left at the edge, to be used, when the men were allowed to sleep, as a roof to catch the snow. There was no question that German forces were out in the woods, because when the winds bore down from the north, we could smell their fires, a luxury I couldn't allow if we hoped to maintain the element of surprise.

Each platoon had responsibility for a flank in our three main perimeters, and we set up a watch schedule and ordered the men to turn in, which many were eager to do, because they were still warm from digging. As I was to learn, it was possible to be too cold to sleep.

Biddy and I took the same hole, which appeared to have been the former command dugout, its architecture a tribute to German precision. It had been cut in a perfect trapezoid that allowed two men to fire side by side, but left more room for living behind them. The face was reinforced by a log retaining wall into which a ledge had been cut for personal possessions. I put books, some hand grenades, and my razor there, not that there was much chance of running water. It seemed odd to be unpacking as if this was a hotel room, but that thought was cut short by Biddy's cursing.

"Left my toothbrush in town," he said. "No shave, no bath. Least you can brush your teeth. Damn." I understood at once that the toothbrush was an emblem of the security we'd relinquished on this quest for a man who'd turned up dead, and I offered him mine.

"We can share it," I said. "It won't be the worst of what we share in this hole." With orders to remain out of sight, we weren't going to be making any trips to the latrine during the day. And Biddy and I were past the point of pride or privacy. The last of that had passed when he scraped me off that snowy field with a load in my pants.

Biddy, though, seemed struck by the gesture. He stared at the brush as if it was burning, before he took it.

Near 9:00 p.m., when most of the men had settled in, I heard the rumble of motors behind us, and one of the machine gunners on the point demanding the password. I had motioned Biddy and one of his squads forward, but he came back explaining that it was Signal Corps. They had driven up the road without lights, a fairly daring maneuver in the heavy darkness left by the thick clouds. The signal team was here to extend lines for field telephone connections for me running to Algar, and to each platoon. I was relieved not to be out here alone, but the signalmen reminded me to use the phones sparingly and only in code. Communications by ground wire were subject to interception sometimes a mile away, a radius that almost certainly included the Germans in the woods. We also had a backpack radio, the SCR-300, in the event we were forced to move.

Before turning in, Biddy and I both inspected positions. He went to look after his platoon, while I checked the forward strongpoints manned by the Browning crews.

"Flash," a gunner called.

"Thunder," I answered, the password G had been using all week, according to Meadows. The Browning crews' holes were dug deeper and rounder than the rest of ours. In the most visible location, the men needed to be entirely below ground level but able to swing the gun in a full circle in the event of an assault. I found each of the three crews pretty much exhausted. The men lay in the holes with their feet sole to sole with the boots of their mates, a device to keep them from falling asleep.

Returning to our hole before Biddy, I could feel at once that my pack was not where I'd left it. By flashlight, I found it had been ransacked. An extra pair of field pants was gone and my second gloves, too. I had already decided to give up what I wasn't wearing, but I regretted that a thief was the beneficiary. He'd taken personal effects, too, including three of the letters from Grace I had been carrying. And the card from Gita.

The adjoining holes, where I'd heard voices when I was coming up, now had fir boughs and ponchos drawn over them. I debated my options, then ran down to Sergeant Meadows to tell him someone had 'acquired' some of my gear. He said it had been going on in G Company from the beginning.

"Don't ask me to make it sensible, Captain. Stand and die beside a man then steal his stuff, I know it's crazy. I'm just trying to tell you that you're not the first."

"But this didn't happen unnoticed, Sergeant."

"Probably not, sir." He looked away and back. "They don't like anybody new, Captain, and new officers most of all."

"Because?"

"Because you don't understand, Captain. Listen, these men will fight for you. I've seen them. They're good men, every one of them, and they'll fight because they know they'll die otherwise. They hate you because they hate being here. Only way out of a rifle company is dead or wounded. It's like those turnstiles that only go in one direction. They let you in, but you can never get out. There ain't a man here, sir, who doesn't start praying at some point, God, please let me get wounded so I can go home. Plenty of them would give up an arm or a foot. I'm telling you what every soldier thinks. And what you're going to be thinking, too. And I can see just looking at you that you don't believe it. And that's why they hate you, Captain. Because you hold a better opinion of yourself than they have of themselves, and they know they're right. But don't worry about it, Captain. None of this will matter much, if we don't have battle. And if we do, they'll be fine with you afterward."

I spent two hours too riled to sleep, and then got up for night guard. As an officer, I wasn't required to take this duty, but we were too shorthanded to stand on formalities, and I thought it would be good for morale. On the way, I stopped in the pump house, a brick box dug into the hill that flanked our rear, fully embedded in the earth to keep the hydroelectric pump from freezing. There were no windows on the single exposed wall, just a half-size wooden door, which my men had broken open. Inside, I found most of the soldiers in the second squad from Meadows' platoon, who'd chosen to play cards by the light of a Coleman lantern rather than sleep. They jumped up and I put them at ease. The pump, an old black hunk of iron, reached down into a well hole, and the men had fanned out around it. I took a moment to ask each of the eight soldiers where he was from, but I got the same surly responses, and headed out.

"You a Yid, Captain?" When I turned back, nobody in the pump house was looking at his cards. The speaker, staring hardest at me, was a Mississippi boy, a private named Stocker Collison.

Every candidate in OTS learns the same thing. Rule one, make sure they respect you. If they like you, that's okay. But if they don't, fear will do.

"Is that a Southern term?" I asked Collison.

"Just askin."

"Does the answer matter to you, Collison?"

Of course it did. It probably mattered to half the men in the company, maybe more.

"No, sir."

"Good. What time you stand guard, Collison?"

"At oh three hundred, sir."

"Why don't you walk the perimeter now to be sure everything's okay."

He spent a long time looking at me before departing. The other men remained silent. I had been better at this than I'd imagined, but I knew whose manner I'd instinctively assumed. Teedle's. I would have to think about that.

I had drawn guard with the platoon of Sal Masi, a shrewd little guy from Boston who was my third sergeant. He'd been promoted from corporal on the battlefield and still had the doglegs on his uniform. Along with two of Masi's soldiers, I had watch on the rear hill, a position I'd assigned myself because it was at the highest point we occupied, and thus the most exposed to the wind.

My spot was about fifteen yards from the pump house, and the tin chimney that poked through the roof was designed to vent the pump's heat in the summer, but now it funneled the sound from within as if it were being broadcast. On their first night here, the men inside clearly didn't realize that. As a result, I spent much of my two hours on watch listening as the north wind carried along the squad's conversations, including their commentary about me, which began when Collison got back from his snowy trip around the perimeter.

"Jesus fucking Christ, Collison. Why didn't you just ask him to stick out his pecker so you could check?"

"Man oughta say what he is. He ain't got no call to hide it."

"Hell, man, you're white trash and I don't see you wearing a sign."

"Aw, go soak your head, O'Brien. The thing with the damn Jews is you don't never know when you got one."

"That's bull, Collison," said somebody else. "You can tell by lookin. You just haven't seen any 'cause you're an ignorant Mississippi pecker-wood."

"You got no call to talk to me like that, Marshall."

"Whatsa matter, Collison, did he hurt your feelings? I'm gonna cry, I'm not kidding. I'm crying already. I ain't cried like this since I read *My Friend Flicka*."

The line, from O'Brien, a thin sharp-faced kid from Baltimore, provoked a storm of laughter inside the pump house. Encouraged, O'Brien took off on Collison.

"Know the difference between a zoo in the North and a zoo in the South?"

Collison didn't answer.

"In the South, they don't just write the name of the animal on the cage. There's also a recipe." The uproar rocked out again. "Know what they call a Mississippi farmer with a sheep under each arm? Huh? A pimp."

Apparently O'Brien decided Collison had had enough. The men went back to playing poker, largely silent except for the grousing when somebody won. Without that distraction, and with nothing to see in the farm field that lay ahead of me, I worried. I worried mostly about whether fear would paralyze me in the midst of combat as it had when I jumped, and what would happen then to the men I was supposed to lead. The moment in the plane had drifted with me all day, like the lingering weakness from a fever. It had taken something away from me, from everything I saw and every breath I drew. I was a coward. I didn't expect myself to be unafraid. But I had been dashed to discover that I could not overcome it. The man who had volunteered to jump, the American who believed in the right things, had no control over the other part of me. It was as Gita had been trying to tell me when she lifted her skirt. Everything except instinct was a pretense.

Hoping for other thoughts, I began searching the sky. The clouds to the south did not look quite as thick. If I was right, that would mean air support, supplies, maybe even reinforcements. I hung, yet again, in that uncertain zone, not knowing if I wanted to be replaced before the

German attack. At least a demotion to platoon leader would let me pull duty I'd prepared for. If Meadows went down, I'd literally have to call Algar every hour for instructions.

As 5:00 a.m. approached, somebody else who'd gotten up for night guard entered the pump house, clearly another squad member, who received a full account of the evening, including the ungodly amount Bronko Lukovic had won, and Collison's encounter with me.

"Oh, Collison, you sure know your oats. Way to impress the new CO."

"I just like orders better comin from a Christian, is all," said Collison. "We're already fightin this fuckin war to save the Jews."

"Jesus, button your flap, Collison. You sound like Father Coughlin."

"Says you. Wasn't them Nazis that attacked us at Pearl Harbor. What the hell we care what ole Hitler's doin? I'm tellin you, it was all them Jews around Roosevelt. That's why we're here fightin."

"Collison, we're all fighting for the same damn reason. Because we have to. Because nobody gave us a choice."

"This platoon," answered Collison, "we got to be the worse-off bunch of doggies on the front. We been gettin nothin but screwed. I'm not kiddin. Two-thirds of our men dead and now they send us this Jew officer when we're surrounded."

"Shit, Collison. Don't snap your cap about Dubin. We've lost every officer we've had. And they knew what the heck they were doing. How long you think it's gonna take before this one stops a bullet? He's still looking around the woods for the men's room."

They all laughed. A minute later, I heard a familiar voice. Biddy had gotten up to spell me on night guard.

"Pipe down in here, y'all. Sound come outta that hole up top like cheers at a football game. Hear y'all fifty yards away." There was silence then. I'd wager some were wondering for the first time how far off I was. "And let me tell you something else. The Captain's a good man, y'all gone see that."

I could hear O'Brien ask, "Is he hep? I just can't take these officers who don't know nothing but what they read in the rule book."

"He's hep," Biddy said. He arrived at my position a minute later. He said nothing, but offered a cut-down salute when I left him to go back to sleep.

18. COLD TRUTH

ill Meadows shook me awake a little after 7:00 a.m., as the faintest light was leaking into the sky. He wanted to go over orders for the day. To conceal our position, we couldn't risk contact with the men on point or relieve them once the sun was up. Meadows wanted to replace the crews who'd been out there freezing all night and I told him to proceed.

Before he left, we took a moment to inspect the terrain. The open, rolling hills—hayfields or grasslands grazed by beef cattle—were now deep in snow with no animals in sight. Most, I imagined, had been killed or eaten long ago. North of us, beyond the railroad tracks and the drifts mounded here and there on the road, several fields undulated, separated only by stone markers. With my field glasses, I saw that the land had already seen combat. The Germans who had once occupied our holes had been hit hard before retreating. The blackened form of a Panzer was out there, with snow heaped on the tracks and the turret, and I also could make out the axle and fenders of a truck. My guess was that there had been more wreckage, which our engineers had towed off to assemble the crude roadblock that stood a couple hundred yards from us. It was comprised of commandeered tractors and two burned-out tanks, one ours, one German.

To the west, in the distance, lay dense green woods of tall pines, where the German grenadiers were probably hiding. Even in daylight the forest appeared black and impenetrable. I thought of the Brothers Grimm, and their goblins and spooks stealing from the trees to snatch souls and visit curses.

The last thing Meadows pointed out was the stand we occupied, a mixture of the same skinny, thick-branched pines that were across the way and deciduous trees, most of them beeches still wearing some of their coppery leaves. The Germans were delivering daily artillery barrages across a broad sector, wherever they figured Americans might be positioned to protect the roads, often utilizing their 20mm antiaircraft guns, which had proven effective as offensive weapons, or the dual-purpose 88s. Fixed on quad mounts and half-tracks, the guns were tilted forward and fired into the treetops. The result was a little like a bomb exploding in midair, raining shrapnel down on everyone below. Algar had sent us north of E's holes in hopes that the Germans might not have been aiming here, but up high the trees were ragged, as if they had been eaten away by moths. Several of the beeches had most of their boughs blown away, the remaining trunks standing like solitary amputees, blackened by the shell bursts. In other words, we were going to get it. The Germans had been firing in the hour after dawn and just before sunset, periods when they could be certain that our planes, which could navigate only by daylight in this weather, would never be in the air.

"I want to tell the boys to stay low when that starts," said Meadows. "Or else get out and go hug the trees."

"Right."

"But the sergeants need to keep watch. It'd be a good time for that Panzer infantry to come out of the woods, with us hunkered down."

"Right," I said again. Commanding with Bill Meadows as your top NCO was a little like driving with a chauffeur. He and I exchanged salutes, but Meadows hung back.

"Captain, I hear you had a hard time with Collison last night."

"It was a short conversation, Bill. Nothing to be concerned about."

"Don't let Collison bother you, Captain. He's not a bad Joe, especially once he gets used to you. We got a lot of country boys in this man's

Army just like him, and it don't matter if they're from Mississippi or the North Woods. First time he lived with indoor plumbing was in basic training. They've been through a lot, Captain, these boys. Sometimes they just talk a little bunk."

When Meadows left, Gideon crawled into his boots and coat to inform his platoon about today's orders. He'd been back in the hole only a few minutes, using my toothbrush for the first time, when the shelling began. If nothing else, the Krauts were punctual.

In the midst of combat, I was to discover that certain phrases would become lodged in my head, as if my brain was a Victrola stuck on a scratch. That day, the saying was "Forewarned is forearmed," mostly because it proved completely untrue. The Germans were employing a technique I'd learned in infantry school called TOT, or time on target. The idea was that their shells would fly at several areas at once, before anyone could scramble back to his hole. Not knowing precisely where we were, the Germans calibrated each gun at intervals of roughly thirty yards.

The first rounds were screaming meemies, rocket-propelled shells that bore down with a constant heart-stalling screech like a car's tires when its clutch is popped, and that proved to be nothing compared to my dread when the ordnance started landing. I had thought it couldn't be worse than the bombing at the Comtesse's, but there was no way to anticipate the emotional effect of being under sustained bombardment. I will never hear anything louder—ears simply can't absorb more sound—and combined with the way the earth rocked, I was soon rattled with a primitive panic whenever I detected the sound of the 88s. It was distinctive as somebody's cough, to which it bore a thunderous resemblance. The shells exploded with a magnificent bouquet of flame and snow and dirt, raining down hot shrapnel, pieces often a foot or two long that ricocheted off the trunks, while huge limbs crashed around us. The closest blast to me, about fifty yards away, made my eyes throb in their sockets and squeezed my chest so hard I thought something was broken. After each detonation, just as a way to hold on, I promised myself it was the last, trying to believe that until I heard the throaty rumble of the artillery firing and the keen of the next shell heading in to knock us flat.

And then after almost an hour on the dot, it stopped, leaving the air hazy and reeking of cordite. In the sudden silence, you could hear only the wind and the thud of branches that continued to fall from the trees. After the first few minutes of the shelling, between explosions, a scream had gone out for medics and that shouting resumed now. I phoned Second Platoon. Masi told me that two men in the same hole had been struck by a tree burst. I didn't know what the CO should do, but I couldn't believe hiding was the answer, and I scrambled up there, weaving between the trees. The Krauts couldn't see much anyway, with all the smoke and dust in the air.

Arriving, I found a red-haired kid named Hunt dead from a piece of shrapnel that had descended like an arrow from an evil god and penetrated the soft spot beside his clavicle, plunging straight into his heart. He was lying in the hole, his eyes open and still. I was most struck by his arms, thrown back at an angle no one could have maintained in life.

The other man was being attended by a medic. His leg below the knee was a red mash. The bone was shattered and he was crying from the pain, but the medic thought he would live. They would move him out, once night fell, for what little good it would do. At this stage, this man, Kelly, was facing roughly the same chances for survival as soldiers wounded during the Civil War. The medics were using some sulfa powder, which they had been pilfering from the aid kits of the dead for days, in hopes of disinfecting the wound. Kelly would be transferred to an aid station Algar had set up yesterday at the church where we'd slept in Hemroulle. Back in my own hole, I took reports from the other platoons by phone. Only two casualties. Doing the arithmetic, I knew we had come through rather well.

During the barrage, it had started to snow. I had thought it was too cold to snow—we used to say that at home—but apparently the weather in Belgium didn't adhere to Midwestern rules. It was not a storm of great intensity. Instead the large flakes drifted down almost casually. Like most little boys, I had grown up regarding snow as a thrill. It was pretty. It was fun. But I had never endured it in a foxhole. The snow danced down for more than two hours. As soon as Biddy and I shook it off, it collected again. Eventually, we were soaked and frozen. And it kept snowing. With overcoats, Biddy and I were better off than many of our troops, who were sitting in their holes wrapped in their ponchos and blankets, with their cold M1s held next to their bodies to keep the trigger mechanisms from freezing. But I had no feeling in my hands and feet, and I was increasingly amazed that the blood didn't just go to ice in my veins.

Dealing with the cold proved a matter of will. I was desperate for distraction, and on pure whim decided to light one of the cigarettes that had come in my rations. Cigarettes were probably the one thing not in short supply, although the men complained relentlessly about the fact that the cheaper brands—Chelsea, Raleigh, Wings—had been sent to the front.

The skies had remained so dim that it seemed as if the light was oil being poured in by the drop. Now I found myself keeping track of the birds. It was hard to believe any were left. The artillery barrages must have killed most of them, and during the German occupation food had been scarce enough that I'd heard of the locals routinely eating sparrows. A few crows scavenged in the forest, and some swift long-tailed magpies darted by. I pointed out a hawk to Biddy, but he shook his head.

"Ain't no hawk, Cap," he said. "That there is a buzzard."

By midday, we knew there was little chance an attack would come. The offensives were taking place around us—the air spasmed from artillery rounds, and the sputtering of machine guns and the sharp crack of rifle fire a mile this way or that carried distinctly through the cold. In considering things, I'd decided that our most likely role would be as reinforcements if the Germans attacked Savy. But if that happened at all, it would be tomorrow or the day after. While the sun was up, there was little to do but stay out of sight in the hole and battle the cold.

"You think it ever gets this cold in Kindle County?" I asked Bidwell.

"As I recollect, sir, yes. Colder. I still have in mind, Cap, walking up to high school eight blocks, and the mercury stuck clear at the bottom of the thermometer. Colder than twenty below."

I'd made those trips myself and laughed at the memory. Insane with adolescent vanity, I'd refused to wear a hat. I could recall my mother screaming at me from the back porch and the feeling once I'd reached the high school's hallways that if my ears grazed something hard, they'd break straight off my head.

In the middle of the day, there were suddenly shouts from within our midst. I jumped out with my tommy gun, certain the Germans had somehow snuck up on us, only to find that two men in Biddy's platoon had uncovered a discarded Luger in their hole—the breach mechanism had seized up—and a fistfight had broken out between them about who would get the souvenir. I put both men on discipline—meaningless now—and said the Browning crews, who'd been on the strongpoints without communication for hours, could draw straws for the pistol when they were relieved. We had to reassign the two soldiers to other holes, and even though I demanded silence, I could hear both calling one another "motherfucker" as I left. That wasn't a word used much among the officer class, who usually adhered to a certain gentility.

"You ever know of anybody who actually fucked his mother?" I asked Biddy.

"Had a friend in high school who fucked one of my buddy's mothers. I heard of that."

"Well, that's not the same thing."

"No sir, not at all." We fell silent for a while.

"Biddy, where in the world did you go to high school, anyway?" He'd told me before that he hadn't quite made it to graduation. His family needed money.

"No place you'd know, sir."

"Don't bet on that. I think I swam against every school in Kindle County."

"You didn't never hear of Thomas More, sir. Wasn't no swimmers there."

"Thomas More? In the North End? Wasn't that all colored? I didn't know there were any white men in that school."

"Wasn't," he said. "Two white girls. No white men."

I had been looking at the sky, just realizing that blue was starting to edge past the dirty gray masses. That meant the planes would be flying. When I finally processed Gideon's words, I was sure I'd misunderstood. He had removed his helmet and, big as he was, I found him staring down at me, unconsciously drumming one finger on the MP stenciled in white on the front.

"You heard me, Captain."

"What the heck are you telling me, soldier?"

"I'm trusting you is what I'm doing. Against my better judgment."

A hundred things fell into place. After the artillery barrage, I was too drained to feel shock, but I was lost in some fundamental way.

"Now what're you thinking?" he asked me.

"Truthfully? I don't think I believe you."

"You better. Because this here's no off-time jive." He was sullen and probably more astonished with himself than I was. His choice of words, however, went to make his point.

Now that he'd said it, of course, now that I was actually looking, appraising his nose, his hair, I suppose I could see how he might have been colored. But there were men in the next hole, Rapazzalli and Gomez — not to mention me — who were probably darker complected, and none of us with eyes as light as Biddy's green peepers.

"I got my draft notice," he said. "I went down there. I didn't never say one way or the other. They just looked at me and put me in. You know, I'd always had that, folks saying as how I could pass. When I was a kid in Georgia, and we was away from home, I always knew I could go strolling free as a bird into places my brothers couldn't. It didn't seem to matter all that much once we got North. But there I was now. I come home and told my folks.

"'Did you lie?' my daddy asked me.

"'Not a solitary word.'

"My mom and he really got going. She wanted me to head straight down there and tell the truth. If the Army didn't want me doin no fighting, she was in no mind to quarrel. But Daddy wudn't hear none of that. 'What truth is that? That even though he looks every bit as good as any other man, even though he *is* every bit as good as any other man, he ought not get treated like it 'cause he's actually colored. Is that the truth? The day ain't dawned yet where I'll let a child of mine say that. Not yet.' I'm not sure the two of them have patched it up completely even now.

"But how it was really, Captain, I went along with it mainly because I was just like you. I wanted to fight. I wanted to be like Jesse Owens and rub old Adolf Hitler's face in the dirt so hard that that damn mustache come off his face. And I knew they wouldn't see hide of many colored troops near the front.

"Once I got in the middle of Omaha Beach, I gave that another think, all right. I'd'a been just as happy to set 'em straight and go back to England. It's full crazy, what I got myself into. Ain't a day that passes I don't think once or twice I should have listened harder to my mom. Times I feel like I'm not being true to my own, even though I never said a false word to nobody. And I'm always tellin myself I gotta get home alive, just so ain't nobody there sayin how it's a mistake for a colored man to think he can do the same things as white folks. It's just all one hell of a mess."

He peeked over at me again and reached onto the ledge for my toothbrush, which he'd pulled from his mouth and thrown in there as the shelling began.

"You want this back?"

The word 'yes' was halfway to my lips, but I retrieved it without a flicker.

"Yeah, damn it, I want it back," I said then and snatched it from him, jamming it into my mouth. The toothpowder had frozen hard on the bristles. "I didn't get a chance to use it this morning. And tomorrow I'm first. You can be first the day after that."

He looked at me for a while.

"Yes, sir," he said.

19. THE SKIES

Late in the day, American C-47s passed overhead. Looking back toward Savy, we could actually see the chutes and supplies drifting down out of the big Gooney Birds, and the glowing trails of the German antiaircraft fire darting at them like malign june bugs. The parachutes, red, yellow, and blue, resembled blossoms, a lovely sight in the clean sky, but not one we enjoyed for long. Nazi bombers and fighters appeared from the other direction, and the fierceness of the AA soon cleared the skies. Once our planes were gone, the Germans repositioned their guns and another artillery barrage began. They clearly feared that with their AA occupied, the Americans might have moved out ground forces, and the new volleys seemed to go on twice as long as they had in the morning. As we huddled in the hole, I felt my teeth smash against each other so hard I thought I might have broken one of my molars.

Once it was over, the field telephone pealed. It was Algar, who'd chosen the code name Lebanon.

"What's the condition out there, Lawyer?"

We'd sustained two more wounded from the last barrage, both relatively minor injuries. One man would need to be moved back to town, along with the young fellow with the leg wound. Algar promised that the ambulances would be there after dark.

"I'm hearing that your Army commander has broken through to the south," Algar said. "Punched a hole, they're saying. We should start seeing reinforcements. Make sure your men know. We had a hundred sixty supply drops here, now. Not enough. But there's some ammo. Medicine."

"Yes, sir." The news about Patton was welcome, but my men would believe only what they saw. Everything was rumor until then.

"How's the mood?"

The mood, I said, was good, considering. The men realized there was nothing to do about the cold, but they were complaining often about not being allowed out of the holes in daylight, especially to relieve themselves. Orders were to shit in your hat if you had to, but since nobody was going to abandon his helmet with two tree bursts every day, the directive put the troops to a ridiculous choice.

Sunset came shortly after that, a moment of great solemnity, as it signaled a lessening of the dangers. The Panzers wouldn't come at night in these conditions when they could get stuck so easily if they veered off the roads. And the Germans, after the huge push that drove us back from the Ardennes, were too short supplied to engage in the harassing artillery fire they normally would have ordered up in darkness. We had to be alert for Kraut scout teams, who could sneak across the field in an effort to assay our position, but we all knew we had survived and would soon be able to move around. The sun, which had edged in and out for hours, knifed through in the distance, breaching the clouds with an intense coppery shaft blazing on the forest across the field. Biddy grabbed his camera, somehow seeing a black-and-white picture in all that color.

Meadows called and we made night assignments. Bill also had a request. The men wanted to make a fire in the pump house. There would be no light. The issue was the smoke, which might betray our position. But the wind was still coming from the north, which would carry the odor back toward town. It was a calculated risk, but we decided it was worth it. I doubted that even if the wind shifted the Germans would be able to tell our smoke from their own. Each squad would be allowed in the pump house for half an hour to eat their rations, as well as fifteen minutes before and after night guard. The gunners who'd been out on the strongpoints all day without communication would get stretches twice as long and go first.

The ambulance arrived near 6:00 p.m., accompanied by a supply truck. The quartermasters were supposed to be bringing tomorrow's rations, but they had only two C ration containers. It meant I was going to be able to feed the men just once tomorrow.

"Colonel hopes for better Christmas Day," said the quartermaster sergeant. I knew he was husbanding whatever he had for a Yule treat, but starving the troops in advance seemed like a poor way to enhance their appreciation. "He did send these, though. Requisitioned them from a local café in Bastogne. Owner beefed something terrible, but hell, he ain't doing much business these days anyway."

I stuck my field knife into one of the soft pine boxes and found table linens. It took me a moment to catch on, then I summoned my three non-coms, Meadows and Biddy and Masi, to distribute them to their platoons.

"What the hell?" Meadows asked.

I explained that the men could use the white tablecloths as camouflage, if they needed to leave their holes during daylight. We were lucky the linens had been starched. Otherwise they would have been shredded for bandages.

Once he'd handed out the cloths and napkins, Meadows returned. He wanted me to know this had elevated me in the eyes of the men, an effect that would undoubtedly be lost when they got hungry tomorrow. Nevertheless, I appreciated the fact that Meadows was looking out for my morale, too.

"If Algar had any sense, Bill, he'd have made you the company commander."

"Tell you a secret, Captain, he offered. But I don't see myself as officer material. Second lieutenant, frankly, that's the worst job in the Army. At least in the infantry."

Biddy, across the hole, grumbled in agreement. I'd heard the statistics, but I answered, "The food is better at headquarters."

"Suppose that's so," said Meadows. "I'm just not the one to give orders, sir. Not in combat."

"Because?"

"Because if you live through it and your men don't, that's something I don't want to deal with. All respect, sir."

It was another problem I'd never considered, because I was too green, and I dwelt on it in silence while Meadows went on his way.

As captain, I'd assigned myself the last stretch in the pump house, and I decided to try to sleep before then. I took off my overcoat. The snow had frozen it solid and it actually stood up by itself, leaned against one wall in the foxhole. I was too cold to fall off. Instead, near the end, awaiting my turn in the pump house, I actually started counting to myself. When I finally walked in, the heat was one of the sweetest sensations of my life, even though my hands and feet burned intensely as they thawed. The men of Meadows' Second Squad were in there again, taking as long as they could to consume their rations. I knew they'd overstayed by the speed with which they all jumped up when I entered.

"As you were, gentlemen."

O'Brien told me to go slow approaching the fire. These men were familiar with the hazards of frostbite.

"Captain," said O'Brien. "Can I ask you a question? You ever heard of a fella getting frostbite of the dick? Collison's worried that his dick will fall off."

I'd never heard of that. I thought back to high-school biology and explained that what imperiled the extremities was their distance from the heart.

"I told you, Collison," said O'Brien. "You're so dumb, you know what they call the space between your ears? A tunnel. You know what you got in common with a beer bottle, Collison? You're both empty from the neck up."

Collison, on his haunches, looked toward the fire as O'Brien laid into him. I suspected that O'Brien was giving him the treatment for my benefit, after last night.

"Take it easy, O'Brien. Save a few cracks for the rest of the war."

Saved by an unexpected source, Collison looked my way briefly.

"How's he even remember all these? I can't never remember no jokes."

"That's because you're a marching punch line, Collison," said O'Brien.

Meadows came in then to send the squad back to their holes. First Squad was on the way up. I crept closer to the fire and Meadows stayed with me a minute to warm his wire-framed glasses, which were frosting over. The little red dents stood out beside his nose.

"So, Bill, what was your racket before this started?"

"Me? I was on hard times, Captain, if you want to know the truth of it. I grew up in California, close to Petaluma. My folks were farmers but

I got myself down to Frisco, worked as a longshoreman and made a good buck, too. But there was no work come '34 or '35. It didn't go right between me and my wife, then. I was drinking. Finally, she took herself and my two boys back to Denver where her people was from, put up with her folks. I just started hopping freight cars, looking for work. But there were lots of chappies like me sittin 'round fires in every freight yard in every city. Those were bad times, Captain. I was first in line at the Army recruiter when the mobilization started in '40. This damn war was a piece of luck for me. If I live through it. Wife remarried but it didn't work out and she's all lovey-dovey now when she writes me. I really want to see those boys. Oldest is sixteen. I sure as hell hope this war ends before he can join up. I don't know how I'd keep my senses if I had to worry about him being in this mess, too. You think it's gonna be over soon?"

I'd thought so, just a week ago. At the moment it looked as if there was more fight in the Nazis than any of us had expected. Still, it seemed important to tell the men I believed victory was not far off. Meadows looked at me hard to see if I really believed it.

I ate a cracker out of today's K ration and decided to save the rest for morning. I caught two hours' sleep, then warmed up again in the pump house before my watch. The men of Masi's platoon, too small to be divided into squads, began filing in. Meadows and I were on the same schedule and headed out together.

"Gee whiz," said Meadows, putting his gloves on again, "how do you figure they took a fella from California and sent him to the European theater?"

"Man, you ain't countin on the Army to make any sense, are you, First Sergeant?" asked one of the men coming in.

We all laughed. I stood outside listening to my men for a minute as their talk rose into the night through the chimney.

"You figurin it's some bad luck we're here rather than the Pacific?"

"Lot warmer in the Pacific, I know that."

"Every letter I get from my brother," said someone else, "is about how damn hot it is. But it's not how that's a blessing or nothing. They get every kind of rash. He says he got stuff growin on him, he didn't even know a man's skin could turn that color. And a boy's got to have some absolute luck to get himself a drink. Ain't like here in Europe with all this wine and cognac, nothing like that. Best that happens is somebody with an in with the quartermaster gets hold of some canned peaches and sets himself up a still, makes something tastes like varnish. Guys is drinkin so much Aqua Velva, quartermaster's never got any in stock. And they-all's fighting among themselves to get it."

"But it ain't cold there."

"Yeah, but I'd rather get killed by a white man, I really would."

"Now what kind of fucking sense does that make?" another asked.

"That's how I see it. I ain't askin you to feel that way, Rudzicke."

"Don't be a sorehead."

"Just how I feel is all. Think it would be a little easier to go out like that. Just don't want the last face I see to be brown."

"I can understand that," said another man.

"I tell you another thing," said the first man, called Garns, "them Japs is savages. They're like the wild Indians, eat a man's heart. They think we're some inferior species like monkeys. They really do."

"They're the ones look like monkeys. Don't they? The Krauts at least, they'll treat you okay if they take you prisoner. Buddy of mine wrote me how he was fighting on this island, Japs caught one of their men. They sliced this guy's backbone open while he was still alive, then they poured gunpowder in there, and lit the poor son of a bitch. Can you imagine? And the rest of his platoon, they're hidin out and listening to this shit."

There were plenty of hideous stories from the Pacific. I'd heard several times that the Japs cut the ears off living prisoners.

"Yeah, but it's warm," said someone. That drew a laugh.

"I don't figure war's much good wherever you are," somebody else said.

"You hear about these Polynesian dames. Buddy wrote me they landed in a couple of places, girls didn't even have no shirts on when they got there. And they fuck sort of like saying hello."

"Ain't no women fuck like saying hello. Ain't no woman do that lest she's gettin somethin out of it. My daddy tole me that and I ain't never seed how he was wrong."

"Yeah, but I still hear these dames in the Pacific, they're something else. This buddy said one of these dolls, she could pick up a silver dollar with her you know what. Finally, somebody got the idea of taking out his business and laying the dollar on there and this girl she took up both. That musta been a sight."

"You think it's true what they say?"

"How's that?"

"That the Nazis travel with whores. They bring them along."

"Sounds like Nazis."

"Yeah, we're goddamn Americans. We believe in freedom. The freedom not to get laid."

Meadows came crunching back through the snow. He gave me a wink, then opened the door to tell the men to keep it down.

"Krauts are still there," he said.

When I left, a soldier named Coop Bieschke was carving his name in a copper beech about halfway to my guard position. He'd been at it both nights, using up his sleeping time for this enterprise. I thought to ask him what was so important, but I wasn't sure Coop could explain it. Maybe he was planning to come back here after the war ended, or perhaps he wanted his people to know the spot where he'd died. Maybe he simply hoped to leave a mark on the earth that was definitively his. I watched him at work with his jackknife, oblivious to me and everything else, then continued up the hill.

After guard, I returned to the pump house, then rushed back to our foxhole before my boots could freeze again, placing them under my legs, in the hopes that my body warmth would keep them from hardening overnight. It was a wasted effort. When I woke up, my pants legs had actually frozen together and it was a struggle even to get back on my feet.

The morning of December 24 was cloudless and our Air Corps was in the sky not long after first light. As the formations of bombers, and the P-47s to protect them, roared overhead, my men waved from inside their foxholes. The German antiaircraft was intense, especially as our planes penetrated German territory. We could see the red trails of the AA rising, and several times aircraft suddenly becoming a star of flame. But the ranks of bombers and supply planes kept appearing for nearly five hours, vapor trails behind each motor, making the sky look a little like a plowed field. The escorts weaved up and down, on the lookout for German fighters, while the chutes on the supply drops continued to unfurl in the skies near Savy. Occasionally, when the wind died down, we could hear the rumble of the trucks fetching the medicine and food and ammunition back into Bastogne.

The men remained in their holes, but now with the camouflage, I was able to move out every hour or so to check our positions. I dashed through the woods, wrapped in a tablecloth, with a linen napkin knotted beneath my chin like my grandmother's babushka. When I ran up to their holes, several soldiers looked at me and said, "Trick or treat."

For the most part, I was in the hole with Biddy, trying to tell myself that I had borne the cold yesterday, so I could make it today. Today would be easier, I told myself, because now I knew there would be a fire in the pump house later. But perhaps that made it worse, since I could recall now what it felt like to be warm.

Every hour, I lit a cigarette. In the interval, I took to sniffing the odor of the tobacco on my gloves. I couldn't understand the odd comfort it seemed to bring me, until I thought of Gita Lodz and the strong scent of her hair and clothing. I wondered if I'd ever see her again. Or if I cared to. Then I asked myself the same thing about Grace. And my parents. If I had to choose only one of them to be with last, who would it be?

"Lord, Biddy," I said suddenly, "doing nothing but standing in this hole and thinking is enough to make a man stark raving mad."

He grunted as a form of agreement.

"I wonder if we'd be better off if the Germans just came and we got it over with."

"Captain, you don't want to say that. Take it from me."

I asked him to tell me about Omaha Beach.

"I don't know, Captain. It ain't nothing like whatever we-all gonna get ourselves into here. The thing of D-Day was the size of it. I was there D plus one. And it was war everywhere, sir. Them battleships was behind us firing at the Germans on the cliffs, and the Germans was shooting down. Our bombers was up above and the Kraut AA batteries were roaring. And you had thousands of soldiers running up that beach, shooting whatever there was to shoot at. It was fighting everywhere, men giving battle cries, and all that moaning and screaming of the wounded. When the troop carrier dropped us and we sloshed up through the water there, it was red as a stop sign from the blood, and I couldn't see how we'd ever get to the rendezvous point. There were bodies all over. You couldn't pick a straight line up that beach without tromping on the dead. And each step, I looked at them and thought: This here is my last step, the next one, it's going to be me. When I got my squad assembled, I turned back and I realized it was just like I'd imagined it. I'd imagined this my whole life."

"War, Biddy?"

"No, sir. Hell. It was the devil's hell, all right. Sitting in church, having the preacher tell me where the sinners was gonna find their ugly selves, and thinking so hard about it, that was what I'd seen. The banging, the screaming, the pain. Even the smells of the bombs and the artillery rounds. That's a saying, sir, you know, war is hell, but it's a truth. The souls screaming and sinking down. And the skies falling. When I get to thinking about it, sometimes I wonder if I'm not dead after all." He shook his head hard as if to empty it of thought. "I don't like going on about this, Captain."

I told him I understood. He was silent for a second.

"You know, Captain, about Martin?"

"What about him?"

"Men like that who've been at war for years now. I understand why they keep doin it. Because it's the truth, sir. It's hell. And it's the truth, too. Ain't nothin else so real. Can you figure what I'm saying?"

I couldn't really. But the idea frightened me as much as the thought of the Germans waiting to attack.

We were an hour from sunset when there was a little aimless putt-putting overhead. My first thought was that it was German buzz bombs, the V-1s that I'd heard about, but when I got my binoculars, I followed the sound to a little single-engine plane. The field telephone growled at once. It was Meadows, telling me the aircraft was a Nazi scout and that we should yell to all the men to get their tablecloths on and hunker deep in their holes. But about five minutes later, the plane circled overhead again. When I heard the engine nearing for a third pass, I knew we'd been observed. I raised Meadows.

"Any question he's seen us?"

"No, sir."

"Well then, let's try to shoot him down."

"We don't have bullets to waste, Captain."

We agreed that the Browning crews had the only real chance of hitting a target at five hundred feet and we both dashed forward to the strongpoints to issue that instruction. It seemed to take the three-man crews forever to get the unwieldy machine guns elevated, but even at that, one round took a piece out of the plane's left wing, before the craft climbed out of range.

I called Algar.

"Shit," he said. "Any chance the plane didn't make it back?"

There was a chance, but it was still in the sky when we'd last seen it. If it made it, we'd be sitting ducks for the Kraut artillery. We had to move out, but not until we had another defensive position as good as the one we were giving up. Algar also wanted to see if our recon had provided any clues about where the Germans were in the woods. Putting down the phone, I thought the same thing all my men would. Another position meant giving up the pump house.

Algar was back to me in a few minutes. Both intelligence and operations thought that the Germans were repositioning much of their artillery in light of the morning overflights. If so, they were probably not ready yet to fire on us, and both G-2 and G-3 doubted that the Germans would risk a barrage at night, which would pinpoint their guns' new positions to air surveillance, inviting bombing at dawn.

"It's your choice," Algar said about staying put for the moment. "We'll reposition you by morning, either way."

This was my first real decision as a commander. For the sake of the pump house and the fire, I decided to remain here, but in the next thirty minutes, every creak of the trees in the wind seemed to be the first sound of incoming shells. I stood up in the hole, examining the skies, hoping to smell out the artillery like a pointer. The field telephone rang as soon as darkness began to settle over us. It was Meadows.

"Captain, a lot of these men, they'd like to get that fire going. It's Christmas Eve, sir. They want to have a little service. I guess they figure that if God's gonna protect them, it has to be tonight." I gave permission.

Having gone last to the pump house the night before, I was entitled to an early trip and I took it, before the prayer service began. As Meadows had predicted, coming up with the table linens had broken the ice for me with some of the men, and I found one of Biddy's squads in there anyway, troops better disposed to me for his sake. A lanky Texan, Hovler, had taken a place on a stone near the fire, and looked up at me as I warmed my hands beside him.

"Captain, you married?"

"Engaged," I said, although life in a foxhole made that seem more chimerical every minute. Home was so far away.

"Pretty," Hovler allowed, when I found my wallet. "This here is my Grace," he said.

"Grace. Why, that's my girl's name, too." We marveled at the coincidence. His Grace was sunny and buxom. In the snapshot, her hair was flowing behind her in a wind that also formed her dress against her.

"Fine-looking."

"She shore is," he said. "Shore is. Only thing is, that works on my mind. You think your Grace is gonna wait for you?"

Eisley and I had bunked at the Madame's with two different fellows in Nancy whose women had Dear Johned them. I wondered how it would feel, if Grace got some intimation of my fling with Gita and abandoned me. I'd excused myself because of the excesses of war, but what if she didn't? Grace had two suitors left at home, boys she had been going with before me, one a 4-F because of a glass eye, and the other running a factory critical to the war effort. Now and then, when I listened to men like Hovler worry that their gals could two-time them, the idea that Grace might take up with one of these boys would pierce me like an arrow, and then, like an arrow pass through. I did not believe she would do it. It was that simple. Boredom, longing, loneliness—even jealousy and anger—were not forces capable of conquering Grace's virtue. Until I met Gita, I might have called it principle. But even by Gita's view, even if she were correct that every man and woman was a story they had made up about themselves and tried to believe, that was Grace's—that she was a person of virtue so lightly borne that it did not really touch the earth. She could never do that to me. Because, in the process, she would destroy herself.

"I hope so," I answered.

"Sitting out here, it kinda gets in my mind that she can't possibly wait for me. She got any sense, she'd know I'm three-quarters of the way to dead anyhow, being out here surrounded. And likely to come back with some piece of me missin, if I make it. Why should she wait? There all those 4-Fs and smart guys and USO commandos at home, makin good money 'cause there ain't many men left. Why shouldn't a dame get herself a beau?"

I still had the picture in my hand.

"She doesn't look like the kind of girl to do that, Hovler."

"I hope not. I'd hate to live through all this just to come home to a broken heart. I don't know what I'd do. I'd mess her up, I think." The thought made him so unhappy that he left the fire and went back to his hole.

At 9:00 p.m., a jeep came creeping up the road. I'd been summoned into town to see Algar. He was at the same desk where I had met him, now trimmed out with pine boughs. His pipe was in hand, but I could tell from the aroma that he'd been reduced to filling it with tobacco from cigarettes.

"Merry Christmas, David." He offered his hand. He and his staff had been contemplating my company's situation and the way it fit into the overall picture. Creeping ever closer, the Krauts had issued an edict today to McAuliffe to surrender and he'd reportedly said "Nuts" in reply. There was reason to think he'd made a good decision. Patton's forces were said to be advancing down the Assenois road on Bastogne now, and more than 1,200 loads of supplies had fallen by parachute today. As a result, General staff was convinced that the Germans had no choice but to mount an all-out attack tomorrow. They could not position their tanks to take on Patton without control of Bastogne. And they knew that with every hour, supplies were being distributed to peripheral forces, meaning the longer they waited, the stiffer the resistance.

Given the scout plane, Algar figured there was now some chance that one of the Kraut attacks might come from the west, perhaps through Savy. Perhaps even through Champs. There was no telling. And in any event, whatever force was in the woods would move on us, at least for a while, to keep the company in place. So Algar and his staff still wanted us in position to hold that road. They were just going to move us a little, into the woods on the eastern side, in order to lessen the chances of the German guns fixing on us. If the first attack came at us, we were to move north and contact the enemy. With luck, we'd catch them by surprise and be able to flank the Panzer grenadiers. Either way, we were better off attacking than waiting for the Germans to mass and pin us down. If we did get the first attack, Algar would send tanks and reinforcements, even call in air support if the weather held. It was more likely that we'd get called to reinforce Savy. Those were the orders.

Ralph, the Exec, came in to report on a conversation with McAuliffe's staff in Bastogne, who were suddenly disheartened about Patton's progress.

"Ham, I don't know what to make of this, but this guy Murphy, he was sort of implying that maybe Bastogne is bait."

"Bait?"

"That Ike wants to draw as many of the German assets as possible tight around the town, and then bomb it to all hell. Make sure there's never another offensive like this. Better in the long run."

Algar thought about that, then gave his head a solid shake.

"Patton might bomb his own troops. Never Eisenhower. We want to keep that one to ourselves, Ralph."

"Yes, sir."

When Ralph left, Algar looked at me. "Here's another thing to keep to ourselves, David. A couple of things. I don't like to say either of them, but we're all better off being plain. Don't let your men surrender to the Panzer forces. Name, rank, and serial number won't get them very far. After the job we've done on the Luftwaffe, most of their intelligence comes from what they can beat out of our troops. Once they've got what they want, the buggers have no means to keep prisoners. And they don't. Word is they flat-out shot dozens of our troops at Malmédy. But understand what I mean. I was with Fuller at Clervaux, when Cota wouldn't let us retreat. I'm never going to issue that command. I don't want to lose that road. But I don't want a bunch of soldiers with rifles trying to stop tanks. Fight like hell, as long as you can, but protect your men. Those are your orders."

I saluted.

I passed through our strongpoints, giving the password. Walking up, I encountered another member of Masi's platoon, Massimo Fortunato, a huge handsome lump, on guard duty. An immigrant, Massimo claimed to have lived in Boston "long time," but he spoke barely a word of English. Even Masi, who said he knew Italian, generally communicated with Massimo by hand signals like everybody else. Fortunato had come in as a replacement, but one with combat experience, which meant that he was not subject to the usual ridicule. He had fought through North Africa and Italy, until a sympathetic commander transferred him to Europe, following an incident in which Fortunato believed he was firing at a boy he'd grown up with.

I asked Fortunato if all was quiet.

"Quite," he answered. "Good quite."

I went back to the pump house to find Meadows. O'Brien was helping Collison with a letter home, writing down what Stocker told him, sometimes framing the words for him. Bill and I agreed that he'd send a scout team across the road to assess our new position. After that, we'd give the men orders to pack up. Bill went out to make the assignment, as Biddy's platoon was filtering in.

"Think we'll ever have a worse Christmas, Captain?" Biddy's second-in-command, a PFC named Forrester, asked me.

"Hope not."

"Nah. Next Christmas, we'll be dead or the war'll be over. Right?"

"It'll be over. You'll be home. That'll be your best Christmas, then."

He nodded. "That'd be nice. I'm not sure I ever had a best Christmas." I didn't say anything, but I'm sure my face reflected my curiosity. "I was adopted, Captain. Old man got it at Verdun. My mother, she ran out of gas somehow. Some friends of my aunt's took me in. They had six other kids in that house. I don't know what made them do it. Good sods, I guess. Irish, you know. Only Christmas, somehow, that was always strange. They were Catholic, went to midnight Mass. My family was Scotch-German, Presbyterians. Not such a big deal, but Christmas would get me thinking. These here ain't my real brothers. Ma and Pa ain't my real ma and pa. Adopted like that, Captain, at that age, it didn't seem there was anything real in my life. Not like for other people." He looked at me again. I couldn't think of anything to do but clap him on the arm, yet the gesture drew a smile.

When I returned to our forward position, I wrote letters to my parents and to Grace, as I had in the hours before we'd attacked La Saline Royale, just on the chance the messages might somehow reach them if worse came to worst. Writing to Grace was getting harder. I knew what to say, but I seemed to mean less of it each day. It was not my stupidity with Gita Lodz, either. Instead, there was something about my feelings for Grace that seemed to suit me less and less. After standing there with

Hovler, thinking about whether Grace could do me wrong, I now experienced a pinch of regret that stepping out was beyond her, since it might even have been for the best.

While I was writing, I gradually became aware of music. The German troops were in the woods singing Christmas carols, the voices traveling down to us on the wind. Many of the tunes were familiar, despite the foreign tongue, whose words I could make out here and there because of my limited Yiddish. *"Stille Nacht,"* they sang, *"Heilige Nacht."* Rudzicke scrambled up to my hole.

"Captain, I was going to sing, too," he said. "A lot of us wanted to. Seeing as how we're moving out anyway."

I debated, undertaking the unfamiliar arithmetic of pluses and minuses that an experienced combat officer probably had reduced to instinct. Would I mislead the Germans about our position in the morning, or give something away? With an assault in the offing, could I deny the men one meager pleasure of Christmas? And how to cope with the ugly worm of hope that this demonstration of fellowship might make the Krauts less savage at daybreak?

"Sing," I told him. And so as we packed up, G Company sang, even me. Christmas was nothing in my house, a nonevent, and I felt as a result that I was not a participant in the festival of fellowship and good feeling that Christmas was everywhere else. But now I sang. We sang with our enemies. It went on nearly an hour, and then there was silence again, awaiting the attack which all the soldiers on both sides knew was coming.

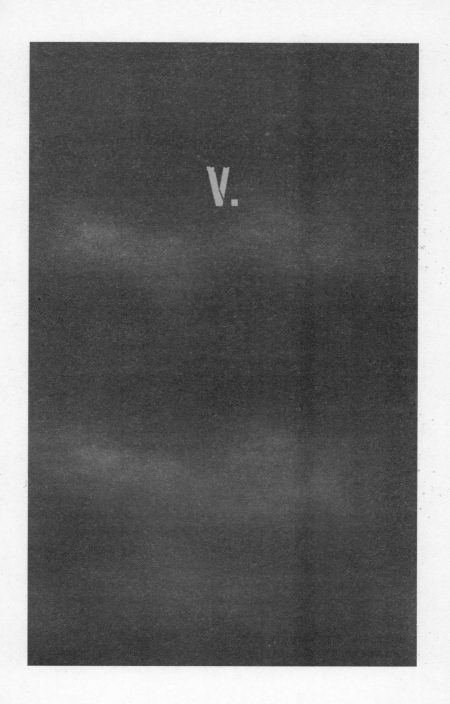

V.

20. DON'T TELL THE CHILDREN

ong after I first read what my father had written for Barrington Leach, one question preoccupied me: Why had Dad said he desperately hoped his kids would never hear this story? Granted the tale ended with what I viewed as an episode of heartbreaking gullibility, not to mention dead-bang criminality. But there were oceans of valor before that. What did Dad want to protect us from? I would have thought he'd learned too much to believe that anybody could be harbored from the everlasting universe of human hurt at human hands. Instead, Dad's decision to suppress everything could be taken only as the product of his shuttered character, and one more occasion for regret. God knows, it would have meant the world to me at a hundred points as I grew up to know even a little of what he had written.

Like every boy my age, soaked during the 1950s in World War II epics on TV and in the movie houses, I had longed to know that my daddy had done his part—best if he were another Audie Murphy, but at least someone who'd brought his rightful share of glory to our household. Instead my questions about the war were perpetually rebuffed by both parents.

The silence was so complete that I didn't even know whether Dad had seen action. I believed he had, because of the profound stillness that gripped him when battle scenes from WWII appeared on *The Way It Was*, my father's favorite show. It was TV's first video history, hosted by the sage and solemn Eric Sevareid. I would watch the black-and-white images leap across my father's unmoving eyes. There were always artillery pieces firing with great flashes, their barrels rifling back and mud splattering as the massive armaments recoiled into the ground, while aircraft circled in the distance overhead. The grimy soldiers, caught in the camera's light, managed fleeting smiles. It became an article of faith to me that Dad had been one of them, a claim I often repeated when my male friends matched tales of their fathers' wartime exploits.

Yet all I knew for sure was that both my parents regarded war as a calamity which they often prayed would never be visited on Sarah and me. No one was more determined than my father and mother that I not go to Vietnam when my number came up in 1970. They were ready to hire lawyers, even leave the country, rather than allow me to be drafted. The sight of Richard Nixon on TV inspired Dad to a rare sputtering fury. He seemed to feel a basic deal America had made with him was being broken. Simply put, he had gone to war so that his children would not have to, not so they could take their turn.

But that period might have been less unsettling for me if I'd known a little more about my father's wartime experiences. At the U., among the antiwar types, there were occasional debates about the ethics of avoiding the draft. Logic said that some kid, working class or poor, was going to take my place. Four decades later, I still accept my rationale for wiggling out with a medical exemption due to a deviated septum, a breach between my nasal passages, which, in theory, might have led to breathing problems on the battlefront. My first responsibility was for my own actions. Understanding how misguided Vietnam was, I faced a clear moral imperative against killing—or even dying—there.

But for those of us who didn't go, there was always a lurking question. Granted, we were privileged, moralistic, and often ridiculously rude. But were we also cowards? Certainly we had planted our flag in new ground. Before 'Nam, the idea had been handed down since the Revolution, like some Chippendale heirloom, that braving death in defense of the nation was the ultimate measure of a true-blue American guy. Knowing a few details of how my father had passed this fierce test of patriotism and personal strength might have given me some comfort that I could do it, too, if need be, and made me more certain I was standing up, rather than hiding.

Instead, the only story about my father's war I ever heard came from his father, my grandfather the cobbler. Grandpa was a wonderful raconteur in the Yiddish tradition and, when Dad was not around, he told me more than once the colorful tale of how my father had entered the service. In 1942, after Dad had decided he could no longer wait to do his part, he had gone for his induction physical and been promptly rejected because of the deviated septum I ended up inheriting from him (and which, when I faced the draft, he wisely suggested I ask an ENT to check for).

My father was so upset at being turned down that he finally persuaded my grandfather to go with him to visit Punchy Berg, the local Democratic committeeman, who was able to influence the course of most governmental affairs in Kindle County. Punchy received entreaties in the basement of a local county office, where boxes of records were stacked on steel shelving. There beneath a single lightbulb, Punchy sat among his henchmen at a teacher's desk while he pondered requests. He either said no, or nothing at all. In the face of silence, one of Punchy's sidekicks would step forward and whisper a price—$5 to allow a child to transfer to a better school, $15 to get a driver's license after failing the exam. Favorable verdicts in the Kindle County courts were also available, but at costs beyond the means of workingmen.

My father stood before Punchy and poured his heart out about not being allowed to serve his country. Punchy had expected something else, a request, of which there were a number, that a draft notice be delayed or, better yet, forgotten. My grandfather said that Punchy, a former boxer whose nose was flattened on his face like the blade of a shovel, spent a minute shaking his head.

"I'll tell you, kid. Maybe you want to think about this. I know your old man a long time. Schmuel, how long it's been you fixed my shoes?"

My grandfather could not remember that far back.

"A long time," Punchy said. "You're the firstborn son. That makes you an important guy to your folks."

This remark provided the only encouragement my grandfather needed to let fly with his own opinions about what my father wanted. It was pure craziness to Grandpa's way of thinking. He had come here to America, like his brothers, so that they did not get dragooned for the Tsar's army, as Jews so often were. And now his son wanted to go back across the same ocean and fight, beside the Russians no less?

"Your old man's got a point," Punchy allowed.

My father was adamant.

"Well," said Punchy, "this is hard to figure. How I hear tell, it's costing families twelve hundred to keep their sons out. But gettin in?" Punchy rubbed his chin. "All right, kid," he said. "I gotta tell you. I'm pretty red, white, and blue myself. Half the time I'm cryin that I'm too old to go over there and take a bite out of Hitler's dick. In you want, in you get." And then Punchy proved what a true patriot he was. "Kid," he said, "it's on the house."

21. COMBAT

Dear Grace —

I am writing to wish you and your family a wonderful Christmas holiday. I imagine all of you together, cozy around a fire, but perhaps that's just to comfort myself, because right now I'm colder than I have ever been in my life. At the moment, I'm convinced we should honeymoon in Florida and I am trying to warm myself up by imagining that.

I assume news of the German offensive has reached you, but the commanders here are encouraging. This is magnificent, scenic country, tremendous hills of trees, deep with snow, and beautiful little towns nestled between, but combat has blown many of them to smithereens. I arrived as part of the investigation I have mentioned now and then, and given the circumstances have actually been pressed into combat as the leader of a rifle company. Finally, a chance to put that training to good use! At last I'll have a little story or two to tell you and our children.

Please give my warm regards to your family. I assume you will
be praying tonight. I'm not much of a prayer-sayer myself, so
please put in a few extra for me, fortissimo. I want all the help we
can get.

Well, that's enough blabbing for tonight. Remember I love
you, darling.

David

At 2:00 a.m., we moved out on the route the scout team had traced along the edge of the forest, following their tracks in the snow. Orders went down the line in a whisper. "Scouts out first in each squad. Patrol discipline. Silence. Move fast and low. Don't lose sight of the man in front of you."

In all, we advanced about four hundred yards to another incline on the eastern side of the road, settling in a small notch in the forest. It was not as good a position as the one we had deserted. We were about thirty yards from the roadside here, and even when we fanned out, we could not really see well to the north. A small creek was east of us, however, a good defensive perimeter. It must have been fed by an underground spring, because it was still running, even in the intense cold.

There had been no prior encampment here, which meant the men had to dig in through the snow and the frozen ground. It was hard work and we agreed we'd assign four soldiers to each hole, and let them sleep in shifts. Bidwell and I were still shoveling with our entrenching tools when Masi came up. He turned his angle-necked flashlight on to show me a German ration can. There was no rust on it, and the streaks of the meat that had clung to the side hadn't frozen yet.

"There was a pile of shit no more than ten yards away from it, Cap. Hot enough to have melted a little hole in the snow, and still soft when I put a stick to it."

I took the can to Meadows.

"Where are they?" I asked Bill.

"Back there somewhere," he said, pointing to the woods half a mile off. "Probably just following up on the scout plane, Captain. Good thing we changed position."

I wasn't as confident. The Krauts were paying a lot of attention to us, if they didn't intend to come down this road. We agreed we'd send out scouts at first light to follow the tracks and get a fix on the German forces. We also doubled tonight's guard. That was better anyway, given our shortage of deluxe accommodations.

Despite my concerns, I was calm. I seemed to have simply worn out my nervous system, subsiding to the resignation true soldiers acquire. If it happens, it happens. I slept for an hour or so, until heavy booms woke me, and I saw the light dancing up from Bastogne. The Germans were bombing there, giving General McAuliffe a Christmas present after the warm greetings he had sent them. The air assault went on about twenty minutes.

I fell off again before Biddy shook me awake for guard duty an hour later. I had been dreaming of home. There, it was the usual chaos. I was knocking at the front door and could not get in. But through the window I had a clear view of my parents and my sister and brother around the kitchen table. My mother, stout, voluble, enveloping, was ladling soup, and through the glass I could somehow enjoy the warmth and fragrance from the bowls she placed on the table. When the image returned to me now, I emitted the minutest moan.

"What?" asked Biddy. He was climbing into his bedroll. There was already some light in the sky, but we'd all been up most of the night. In the distance, the German artillery was pounding already. The Krauts were at work early.

I told him I had been dreaming of home.

"Don't do that," he said. "Best I can, sir, I try to never let my mind go runnin off in that direction. Just makes a body feel badly." That had been Martin's reasoning with Gita.

"You figure you'll go back home, Biddy? I mean afterward. You know. To stay?" I'd been deciding whether to ask this question for the last couple of days.

"You mean, am I gonna go back home and be myself? Who I was? Or go any other place and be who I am to you?"

That was what I meant. His big body swelled up and deflated with a long sigh.

"Captain, I been thinking on that so long, I'm just plain sick of it. Truth, Cap, I don't mind this here at all, not being every white man's nigger. It's okay—most of the time. Over there in England, lot of those English girls preferred the colored soldiers, said they was more polite, and I was trying to make time with one and she slapped my cheek when I said I was a Negro. Aside from that, it's been all right.

"But I can't go home and not claim my own. I can't go walking down the street pretending like I don't know the fellas I do, men I played ball with and chased around with, I can't do that. That boy I was having words with last week—that's what it was about, and I wanted to crawl into a hole after you lit into me. I can't hardly do that. And I can't turn tail on the folks who love me neither. I'll go back. That's what I reckon. But no matter what, Captain, it ain't gonna feel right."

"It won't make any difference, Biddy. You go back, get some more schooling for your photography. It won't make any difference."

"Captain, you don't really believe that."

"I do indeed, Biddy. I know what it's been like. But we can't take up the same stupidity now. Here we've had Southerners and Northerners, rich and poor, immigrants from every nation, fighting and dying for this country. People can't go back home and tell themselves we're all different when we're not. You be your own man, Biddy, nobody's ever going to judge you, white or colored."

"Captain," he said. He stopped to think, then started again. "Captain, I want you to know something. You're a good man, all right, you truly are. You're as straight and honest an officer as I've met. And you ain't hincty—you don't get up on yourself too much. But Captain, you don't know what the hell you're talking about now. That's the last we-all gonna say on this."

I had no chance to argue further because the first artillery shell came wailing in then. It landed about two hundred feet away, rocking the earth and igniting a plume of flame that irradiated the near darkness. I rose, still without my boots, and hollered for everyone to get down, just in time to witness another detonation that hurled a private at the perimeter into a thick tree, shoulder first. It was Hovler, the Texan who'd worried about his girl stepping out on him. The sheer force threw his arms and legs behind his back so hard that they wrapped around the trunk, before he slithered down in dead collapse.

What followed was twice the intensity of the TOT barrages. This was not random shelling at thirty-yard intervals from converted light AA or mortars. This was fire from bigger German guns, the 88s and even the heavy loads of Nebelwerfers, all precisely targeted and seeming to cover every inch of the forest incline we occupied. On impact, the ordnance spit up flames and snow and soil in the dark like giant Roman candles. Slumping back, tying my boots, listening to the outcry all around me, I realized that the Germans knew exactly where we were, despite our move. The earth rocked and things went flying the way they did in the newsreels of tornadoes—rifles, soldiers, and tree trunks zooming through the air in the orange light of the explosions and the resulting fires. Chunks of steel sizzled as they sank into the trees, from which smoke, like blood, leaked forth. But the noise, as ever, was the worst of it, the whistling metal raining down, the titanic boom of the shells, and the seconds in between when the panicked voices of my men reached me, shrieking in anguish, yelling for medics, begging for help. Peeking out, I saw direct hits on two holes at the far perimeter and the soldiers, already dead, flying toward me. In the uneven light, one of them, Bronko Lukovic, the poker champion, seemed to break apart in descent. He landed twenty yards from me on his back. His arms and legs were spread as if he was floating in a pool in the sun, but his head was gone, a bloody mess sprouting from his neck like the teased ribbon on a gift box.

"Move 'em out," I started screaming. I clambered from the hole, waving my arms, giving orders to Biddy and Masi, and Forrester. Bill Meadows, unaccountably, was nowhere to be found. I located him, blundering around in his hole on his hands and knees.

"Lost my specs, Captain, I'm blind without those specs." I jumped in, groping with him for an instant, then climbed back out, running from hole to hole to get the men in his platoon moving. By now I knew that if we didn't go, most of us would be blown to bits, and the remainder killed in the ground assault that was sure to follow. Even so, a couple of soldiers had lost control of themselves in the relentless bombardment. In one hole, a private named Parnek was on his knees, sobbing hysterically, as he tried to claw a hole in the frozen ground with his fingers. Another man in his squad, Frank Schultz, wouldn't leave because he couldn't find his helmet.

"Where's my hat," he yelled, "where's my hat?" I grabbed him by the shoulders to tell him it was on his head. He touched it and fled.

With the creek behind us, we could only go toward the road, and as we tumbled off the incline, I could hear the roar of tanks approaching. My men dashed forward, including the wounded who were mobile.

O'Brien, the wiseacre from Baltimore, was hobbling behind me. His whole lower leg was gone, even the trousers, and he was using his M1 as a crutch. As we broke into the clearing, I was following Biddy and his platoon, and his troops were suddenly falling to their bellies in front of me. My instinct was to order them back to their feet until I found myself facing the black mouth of a 75mm tank gun aimed at us from no more than one hundred yards. As I crushed myself against the snow, a rocket went right over our heads, exploding in the midst of the holes we'd just left. Most of Meadows' platoon was still back there and I could hear the shrieking. On our left, a machine gun began barking, joined almost immediately by rifle fire from the foxholes we'd abandoned last night across the way. There were two tanks in the road now, both Mark IVs that had been painted white, their big guns flashing and recoiling as they spit shells into the woods. About fifteen infantrymen were riding on each tank and firing their rifles at us.

It was havoc. Fortunato was on his feet, looking on like a spectator, with the SCR-300 on his back. Who had given the radio to the man who couldn't speak English? Several of our soldiers were on the ground, doing nothing. "Shoot," I yelled, and raised my Thompson. I was sure no one could hear me, but on one of the tanks, a grenadier was struck and pitched forward into the snow. Ten feet to my left, Rudzicke, who'd wanted to sing Christmas carols, was hit in the back. The bullet left a clean hole that looked like it had been sunk by a drill bit. From the way he jerked forward, I was afraid he'd been shot by one of my troops, but the Germans had fallen upon us from all directions and the men had no idea even where to aim. Behind us, in the woods, grenades exploded, and in the fires burning back there, I recognized Volksgrenadiers, regular infantry who'd been able to sneak close in white snow-combat suits. They were cleaning out those of Meadows' men who'd remained in their foxholes. Amid the machine-gun and small-arms fire, there was a great jumble of voices, buddies crying out directions, but also men screaming in pain and terror. Stocker Collison teetered by, blood-soaked hands over his abdomen. I had the impression that he was holding a cauliflower against his uniform until I realized that the blue-white mass was his intestines.

Biddy had his bazooka team taking aim at the tanks, but they got off no more than one round before a grenade landed in their midst. I wanted Masi to return with his platoon to attack the grenadiers in the trees to our rear, but he went down as soon as I reached him. It was a leg wound, but a bad one. Blue-black blood surged forth with every heartbeat. He cast me a desperate look, but by the time I thought of applying a tourniquet he had fallen backward. There were two final feeble squirts and then it stopped completely.

When the crossfire had started, probably two-thirds of the company had emerged from the woods, strung out over forty yards. At least half had gone down in no more than a minute. Amid the great tumult, I turned full circle. The sun was coming up and in the first hard light the world was etched with a novel clarity, as if everything visible was outlined in black. It was like that moment of impact I'd felt once or twice in a museum, but more intense, for I was beholding the gorgeousness of living.

Somehow, in that instant, I understood our sole option. Algar had told me not to surrender, a point proven by the slaughter behind me in the woods. Instead I dashed and rolled among the men, yelling one command again and again, "Play dead, play dead, play dead." Each of them fell almost at once, and I too tumbled down with my face in the snow. After a few minutes the firing stopped. I could hear the explosive engine roar of Panzers thundering by and orders being shouted in German. Not surprisingly, Algar seemed to have been good to his word. The rocking blast of mortars was nearby. I gathered that Algar had brought his armor up fast and had apparently engaged the Panzers a mile farther down, where machine-gun fire and the boom of the tank rockets was audible. Near us, I could make out different engines, probably armored troop carriers, into which the unit that had killed most of my men seemed to climb to join the battle up the road. Even as the shouts sailed off, two grenades exploded in the broad clearing where we lay, rattling the earth and leaving more men screaming.

That was the principal sound now, men moaning and crying. Stocker Collison was calling out, "Mama, Mama," a lament that had been going on for some time. The wounded were going to die fast in this weather. Soaked in their own blood, they would freeze soon, a process that would accelerate due to their blood loss. When the last German voice disappeared, I hoped to find the radio.

I was about to get up, when a single shot rang out, a parched sound like a breaking stick. The pricks had left a sniper behind, at least one, who'd probably fired when somebody else moved. I thought of calling out a warning, even though it would have given me away, but that would reveal that many of the others lying here were alive. I could only hope the men would understand on their own.

Instead, to betray no sign of life, I worked on slowing my breathing. The smell, now that I was aware of it, was repulsive. No one ever told me there is a stench of battle, of cordite and blood, of human waste, and as time goes on, of death. I had chosen a terrible position—I was lying on the submachine gun and after only a few minutes the stock had begun to sink into my thigh, so that I was being bruised under my own weight. But I would have to bear it. In some ways I welcomed the pain as my just deserts as a failed commander. I wondered how the Germans had found us. Their scouts must have been out in the darkness and followed our tracks through the snow. They may even have seen us cross the road. I reviewed my decisions repeatedly. Should I have recognized there was such a large force out here? Would we have been better off, in the end, staying in the first foxholes and fighting from there? Could we have held the Krauts off longer, inflicted more losses? After days of suffering in the cold, we had not detained the Germans more than a few minutes as they came down the road.

I was freezing, of course. I had been freezing for days, but lying in the snow without moving was worse. My limbs burned as if my skin had been ignited from inside. Near me, someone moaned now and then for water and Collison was still asking for his mother. He went on for at least another hour and then a single sniper's bullet rang out and the calling stopped. I wondered if they'd shot him out of mercy or contempt. But within a second, there were several more bullets and a haunting punctured sound emerging from each man they struck. The snipers—I now thought there were two—seemed to be systematically picking off our wounded. I awaited my turn. I had gone through the entire battle, the few minutes it all had lasted, with no conscious fear, but now that I realized they were killing any man showing signs of life, I felt the full flush of terror. A thought struck through to the center of me like an ax: I was going to find out about God.

But I did not die. After five or six shots, the firing ceased. The wounded, at least those moaning or begging for water or help, had gone still, and there was now a harrowing silence in the clearing. I could hear the noises of the morning, the wind in the trees and crows calling. The submachine gun was still beneath me. From the last shots, I believed the snipers were across the road in the same woods we'd left. I had no idea how many men who lay here were still alive. Ten perhaps. But if we all stood and fired, we'd have a chance to kill the snipers before they killed us. Those would be my orders if the sharp-shooting started again.

With no voices here, the fighting down the road was more audible. The rumbling explosions echoed and reechoed between the hills. Late in the morning, the drone of aircraft joined it and bombs shook the air. I hoped we were dropping on the Panzers, but couldn't be certain.

Several hours along, I opened my eyes briefly. Near me Forrester, who'd been abandoned by his widowed mother, was jackknifed. A ragged bullet hole was ripped in the back of his neck. His carotids had emptied through it, staining his jacket, and he'd messed his trousers as he was dying, an odor I'd smelled for quite some time. But I hadn't looked out to count the dead around me, or even the living. With the planes aloft, I knew the sky was clearing, and I longed for one last sight of that fresh blue, so full of promise. I looked while I dared, then closed my eyes. I missed the world already.

By now, my bladder was aching. Urine, however, would eat through the snow and potentially give me away to the snipers. More important, I was likely to soak myself and freeze to death. For a while, I decided to count, only to know time was passing. Finally, I thought about the people at home. Lying there, I was full of regret about Gita. For weeks, I had been too confused to feel the full measure of shame that visited me now. It was the images of my morning dream that haunted me, a tender rebuke. I wanted home. I wanted a warm place that was mine, a woman within it, and children, too. I saw that spot, a neat bungalow, from outside, as clearly as if I were at the picture show. The light, so bright through the broad front window, beckoned. I could feel the warmth of the house, of the fire that burned there, of the life that was lived there.

Someone broke through the trees. Had the Germans come to finish us? But the tread was lighter, and too quick. Eventually I concluded an animal was lingering among us, some carrion eater, I feared, meaning I would have to lie here while it gnawed the dead. At last the footfalls reached me. I recognized the heat and smell of the breath on my face instantly, and had to work to hold off a smile as the dog applied his cold snout to my cheek. But my amusement quickly sluiced away in fear. I wondered if the Krauts were using the animal for recon. Could the dog tell the quick from the dead or was he sent to test our reactions? I refused to move although I could feel the mutt circling me. He lowered his muzzle yet again for a breath or two, then suddenly whimpered in that heartbreaking way dogs do. I could hear him padding around, nosing among the men. He cried out one more time, then went off.

Late in the afternoon, the battle appeared to shift toward us. I reasoned it through. We were winning. We had to be winning. There was gunfire only a few hundred yards away, on the western side of the road where we'd been yesterday. That meant Americans were nearby. An hour later, I heard English on the wind and debated whether to cry out. As soon as it was dark, I decided, we'd move.

When I opened my eyes again, it was dusk. Forty minutes later, the light was gone and I began to drag myself on my elbows through the clearing. I wanted to crawl toward the Americans, but the snipers' shots had come from there, and so I crept back to the woods where so many members of G Company had been slaughtered this morning. I was slithering on my belly into a black maze, through the snow and blood and shit and God knows what else, thinking in my brain-stuck way about the serpent in Eden.

I touched each body I passed. It was easy to tell the living, even with a gloved hand that was like lead. In the dark, I could see eyes spring open, and I pointed to the woods. I reached a form I recognized as Biddy's and hesitated. Please, I thought. He was alive.

I dragged myself around for nearly an hour, gathering the men who were able to move, and sending them scraping toward the woods, like a nighttime migration of turtles. Covered in sweat now, I'd worn the skin off my elbows and knees. I could make out the trees ahead of me, but stopped when I suddenly heard voices. Germans? After all of this we were crawling back into the arms of the Krauts? But I was too miserable to devise alternatives. Nearing the border of the woods, I realized someone was creeping toward me. I grabbed my gun while the other form continued forward on his belly. Then I saw the Red Cross on his helmet.

"Can you make it?" he whispered.

When I reached the trees, two more medics swept forward to grab me. As I stood up, the urge from my bladder overwhelmed me and I barely made it to a beech where I relieved myself, savoring the warm fog rising in the cold. I had a terrible cramp in one leg, and feared I would fall over and look like a fountain.

The medics explained the situation. The Germans who had passed by here had been routed. McAuliffe had brought up reinforcements and the firefight went on long enough for American bombers to get here and blow all of the Panzers off the road. More than one hundred grenadiers had surrendered, but one band had fallen back into the trees on the other side of the road. Algar was going to call in artillery, but he'd demanded that the medics first try to collect the survivors of G Company. The corpsmen had driven jeeps down the cow path from the west, then walked in nearly a quarter of a mile before they made out the dozen or so of us bellying our way through the snow.

Here, in what remained of the foxholes we'd been in this morning, the medics moved among the dead with gruesome efficiency, checking wrists and throats for the sign of a pulse, and when that was lacking, as it almost always was, pulling the dog tags through the shirtfronts to make work easier for those in the Quartermaster Corps Graves Registration Detail. With the medics, I talked about how to bring in the wounded still out in the open. We had to figure there were Germans in the woods across the road, but the medics understood I couldn't leave without the eight men I'd found in the clearing, still breathing but unable to move. Biddy and I crawled back out with two corpsmen. We formed litters by retying each man's belt under his arms, then peeling his field jacket back over his head and folding his rifle within the fabric. One of the medics gave a signal and I stood up first and began dragging the man I had, O'Brien, toward the trees. I waited to die, yet again, but after even a few yards, it was clear there was no one on the other side now, at least no one willing to give himself away by shooting. As I dragged O'Brien along, the dog followed.

From the woods, the corpsmen radioed for a convoy and ambulances, which met us on the other side of the creek where the cow path joined the woods. In the lights of the vehicles, I caught sight of a C ration cracker in cellophane lying unharmed in the snow. I broke it in pieces and passed it out to the three other men who were waiting with me. We ate this morsel in total silence.

"Damn," one of them, Hank Garns, finally said.

We were back at Algar's headquarters in minutes and ushered into the cold barn. There were thirteen of us. Counting the wounded, twenty-two men in G Company had made it, out of the ninety-two we'd had at the start of the day. Meadows and Masi were dead.

"Jesus, that was rough," said a dark man named Jesse Tornillo. "We came in on our chinstraps."

"Yeah," said Garns. "Guess you're right. Hadn't noticed till you mentioned it." Garns was smiling and seemed to take no notice that his entire body was rattling as if he had a mortal chill.

"Captain," said Tornillo, "it might be that mutt of yours saved our lives." I had not registered that the animal had followed me inside but he was looking around the circle as if he could follow the conversation, a black mongrel with a brown star on his chest and one brown paw. "When he started in with that whimpering, maybe he made those snipers think we were all of us dead." Tornillo bent to scratch the dog's ears. "Saved our lives," he said. "How you like that? I was laying there, listenin to him scratch around. Soon as I figured out it was a dog, hombre, I was praying for just one thing. 'Oh, Lord,' I kept sayin, 'if these Krauts gotta shoot me, please don't let this damn pooch piss on my head before that.'"

We laughed, all of us, huge gusts of laughter, full of the sweet breath of life. As for the dead, there was no mention of them now. They were, in a word, gone. I didn't doubt that these men, some of whom had been together for months, mourned. But there was no place in our conversation for that. They were dead. We were alive. It wasn't luck or the order of the universe. It was simply what had happened.

Algar came in then and I gave him my report.

"Good thinking, good thinking," Algar kept saying when I admitted how we'd survived by playing dead.

"It was an ambush, Colonel."

By now we both knew that G Company had been given a suicidal assignment. We did not have enough men or firepower to hold that road, no matter what our position. I didn't say that, but I didn't have to.

"Dubin," Algar said, "I'm sorry. I am the sorriest son of a bitch in the Army."

I went to the battalion aid station to check on the wounded from G, but they were already on the way back to the field hospital by ambulance. There were doctors in Bastogne now, four surgeons who'd landed this morning by glider.

When I returned, Algar had found the cooks and ordered them to re-open the mess to serve us Christmas dinner. We had fried Spam and de-hydrated potatoes, with dehydrated apples for dessert. As a treat, there were a few fresh beets. We'd eaten one meal in the last two days, and I felt the full measure of my hunger as the heat and aroma of the food rose up to my face. I count that Christmas meal in that cold mess eaten off a tin plate as one of my life's culinary highlights.

Biddy sat down beside me. We didn't say much while we ate, but he turned to me once he was done.

"No disrespect to the dog, Captain, but it was you that saved our lives."

A couple of the other men murmured agreement. But I wanted no part of being treated as a hero. There were isolated instants when I had actually led my men, scrambling from hole to hole amid the initial ar-tillery barrage, even when I waved them so disastrously into the clearing. In those moments, a tiny voice trapped somewhere in my heart had spo-ken up in utter amazement. Look at me, it said, I'm commanding. Or more often: Look at me, I didn't get hit. But I held no illusion that was fundamentally me. We can all play a part for a few minutes. But I was not like Martin—and it was he I thought of—able to do it again and again.

The real David Dubin had fallen to the earth and played dead, where he had eventually surrendered to terror. I had given my men sav-ing advice mostly because it was what I had wanted to do, to lie down like a child and hope that the assault—the war—would be over soon. True, it was the wiser course. But I had taken it because at the center of my soul, I was a coward. And for this I was now being saluted. I was grate-ful only that I did not feel shocked at myself or overwhelmed with shame. I knew who I was.

The men began to talk a little about what had happened, especially the eight or nine hours we had lain in the snow.

"Praise God, man, these are the shortest days of the year."

"Lord, poor fucking Collison, huh? I ain't gonna sleep for three nights hearing that."

But as I sat there, finishing off my dinner, my will, indeed all that re-mained of my being, was summoned in a single desire: I was going to make sure I never set foot on a battlefield again.

22. THE REMAINS

My wish to avoid combat, like so many other wishes I made, did not come true. There were more battles, but never another day like Christmas. Patton's forces continued pushing on Bastogne from the south, and more and more supplies made it through. Like an eager audience, we cheered the sight of every truck carrying cases of C rations bound in baling wire, the brown-green ammo boxes, or the gray cardboard tubes containing mortar and bazooka rounds.

On December 27, the 110th was re-formed with elements of the 502nd Parachute Infantry Regiment. Algar became battalion commander. G Company was now E Company, but I remained in charge. With six days in combat, I was one of the more experienced field officers Algar had. A second lieutenant named Luke Chester, literally a month out of OCS, became my second-in-command. He was a fine young soldier, a serious man, who spent most of his free time reading the Bible. But he was not Bill Meadows.

We pushed farther down the road through Champs, where so many of my men had died, then swung north and east into Longchamps. Although it did not seem possible, the weather was worse, less snow, but the kind of brittle, devastating cold that had seemed liable to snap the ears off my head in high school. However, our assignments allowed us to be quartered indoors for a portion of most nights. Algar protected my company. We were not the forward element on many operations. Instead, we generally followed armored infantry, covering the flanks. We fought brief battles, two or three times a day, knocking back smaller German units, repelling commandos, securing positions other forces had already overrun, and often taking prisoners, whom we'd hold until the MPs arrived.

But it was war. We still entered scenes that, as Biddy had characterized them, seemed to have come from the *Inferno*: the dead with their faces knotted in anguish, weeping soldiers immobilized by fear, vehicles ablaze with the occupants sometimes still screaming inside, soldiers without limbs lying within vast mud-streaked halos of their own blood, and others careening about, blinded by wounds or pain.

Every morning, I awoke to the same sick instant when I realized I was here fighting. I thought the same things so often that they were no longer thoughts at all. The questions simply circulated through my brain with the blood.

Why was I born?

Why do men fight?

Why must I die now, before living my life?

These questions had no answers and that fact often brought pain. It was like running full tilt again and again at a wall. The only comfort— and it was a small one—was that I saw these thoughts passing behind the eyes of every man I knew. They danced, like skinny ballerinas, across the thin membrane that separated everything from a molten surface, which was my constant fear.

I nearly did not make it to 1945. We were throwing the Germans back, inch by inch, but the control of terrain remained extremely confused. The Nazi lines, once drawn so tight around Bastogne, had been shredded, but not always with sufficient force to fully subdue the Krauts. On the maps, the intermingled American and German positions looked like the webbed fingers of joined hands.

On December 31, Algar sent us out to secure a hill on the other side of Longchamps. Our artillery had rained down already, and the enemy figured to have retreated, but as the first platoon started up, shots snapped in from above. Two men died and two were wounded. I was in the rear, but I scrambled forward to order everyone to dig in. A shot rang off a stone near my feet. I saw the German who had been shooting. He was up the hill, perhaps two hundred yards from me, peeking out from behind an outhouse in his large green coat with its high collar and the helmet that I still thought made every Kraut look half comic, as if he was wearing a coal scuttle. As he watched me through his rifle sight, I could see that killing me was a crisis for him. I had the nerve somehow to nod in his direction, and then scurried off on all fours, leaving the German infantryman little time to think. When I looked back, he was gone. I promised myself that I would spare one of them when the shoe was on the other foot. I tried to work out how fast the phenomenon of troops giving grace to one another would have to spread before the men in combat had made an armistice of their own.

I killed, of course. I remember a machine-gun nest we had surrounded, pouring in fire. A German soldier literally bounced along on the ground every time my bullets struck him, almost as if I was shooting a can. Each of these deaths seemed to enhance the power of the Thompson .45 submachine gun with which I'd parachuted, and which Robert Martin had borrowed, so that I sometimes felt as if I'd lifted a magic wand when I raised the weapon.

By now, I also thought I was developing animal senses. I knew the Germans were nearby even when they could not yet be seen or heard. In that instant before combat began, I passed down a bizarre passageway. Life, which had seemed so settled, so fully within my grasp, had to be renounced. I would now shoot my way across a bridge between existence and nonexistence. That, I realized mournfully, was what war was. Not life-essential, as I'd somehow believed, but a zone of chaos between living and dying. And then the bullets would fly and I would fire back.

On New Year's Day, after we'd turned east toward Recogne, we came upon a few advance scouts, Waffen troops. There were only four of them. They'd been hiding behind a crisscross of felled pines in the forest, and should have let us pass whatever their intentions, whether to ambush us or simply to report our whereabouts. Instead one of them spooked and fired at first sight of our uniforms. The four were no match for a company. Three were dead after less than a minute of fighting, while several of my men saw the fourth scout stumbling off into the brush. Reaching the three corpses, we could see the blood trail the fleeing German had left, and I dispatched Biddy's platoon to find him before the man got back to his unit.

When Bidwell returned half an hour later, he was morose.

"Bled to death, Cap. He was just laid out in the snow, with his blue eyes wide open, lookin at this here in his hand." Biddy showed me a tiny snap the size of the ones he was always taking, but this was of the German soldier's family, his thin wife and his two little boys, whom he'd been staring at as he died.

On January 2, 1945, E Company received reinforcements, nearly thirty men, all newly arrived replacements. I hated them, with the same intensity my men had hated me only a few days ago. I could barely stand to command these troops. I hated being responsible for them and knowing how much danger they were destined to expose us to. One of them, Teddy Wallace from Chicago, told anybody who'd listen that he had a family at home. Fathers had been the last drafted and he worried aloud about what would become of his sons if something happened to him, as if the rest of us didn't have people who loved us and needed us, too. His first action required his platoon to clean out a German mortar team. Two squads had surrounded the position and then tossed in a grenade. When I arrived, I found Wallace on the ground. After falling on a rock, he had pulled his pants leg up to study the bruise, rubbing it repeatedly, while two men with bullet wounds groaned within feet of him.

He died the next day. We were trapped in the woods, while inching our way north and east toward Noville. The artillery again had devastated the German position, but two snipers had climbed into the trees, trying to shoot down on us as if they were hunting deer. In the process, they made themselves insanely vulnerable, but rather than trying to lob bazooka rounds at them, I radioed for tank support, and ordered my men to dig in on the other side of one of those thick-walled Belgian farmhouses. Suddenly, Wallace stood up, as if it was a new day and he was getting out of bed. I don't know what he figured, that the snipers were disposed of, or perhaps the battlefield had simply gotten to him. In the instant I saw him, he looked as if he had a question in mind, but a shot ripped all the features off his face. A buddy pulled him down. I thought

Wallace was now going back to his family, albeit without a nose or mouth, but when I crawled up later, he was gone. I wrote to his wife and sons that night, describing his bravery.

In the wake of battle, one of the principal preoccupations of my company, like every fighting band, was collecting souvenirs. German firearms, Lugers and Mausers, were most prized, and everyone, including me, eventually acquired one. One of the men found a good Zeiss photographic lens and gave it to Biddy. My troops also removed wristwatches, flags, pennants, armbands—and cut off ears, until I put a stop to that. I understood this trophy hunting, the desire to have some tangible gain for what they had been through.

The day that Wallace went down, after two Sherman tanks had arrived and blown up the trees where the German snipers had perched, I watched another replacement soldier, Alvin Liebowitz, approach Wallace's body. I hated Liebowitz most among my new men. He was a lean boy, red-haired, with that New York air of knowing every angle. During several of the brief firefights we'd had, he'd seemed to disappear. Wallace and he had come over together, and I thought Liebowitz was reaching down to pass some kind of blessing. I was shocked when the sun gleamed before his hand disappeared into his pocket.

I came charging up.

"What?" Liebowitz said, with ridiculous feigned innocence.

"I want to see your right pocket, Liebowitz."

"What?" he said again, but pulled out Wallace's watch. He could have told me he was going to send it to Wallace's family, but then he might have had to hand it over. Alvin Liebowitz wasn't the kind to give up that easily.

"What the hell are you doing, Liebowitz?"

"Captain, I don't think Wallace here's going to be telling much time."

"Put it back, Liebowitz."

"Shit, Captain, there're guys over in the woods picking over the Krauts' bodies right now. Germans, Americans, what's the difference?"

"They're your dead, Liebowitz. That's all the difference in the world. That watch may be the only thing Wallace's sons ever have of their father's."

"Hell, this is a good watch, Captain. It'll disappear a long time before that body finds its way home."

That was Liebowitz. Smart-ass answers for everything. The Army was full of Liebowitzes, but he got under my skin to a degree unrivaled by any other man I'd commanded, and I felt a sudden fury that did not visit me even in battle. I lunged at him with my bayonet knife, and he barely jumped out of the way as he yelped.

"What the fuck's wrong with you?" he asked, but put the watch down. He went off, looking over his shoulder as if he was the aggrieved party.

Biddy had witnessed the incident. When we were settling in the empty train car where we billeted that night, he said, "That was dang good, Cap. Lot of the men liked seeing you put Liebowitz in his place, but it looked for all the world like you was actually gonna cut him."

"I meant to, Biddy. I just missed."

He gave me a long look. "I guess we all harder on our own, Captain."

By January 8, the battle had turned. Every day we were securing large chunks of the ground the Germans had taken back with their offensive. I woke that morning with a dream I'd had once or twice before, that I was dead. The wound, the weapon, the moment—I felt the bullet invade my chest and then my spirit hovering over my body. I watched the Graves Detail approach and take me. Fully awake, I could only say as everybody else did: Then that is what will happen.

It was Bidwell who had roused me inadvertently. He had my toothbrush sticking out of the corner of his mouth. We were quartered in a church school and Biddy, without apology, had taken a little water from a sacramental font.

"I dreamed I was dead, Biddy. Have you done that?"

"Captain, it ain't any other way to be out there but that." Then he pointed to the doorway, where a young private stood. He'd come to tell me that Lieutenant Colonel Algar wanted to see me on the other side of Noville.

Algar, as ever, was at his desk, looking at maps. He'd acquired a supply of narrow black cheroots and had one in his mouth whenever I saw him these days. He answered my salute, then pointed me to a canvasback chair.

"David, I got a teletype this morning from a Major Camello. He's General Teedle's adjutant, or assistant adjutant. They were trying to determine your whereabouts. When I answered you were here, he wrote back wanting to know when you could resume your assignment. They're concerned for your welfare."

They were concerned about Martin, at least Teedle was. I asked if he'd told them Martin was dead.

"I thought I'd leave that to you. Besides, you said you needed to see a body. I asked General Teedle for your services for one more week. We're going to be a long way toward kicking Dietrich out of the Ardennes by then. If things go well, I hope to be able to relieve your entire unit."

I found the thought of Teedle, still up in the middle of the night, still incensed as he thought about Martin, richly comic. I would have laughed, except that I knew I was going to get killed in the next seven days. That was a certainty. If I didn't, then it would be Biddy. But I said, "Yes, sir."

"You've done your part. There's a first lieutenant in A who's ready to take over a company. So I'm relieving you, effective January 15. You and Bidwell. You're to follow your prior orders and, when complete, report to General Teedle." The 18th Armored had met the 6th Panzers and contained them, and was now pushing them back. They were south of us in Luxembourg.

Algar said he'd have written orders in the morning. With them, we'd find he had put Bidwell and me in for medals. The Silver Star, he said. For our jump and for volunteering for combat.

"A Section Eight would be more appropriate," I said.

He said he felt a Distinguished Service Cross was actually in order, but that required an investigation which might reveal the condition of my trousers when I'd hit the ground in Savy.

We laughed and shook hands. I told him what a privilege it had been to serve under him.

"I'm going to look you up, if I get to Kindle County, David."

I promised to do the same when I was in New Jersey, another wish that went unfulfilled. Hamza Algar was killed in July 1945 in Germany, after the surrender, when his jeep ran over a mine. By then, 4,500 soldiers out of the 5,000 men in the 110th Regiment which had faced the first German assault of the Ardennes campaign along Skyline Drive were dead or wounded. So far as I know, Hamza Algar was the last casualty.

★★★

On the morning of January 15, Luke Chester assembled E Company and First Lieutenant Mike Como formally took command. It had been a hard week. The Germans seemed to be resisting Patton and the 11th Armored Division, behind whom we'd been fighting, with much greater ferocity than the armies of Montgomery and Hodges coming down from the north. I think Dietrich was unwilling to abandon his dream of capturing Bastogne, or perhaps he simply wanted to waste his last fury on the forces that had stopped him. My company lost six more men that week, and suffered thirteen wounded, all but four seriously. But there would be no casualties now for a few days. Most of the infantry elements in the 502nd, including E Company, were being relieved by the 75th Infantry Division. My men would head for Theux for a week's R & R, battlefront style, which meant nothing more than warm quarters and running water. Nonetheless, I told them they would have my enduring envy, because each man was guaranteed a bath. It had been a month since any of us had washed, other than what was possible by warming snow in a helmet over a camp stove, which generally meant a fast shave once a week when we were housed indoors. The smoke and grease from our guns had more or less stuck to our skin, turning all of us an oily black. We looked like a minstrel troupe, which made for a few private jokes between Bidwell and me. Now standing next to Como, I told the men that it had been the greatest honor of my life to command them and that I would remember them as long as I lived. I have never spoken words I meant more.

The dog, whom the men had named Hercules, presented a problem. Hercules was deaf, probably as the result of getting caught too close to an explosion. He fled yelping at the first flash of light on the battlefield, and we speculated that that was why whoever owned him had turned him out. Despite his handicap, he had made himself increasingly popular in the last two weeks by proving to be an able hunter. He'd snatch rabbits in the woods which he would deposit at my feet several times a day. We packed them in snow until he had caught enough for the cooks to give a ribbon of meat to each man as a treat with his rations. Hercules would sit at the fire and make a meal of the viscera, and, once he'd finished, the soldiers came by to ruffle his ears and praise him. I regarded him as a company mascot, but because Biddy and I fed him, he jumped into our jeep after I'd transferred command. We pushed him out at least three times, only to have him leap back in, and finally gave up. Half the company came to bid Hercules farewell, exhibiting far more affection than they'd shown Gideon and me.

Then we drove south and west, beyond Monty, to find out what had happened to Robert Martin and his team. The hill where they'd fallen had been retaken only in the last thirty-six hours and the bodies of the men who had died there were yet to be removed. Graves Registration Detail had arrived, but most of the GR troops were at work on a hillock to the west. In their gloves, they rooted for dog tags in the shirtfronts of the dead, bagging any possessions they found on a body and tying it to the man's ankle. Then they sorted the corpses by size, so that the cordon they were going to assemble would be stable. Quartermaster Salvage was with them, picking over the inanimate remains. During the stillborn portion of the war in September, Salvage went over some battlefields so closely you couldn't find a piece of barbed wire or a shell casing afterward. But right now they were interested in weapons, ammunition, and unused medical supplies. Even before GR got to most of the corpses, I noticed they had been stripped of their jackets and boots. It was probably the Germans who'd done that, but it could have been our troops, or even locals. I didn't begrudge any of them whatever it had taken to survive the cold.

Biddy and I walked up the hill. Most of the men in the team Martin had led here had been mowed down as they fled by the machine guns mounted on the Panzers. The corpses were frozen solid like statues. One man, on his knees in an attitude of prayer, had probably died begging for his life. I walked among the dead, using my helmet to clear off enough of the snow that had drifted over them to make out their features, giving each man a moment of respect. By now, their flesh had taken on a yellowish color, although I uncovered one soldier whose head had been blown off. The frozen gray brain matter, looking like what curdles from overcooked meat, was all around him. Somehow the back of his cranium was still intact, resembling a porcelain bowl, through which the stump of his spinal cord protruded.

Biddy and I passed several minutes looking for Martin. Four weeks ago I had seen nothing like this. Now it remained awful, but routine. And still, as I often did, I found myself in conversation with God. Why am I alive? When will it be my turn? And then as ever: And why would you want any of your creatures treated this way?

The lodge which had been Martin's observation post was about fifty yards west. According to Barnes and Edgeworthy, it had gone down like a house of cards. Everything had fallen in, except the lower half of the rear wall. The crater from the tank shells reached nearly to the brick footings and was filled with the burned remains of the building—cinders and glass and larger chunks of the timbers, and the blackened stones of the outer walls. We could see the view Martin had as he looked west where the American tanks had emerged like ghosts from the morning blizzard. He had died in a beautiful spot, with a magnificent rolling vista of the hills, plump with snow.

I summoned the GR officer and he brought over a steam shovel to dig through the stony rubble, but after an hour they were unable to find a whole corpse. In the movies, the dead die so conveniently—they stiffen and fall aside. Here men had been blown apart. The flesh and bone, the shit and blood of buddies had showered over one another. Men in my company had died like that on Christmas Day, and among the burdens I carried, along with the troubled memory of the gratitude I'd experienced that it had been them and not me, was the lesser shame of feeling revolted as the final bits of good men splattered on me. Here, of course, if anything remained of Robert Martin, it probably had been incinerated in the burning debris. Biddy motioned toward a tree about twenty yards off. A ribbon of human entrails hung there, ice-rimed, but literally turning on the wind like a kite tail.

Edgeworthy and Barnes had placed Martin at the second-floor window, surveying the retreating Germans, when the first tank shell had rocketed in. Working from the foundation, it was not hard to figure the spot, but his remains could have blown anywhere within two hundred yards. The sergeant had his men dig in the area of the west wall for close to an hour. A pair of dog tags turned up, neither Martin's.

"They don't usually burn up," the sergeant said, meaning the tags. He expected eventually to identify Martin somehow. Dental records, fingerprints, laundry marks, school rings. But it would take weeks. As we were getting ready to leave, a hand and arm were discovered, but there was a wedding ring on the third finger. It wasn't Martin.

"Panzers didn't take many prisoners," said the sergeant, "but the Krauts are the Krauts. They'd have treated an officer better, if they found him alive. Only thing is, anybody who made it through this didn't live by much. Have to be in a POW hospital, wouldn't you think? And the Krauts don't have medicine for their own. I wouldn't think your man would be doing too well."

I sent a signal to Camello reporting on our findings and asking for the Third Army to contact the Red Cross, which reported on POWs. At this stage, it could take a month at least to be sure the Germans didn't have Martin, and even that wouldn't be definitive. General Teedle had another suggestion on how to fully investigate Martin's fate. The idea had occurred to me, but I had been unwilling. Lying in that snowy field on Christmas Day seemed to have put an end to my curiosity. Now I had a direct order, a three-word telegraphic response.

Find the girl

23. REUNION

I gave no credence to what Martin had told me in Savy about Gita's whereabouts, even though it had been vaguely corroborated by the little private, Barnes, and his memory of the girl with the farm family Martin contacted near Skyline Drive. Instead, we decided to retrace the initial intelligence which had placed Gita near Houffalize. After several signals, we were advised to see the leader there of the Belgian resistance, the Geheim Leger, the Secret Army, a woman named Marthe Trausch.

Traveling took two days, because Houffalize was not fully liberated until January 16, when the First Army's 84th Infantry and Patton's 11th Armored met at the town and began driving east. Like so much of the Ardennes, Houffalize sat handsomely in a snowy forest valley carved by the Ourthe River, a narrow tributary of the Meuse, but the town itself was now all but obliterated. The American bombers had leveled every structure large enough to be used by the Germans as a command center, killing hundreds of Nazis, but dozens of Houffalize residents as well. We rode in to indifferent greetings. For these people, when it came to war and warriors, the sides were less and less consequential.

Madame Trausch proved to be a seventy-year-old tavern keeper, a fleshy widow with a bright skirt scraping the floor. She had taken over her husband's role in the resistance when he died, her saloon providing an excellent site both for eavesdropping on the Nazis and for passing information. About half of the old stone inn had survived and I found her calmly clearing debris with two of her grandchildren. Her native tongue was Luxembourgian, a kind of Low German, and her accent made her French hard for me to follow, but she responded promptly when I mentioned Martin and Gita.

For once, Robert Martin appeared to have told the truth. Madame Trausch said Martin had been intent on getting into southern Germany, and asked for help setting up Gita in Luxembourg near the German border. The Luxembourgers had not put up the same fight against the Nazis as the Belgians, but a loose network existed there of residents who assisted the Geheim Leger when they could. More than a month ago, Gita had been placed with one of these families on a small farm in sight of the Ourthe River, on the steep hills beneath Marnach. Gita posed as a milkmaid, taking the family cows to pasture and back each day. These rambles allowed her to watch the movement of the German troops from the heights over the river, leading to her unheeded warnings about tank activity near the German town of Dasburg.

"In war, it is all noise, no one listens," said Madame Trausch. She had no idea whether Gita or the farmer or their house had survived the battles. No one had yet been heard from, but it was unclear whether the Germans had even been pushed back there. We started east, were roadblocked by combat, and did not get to the hamlet of Roder until the afternoon of January 19. By then the fighting was about two miles east.

Here, as in Belgium, the ocher farmhouses and barns, rather than being scattered over the landscape, were arranged in the feudal manner around a common courtyard with each family's land stretching behind their abode. The medieval notion was common protection, but now this clustering had made all the structures equally vulnerable to modern explosives. Every house was damaged, and one had fallen in entirely, with only two walls of jointed stone partially standing in broken shapes like dragon's teeth. The round crosshatched rafters of the roof lay camelbacked between them, beside a heap of timber and stone over which a family and several of their neighbors were climbing. Apparently searching for any useful remains, they proceeded in a determined and utterly stoic manner. At the top of the hill of rubble a man picked up scraps of paper, sorting them in a fashion, some in his trouser pockets, others in his coat. Another fellow was already at work with a hammer, knocking loose pieces of mortar from the stones, probably quarried a century ago, and stacking them so that they could be used to rebuild.

But I sensed this was the place I was looking for, due not so much to Madame Trausch's information as to what I'd heard from Private Barnes. He'd described the lady of the house as "a round old doll," and there would never be better words for the woman wobbling along near the top of the pile.

I had started toward her, when I heard my name. On the far side of the heap, Gita held a hand to her eye. She was dressed in a makeshift outfit—a headscarf, a cloth overcoat with fur trim on the sleeves, and torn work pants.

"Doo-bean?" She seemed only mildly surprised to see me, as if she presumed I'd been searching for her for weeks. She climbed up grinning and struck me on the shoulder, speaking English. It was only my physical appearance that seemed to inspire her wonder.

"You soldier!" she cried.

Despite all the vows I had made on the battlefield, I found myself enjoying her admiration. I offered her a cigarette. She shrieked when she saw the pack and dragged on the smoke so hungrily that I thought she would consume the butt in one breath. I told her to keep the package, which she literally crushed to her heart in gratitude.

We reverted to French. I said I was looking for Martin.

"*Pourquoi?* Still all this with Teedle?"

"There are questions. Have you seen him?"

"*Moi?*" She laughed in surprise. The round old doll teetered over to see about me. Soon, the whole family was describing the last month. In Marnach, like everywhere else, collaborators with the Germans had been severely punished when the Allies took control, and thus, once the Germans returned, those known to have aided the Americans were endangered, less by the SS than by their vengeful neighbors. Gita and the Hurles had endured many close calls. For several days, they had scurried like wood mice through the forest, eventually stealing back here and remaining in the woodshed of family friends. No one had food, and there was little way to know which side would bomb or shoot them first. The

Hurles still had no idea who had destroyed their house, nor did it matter. All was lost, except two of their twelve cows. But the father, the mother, and their two married daughters were safe, and they all continued to hold out hope for their sons, who like most of the young men in Luxembourg had been forced into the German Army and sent to the eastern front. Madame Hurle remained on the Americans' side, but wished they would hurry up and win the war.

"*Qu'est-ce qu'ils nous ont mis!*" The Germans, she said, had beaten the hell out of them.

"But no sign of Martin?" I asked Gita. She had not really answered the question.

"*Quelle mouche t'a piqué?*" she answered. What's eating you? "You are angry with Martin, no? Because he played a trick. And me, too, I suppose."

"I received your postcard," I answered.

"Robert was very put out when I told him I wrote. But I owed you a word. I was afraid you would be hurt when you woke."

"And so I was."

"It was a moment, Dubin. An impulse. War is not a time when impulse is contained."

"I have had the very same thoughts in the days since."

"Ah," she said. "So between us, peace is declared."

"Of course," I said. We were both smiling, if still somewhat shyly. "But I must know about Martin. Tell me when you last saw him."

"A month, I would say. More. Since I am with the Hurles. When the battle is done, he will find me here. He always does." She was blithe, even childish in her conviction. Assaying her reactions, the question I had been sent here to pose seemed answered. Martin had made no miraculous escape, had sent no secret emissaries.

"Then I am afraid Martin is dead," I said.

"*Qu'est-ce que tu dis?*"

I repeated it. A tremor passed through her small face, briefly erasing the indomitable look that was always there. Then she gave a resolute shake to her short curls and addressed me in English to make her meaning clear.

"Is said before. Many times. Is not dead."

"The men in his company saw him fall, Gita. Tank shells struck the building where he was. He died bravely."

"*Non!*" she said, in the French way, through the nose.

I had watched myself, as it were, throughout this exchange. Even now, I could not completely fight off the fragment in me that was dashed that she took Martin so much to heart. But I felt for her as well. When I wondered where she would go next, I recognized much of the motive for her attachment to him. She was again a Polish orphan in a broken country. Even her time as warrior was over without Martin.

"I had very faint hopes, Gita. Hope against hope, we say. That is why I came. If he survived, I knew he would have contacted you."

She agreed with that in a murmur. I had toyed with the truth in my role of interrogator, and she might well have shaded her answers to me. After all, she wanted to be Bernhardt. But her grief looked genuine. She wandered down the mound by herself. She was not crying, though. Then again, I wondered if Gita ever wept. She stood alone, looking out at a field where a dead cow was frozen in the snow.

I asked Biddy how she appeared to him.

"Bad off," he answered. "I don't take her for foolin.'"

In a few minutes, I skirted the rubble heap to find her.

"You should come with us," I told her. She had nowhere else to go. "Even the cows you herded are gone. And my superiors may have questions for you. Best to deal with them now." I suspected OSS would want to glean what they could from her about Martin.

She nodded. "I am another mouth to them," she said looking back to the Hurle family.

We headed for Bastogne. Biddy drove and Gita and I sat in the back of the jeep, smoking cigarettes and chatting while she stroked Hercules, who took to her quickly. We all agreed his prior master must have been a woman.

For the most part, we talked about what we had been through in the last few weeks. I described our airborne arrival in Savy, including the condition of my trousers. Every story with a happy ending is a comedy, one of my professors had said in college, and our tale of parachuting without training into a pitched battle had all three of us rolling by the time we'd finished.

"But why so desperate to reach Bastogne?" she asked. I had given away more than I wanted to, but had no way out except the truth. "'Arrest Martin'!" she responded then. "These are foolish orders, Dubin. Martin played a trick. That is not a terrible crime. He has done nothing to harm the American Army."

I told her Teedle thought otherwise.

"*Merde. Teedle est fou. Martin est un patriote.*" Teedle is nuts. Martin is a patriot.

"It does not matter now," I said somberly.

With that her eyes were glued closed a moment. I offered her another cigarette. I'd acquired a Zippo along the way and lit hers before mine. She pointed to me smoking.

"This is how I know for sure you are a soldier now."

I showed her the callus I'd worn on the side of my thumb in the last month with the flint wheel of the lighter.

"You see, in the end, Martin was good for you, Dubin. You should be grateful to him. No? To fight is what you craved."

I was startled I had been so transparent. But that illusion was all in the past. I had not yet found a way to write to Grace or my parents about Christmas Day, but I told Gita the story now, quietly. Biddy stopped and got out of the jeep. He said he needed directions to Bastogne, but I suspected he wanted no part of the memories. I told her about lying in the snow in that clearing waiting to die, while the men nearby preceded me, and about feeling so shamed by my desperation to live.

"I thought all my last thoughts," I told her. "Including, I must say, about you."

Her full eyebrows shot up and I hurried to clarify.

"Not with longing," I said.

"Oh? What, then? Regret?" She was teasing, but remained attentive.

"I would say, with clarity," I said finally. "Our moment together had given me clarity. I longed for home and hearth. A normal life. To gather my family around a fire. To have children."

She had taken the Zippo and held its flame to the tip of a new cigarette for a long time. Through the blue scrim, she settled a drilling look on me, so intense my heart felt like it skipped.

"And I am what, Dubin? A vagabond? You think I care nothing for those things? The fire, the warm meal, the children underfoot?"

"Do you?" I answered stupidly.

"You think I do not wish to have a place in the world, as other persons have a place? To want what you or any other person wants? To have a life and not merely to survive? You think I have no right to be as weary of this as everyone else?"

"I hardly meant that."

"No," she said. "I heard. I am not fit for a decent life."

She suddenly could not stand to look at me. She released the car door and jumped outside, where I felt I had no choice but to pursue her. Her dark eyes were liquid when I caught up, but her look was savage. She swore at me in French, and then, as an astonishing exclamation point, hurled the pack of cigarettes at me.

I was flabbergasted. Men always are when they sacrifice a woman's feelings, I suppose. But I had known better. I had glimpsed the fundamental truth of Gita in the instant she had raised her skirt in that barn. She would always be the spurned offspring of the town pariah. Everything about her character was built over an abyss of hurt.

I followed her farther out into the snow. She was already attracting attention from some of the soldiers on their guard post nearby. Her face was crushed on her glove and I touched her shoulder.

"I mourn Martin," she said. "Do not think your chatter about yourself has upset me."

"I had no such thought." I knew better than to tell her she wept for herself. "But I am sorry. I should not have said that. About what I thought. That I felt no longing. I am sorry."

"'No longing?'" She pivoted. If possible, she was even more furious. "You think I care about *that*? You think *that* damaged my pride?" She smashed the last of her cigarette underfoot and stepped toward me, lowering her voice. "It is your poor opinion of me I revile, not your desires. You know nothing, Dubin. You are a fool. No longing," she huffed. "I do not even believe it, Dubin." Then she lifted her face to me, so that there was only a hairbreadth between us. "Nor do you," she whispered.

She was an iceberg, of course, on the remainder of the ride, tomb-silent except to the dog, to whom she spoke in whispers he could not hear. I sat in front with Biddy, but he could tell there had been a personal eruption and said little. As we approached Bastogne, Gita announced that she wanted to be taken to the military hospital, where she would find work as a nurse. Trained assistance was never spurned in a war zone. In so many words, she was saying she needed no help from me.

Arriving in Bastogne, I was startled by its size. It was hard to believe thousands of men had died for the sake of such a small place. The town had only one main street, rue Sablon, although the avenue sported several good-size buildings, whose fancy stone façades were now frequently broken or scarred by shrapnel and gunfire. Iron grates framed tiny balconies under windows which, for the most part, had been left as empty black holes. Here and there one of the steep peaked roofs characteristic of the region lay in complete collapse as a result of an artillery strike, but in general the poor weather had kept Bastogne from more severe destruction by air. The cathedral had been bombed as part of the Germans' Christmas Eve present, a crude gesture meant to deprive Bastogne's citizens of even the meager comfort of a holiday prayer, but the debris from the buildings that had been hit had already been shoveled into piles in the streets, and was being removed by locals in horse-drawn carts. Last night there had been yet another heavy snowfall, and soldiers on foot slogged along while the jeeps and convoys thick on rue Sablon slid slowly down the steep avenue.

I had no way to temporize with Gita. Instead we simply asked directions to the American field hospital, which occupied one of the largest structures of the town, a four-story convent, L'Établissement des Soeurs de Notre Dame de Bastogne. Despite the fact that the roof was gone, the first two floors remained habitable, and the Sisters had given up their large redbrick school and the rear building of their compound to the care of the sick and wounded. The snow from the street had been pushed onto the walks and sat in frozen drifts, some the height of a man. Between them, several ambulances were parked, the same Ford trucks that served as paddy wagons at home, here emblazoned with huge red crosses. Gita snatched up the small parcel she had gathered from the remains of the Hurles' home and marched inside. I followed in case she needed someone to vouch for her.

At the front desk sat a nun whose face, amid a huge starched angelwing habit, looked like a ripe peach in a white bowl. She made an oddly serene figure in the entryway, which had been strafed. There were bullet holes in the walls and in the somewhat grand wooden rococo balustrades leading to the upper stories, while some kind of ordnance had blown a small crater in the inlaid floor, leaving a hole all the way to the cellar. After only a few moments of conversation, Gita and the nun appeared to be reaching an agreement.

Watching from a distance, I was surprised to hear my name from behind.

"David?" A doctor in a green surgical gown and cap had both arms raised toward me, a short dark man who looked a little like Algar. Once he removed the headgear I recognized Cal Echols, who had been my sister's boyfriend during his first two years in med school. Everyone in my family had loved Cal, who was smart and sociable, but he'd lost his mother as a four-year-old, and Dorothy said his clinging ultimately drove her insane. We'd never seen that side of him, of course. Now Cal and I fell on each other like brothers.

"Jeepers creepers," he said, when he pushed me back to look me over, "talk about the tempest tossed. I thought you lawyers knew how to worm your way out of things."

"Bad timing," I said.

He figured I had come to the hospital to visit a soldier, and I was immediately embarrassed that my preoccupation with Gita had kept me from realizing that several of the wounded men from my company were probably here. Cal had finished his surgical shift and offered to help me find them. When I turned to the front desk to attempt some awkward goodbye with Gita, she was gone.

Once Biddy had found a place for the jeep, he and I went over the hospital roster with Cal. Four of our men were still on hand. A corporal named Jim Harzer had been wounded by a mortar round during a hill fight near Noville. He was another of the replacement troops, the father of two little girls, and when I'd last seen him he was on the ground, with the corpsmen attending him. They had a tourniquet above his knee; down where his boot had been it was primarily a bloody pulp. In spite of that, Harzer had beamed. 'I'm done, Cap,' he said. 'I'm going home. I'm gonna be kissing my girls.' I found him in a similarly buoyant mood today. He'd lost his right foot, but he said he'd met several fellas missing their lefts and they planned to stay in touch so they could save money on shoes.

In the convent, all the class space had been converted to hospital wards. The long wooden desks at which students once sat facing the blackboards were being used as beds, with more cots placed in between. The valuable classroom equipment, bird exhibits for science, chem lab beakers, and microscopes, had been preserved in the closets.

Almost every patient had had surgery of some kind, the best-off only to remove shrapnel from nonmortal wounds. But on the wards were also the limbless, the faceless, the gut-shot, who too often were only days from death. The cellar that ran the length of the building now served as a morgue.

At the far end of the second floor, an MP stood outside a full ward of German POWs here as patients.

"We give them better than our boys get, that's for sure," said Cal. Indeed, several of the Germans waved when they recognized Cal in the doorway. "Nice kid, from Munich," said Cal about one of them. "Speaks good English, but both parents are Nazi Party members."

"Does he know you're Jewish?"

"That was the first thing I told him. Of course, all of his best friends at home were Jewish. All. He gave me a whole list." He smiled a little.

Cal had been here since the day after Christmas, and I began asking about the other men from my company who'd left the front in ambulances. He remembered a number. Too many had died, but there was some good news. Cal himself had operated on Mike O'Brien—the joker who'd enjoyed giving it to Stocker Collison—whom I'd dragged from the clearing on Christmas Day. He had lived. So had Massimo Fortunato, from whose thigh Cal had removed a shrapnel piece the size of a softball. He had been transferred to a general hospital in Luxembourg City, but Massimo had done so well that Cal thought he would be sent back to my former unit in a month or two.

Cal offered us billets in the convent, which we eagerly accepted, since it saved me from a problematic reconnaissance in the overcrowded town. The enlisted men, medical corpsmen for the most part, were housed in a large schoolroom converted to a dormitory. Their quarters were close, but the men weren't complaining, Cal said. The building had electricity from a field generator and central heat, coal-fired, although there was not yet running water in the tiled baths and shower rooms. Better still, the enlisted men were right next to the mess hall and on the same floor as the nuns and nurses, a few of whom were rumored to have dispensed healing treatments of a nonmedical variety. True or not, the mere idea had revived the men.

The docs were boarded on the second floor in the nuns' former rooms, which the Sisters had insisted on surrendering. These were barren cubicles, six feet by ten, each containing a feather mattress, a small table, and a crucifix on the wall, but it would be the first privacy I'd had for a month. Cal's room was two doors down. He had received a package from home only a day ago and he offered me a chocolate, laughing out loud at my expression after the first bite.

"Careful," he said. "You look close to cardiac arrest."

Afterward, in officers' mess where we had dinner, I again recounted Christmas Day. Despite all the fighting I'd seen following that, my stories never seemed to get any farther.

"This war," said Cal. "I mean, being a doc—it's a paradox, I'll tell you, David. You try like hell to save them, and doing a really great job just means they get another chance to die. We had a young medic who came in here yesterday. It was the third time in a month. Minor wounds the first couple of times, but yesterday just about his whole right side was blown away. What a kid. Even in delirium, he would reply to all of my questions with a 'Yes, sir' or 'No, sir.' I stayed up all day with him, just trying to coax him to live, and he died not ten minutes after I finally went off." Cal peered at nothing, reabsorbing the loss. "A lot of these boys end up hating us when they realize they're going back. You know the saying. The only thing a doctor can give you is a pill and a pat on the back and an Army doc skips the pat on the back."

It was nearly 8:00 p.m. now, and Cal's surgical shift was about to begin. He would operate until 4:00 a.m. The surgical theater was never empty. Before he went back to work, he brought a bottle of Pernod to my room. After two drinks, I passed out with my boots still on.

I woke in the middle of the night when my door cracked open. At first, I thought it was the wind, but then a silhouette appeared, backlit by the brightness from the hall.

"*Ton chien te cherche*," Gita said. She slid through the door and closed it and flicked on the light. She had hold of Hercules by the woven belt that one of the men in my company had given him as a collar. Her hair had been pinned up under a white nurse's bonnet and she was dressed in a baggy gray uniform. The dog, which Biddy had left outside in the convent's one-car garage, had been found trotting through the wards. Harzer and a couple of others recognized him and swore that Hercules had come to pay his respects before moving on in his apparent search for Biddy or me. When she let him go, the dog bounded to my side. I scratched his ears, before I faced her.

Cal's stories about nurses scurrying through the halls at night had briefly sparked the thought that Gita might arrive here. It seemed unlikely given her mood when we parted, but before falling off I'd had a vision so clear I had actually deliberated for an instant about whether I would tell her to stay or to go. Yet in the moment there was no choice. As always, she presented herself as a challenge. But I doubted her boldness was only to prove her point about my longing. Her need was as plain as my craving for her, which just like my paralyzing fears in the air over Savy was not subject to the control of preparation or reason. I beckoned with my hand, the lights went off, and she was beside me.

As I embraced her, I apologized for my grime and the odor, but we met with all the gentleness our first time together had lacked, softened by what each of us had endured in the interval. Even as I savored the remarkable smoothness of her stomach and back, the thrill of touching a human so graceful and compact, something within me continued to wonder if this romance was a fraud, merely the overheated grappling of the battlefront. Perhaps it was just as Teedle had told me. When a human is reduced to the brute minimum, desire turns out to be at the core. But that did not matter now as we lay together in the tiny convent room. In the tumult of emotion Gita consistently provoked in me, there was a new element tonight. I had been fascinated from the start by her intelligence and her daring; and my physical yearning for her was greater than I'd felt for any woman. But tonight, my heart swelled also with abounding gratitude. I pressed her so close that I seemed to hope to squeeze her inside my skin. I kissed her again and again, wishing my appreciation could pour out of me, as I, David Dubin, recovered, if only for a fragment of time, the fundamental joy of being David Dubin.

24. ALIVE

We remained in Bastogne two more days. I had signaled Teedle that Gita was here if OSS wished to interview her, and awaited his order to formally abandon the effort to arrest Martin. Pending a response, I worked on a long report about the past month for Colonel Maples, who had moved to the new Third Army Headquarters in Luxembourg City. I also spent a couple of hours both days with the men from my former command who were hospitalized here. But every minute was only a long aching interval, waiting for dark and the end of Gita's shift, when she would slip into my room.

"You are an unusual woman," I had told her again that first night after she had come to me, as we lay whispering in the narrow bed.

"You notice only now?" She was laughing. "But I do not think you mean to praise me, Dubin. What do you find so uncommon?"

"That you mourn Martin and are with me."

She thought a moment. "No soldier in Europe more eagerly sought death, Dubin. I knew that, no matter how often I tried to say otherwise. Besides, if my father died or my brother, would it be unusual, as you say, to find comfort in life?"

"Martin was not your father or your brother."

"No," she said and fell silent again. "He was both. And my salvation. He rescued me, Dubin. When I met him I was on the boil, furious at all moments except those when I simply wanted to die. He said, 'If you are angry, fight. And if you wish to die, then wait until tomorrow. Today you may do some good for someone else.' He knew the right things to say. Because he had said them to himself."

"But you do not mourn him as your lover?"

"*Qu'est-ce qui te prend?*" She raised her head from my chest. "Why does that matter so much to you—me with Martin? Do you fear that I liked Martin better this way than I like you?"

"You think that is the issue?"

"It is the issue with every man at times. And it is stupid. With each person it is different, Dubin. Not better or worse. It is like a voice, yes? No voice is the same. But there is always conversation. Does one prefer a person for the voice, or the words? It is what is being said that matters far more. No?"

I agreed, but pondered in the dark.

"Doo-bean," she finally said, more emphatically than usual, "I have told you. With Martin and me that aspect was long over. It became impossible."

"Because?"

"Because this is no longer an activity for him."

I finally understood. "Was he wounded?"

"In the mind. He has not been good that way for some time. He punishes himself perhaps, because he likes the killing too much. He has clung to me, but only because he believes there will not be another woman after me. *Comprends-tu?*"

Surprisingly, something remained unsettled. I looked into the dark seeking the words, as if attempting to lay hold of a nerve running through my chest.

"When I think of Martin," I said then, "I wonder what interest I could have to you. I am so dull. My life is small and yours with him has been so large."

"*Tu ne me comprends pas bien.*" You do not understand me well.

"'Well'? You are the most mysterious person I have ever met."

"I am a simple girl, with little education. You are learned, Dubin.

Occasionally humorous. Brave enough. You are a solid type, Dubin. Would you drink and beat your wife?"

"Not at the same time."

"*Tu m'as fait craquer.*" I cracked, meaning, I couldn't resist. "Besides, you are a rich American."

"My father is a cobbler."

"*Evidemment! Les cordonniers sont toujours les plus mal chaussés.*" The shoemaker's son always goes barefoot. "I have miscalculated." Once we had laughed for some time, she added, "You have a conscience, Dubin. It is an attractive quality in a fellow in a time of war."

"A conscience? Lying here with you when I have promised myself to someone else?"

"Eh," she answered again. "If you and she were destined for each other, you would have married before you departed. What woman loves a man and allows him to leave for war without having him to her bed?"

"It was not solely her choice."

"More the point, then. You are not so scrupulous here, when there are no expectations." She laid her fingertip directly on the end of my penis to make her point. "You chose to be free, Dubin. No? *Qui se marie à la hâte se repent à loisir.*" Marry in haste, repent at leisure.

Gita's observation, made in her customary declarative fashion, seemed too stark to be true, but there was no avoiding it. I yearned for the aura that surrounded Grace like a cloud—her gentility, her blonde hair and soft sweaters, the way she glided through life, her pristine American beauty. But not enough to separate myself from my parents in the irrevocable way our marriage had called for. My sudden decision to enlist, rather than wait out my fortunes with the draft, seemed highly suspect from the distance of a convent bed in Belgium. But so did the balm these conclusions gave to my conscience.

"At any rate, Dubin, you are here with me now. Even though you felt no longing." She stroked now where she had left her finger, and I responded quickly. "Aha," she said. "Again, Dubin, you are betrayed."

"No, no, that is merely to save your feelings."

"Then, perhaps I shall stop," she said.

"No, no, I am much too concerned for you to allow that."

Afterward, we slept, but in time I was awakened by growling. I had heard it in my dreams for a while, but it grew insistent and I stirred, ready to scold Hercules. Instead, I found Gita snoring. Her constant smoking had apparently done its work on her sinuses. From an elbow, I studied her in the light borrowed from the hall. Lying there, she seemed, as we all do in slumber, childlike, her small sharp face mobile in sleep. She suckled briefly; an arm stirred protectively, and her eyes jumped beneath her lids. I was impressed by how small she appeared when the current, as it were, was turned off on her imposing personality. I watched several minutes. As she had been trying to tell me, she was, at heart, a far simpler person than I supposed.

After Gita had snuck back downstairs the first night we'd arrived in Bastogne, I met Cal for breakfast at the officers' mess, as planned. He had been in surgery until 4:00 a.m., then had made rounds to see his patients. He was still in a bloody gown, gobbling up something before he grabbed a few hours' sleep. Apparently, it was he who had directed Gita and the dog to my room, and he let me know promptly that he'd guessed the score.

"So how did your quarters work out? Bed a little tight?"

I could feel myself flush, and then, like a switchboard operator plugging in the lines, I made a series of connections which, when complete, brought me up short. Cal would write home that he had seen me. He would say I had a woman here. Grace, in time, would hear.

"Oh, don't worry," he said, when he saw my expression. He made that zipper motion across his lips.

But somehow I was caught up in a vision of Grace reacting to this news. Would she rely on some bromide about how men will be men? Or take comfort from the extremities of war? My mind continued tumbling down the staircase, descending into various images of what might occur when word reached Grace, until I finally crashed and came to rest at the bottom. In a figurative heap, I checked myself and was shocked to find myself frightened but unhurt—no bruises, no broken bones—and thus I knew at that moment, absolutely and irrevocably, that I was not going to marry Grace Morton. I cared intensely about Grace. I still could not imagine being the brutal assassin of her feelings. But she was not a vital part of me. Gita's role in this seemed incidental. It was not a matter of choosing one woman over the other, because even now I continued to doubt that Gita's interest would last. But, in the light of day, what I'd recognized lying beside Gita remained. Grace was an idol. A dream. But not my destiny.

With some bemusement, Cal had watched all this work its way through my features.

"Who is this girl, anyway, David? I asked the nuns about her. They say she knows her bananas, bright, works hard. Bit of a looker," said Cal, "if you'll forgive me. Every man in this hospital will be pea green with envy, even the ones cold down in the morgue."

I smiled and told him a little about Gita. Runaway. Exile. Commando.

"Is it serious?" he asked.

I shook my head as if I didn't know, but within a distinct voice told me that the correct answer was yes. It was gravely serious. Not as Cal meant. Instead it was serious in the way combat was serious, because it was impossible to tell if I would survive.

Gita's nursing duties included washing bedridden patients. Imagining her at it made me nearly delirious with envy, although I admitted to her that I was uncertain if I was jealous of her touch or of the chance to bathe. When she arrived on the second night, she swung through the door with a heavy metal pail full of hot water. It had been boiled on the kitchen stove, the only means available in the absence of working plumbing.

"You are an angel."

"A wet one." The sleeves of her shapeless uniform were black.

"So you can no longer tolerate the smell of me?"

"You smell like someone who has lived, Dubin. It is the complaining about it I cannot stand. Get up, please. I will not bathe you in your bed like an invalid."

She had brought a cloth, a towel, and another bowl. I removed my clothes and stood before her, as she scrubbed and dried me bit by bit. My calf, my thigh. There was a magnificent intermezzo before she went higher to my stomach.

"Tell me about America," she said, once she continued.

"You want to know if the streets are lined with gold? Or if King Kong is hanging from the Empire State Building?"

"No, but tell me the truth. Do you love America?"

"Yes, very much. The land. The people. And most of all the idea of it. Of each man equal. And free."

"That is the idea in France, too. But is it true in America?"

"True? In America there was never royalty. Never Napoleon. Yet it is still far better to be rich than poor. But it is true, I think, that most Americans cherish the ideals. My father and mother came from a town very much like Pilzkoba. Now they live free from the fears they grew up with. They may speak their minds. They may vote. They may own property. They sent their children to public schools. And now they may hope, with good reason, that my sister and brother and I will find an even better life than theirs."

"But do Americans not hate the Jews?"

"Yes. But not as much as the colored." It was a dour joke and she was less amused than I by the bitter humor. "It is not like Hitler," I said. "Every American is from somewhere else. Each is hated for what he brings that is different from the rest. We live in uneasy peace. But it is peace, for the most part."

"And is America beautiful?"

"*Magnifique.*" I told her about the West as I had glimpsed it from the train on my way to Fort Barkley.

"And your city?"

"We have built our own landscape. There are giant buildings."

"Like King Kong?"

"Almost as tall."

"Yes," she said. "I want to go to America. Europe is old. America is still new. The Americans are smart to fight on others' soil. Europe will require a century to recover from all of this. And there may be another war soon. *Après la guerre* I will go to America, Dubin. You must help me."

"Of course," I said. Of course.

By the next morning, it seemed as if every person in Bastogne knew what was occurring in my quarters at night. Gita had made a clanging commotion dragging her pails up the stairs. I worried that the nuns would evict both of us, but they maintained a dignified silence. It was the soldiers who could not contain themselves, greeting me in whispers as "lover boy" whenever I passed.

Third Army had established a command center in Bastogne, and Biddy and I walked over there every few hours to see if Teedle's orders had come through. For two days now, no shells had fallen on the city, and the civilians were in the streets, briskly going about their business. They were polite but busy, unwilling to repeat their prior mistake of believing this lull was actually peace.

As we hiked up the hilly streets, I said, "I find I'm the talk of the town, Gideon."

He didn't answer at first. "Well, sir," he finally said, "it's just a whole lot of things seem to be moving around in the middle of the night."

We shared a long laugh.

"She's a remarkable person, Biddy."

"Yes, sir. This thing got a future, Captain?"

I stopped dead on the pavement. My awareness of myself had been growing since my conversation with Cal at breakfast yesterday, but trusting Biddy more than anyone else, things were a good deal clearer in his company. I took hold of his arm.

"Biddy, how crazy would it sound if I said I love this woman?"

"Well, good for you, Captain."

"No," I said, instantly, because I had a clear view of the complications, "it's not good. It's not good for a thousand reasons. It probably conflicts with my duty. And it will not end well." I had maintained an absolute conviction about this. I knew my heart would be crushed.

"Cap," he said, "ain't no point going on like that. They-all can do better telling you the weather tomorrow than what's gonna happen with love. Ain't nothing else to do but hang on for the ride."

But my thoughts were very much the same when Gita came to my bed that night.

"Your phrase has haunted me all day," I told her.

"*Laquelle?*"

"'*Après la guerre.*' I have thought all day about what will happen after the war."

"If war is over, then there must be peace, no? At least for a while."

"No, I refer to you. And to me. I have spent the day wondering what will become of us. Does that surprise you or take you aback?"

"I know who you are, Dubin. It would surprise me if your thoughts were different. I would care for you much less."

I took a moment. "So you do care for me?"

"*Je suis là.*" I am here.

"And in the future?"

"When the war began," she said, "no one thought of the future. It would be too awful to imagine the Nazis here for long. Everyone in the underground lived solely for the present. To fight now. The only future was the next action and the hope you and your comrades would survive. But since Normandy, it is different. Among the *maquisards*, there is but one phrase on their lips: *Après la guerre*. I hear those words in my mind, too. You are not alone."

"And what do you foresee?"

"It is still war, Dubin. One creeps to the top of a wall and peeks over, I understand, but we remain here. If one looks only ahead, he may miss the perils that are near. But I have seen many good souls die. I have promised myself to live for them. And now, truly, I think I wish to live for myself as well."

"This is good."

"But you told me what you see, no? The hearth, the home. Yes?"

"Yes." That remained definitive. "*Et toi?*"

"*Je sais pas.* But if I live through this war, I will be luckier than most. I have learned what perhaps I most needed to."

"Which is?"

"To value the ordinary, Doo-bean. In war, one feels its loss acutely. The humdrum. The routine. Even I, who could never abide it, find myself longing for a settled life."

"And will that content you? Is it to be the same for you as me? The house, the home, being a respectable wife with children swarming at your knees beneath your skirt? Or will you be like Martin, who told me he would soon look for another war?"

"There will never be another war. Not for me. You said once that a woman has that choice, and that is the choice I will make. 'A respectable wife'? I cannot say. Tell me, Dubin"—she smiled cutely—"are you asking?"

Lightly as this was said, I knew enough about her to recognize the stakes. She would chuckle at a proposal, but would be furious if I was as quick to reject her. And at the same time, being who she was, she would chop me to bits for anything insincere. But having left one fiancée behind for little more than a day, I was not ready yet for new promises, even in banter.

"Well, let me say only that I intend to pay very careful attention to your answer."

"You sound like a lawyer."

We laughed.

"Martin once said you will never be content with just one man."

"Eh, he was consoling himself. Believe me, Dubin, I know what I need to know about men. And myself with them. But one person for-ever? For many years that sounded to me like a prison sentence."

"May I ask? Was that perhaps your mother's influence?"

"I think not. My mother, if she had any influence, would have told me to find a fellow like you, decent and stable, and to stand by him. 'One craves peace,' she said always." She sat up into the borrowed light. Gita was more physically shy than I might have expected and I enjoyed the sight of her, her small breasts rising perfectly to their dark peaks.

"But she did not succeed herself."

"She had tried, Dubin. When she was seventeen, her looks attracted the son of a merchant, a wool seller from the city. She thought he was rich and handsome and a sophisticate and married him on impulse."

"This was Lodzka?" I tried to pronounce it correctly.

"Lodzki, yes. He was a cad, of course. He drank, he had other women, he was stingy with her. They fought like minks, even battled with their fists, and naturally she took the worst of it. One day she left him. She returned to Pilzkoba and announced that her husband was dead of influenza. Soon she had suitors. She had been married again for a month, when it was discovered that Lodzki was still alive. It was a terri-ble scandal. She was lucky they did not hang her. She always said she would have left, but it would have given everyone in Pilzkoba too much satisfaction." Gita stopped with a wistful smile. "So," she said.

"So," I answered, and drew her close again. One craves peace.

The next day, late in the afternoon while I was on the wards visiting, a private from the signal office found me with a telegram. Teedle had finally replied.

Seventh Armored Division captured Oflag XII-D outside Saint-
Vith yesterday a.m. STOP Confirms Major Martin alive in
prison hospital STOP Proceed at once STOP Arrest

I had been with Corporal Harzer, the soldier who had lost his foot,
when the messenger put the yellow envelope in my hand.

"Captain, you don't look good," he said.

"No, Harzer. I've seen the proverbial ghost."

I located Bidwell. We'd head out first thing tomorrow. Then I walked
around Bastogne, up and down the snowy streets and passageways. I
knew I would tell Gita. How could I not? But I wanted to contend with
myself beforehand. I had no doubt about her loyalties. She would desert
me. If she did, she did, I told myself again and again, but I was already
reeling at the prospect. I concentrated for some time on how to put this
to her, but in the event, I found I had worked myself into one of those
anxious states in which my only goal was to get it over with. I waited for
her to emerge from the ward on which she was working and simply
showed her the telegram.

I watched her study it. She had left the ward smoking, and as the
hand that held the cigarette threshed again and again through her curls,
I wondered briefly if she would set fire to the nurse's bonnet on her head.
Her lips moved as she struggled with the English. But she understood
enough. Those coffee-dark eyes of hers, when they found me, held a hint
of alarm.

"*Il est vivant?*"

I nodded.

"These are your orders?"

I nodded again.

"We talk tonight," she whispered.

And I nodded once more.

It was well past midnight before I realized she was not coming, and
then I lay there with the light on overhead, trying to cope. My hurt was
immeasurable. With Martin alive, she could not bring herself to be with
me. That was transparent. Their bond, whatever the truth of their relationship, was more powerful than ours.

In the morning, as Bidwell packed the jeep, I sought her out to say goodbye. I had no idea whether I could contain my bitterness, or if I would break down and beg her to take me instead.

"Gita?" asked Soeur Marie, the nun in charge, when I inquired of her whereabouts. "*Elle est partie.*"

How long had she been gone, I asked. Since dark yesterday, the Sister told me.

It took nine hours to reach Saint-Vith and I realized well in advance what we would find. The MP at Oflag XII-D said that a Red Cross nurse, accompanied by two French attendants, had come hours ago to transport Major Martin to a local hospital. We followed his directions there, where, as I had anticipated, no one knew a thing about the nurse, the attendants, or Robert Martin.

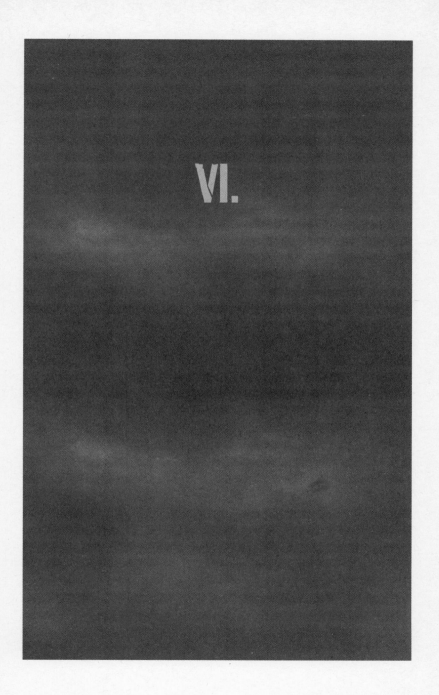

VI.

25. WRONG DISH

When I was a senior in high school, I was desperately in love with Nona Katz, the woman I finally married six years later. The mere thought of parting from her for college left me desolate. I had been admitted to the Honors Program at the U., here in Kindle County. Nona, on the other hand, was never much of a student. She had been lucky to get into State, originally called State Agricultural College, which was not an institution in the same circle of heaven as the more famous university to the north. Not to be overlooked either was the fact that my admission to the U. Honors Program included a tuition waiver and a $1,500 stipend for room and board. My parents used endless ploys to get me to go there. From Kindle County, it was no more than a five-hour drive to State, they said, even in winter weather. They promised to help me buy a used car and pay my phone bills.

"You don't understand," I told them. "You don't understand what this feels like."

"Of course not," said my mother. "How could *we* understand? Ours must have been an arranged marriage."

"Ma, don't be sarcastic."

"It is you, Stewart, who does not understand. I met your father at perhaps the darkest time humanity has ever known. We fully comprehend the wonder of these feelings. That is not, however, all there is to consider."

"Ma, what else matters? What's more important than love?"

My father cleared his throat and took a rare part in our debates.

"Love in the form you are talking about, Stewart, does not remain unchanged forever. You cannot lead your life as if you will never have other concerns."

I was thunderstruck by this remark. First, because my mother looked on approvingly. And second, by the sheer notion that Dad was asserting so coolly. Nona—the discovery that there was some complementary principle in the world—had lifted the stinking fog from my morbid adolescence. My father's blasé assertion that love would somehow evaporate was like telling me I was going to be thrown back into a dungeon.

"You're wrong," I said to him.

"Well, consider that I may be right. Please, Stewart. Love in time takes a form more solid but less consuming. And thank the Lord! No one would ever leave the bedroom. There is work to do, families to raise. It changes, Stewart, and you have to be prepared for what happens next in life."

I did not hear much after that. It was the "thank the Lord" that always stuck with me, evidencing my father's frank relief that he had been able to escape from something as messy and demanding as passion.

And yet it was that selfsame guy I had to contemplate in the arms of Gita Lodz, so nuts with lust that he was rutting in a barn with the farm animals, and then, even more sensationally, getting it on in the bed of a nun. Yet I didn't feel as much discomfort with these scenes as I might have expected. For one thing, when you're big enough to think, on bad days, of replacing your bathroom scale with the ones they use at highway weigh stations, you accept one of life's most cheerful truths. Everybody fucks. Or at least they want to. Notwithstanding American advertisers, it's a universal franchise. The bald truth was that after several months of separation, Gita Lodz struck me as a pretty hot dish. Like my father, I've always been attracted to small women—Nona is barely five feet.

More to the point, I knew the end of the story. Mademoiselle Lodz was just a pit stop on Dad's voyage from Grace Morton to my mother. Irony being the theme song of life, middle-aged Stewart sat in the passenger lounge of the Tri-Counties Airport reading the end of Dad's account and warning young David to think twice. It was only going to turn out badly, I told him. Anticipating a train wreck, I was not surprised to see one at the end.

When I made my second visit to Bear Leach in November 2003, five weeks after our first meeting at Northumberland Manor, I wanted to know the aftermath of all the characters in my father's story. This led into the region where Bear had told me he might not be free to go, and at moments he chose his words carefully. As it turned out, there was plenty he could say about the fate of Robert Martin, and even a little about General Teedle. But asking what had happened to Gita Lodz stopped him cold. I'd brought Dad's manuscript along to illustrate my questions and Bear actually thumbed through the pages in his lap briefly, as if trying to refresh his memory when I mentioned her name.

"Well," he said finally, "perhaps it's most helpful if I give you the sequence, Stewart. I initially made an effort to locate Miss Lodz, believing she could be an important witness to mitigate your father's punishment. That was to be the principal issue at trial, of course, in light of David's intended guilty plea. Your father's service near Bastogne remained my ace in the hole; it was amply documented in his service record, especially in the papers recommending him for the Silver Star, which was approved, by the way, in the War Department, but never awarded as a result of the court-martial. However, I also wanted to show, if I could, that David had fought beside Martin. It would not excuse letting Martin go, but any soldier worth his salt who sat on the court-martial panel would understand an act of mercy toward a comrade-in-arms.

"Accordingly, I hoped to offer a first-person account of the incident in which your father had helped destroy the ammunition dump at the Royal Saltworks, which I learned of when I interviewed Agnès de Lemolland. I pressed the Army for the whereabouts of all the persons who had worked on that operation.

"When I informed your father about that, he became extremely agitated. 'Not the girl,' he said. Since he still refused to tell me anything about what had actually transpired, this frustrated me to no end and I said so.

"'It's beyond discussion,' he said. 'It would be a complete disaster.'

"'For your case?' I asked.

"'Certainly for my case. And personally as well.'

"'And what is the personal stake?' I asked.

"He yielded slightly in his usual adamantine silence and said simply, 'My fiancée.'"

I interrupted Bear. "Grace Morton?"

"Surely not. That was long over by then."

"My mother?"

Leach took his time before finding his way to a dry smile.

"Well, Stewart, I wasn't present when you were born, but you say your mother was an inmate at the Balingen camp and that was certainly the residence of the woman whom your father by then intended to marry."

He studied me with his perpetual generous look to see how I assembled this information.

"So he said, my dad said, it would be a disaster if Mom met Gita Lodz? Or found out about her?"

In a typically aged gesture, Bear's mouth moved around loosely for quite some time as if he was attempting to get the taste of the right words.

"David said no more than what I have stated. I drew my own conclusions at the time. Naturally, I had a far fuller picture when I eventually read what your father had written, which you now have done, too. The personal aspects, I ultimately decided, were best left without further inquiry. But, as a lawyer, I was relieved that your father had prevailed on this point. As I have said, his judgment as a trial attorney was first-rate. Calling Miss Lodz to testify and subjecting her to cross-examination would have been very damaging for his cause."

Having read the whole story by then, I understood. Had Mademoiselle Lodz told her story, Dad's decision to let Martin go could not have been made to look like an act of charity toward a buddy from combat, not even by a trial lawyer as skilled as Leach. In fact, as Bear had said last month, it could have raised the specter of murder in the mind of an imaginative prosecutor.

But that, I figured, was the least of it. Dad might have wanted to shield my mother from the details of his recent love affair. But I was sure the person he most wanted to protect was himself. Having gone on with his life, the last thing Dad needed was to see Gita Lodz. It would have made for a moment of unequaled bitterness, sitting there, knowing he was on the express for Leavenworth, while he looked across the courtroom at the woman who'd used every trick to abet Martin's countless escapes, including, as it turned out, dancing on my father's heart.

I was aware that Bear was watching me closely, but I was in the full grip of the illusion that I finally had some insight into my father, and had suddenly harked back to Dad's advice when I was eighteen. In telling me to base my college choice on something besides the bulge that arose in my trousers at the first thought of Nona, Dad, I saw, was speaking from experience, rather than his native caution. He wanted to keep me from taking my own helping of a dish that had been served cold to him decades ago by Gita Lodz.

26. CAPTURED

Outside the former French Army garrison building which had been used as a civilian hospital in Saint-Vith, Biddy and I awaited the organization of a posse of MPs, while I smoked in the cold. The fighting had taken an enormous toll on this town, too. Almost nothing remained standing. The hospital had survived only because of the huge red crosses painted on its roof.

The Provost Marshal Lieutenant who had surrendered Martin to the nice-looking little nurse was abject when he learned that the Major was a wanted man, but he insisted they could not have gotten far. The explosion in December that had leveled the lodge had also blown off Martin's left hand and a piece of his thigh, as well as layers of hair and flesh on the side of his head. A month later, he still had open burn wounds and had departed from the hospital in a wheelchair.

"If we don't find them," I told Biddy, "Teedle will court-martial *me*. Mark my words. Showing my orders to the known consort of a spy—what was I thinking?"

Biddy cocked a brow at the word 'consort.'

"Cap," he said finally, "let's just get 'em."

My grief over my professional failures seemed trivial, however, compared to the personal devastation. I had assumed Gita would disappoint me, but I'd never imagined she would play me entirely false. One question seemed to peck at my mind like an angry crow. Was she really the new Bernhardt? Had everything she'd exhibited toward me been part of a role? Even while my heart struggled for some other solution, I could not reason my way to any answer but yes. Martin and she were the worst kind of people, I concluded, manipulators willing to prey on the softest emotions. If I saw either, I might reach for my pistol.

According to the U.S. personnel who'd taken over at Oflag XII-D, Martin had been driven off in a horse-drawn cart with a long-haired Gypsy holding the reins. A team of six MPs was gathered to search the town. Biddy and I went to the rail yard, but there were no trains moving yet, not even military ones, and it seemed impossible that Martin could have escaped via his favorite route. I took a point from that. Here in Belgium, Martin had feeble alliances. His chances were better in France—or Germany, where he could rely on what remained of his old network. Heading that way would also allow Martin to continue doing his work for the Soviets. Whichever direction he went, he would need medical attention—or at least medical supplies. And the only reliable source for them was the U.S. Army. Overall, he figured to follow Patton's forces, some of whom would remain friendly to him, especially since, at OSS's insistence, the fact that Martin was wanted was not widely known.

I cabled Camello, stating that Martin had escaped and that we wanted authority to pursue and arrest him. We received a one-word response from Teedle: "Proceed." I was still not sure which of the two I was actually searching for.

Although it was a little like playing pin-the-tail-on-the-donkey, Biddy and I chose to follow the 87th Infantry as it moved out of Saint-Vith toward Prüm. We had encountered battalion commanders of the 347th Infantry Regiment in town and they had agreed to let us accompany them.

Virtually all the territory lost in the Ardennes offensive had been regained and some of Patton's elements were now mounting assaults against the massive concrete fortifications of the Siegfried line at the

German border. The battle was progressing inch by inch, an advantage to Biddy and me, since it would make it hard for Martin to get far. Bidwell and I drove along just behind the fighting, going from one medical collecting company to another. By the third day, we had twice received reports of a little Red Cross nurse who'd presented herself at battalion aid stations. She'd helped minister to the wounded briefly and then disappeared with an armload of supplies.

On the front, the battle lines were constantly shifting, with each side making swift incursions and then drawing back. Several times Biddy and I found ourselves driving into firefights. However slowly, though, the Americans were gaining position and our troops were in a far different mood here than they'd been in during the Bulge. They were not simply more confident, but also hardened by being on enemy soil. Late on our third day, Biddy and I encountered an infantry platoon that had just taken a high point dominated by the house of a prosperous burgher.

A sergeant came out to greet us. "You figure this here is Germany?" he asked. I didn't know from hour to hour if we were in Belgium, Germany, or Luxembourg, but we compared maps and I agreed with his estimate. He then issued a hand signal to his troops and they rushed into the house, emerging with everything of value they could find. China. Candlesticks. Paintings. Linens. Two soldiers struggled through the door with an old tapestry. I had no clue how they even imagined they could get it back to the U.S. The homeowners had made themselves scarce but an old maid had remained and she followed the troops out, shrieking about every item, trying once or twice to grab them from the men's arms. When she would not desist, a thin private pushed her to the ground, where she lay weeping. A corporal delivered a set of silver wine goblets to the sergeant, who offered a couple to Biddy and me.

"I don't drink wine," Biddy said, which was untrue.

"Learn," the sergeant told him, and insisted on heaving them into our jeep.

We stayed the night in the house, where every man in the platoon seemed determined to consume the entire store of liquor they had discovered in the cellar. One literally drank himself into a coma. When a buddy tried to revive him by throwing schnapps in his face, the liquid splattered into the wood-burning stove in the center of the room and the flame leaped up into the bottle, which exploded. Several men were pierced by flying glass, and the couch and the carpet caught fire. The troops were so drunk they howled in merriment while they stomped out the flames, but the lieutenant in charge was irate, inasmuch as four soldiers had to be removed to the aid station.

In the morning, Biddy and I headed south. We were in American-held territory, no more than half a mile from the house, when half a dozen Germans, dressed in black leather coats and armed with Schmeisser machine pistols, leaped up from the ditches on either side of the road and surrounded the jeep. I could see they were SS, rather than Wehrmacht, because of the silver death's-heads over the bills of their caps and the Nazi runes on their coats.

My instinct was to shout out a stupidly casual remark like "Our mistake," and head the other way, but as the six came forward to disarm us, the full gravity of the situation settled on me. I had been off the battlefield ten days now, but I found it had never left me, as I suppose it never will. Within, my spirit shrunk to something as small and hard as a walnut and piped out its familiar resigned message: So if you die, you die.

They ordered us out of the jeep and drove it into a wayside of heavy bushes, marching Biddy and me behind it. As we walked through the snow, Hercules sat in the back of the vehicle, Cleopatra on her barge, surveying the scene with a struggling curiosity like the RCA hound staring into the trumpet of the Victrola. "Look at that dog," Biddy muttered, and we managed a laugh.

Once the jeep was out of sight, the Germans searched us, taking anything useful we had. Compass. Trench knives. Grenades. Watches. And, of course, Bidwell's camera. One of the soldiers looked at the lens and recognized it as German.

"*Woher hast du die?*" he asked Biddy.

Biddy acted as if he did not understand and the SS man raised his Schmeisser and asked the question again. Fortunately, he was distracted when the others found our store of K rations. They each tore through several boxes, tossing aside the cardboard covers with their wavy designs as they ate with feral abandon.

"Cut off from their unit?" I asked Biddy.

He nodded. They clearly hadn't seen food for days.

"Run for it?" he asked. I was still debating, when the German lieutenant came back our way and began to question me in terrible English.

"Vhere Americans? Vhere Deutsch?" They obviously wanted to get back to their side.

I answered with my name, rank, and serial number. The Germans were far too desperate to be bothered with the Geneva Convention. The lieutenant motioned to two of his men, who took me by the shoulders while the lieutenant kicked me three times in the stomach. I was brought back instantly to the schoolyard, the last time I'd survived this panicked breathless moment when the diaphragm stops functioning after a blow to the gut. To make matters worse, when the air finally heaved back into my lungs, I vomited my breakfast on the lieutenant's boot. In reprisal, he struck me in the face with his gloved fist.

My vomiting seemed to catch Hercules' attention. Up until now, the deaf dog had been more interested in the discarded ration tins, but when I was hit this time, he bounded forward and started an enormous racket. He did not attack the German lieutenant, but came within a few feet, rocking back on his paws with his hot breath rising up in puffs, almost like punctuation, as he barked. The Germans immediately began glancing down the road while they futilely attempted to quiet the animal, raising their fingers to their lips, shouting at him, and finally reaching out to subdue him. When the men came after him, Hercules snapped at one and caught his hand, biting right through the leather glove as the German yelped somewhat pathetically.

There was then a single gunshot. The same SS man who'd been questioning Biddy had his pistol out. A little whiff of smoke curled up over the barrel and the dog lay in the snowy road motionless, with a bloody oval like a peach pit where his eye had been. Several of his comrades began shouting at the soldier who'd fired, afraid of the attention the shot would attract. In the confusion, Bidwell joined in.

"What the hell you'd go and do that for?" he demanded. The German soldier with the drawn Schmeisser appeared to have no idea how to respond to the berating he was receiving from all sides. When Biddy strode forward, intent on looking after the dog, the German recoiled slightly and his pistol ignited again in a short automatic burst. Gideon toppled, rolling to his back with three clean bullet holes in his stomach. It had happened so simply, with no preparation at all, and was so pointless, that my first reaction was that it could not be true. How could the world, which has always been here, undergo such a fundamental transformation in two or three seconds?

"Oh my God!" I yelled. I screamed again, one long lament, and for an instant broke away from the two men who were holding me, but they, along with the lieutenant, dragged me down into the ditch. I twisted, cursing them until the lieutenant put the pistol barrel straight to my forehead.

"*Schrei nicht. Schweigen Sie. Wir helfen deinem Freund.* We help." I quieted to see if they'd aid Biddy as promised, and one of them scrambled up to the road. He was back in a second.

"*Er ist tot,*" he said.

The lieutenant could see I understood and immediately placed the icy pistol muzzle to my forehead again. The idea of some vain act of resistance passed through my mind like a weak current. But I'd already learned on the battlefield the desperate, humiliating secret of how badly I wanted to live, and I said nothing, allowing the Germans to drag me along in despair.

With any kind of luck, we'd have encountered American troops, but it was, simply put, not a lucky day. The Germans nearby were mounting an offensive action and my captors moved toward the sounds of the battle. Near nightfall, they hooked up with a German antitank unit, which turned out to have taken a number of Allied prisoners. The unit was being redeployed and we marched at the end of their column, with our hands behind our heads. As the only officer, I was separated from the dozen or so enlisted men by the buffer of a single guard.

We were clearly inside Germany, because at one point we passed through a tiny village where several locals came out to observe us. An old woman rushed from her little house and spat on the first American in line. She was followed by another, younger woman who began to scream, while several more people stepped from their houses. Perhaps to pacify them, one of the German officers ordered us to surrender our coats to the residents. I couldn't see exactly what had happened in this town. Probably nothing different than in any other town. There were still bodies of American and German soldiers pushed to both sides of the road.

We slept that night in an open field. Another prisoner thought we were somewhere near Prüm. We were each issued a worn army blanket but no food. One man, a Brit, had been a prisoner for two days now. He said this was the second time he'd been captured. The first was during Market Garden, the invasion of the Low Countries, and he'd been shipped back to a German stalag in Belgium, not all that far from here, from which he and everyone else had escaped when it was bombed. As the only veteran of captivity, he did his best to remain sunny. If I'd been in a mood to like any human being, I probably would have liked him.

"POW ain't the end of the world, mate, not by my lights. Cuisine ain't the Savoy, but there been days when I ain't et in my own army. It's those blokes out there gettin shot at are 'avin the rough time, if you ask me. This 'ere, it's just boring."

One of the enlisted men asked what the former prison camp had been like.

"Jerries are completely crackers. All day long, they was counting us, mate. Stand up. Sit down. *Eins, zwei, drei.* Not like they were going to give us anything. Food was bread once a day, and couple times this awful potato stew. One day the commandant comes in. 'I have goot news and bat news. Goot news. Today each man will get a change of underwear. Bat news. You must switch with the man next to you.' Only a joke," he added.

Our laughter attracted the German guards, who stomped among us, demanding silence. Nonetheless, the talk resumed shortly. Sooner or later, we were going to be handed off to the Kraut equivalent of the MPs. The Brit didn't think we were going to a stalag. Before his capture, he'd heard that they were housing prisoners in the German cities which the Allies had begun to bomb.

This time, when the two guards heard us talking, they didn't bother with more warnings. They charged around, knocking heads with their rifle butts. I barely ducked when the soldier came at me and I took the blow with little reaction. The pain resounded. But I did not care much. Sooner or later, I realized, they'd take a proper inventory of us and notice the 'H' on my dog tag. At that point, things for me were likely to get considerably worse. But I could not hold on to any concern about that. I did not feel part of this world any longer. It was as if I had sunk one foot inside myself. I often wonder if I will ever fully return.

★★★

The Germans woke us a little before daybreak. We were issued our ration for the day, a roll to be split between two men.

"Eat it now," the Brit said. "Someone will steal it, if you try to save it."

As the guards got us to our feet, the SS lieutenant who'd put the gun to my head passed by. He looked at me and then came over.

"*Wie geht's?*" he asked, manifestly more at ease now that he was back among his own. He thought I spoke more German than I did. I'd been muddling along with my grandparents' Yiddish, and I answered only with a shrug. Even at that, I felt I was a coward. He had perfect blue eyes and he looked at me a moment longer. "*Bald schiessen wir nicht mehr,*" he whispered and gave me a weary smile. He was saying that the shooting was going to be over soon, and didn't seem to hold any illusion he would be on the winning side.

We marched most of the morning. I don't know where the Germans thought they were headed, probably to bolster more of the troops we could hear fighting, but they never got there. As we passed a wood, an American armored cavalry unit appeared out of nowhere. Six Shermans rolled in literally from every direction with their big guns leveled. The German commander surrendered without a shot. Apparently, he had the same view of the war's progress as the lieutenant.

The American troops rushed forward. The Germans who'd been our captors were forced to their knees with their hands behind their heads, while we were greeted like heroes. Two of the men who'd been prisoners had minor wounds, and they were whisked off for medical attention. The rest of us were loaded on a truck and transported to the regimental headquarters, while the Germans marched at gunpoint in the rear. This was the 66th Tank Regiment of the 4th Armored Division. While most of the division had been allowed a respite in Luxembourg after Bastogne, these tankers had been brought in to flank the 87th Infantry. They were doing one hell of a job as far as I was concerned.

Their mobile headquarters, about two miles behind the lines where we'd been captured, consisted of an array of squad tents in a snowy field. Each of the freed Americans was interviewed by regimental G-2. Since I had been the lone officer in captivity, the staff G-2, Major Golsby, interviewed me personally in his tent. He was confused about my orders, which I still had in my pocket, the only thing the Germans hadn't taken.

"I have to go back to Third Army JAG," I told him. If the MPs hadn't found Martin and Gita by now, there was no point in pursuing them now that they had another two days' lead time. More important, I had lost all interest in the mission. I knew as a matter of historical fact that it was my fault Bidwell was dead. My adolescent fascination with both Martin and Gita had led, as tragic errors always must, to tragedy—to combat, capture, and now Biddy's grave.

When I told Golsby what had happened to him, I realized I sounded remote. "I bawled my eyes out yesterday," I added. It was an absolute lie. I was yet to shed a tear. Instead, all my grief about Biddy had energized another of those circling thoughts, this one about why I'd never gotten around to telling him to call me David.

"They shot a POW?" he asked me, repeating the question a few times. "Unarmed? Stay here." He returned with Lieutenant Colonel Coleman, the deputy regimental commander. He looked like a former football player, big and stocky and quick to anger, and he was angry now, as he should have been, at my account of how Biddy died.

"Who did this to your sergeant? Are the men here who did this? Did we capture them?"

Coleman ordered a second lieutenant and a sergeant to accompany me through the camp to look for the SS men. The sergeant was carrying a Thompson submachine gun. The weapon was uncommon enough that I wondered if it was mine, reacquired from the Germans who'd taken it. The captured Krauts had just arrived on foot and were seated in rows with their hands clasped behind their heads. The MPs had made them remove their boots to safeguard against any effort to run. I walked up and down the rows. I had no illusions about what was going to happen.

The SS man who'd killed Bidwell saw me coming. Our eyes had found each other's almost mechanically several times in the last two days. I would steal hateful glances at him, but when his gaze caught mine, I hurriedly looked away, knowing he was easily provoked. Now it was he who turned in the other direction. He wasn't very old, I realized, perhaps twenty-one.

"This one," I told the second lieutenant.

"Get up." The second lieutenant kicked the German's foot. "Get up."

The German was not going to die well. "*Ich habe nichts getan.*" I have done nothing. He shouted it again and again.

The second lieutenant told him to shut up.

"Were there others with him?" I looked down the rows. I found three more, including the German lieutenant who had told me the shooting would end soon. He raised his perfect blue eyes to me, a single look of dignified entreaty, then cast his glance down. He had been at war too long to believe in much.

The four were marched, shoeless in the snow, back to the Lieutenant Colonel. Two of the Germans were virtually barefoot, their socks worn through at the toes.

"Which one did it?" Coleman demanded.

I pointed.

Coleman looked at the man, then withdrew his pistol and put it to the German's temple. The young SS soldier wept and shouted out in his own language yet again that he had done nothing. But he was too frightened to withdraw his head even an inch from the gun barrel.

Coleman watched him blubber with some satisfaction, then holstered his sidearm. The German went on heaving, his protests continuing, albeit in a reduced voice.

"Take them in back," Coleman said to the second lieutenant. I followed along, entirely a spectator, suddenly uncertain about what was to occur. I had been afraid that the Lieutenant Colonel was going to offer me the gun, but I had been disappointed when he decided not to pull the trigger. Now it seemed for the best.

The second lieutenant led the men behind Coleman's tent at the boundary of the camp and ordered the four to turn around with their hands behind their heads. He looked toward me, not long enough to allow much in the way of a reaction, then pointed to the sergeant with the tommy gun, which seemed to have begun firing almost before the weapon was aimed. Afterward, I figured that the sergeant had just wanted to get it over with. A thought arose to say a word for the German lieutenant, but I didn't. The machine gun's spastic bark resounded in the quiet camp and the four Germans went down like puppets cut from their wires.

At the sound, the Lieutenant Colonel came around the tent. Coleman walked along inspecting the four bodies. "Rot in hell," he told them.

I had watched all of this, there and not there. I had been unable to move since the Germans fell. I had been so pleased by the SS man's terror. Now it was as if I was groping around within myself, trying to find my heart.

27. LONDON

February 5, 1945

Dear Folks—

R & R in London. I have a chance at last to describe what we have been through, but at the moment I am in no mood to relive any of it. The war goes well, and I have done my part. But in thinking over everything I have seen, I cannot imagine how I will return home anything but a pacifist. Military calculations are so tough-minded—they must be, clear-eyed determinations of how to win and who must die. But employing the same kind of unsentimental reasoning, it is hard to understand how war—at least this war—has been worthwhile. The toll of daily oppression Hitler would wreak on several nations, even for years, cannot equal the pain and destruction that is being caused in stopping him. Yes, Europe would be in prison. But it is in rubble instead. And is a matter of government worth the millions upon millions of lives lost to this carnage? I came thinking that freedom has no price. But I know now that it is only life about which this may truly be said.

*I send my love to all of you. I cannot wait to be with you
again.*

David

I returned to Third Army Headquarters in Luxembourg City on February 1, 1945. Because the Luxembourgers were regarded as inappropriately accommodating to the Germans, Patton had treated them with little sympathy and had literally turned out the elderly residents of the national old people's home, the Fondation Pescatore, taking it for his headquarters. It was a castle-size structure of orange limestone squares and, with its two projecting wings, vast enough to accommodate both the forward- and rear-echelon staffs. Colonel Maples had been favored with a third-floor salon, where invalids formerly sunned in the banks of high windows, and he was extremely pleased with his surroundings. He walked me to the glass to ensure that I saw his view of the dramatic gorge that plunged several hundred feet, bisecting Luxembourg City. The furnishings in his office, like those of others in the senior staff, had been provided by a cousin of the Grand Duc's, whose generosity only enhanced the suspicion that he had collaborated with the Germans. The Colonel took a moment to point out the gold-mottled tortoise-shell inlay on his desk and credenzas, priceless heirlooms created in the time of Louis Quatorze by the cabinetmaker Boulle. Logs blazed in the marble fireplace, beside which the Colonel and I drew up two damask-covered chairs. The contrast to the frozen holes in which I had been dwelling only weeks ago was unavoidable, but my mind seemed incapable of making anything from it. There were no conclusions, except that life and, surely, war were absurd, something I already felt as palpably as the bones within my body.

The Colonel leaned forward to clasp my shoulder.

"You look a little worse for wear, David. Thinner and perhaps not the same bright look in your eye."

"No, sir."

"I've seen some papers for medals. You've done quite remarkably."

I recounted my failures for the Colonel. I'd lost the best man I'd met in the service and let Martin get away as the result of my own cupidity. This candor was characteristic of my exchanges with virtually everyone. I steadfastly rejected the fawning of colleagues like Tony Eisley, even while I became quietly furious with one or two people who treated me as if I'd been AWOL or, worse, on vacation. The truth was that no one's reactions pleased me. But because Colonel Maples had fought across the trenches a quarter century ago, a bit of my perpetual bitterness eased in his presence. If anything, my respect for him, never insubstantial, had increased, knowing he had volunteered to return to war. I would never do that. Nor could I imagine acquiring his avuncular grace. Today I could only picture myself as an irascible old man.

The Colonel, with his soft gray eyes, listened for a while.

"You are grieving, David. No one ever mentions that as an enduring part of war. You need some time."

I was given two weeks R & R. Most officers on leave retreated to Paris, where the joy of liberation was enshrined in an atmosphere of guiltless debauchery, but that hardly fit my mood. I chose London, where I found a tiny hotel room off Grosvenor Square. I had made no plans other than to sit in a hot tub for hours, and to review the foot of mail that had awaited me in Luxembourg City. I wanted to sleep, read a few novels, and when I was able, write several letters.

In retrospect, I suppose I had crossed the Channel with the unspoken thought of again being whoever I was before I'd set foot on the Continent. But the war followed me. I'd barely slept longer than two or three hours in a row since Biddy and I had first been dispatched to arrest Martin. Now I was startled to find that I could not sleep at all. I had not spent a night entirely alone within solid walls for months, and I had the feeling they were encroaching. Often I couldn't even stand to close my eyes. The second night I bought a bottle of scotch. But several belts did not make things any better. The ghouls of war took control. Each time I drifted off some panicked sensory recollection raced at me—the keening of incoming artillery, the sight of Collison with his intestines in his bloody hands, the three holes in Biddy's stomach, the earthquake and thunder of the 88s, or the unbearable cold of Champs. And always there were the dead and, worse, the dying, screaming to be saved.

In the aftermath of all that, I guess I expected to feel some gratitude for being alive. But life had been a far sweeter affair without being confronted by the dread of extinction. I had become so accustomed to being afraid that fear was now a second skin, even in the relative safety of London. I awaited artillery blasts in the parks, snipers in every tree. I was ashamed of my fear, and frequently angry. I wanted to be alone, because I was not sure I could treat anyone else decently.

The letters I expected to write came hard. So much seemed beyond words. I wrote to Biddy's family for more than two days, draft after draft, and ended up with something barely longer than a note. I found it impossible to describe the bathos of his death, hoping to comfort a dog, after summoning such valor on so many prior occasions. The only solace I could offer was to enclose hundreds of his photographs which I'd gathered from his belongings. I promised to visit the Bidwells, if I was lucky enough to return alive. In the days that I had composed and recomposed this letter, I had envisioned putting the pen down at the end and, in utter privacy, finally sobbing. But I had never been a weeper, even in the later years of childhood, and tears still would not come, leaving me in a state of constipated agitation.

Then there was Grace. In my two days of German captivity, when the combination of Biddy's death and Gita's desertion had left me feeling certain that I was going to die of heartbreak, I'd had second thoughts about Grace. She was beautiful and brilliant and steady. The one thing I could say with utmost sincerity was that I wished that I could see her, because I had learned that presence meant everything. But without a photo in my hand I could barely bring her to mind. If we were together, if Grace were in my arms, then I might have had some chance of retrieving our life. "Here, here, here," I kept repeating to myself whenever I thought of her, feeling largely enraged that something so dignifying and eternal as love could be defeated by distance. Yet the memory of Gita, of her bare skin and the moments when we'd seemed to fuse souls, easily withstood whatever had been left behind for thousands of miles and many months. By now, I was willing to say only to my most private self that I did not fully regret Gita. I had told Biddy that I was in love with her. That seemed ludicrous. I had been the kind of fool men often were for sex. But even so, I found certain images of her recurrent and fabulously arousing. Again and again I saw her looming over me naked, stimulating me with unashamed intensity. Fantasies of how I might come to find her again in the burning ruins of Europe revolved through me, even as I sometimes begged myself not to abandon the decent life I knew I could make with Grace. But it was not a time for logic. I desired Gita against all reason, and my inability to control my passions seemed part and parcel of the harsh season I was experiencing within the narrow cold confines of my room.

I made it a point to walk as much as I could, but even on the London streets I found my thinking little more than a procession of spotlighted theater scenes, in which various figures, the dear and the dead and the dreaded, made unpredictable leaps onto center stage. Often I saw Robert Martin and Roland Teedle there. In most moods, I hated both of them for letting loose the torrent of events in which I was now drowning. In better moments, I realized that one of the barriers to righting myself was the fact that I still did not know which of them to believe. I despised Martin for his deceptions, but I remained unconvinced at the deepest level that the man I had seen swing down into the Seille like a real-life Jack Armstrong would stoop to spying. Even at this late date, some part of what I'd been told seemed untrue, and that in turn seemed to emanate somehow from the core of uncontrolled excess I'd always sensed in Teedle. Amid all the disgraces I'd suffered, my doubts about the bona fides of the commands that had led me to peril and ruin seemed intolerable.

My tours around the West End took me several times down Brook Street. I recalled the address from Teedle's order to Martin to return to London. What I found at number 68, a block from the U.S. Embassy and across the street from Claridge's, was an ordinary West End row house, with a dormered fourth floor, a limestone exterior on the ground level, and a roofed entryway. This presumably was the OSS, or at least one arm of it. There was no plate identifying the building's occupants, but after passing by a few times I noticed enough foot traffic in and out to convince me that an organization of one kind or another was housed there, and on my fifth or sixth morning in London, I unlatched the iron gate and walked up to the door. Inside, I asked the tidy middle-aged receptionist if I could speak to Colonel Bryant Winters. I gave her my name.

"Regarding?"

"Major Robert Martin." The faintest lick of reaction trickled into her bland face. I was directed to a straight-backed chair across the way. She had other business to occupy her, but eventually spoke into her phone.

I'd had very little notion of the OSS before I'd been assigned to Martin's case, but its mythology had grown in my mind and those of most other soldiers in the European theater. The stories of derring-do in France, Italy, and Africa were, even if untrue, greatly entertaining, and had become staples in the constant gossip and apocrypha that provided important diversions in a soldier's day-to-day life: OSS had wiped out a battalion of German artillery to the man by poisoning their rations. Special Services agents had dropped from the sky, surrounded Rommel's tent, and spirited him back to Rome, where he was being questioned.

Within the inner sanctum, however, the atmosphere was anything but swashbuckling. It was, rather, very much like the Yale Club, which I'd once visited in Manhattan, where everyone seemed to speak with his jaw tightened and where I sensed that Jews or Catholics would always be treated with a courtesy that would never embrace complete welcome. NOK, as some of the more genteel fraternity boys at Easton were apt to put it—not our kind. The men here had good American names and many had eschewed military attire in favor of tweed jackets. Something about the milieu appalled me, especially the degree to which I knew I had once hungered after this like a hound perched beside a table. Whatever had happened to me, I was well beyond that now.

I was absorbed with these reflections when a tall man in a uniform presented himself. I jumped up to salute. This was Colonel Winters. He smiled like a graceful host.

"Captain, we had no word you were coming. My aide is back there thumbing through the cables, but I recognized your name. Judge Advocate, right? I take it it's the usual signal foul-up?"

I shrugged, the familiar gesture of eternal helplessness that was part of life in the Army.

"Well, come along." He had a small office with full bookshelves among the freshly painted white pilasters and just enough room for two small ebony chairs, on which we sat facing each other. His large desk was columned with bound reports. As he closed the door, he permitted himself a well-behaved laugh. "That was a bit of a stir you created. We don't have soldiers wandering in off the street to talk about our operatives."

"No, of course not. But it's official business." I tried to avoid outright lying, yet I said nothing to dispel the idea that Maples had signaled ahead of me. I simply indicated that as long as I was in London, I had decided it was best to formalize certain matters in my investigation, which had to be completed if Martin's court-martial were ever to proceed someday.

"Of course, of course," answered Winters. He was impeccable, with a long handsome face and brilliantined hair sharply parted. But he had an easy air. Despite Winters' uniform, I didn't feel as if I were in a military environment. No colonel, not even Maples, would have come to greet me, and we chatted amiably about London and then the war. He asked what I could tell him about the front. We were going to win, I said. That conviction had returned to me. I told him about the German lieutenant who had expected an end to shooting soon, but made no mention of his death.

"Good, good," said Winters. "And tell me, then, Captain, what information is it you wish from us?"

I named several points on which direct confirmation from OSS was still required, reciting all of it in a drone meant to suggest my regrets about the punctiliousness of the law to which I was a slave. First, we needed to confirm that Martin had been ordered back to London by OSS. Second, that he had not been directed by OSS to blow the Saline Royale ammo dump when he had. Third, that Major Martin was a Soviet spy.

At the last request, Winters frowned noticeably.

"That's Teedle's word, then. That he is a Soviet spy?"

When I said yes, Winters reached down to fuss with his trouser cuff.

"I can confirm for you," he said, "that Martin has been insubordinate. That he has disobeyed direct orders, and conducted important military operations without final authorization. And that OSS supports his apprehension."

"And his court-martial?"

"In all likelihood. After we've spoken with him."

"But not charges as a spy?"

Winters raised his eyes to a window and the trees on Brook Street.

"Correct me, Captain. Are you the one who parachuted into Bastogne?"

"There were actually two of us," I said. "My sergeant and me. And no one had to kick Bidwell in the behind to get him out of the plane."

Winters smiled. Throughout the war, OSS operatives had done things like we had. Those acts were, in fact, the calling card of the agency, and I found it a bitter irony that so many of these mild, bookish types defined themselves by those exploits. If I hadn't made that jump, Winters probably would have left me in his reception area, never bothering to receive me. But I didn't feel like a member of their club. The soldiers at the front had few illusions about what they had endured.

These men, with their self-congratulations and sense of noblesse oblige, lived on their own myths and probably refused to share with one another the essential information that those who carried out their operations did so in terror. In that, Winters appeared slightly different, and was seemingly pleased I was not seeking to impress him.

"And you jumped because Teedle told you Martin was a Soviet spy?"

I no longer remembered why I had done that. Probably because I did not yet understand how terrible it was to die. But I knew a leading question when I heard one, and nodded. Colonel Winters drew his hand to his mouth.

"I have great regard for Rollie Teedle. He's a magnificent commander. There's no other brigadier general in the Army bearing that kind of responsibility. He should have had his second star long ago, but for all the rumor-mongering."

I didn't bother asking what the rumors were.

"I have no doubt that someone here offered Teedle that surmise about Martin," said Winters. "That's surely the prevailing opinion. But it's only an opinion. Candidly, Captain, no one knows precisely what Martin is up to. Certainly it's not anything we've told him to do. Which lends itself to the idea that he's serving someone else's commands. And the Russians, given his background—that's the logical conclusion. Clearly, we can't have him out there on the loose. It's a very dangerous situation."

Even I could see that. "Were there prior signs he was disloyal?"

"No, but the truth is that he'd never been put to the test. This fall Martin was given a top secret briefing back here in London concerning a project we wanted him to undertake in Germany. And the information he learned then would be of special consequence to the Soviets. He made some remarks at the time which unsettled folks here. That's why, after some second thoughts, he was ordered to return. Wrong man for the job, we decided. It wasn't until he ran off that it occurred to anyone that he'd head into the Russians' arms. But if you knew the details, you'd agree it's the most reasonable conclusion. I'm sorry, Dubin, to be so cryptic. I can't say more."

I told him I understood.

"Personally," said Winters, "I hold to a sentimental belief that these conclusions are wrong. But it's a view I keep to myself, because, frankly, I have no other explanation for his behavior."

"Anyone having any better luck finding him than I did?" I'd relinquished the search for Martin when I got back to Luxembourg City and had had no news since. Robert Martin had made nothing but misery for me. Revenge being what it is, I might have relished the sight of him in handcuffs. But I felt that the best homage I could make to Biddy was to give up the quest, without which he'd be alive.

"We'll catch up with him in time. We don't want the Provost Marshal posting an all-points bulletin that might tip the Russians. We'd like to pull Martin in quietly. But he recruited many of the contacts we have in Germany, and a lot of them are leftists, union people, whose leanings these days, as between the Soviets and the other Allies, are a matter of doubt. And beyond that, it's a difficult proposition to tell them to turn their back on the man whom they've always seen as the face of this organization. It's all rather delicate. We've had several reports after the fact. Martin's been in touch with some of his old contacts, but only asks assistance in making his way. He presents himself as on a very sensitive mission. Once or twice, he's asked to be hidden. Him and the girl."

"The girl is with him?"

"I take it you've met her. Beguiling as they say?"

"In her way," I answered.

"I've never had the pleasure. She has her own legend around here. Martin recruited her out of a Marseilles hospital where she was working as an aide. A genius at playing her parts, whatever they are, and willing to do anything. Made the ultimate sacrifice, if you know what I mean, to get information out of a German officer a few years back, fellow who'd been a patient and continued to pursue her. Critical information about the bombing of London. She deserves a medal, if you ask me, but people in this building get squeamish about acknowledging those kinds of activities. Oldest trick in spying, really, sleeping with the enemy, but that's one of our dirty little secrets." He smiled, enjoying his double entendre.

He continued by telling the story I'd heard before about Gita rescuing Martin from the Gestapo by feigning pregnancy. It was fortunate Winters had gone on speaking, because I was not able to. Sleeping with the enemy. I stared at the intricate weave of the Colonel's carpet, which probably had been trod on for a century, trying to calculate what all of this meant for me. Every time I thought I'd absorbed the last from this woman there was more.

"And is she, the girl—is she with the Soviets, too?" I asked.

Winters shrugged. "Unclear. If Martin is really in this game, he might have shared his goals with no one. And then again—" He lifted a hand with elegant understatement. "Anyway, we're a bit astray."

I stood. He offered to buy me dinner one night while I was here, but I doubted, after hearing this information, that I'd have the heart to see him. I remained vague, and said I'd ring if I found a break in my schedule.

Bad as the period before had been, Winters' news about Gita drove me into a turmoil that was even more intense, making my efforts to focus on the outer world increasingly tenuous. I walked toward Green Park and found, half an hour later, that I was still standing at the edge of one of the paths, with my hand on the cold iron railing, beleaguered by what tumbled inside me. When I looked in the mirror I saw a man of normal appearance, but it was as if that outer self was the backside of a moving-picture screen. On the reverse a movie marathon played, a never-ending splash of imagery and sound, all of it tortured. Often, as I plunged along the streets, I thought, I am having a nervous breakdown, and was propelled back to the present only by the panic that accompanied the thought.

With three days to go on my leave I packed up. Before I left, I wrote briefly to Grace. Dashed by Gita, I still could not rebound toward Grace. I would never explain why deluding myself about one woman had meant a death to my love for the other, but that was clearly the case. Grace was estimable in every way. But she was a piece of a life I would never return to. That much was concluded. And so was my time away from the service. Any further idleness would rot me. I needed work. I would head back to Luxembourg City. There would be cases to try. Men to hang.

But I sensed that even the drama of the law might fail to preoccupy me. If I remained in this abyss, there could be only one choice. I knew instantly and found not the remotest irony in my decision. I would apply for transfer to the infantry and return to combat. The desperation to remain alive, to kill rather than die, was the only reliable distraction from what was rocketing around my mind.

Only as I closed the door on the hotel room, with my duffel slung across my back, did the full import of my plans strike home, and somehow it was Gita who addressed me. I listened to her voice in the same state of fury and surrender that had tormented me for days, wanting not to hear it and hearing it nonetheless.

"You are Martin," she said.

February 11, 1945

Dear Grace,

I have spent the last week in London, attempting to recover from what has transpired. After months of sharing so many impressions with you, I know how sparse I've been with details of the fighting. But there is no point to saying more. Imagine the worst. It is more awful than that. I came across the ocean, regretting that I was to be but a pretend soldier. I have been a soldier in earnest in the last months, and I regret that far more.

I now know, Grace, that I will not be able to come home to you. I feel myself damaged in some essential way I will never fully repair. I thought when I arrived here that love would survive anything. But that was one of many fabrications I carried along. For me, our sweet world has ended.

I know what a shock this letter must be. And I am crippled with guilt and shame when I imagine you reading it. But I am in a mood that seems to require me to cast off all illusions, and that includes the notion that I could return to be a loving husband to you.

I will carry you with me eternally. My regard and admiration are forever.

Please forgive me,

David

VII.

28. VISITING

For several years when Sarah and I were little, my mother would dress us up once each summer and put us in our Chevy with my father. There was a touch of foreboding about these trips, probably because Dad didn't take us many places without Mom, except for baseball games, which she regarded as permanently incomprehensible. It was summer, and Sarah and I were not in school, and this little automobile trip was the last thing either my sister or I wanted to do. Before getting very far, Sarah or I would claim to be carsick. But Dad continued, driving about twenty minutes into the heart of the black belt, proceeding through the most blighted streets until reaching a tidy block of three-flats. There he extracted my sister and me from the auto, notwithstanding our complaints.

Inside, we visited briefly with a soft-spoken light-toned black lady named Mrs. Bidwell. These meetings were palpably painful to everyone. After we'd come all that way, neither my dad nor Mrs. Bidwell seemed to have a clue what to say. In fact, even as a child, I realized that my sister and I had been hauled along principally as conversation pieces, so that the old woman could exclaim over how we had grown and Dad could agree. Race was not the issue. My parents lived in University Park, one of the earliest and most successfully integrated neighborhoods in the U.S., and they were comfortable socializing with black neighbors.

In Mrs. Bidwell's living room, we drank one glass of excellent lemonade, then went on our way. When I asked each time why we had to stop, my father said that Mrs. Bidwell was the mother of a boy he used to know. Period. I didn't even think of her when I started reading Dad's account because she was black, unlike Gideon Bidwell—yet another boat I missed.

Years ago, I broke a story about one of the supervising lawyers in the Kindle County Prosecuting Attorney's Office, whose gambling habit left him indebted to local loan sharks. My source was an FBI agent who was understandably concerned about the perils of having an Assistant P.A. in the pocket of hoodlums, and the Bureau guy even showed me the federal grand jury transcripts so I could reassure my editors before we went to press.

It was a great coup for me. The only problem was that the prosecutor involved, Rudy Patel, was a pretty good friend of mine. Both serious baseball fans, Rudy and I were part of a group that shared season tickets to the Trappers' games. We'd often sit side by side, cursing the Trappers' perpetual misfortunes, high-fiving homers as if we'd hit the balls, and berating the players for strikeouts and errors. Bleeding for the Trappers is a Kindle County ritual and it became a bond between Rudy and me. I gave him good coverage on his trials. And then cost him his job.

Fortunately for Rudy, he got into an impaired lawyers program, enrolled in Gamblers Anonymous, and avoided getting disbarred or prosecuted. Naturally, though, he had to be fired, and was required to live with the ignominy of being outed by me. He ended up as a professor at a pretty good local law school and has gone on with his life, albeit with none of the promise that radiated around him earlier. I took care of that.

Rudy and I still live on the same bus line to Nearing and every now and then in the station we'll see each other. Every time I do, I can feel myself light up instinctively with the affection of our old friendship, and even see him begin to brighten, until his memory returns and he retreats into loathing. Over the years, his look of pure hatred has abated a little. He must know I was doing my job. But the fact is that there's nowhere to go. Even if he forgave me wholeheartedly, our friendship would be part of a past that he's both set aside and overcome.

I mention this because it reminds me a little of my father's visits with Mrs. Bidwell. These brief meetings clearly upset Dad. Driving home, he had a look of quick-eyed distraction, gripping and regripping the steering wheel. I don't know what illusion had brought him to the North End. That he was obliged to keep faith and memory? That by showing us off he could restore just a shred of the stake in the future Mrs. Bidwell had lost with the death of her son? But after the last of these trips, when I was about ten, Dad looked at my mother as soon as we returned home and said, "I can't do that again." My mother's expression was soft and commiserating.

I'm sure Dad kept his vow and didn't go back. As I have said, there was never a living place for the war in my father's life. It was not life. It was war. Loyalty could not overcome that.

Nor, frankly, do I imagine that Mrs. Bidwell ever tried to contact him again. Looking back, I'm struck that neither Mr. Bidwell nor Biddy's brothers were ever there. For them, there was probably never any accommodating themselves to the intolerable irony of losing a son and a brother whose only equal opportunity involved dying.

In the end, Mrs. Bidwell and Dad were a lot like Rudy and me. There was a shared history, but it was a history they were impotent to change. Fate, inexplicably, had favored one and not the other. There was no erasing that inequity, or any other. And because they were powerless in these ways, they could only regard what the past had dished up with great sadness and then move on to the very separate lives that remained.

29. WINNING

From *Don't Be a Sucker in Germany!*, a pamphlet published by the 12th Army Group, found among my father's things:

The facts in this booklet were compiled by the Provost Marshal of the Ninth U.S. Army as a guide for troops in Germany. Nothing here was "dreamed up" by someone behind a desk. This booklet is a summary of the experiences of the French, Dutch, and Belgian underground workers now serving with the American armies. They know the tricks and the answers. That's why they are alive to pass this information on to you.

DON'T BELIEVE IT

Don't believe there are any "good" Germans in Germany. Of course you know good Germans back home. They had guts enough and sense enough to break from Germany long ago.

Don't believe it was only the Nazi government that brought on this war. Any people have the kind of government they want and deserve. Only a few people bucked the Nazis. You won't meet them; the Nazis purged them long ago.

One Belgian major, wounded twice in two wars with Germany, was stationed in Germany from 1918 to 1929. He says:

"A German is by nature a liar. Individually he is peaceful enough, but collectively, Germans become cruel."

If a German underground movement breaks out, it will be merciless. It will be conducted by SS and Gestapo agents who don't flinch at murder. They will have operatives everywhere. Every German, man, woman, and child, must be suspected. Punishment must be quick and severe. This is not the same thing as brutality. Allied forces must show their strength but must use it only when necessary.

We won the war. In February and March, the Allies ground forward. The Germans finally seemed to realize they were overwhelmed—depleted by the Battle of the Bulge (as people were now calling what had happened in the Ardennes), outmanned in the skies, and facing massive Russian forces attacking on their eastern front. *"Bald schiessen wir nicht mehr."*

For the Third Army, the principal problems were weather and terrain. The worst winter in fifty years abated with an early thaw, swelling the rivers and streams in the mountainous landscape on which the Siegfried line had been erected. Waterways that our forces once could have forded on foot now required bridging by the engineers while the troops waited. But Patton, as always, advanced. Nineteenth Tactical Air Command provided comprehensive support for the forward columns. On March 22, Patton defied Supreme Headquarters and secretly mounted a massive assault across the Rhine, thereby depriving Montgomery of the intended honor of being the first general into the German heartland. The fur was flying around HQ for weeks afterward, and I have no doubt that Patton's little mutiny provided much of the impetus that led to him being relieved of command as general of the Third Army by May.

Even with the end in sight, our progress brought none of the jubilation that had accompanied the liberation of France. Our men had been at war too long to celebrate combat, and, far more important, there was the daily evidence of what our victory meant to the local populations. A relentless parade of Germans driven from their homes by the fighting flowed back into our path, marching along with their most valued possessions on their backs. They lived in the open in unhappy packs that were soon breeding grounds for typhus. Some waved the Stars and Stripes as we passed, but we had killed their sons and fathers, and exploded or plundered their houses. For the most part, there was a miserable sulking suspicion between them and us, especially since we knew that many German soldiers had ditched their uniforms to hide among the throngs of the displaced.

Despite mass German desertions, the Third Army alone took 300,000 German POWs in those weeks. They were trucked to the rear, dirty, hungry, defeated men, herded into barbed-wire cages, many of whom, when addressed, prayed for the end of the fighting, which, under the Geneva Conventions, would allow them to go home.

As for me, I remained desolate and occasionally temperamental. I never carried through on my threat to myself to volunteer for combat. Instead, I went through the routines of a military lawyer with proficiency and disinterest. Reports describing thefts, rapes, and murders of Germans arrived on our desks in a tide and were generally ignored. We proceeded only with investigations of serious crimes against our own troops. It was not simply that the Germans were our enemies. Many military commanders, including General Maples—he was promoted April 1—expressed the view that a nasty occupation in Germany was justified, not so much in the name of revenge, but so that the Germans saw firsthand what they had unleashed on the rest of the world. I never contested that point of view.

But I contested little. For me, the war was over. Like the cities and towns of western Europe, my steeples lay in ruins. I wanted only to go home and find time to pick through the rubble. It was the downcast civilians, as much as our own troops, with whom I often felt a bond.

From home, I continued to receive heartsore entreaties from Grace Morton, who refused to accept my judgment that our marriage would never occur. *My darling,* she wrote, *I know how awful this time has been for you and the tragedies you have witnessed. Soon, we will again be together, this madness will be forgotten, and we will be one.*

I wrote back with as much kindness as I could muster, telling her she would save us both continued anguish by abiding by my decision. In response, her letters grew more openly pleading. When they went unanswered, her magnificent dignity wore away. One day I would receive a diatribe about my disloyalty, the next a rueful and lascivious contemplation of how wrong we had been not to sleep together before my departure. I forced myself to read each note, always with pain. I was stunned by the extraordinary contagion bred by war, which had somehow conveyed my madness across the ocean to infect her.

The Third Army moved its forward HQ twice within a week, ending up in early April in Frankfurt am Main, which had been bombed unceasingly before our arrival. Blocks of the city were nothing but hillocks of stone and brick above which a little aura of dust lingered whenever the wind stirred. In the area close to the main train station, a number of the older buildings remained standing and the Staff Judge Advocate set up in a former commercial building on Poststrasse. I was given a spacious office that had belonged to an important executive, and was still unpacking there on April 6 when a chubby young officer came in, twirling his cap in his hands. He was Herbert Diller, an aide to the Assistant Chief of Staff of the Third Army, who wished to see me. I was rushing down the block with him toward the General staff headquarters before he mentioned the name Teedle.

I had not seen the General in person since the day I had slunk back from the Comtesse de Lemolland's to report Martin's initial disappearance. As far as I knew, Teedle had received my written reports, although I'd gotten no response. Now, from Diller, I learned that on April 1, General Teedle had been relieved of command of the 18th Armored, which was being cycled into a reserve position for the balance of the war. With that, Roland Teedle had become Patton's Assistant Chief of Staff. As Diller and I hurried down the broad halls of this former government ministry, I could hear Teedle yelling. His target turned out to be his corporal Frank, who'd been transferred with him.

General Teedle looked smaller and older in the office where I found him, a somber room with high ceilings and long windows. He was on his feet, facing, with evident bewilderment, a desk on which the papers looked as if they'd simply been dumped. I was surprised to feel some warmth for the General at the first sight of him, but I suppose after my visit to OSS in London, I'd come to recognize that he had been right about most things. Whatever else, Robert Martin was both disingenuous and a subversive force in the military. Not that I'd completely forgotten Bonner's accusation. It occurred to me for a second that Teedle might have been moved to HQ so someone could keep an eye on him. But I'd

never know for sure, not whether Bonner spoke the truth, or had mis-
perceived other conduct, or, even if correct, where Teedle's misbehavior
should rank among the war's many other travesties.

I congratulated the General on his new posting. Another star had
come with it. As usual, he had no interest in flattery.

"They're already replacing the warhorses, Dubin. They think diplomats should be in charge. The next phase of the war will be political. I'd
rather be feeding cattle than sitting behind a desk, but at least there's
some work left to do. Patton wants to be in Berlin before the end of the
month, and I believe we will be. So how did you like war, Dubin? A
bitch, isn't it?"

I must have betrayed something in response to his scoffing, because
Teedle focused on me with concern.

"I know you had a bad time, Dubin. I don't mean to make light of it."

"I don't think I'm the only one with sad stories to tell."

"There are three million men here with nightmares to take home
with them, and a million or so more half a world away. Makes you wonder what kind of country we can ever be. So much of civilization, Dubin,
is merely the recovery periods between wars. We build things up and
then tear them down again. Look at poor Europe. Some moments I find
myself thinking about all the fighting that's gone on here and expect
blood to come welling out of the ground."

"You sound like Martin, General." As ever, I was surprised by my for-
wardness with Teedle. But he seemed to expect it.

"Oh, hardly, Dubin. I'm sure Martin wants to put an end to war. I
take it as part of the human condition."

My expression, in response, was undoubtedly pained, but in retrospect I am unsure whether that was because I resisted Teedle's view, or
regarded it as a harrowing truth. Observing me, Teedle leaned back and
drummed a pencil on the thigh of his wool trousers.

"Do you know what this war is about, Dubin?"

Teedle had made Diller wait outside and I could hear voices gathering, meaning another meeting was about to take place, most likely involving officers superior to me. But I wasn't surprised that the General
wanted to take time for this discussion. There had never been any question that Teedle found something essential in his contest with Martin.
He opposed everything Martin stood for—the solitary adventurer who

thought he could outwit the machines of war; a spy who favored deception over hand-to-hand assault; and, of course, a Communist who would give to each man according to his need, as opposed to the fathomless will of God.

I asked if he was referring to the Treaty of Versailles.

"Fuck treaties," he said. "I mean what's at stake. In the largest terms."

I knew Teedle valued my seriousness, and I tried not to be flippant, but the fact was that I had no idea anymore and I said so. Teedle, naturally, had a view.

"I think we're fighting about what will unite people. I think that all of these machines we've fallen in love with in this epoch—the railroad, the telegraph and telephone, the automobile, the radio, the moving-picture camera, the airplane, God knows what else—they've changed the compass of life. A shepherd who tended his flock or a smith at his forge, folks who knew only their fellow townsmen, now contend with people a thousand miles away as an immediate presence in their lives. And they don't know exactly what they have in common with all those distant companions.

"Now, along come the Communists, who tell the shepherd the common interest is the good of man, and maybe he should give up a few sheep to the poor fellow a few towns over. And then we have Mr. Hitler, who tells his citizens that they should be united by the desire to kill or conquer anyone who doesn't resemble them. And then there's us—the Allies. What's our vision to compete with Mr. Stalin and Mr. Hitler? What are we offering?"

"Well, Roosevelt and Churchill would say 'freedom.' "

"Which means?"

"Personal liberty. The Bill of Rights. The vote. Freedom and equality."

"For what end?"

"General, I have to say I feel as if I'm back in law school."

"All right, Dubin. I hear you. I think we're fighting for God, Dubin. Not Christ or Yahweh or wood elves, no God in particular. But the right to believe. To say that there is a limit to this big collective society, there's something more important for every human, and he will find it on his own. But we're trying to have it two ways, Dubin, to be collective and individual at the same time, and it's going to get us in trouble. We can't tolerate Fascists *or* Communists, who want the same answer for every person.

Or the capitalists either, if you want to know the truth. They want everyone to stand up for materialism. And that's a collectivism of its own and we have to recognize it as such."

"There's quite a bit of collectivism in religion, General, people who want you or me to do exactly as they believe."

"That's the nature of man, Dubin. And very much, I think, as God expects. But it's the human mission to welcome all reasonable contenders."

I wasn't following and said so. Teedle circled around his desk, coming closer in a way that felt strangely unguarded for him.

"I believe in democracy," he said, "for exactly the same reason Jefferson did. Because God made each of us, different though we may be. Human variety expresses His infiniteness. But His world still belongs to those who will struggle to do the mission He has chosen for them, whether it's the Trappist contemplating His will in silence, or the titan astride the globe. If God made a world with a billion different human plans, He must have expected struggle. But He couldn't have intended a world where one vision prevails, because that would mean only a single vision of Him, Dubin."

"Is war what God wants then, General?"

"We all think about that one, Dubin. I can't tell you the answer. All I know is He wants us to persevere." He picked up a paper off his desk. "I've been getting reports for a day now from a place called Ohrdruf. Heard anything about that?"

"No, sir."

"Three thousand political prisoners of one kind or another lying in shallow graves, starved to death by the Nazis. The few who remain alive survive in unimaginable squalor. The communiqués keep repeating that words can't describe it. God must want us to fight against that, Dubin."

I shrugged, unwilling to venture onto that ground, while the General continued to scrutinize me. I understood only then what my attraction had been to Teedle from the start. He cared about my soul.

"All right, Dubin. So much for the bright chatter. I have an assignment for you, but I thought we should have a few words first. I heard about your visit to London, checking up on me."

"I did what I always told you I had to, General. Confirm the details."

"You were checking up on me. I don't mind, Dubin. I suspect at this stage you hate Robert Martin more than I do."

"I've come to feel rather neutral, to tell you the truth, sir. I can't really make out what his game is. He might just be mad in his own way."

"He's a spy, Dubin. Nothing more complicated than that. He's on the other side."

There was no question that Martin and the General were on different sides. But so were Teedle and I. Not that I could name any of these camps.

"As you wish, General, but I wasn't trying to be insubordinate. I simply wanted to see matters to a logical end."

"Well, you haven't done that, have you, Dubin? The son of a bitch is still cavorting around."

"He could be dead for all I know, sir."

"That, unfortunately, he is not." Teedle thumbed through the papers on his desk, finally giving up in exasperation and yelling for Frank, who was apparently away. "To hell with it," Teedle announced. "About forty-eight hours ago, a reserve battalion of the 100th Infantry Division encountered a man with one hand who claimed to be an OSS officer. This was down near the town of Pforzheim. He said he was on a special operation and in need of supplies. An officer there with good sense contacted OSS, but by the time they'd alerted the MPs, Martin was with the four winds.

"So he's gone yet again. Amazing. Any idea how the hell the girl found out he was in that hospital last time? I've been wondering for months."

"I told her. It was rather stupid."

He made a face. "I thought that was possible. That's more than stupid, Dubin. Get into your pants, did she?"

I didn't answer.

"You should have known better than that, too, Dubin." But his pinched eyes contained a trace of amusement at my folly. Whatever his complex morality, Teedle was good to his word. Sex, like war, was something God expected humans to succumb to.

"I didn't do very well, General. I'm aware of that. It cost a very good man his life. I'll rue that to the end of my days."

He gave me a kinder look than I expected and said, "If you had the pleasure of being a general, Dubin, you'd be able to say that ten thousand times. It's not much of a job that requires other men to die for your mistakes, is it?"

"No, sir."

"But that's what it entails."

"Yes, sir."

He took a moment. "Here's where we stand. I've been doing the Dance of the Seven Veils with OSS for a couple of months now. Donovan hasn't wanted any Army-wide acknowledgment that one of their own has gone astray. They say that's so they can save a chance to use Martin against the Russians, but it's all politics, if you ask me, and I've put my foot down now. A bulletin is going to all MPs, Third Army, Seventh Army, the Brits, everybody in Europe. And I'd like you in charge, Dubin. You have experience that can't be spared. You know what Martin looks like. More important, you've seen his tricks. I could never tell somebody else to be wary enough. Besides, it will give you a chance to clean up whatever mess you made. That's a fair deal, isn't it?"

I didn't answer. Fair wasn't the point and we both knew it.

"I know you've had enough of this assignment, Dubin. And given what you've said—or haven't said—I can understand why. You did the right thing stepping out. But it's a war and we need you. I've discussed it with Maples. And we agree. Those are your orders, Dubin. Get Martin." The General delivered his edict with his head lowered, enhancing the warning glare from his light eyes. There was no doubt the General meant to teach me a lesson. Running Martin to ground was going to convert me entirely to his point of view. And in that, I suspected he might even have been right. "I assume I don't have to add any cautions here about keeping your other gun in its holster, do I. Once burned, twice wise, correct?"

I nodded.

"Dismissed," he said.

30. BALINGEN

I drove south to interview the infantry officer who'd detained Martin at Pforzheim. The little towns I passed through brought to mind cuckoo clocks, with small narrow buildings set tight as teeth on the hillsides, all with painted wooden decorations along the steep rooflines. The officer who'd detained Martin, Major Farell Beasley, described him as robust in spite of his visible injuries and insisting that in Special Operations he could still be useful with only one hand. Beasley, like so many others before him, had been quite taken with Martin's sparkle and seemed puzzled to think such a fine soldier could have done anything wrong. In fact, Martin had provided excellent intelligence about the German units a mile ahead who were attempting to keep the 100th from crossing the Neckar River. As for his own objectives, Martin had declined to discuss them, except to say that he would be launching a small operation in the vicinity. I did not ask if there was any sign Martin was traveling with a woman.

I remained near Pforzheim for twenty-four hours to coordinate the MPs' search. The local Germans were only marginally cooperative and

Martin was presumed to have melted into the surrounding hills, moving on behind the fighting.

On my return to Frankfurt, I found for the next several days that the teletype Teedle had initiated to MPs throughout the European theater brought numerous reported sightings of one-handed men. None of them, however, had the extensive burns on his left side Major Beasley had seen on Martin. Then late on April 11, I received a telegram from Colonel Winters at OSS in London, with whom I'd visited.

Our man captured STOP Will communicate 0600 tomorrow by secure channels.

He phoned on the dot. For the last three or four days, he said, Seventh Army forces outside Balingen in southwest Germany had been negotiating with the commandant of a German camp holding political prisoners. The Nazis had hoped to exchange them for their own POWs, but the Americans had simply waited out the Krauts and they had finally surrendered control yesterday. Entering the camp, the Americans found an infernal scene of sickness and starvation.

"They say it's quite awful. Most of the SS escaped, of course. But when the intelligence officers went nosing around, inmates pointed out a fellow with one hand who'd appeared in their midst only a few days ago. They all assumed he was a German guard who couldn't get away because of his injury. He claimed to be another internee, a Spanish Jew, who'd been working in Germany when he was deported to another slave camp, but that was plainly a lie. He was too well nourished, for one thing, and spoke terrible German. And when they made him lower his drawers, it was clear he wasn't Jewish. He told several more stories, the last of which was that he was an American OSS officer named Robert Martin. That one was wrung from him only when his interrogators threatened to turn him over to the inmates, who've torn several guards apart with their bare hands. Literally, Dubin. Literally. I can't even imagine what the hell is going on down there. But I guarantee you one thing: Martin won't be getting away. They have him chained to the wall. He will be surrendered only to you."

I asked if Winters had any clue what had brought Martin there.

"I would say, Dubin, that the people around here who took Martin for a traitor are the ones smiling a little more broadly. Once you have him back in Frankfurt, we'd like to send our people to interrogate him at length." He ended the conversation with the familiar apologies for not being able to say more.

I ordered up an armed convoy to transport the prisoner, and immediately headed south in advance to take custody of Robert Martin.

And so, driven by a new MP sergeant to whom I barely had the heart to speak, I traveled to Balingen. It was April 12, 1945, a sweet morning with a spotless sky and a swelling, vital aroma in the air. There had been many reports about the German concentration camps, including one or two published accounts by escapees. But the authors had gotten away months ago, before matters turned dire for Hitler's regime. And even the claims made by the few survivors of the slave camp at Natzweiler in France, which several of us had heard of, tended to be dismissed as propaganda or yet another of the improbable, ultimately baseless rumors of disaster that circulated routinely among U.S. troops: The Russians had given up and Stalin had killed himself. Two hundred kamikaze pilots had flattened large stretches of L.A. Montgomery and Bradley had engaged in a fistfight in front of the troops. The Nazis were exterminating political prisoners by the thousands. The last of these stories had cropped up after the Soviets in Poland captured a supposed Nazi death camp called Auschwitz at the end of January, but these days nobody put much stock in what the Russians were saying.

From outside, the camp at Balingen was unremarkable, a sizable former military post at the margin of town, set on a high knoll amid the larches and pines of the Black Forest. The entire site was encompassed by a tall barbed-wire fence topped by brown electrification nodes, with the yellow-brick administration buildings standing in sight of the entrance. There the swinging gate was open and a lone apple tree was in bloom beside a young soldier, probably an SS guard, who lay dead, facedown, beneath a wooden sign reading ARBEIT MACHT FREI. Work makes freedom. Our troops had simply driven around the corpse—we could see the tanks and half-tracks within—and we followed.

We had not traveled far when my driver tromped on the brake, suddenly overpowered by the stench—excrement, quicklime, decaying flesh. It was crippling, and only grew worse when we finally drove on.

That smell still revisits me without warning, usually propelled by a shock of some kind. At those instants, I imagine that the odor was so potent it somehow burned itself permanently into my olfactory nerves.

The first soldiers to enter the camp yesterday had come from the 100th Infantry Division, the same outfit whose reserve regiments had briefly seized Martin at Pforzheim. There were a few officers from divisional G-3 present now, but most of the troops I saw were with associated armored cavalry units and, a day later, still seemed at a loss over the scene. They stood beside their vehicles while perhaps a dozen of the former inmates in their threadbare striped uniforms teetered around near them, frightful otherworldly creatures. Many were more emaciated than I'd believed human beings could become, veritable skeletons with skin, whose wrists and knuckles bulged hugely within their hands, and whose eyes were sunk so far into their skulls they looked sightless. Several were barefoot, and a number had large spots of feces and urine on their clothing. All of them moved with almost inanimate slowness, staggering inches at a time, with no apparent destination. One of them, a man with arms like mop handles, turned to me as soon as I alighted from the jeep and lifted both hands in a shameless plea.

I still do not know what he wanted, food or just understanding, but I froze there, shocked again to my battered core, and gripped by revulsion. This man, and those around like him, frightened me more fundamentally than the dead on the battlefield, because I recognized them instantly as unmistakable tokens of the limitless degradation a human would endure in order to live.

It was some time before I noticed a lieutenant who'd ventured forward to greet me. A tall, sandy-haired young man from divisional G-3, he gave his name as Grove and told me he had received a signal I was on the way. He motioned where I was looking.

"These are the lucky ones," he said. "Still on their feet."

"Who are they?" I asked.

"Jews," he answered. "Most of them. There are some Polish and French slave workers in one sub-camp. And a few of the Germans Hitler hated in another, mostly Gypsies and queers. But the greatest number of the folks here seem to be Jews. We've hardly sorted them all out. There's so much typhus here, we're afraid to do much."

I gasped then, choked almost, because I'd suddenly recognized the nature of a pearly mound a hundred yards behind the Lieutenant. It was made up of corpses, a nest of naked starved bodies, wracked and twisted in death. Instinctively, I moved a few steps that way. Grove caught my sleeve.

"You'll see a lot of that, if you care to."

Did I?

"I'd take a look," Grove said. "You'll want to tell people about this."

We began walking. Grove said there were probably 20,000 people held here now, many of them having arrived in the last few days. Some had been marched on foot from other concentration camps, with thousands dying along the way. Others, especially the sick, had been dumped here by the trainload. All had been crowded into makeshift wooden barracks, each about 150 feet long, in which there were only empty holes where the doors and windows were intended to be. I could not imagine what the savage winter had been like for the people already here, most of whom had had no more than their thin uniforms to protect them from the cold.

Outside the huts, there were open latrines, all overflowing with human waste because they were plugged intermittently by corpses. American bombing of a pumping station a few weeks ago had put an end to running water, and the prisoners had not been fed with any regularity since early March, when the German commandant had cut off most meals as a cruel means of controlling the plagues of dysentery and typhus that had broken out. For the last week, while the camp was surrounded, those interned here had received nothing at all. Some of those we passed, with their scraps of clothing and impossibly vacant looks, begged for crumbs. Grove warned me not to oblige them. The troops who arrived yesterday had given candy and tinned rations to the first inmates they saw. Rioting had broken out and then several of the prisoners who'd won the grim struggle that ensued had died when their intestinal systems revolted as a result of their gorging.

The huts that had housed these people were miserable, dark and reeking. Piles of feces stood here and there on the straw-covered floors, and in the wood bunks, stacked like shelving, the sick and starving lay side by side with the dead. You could tell the living only by their occasional moans and because the lice were so numerous on the deceased that the bugs appeared to be a moving wave. Hundreds of inmates had died since yesterday, Grove said. The division's docs had arrived this morning but were at a loss for a treatment plan that had any chance of success for those already so sick or that would afford a sanitary means to avoid spreading the typhus, especially to American troops.

As a result, Grove said, we really had only marginal control of the situation. As a case in point, we came upon the remains of a female guard Grove had seen killed earlier this morning. A group of female internees had found her hiding under one of the buildings and had pulled her out by the hair. The guard had screamed and called the prisoners filthy names, while they stomped and spat upon her. Ultimately, several men arrived with discarded pieces of wood to beat her to death. The killings of the kapos—most of them thugs sent here from German penitentiaries—and the Wehrmacht guards the SS had deserted had been going on for a day now, Grove said. A water tower had been converted to a makeshift gallows yesterday, and several of our troops had volunteered and helped with the hangings.

Back near the yellow-brick administrative cluster, out of sight of the huts, was a square building that contained an enormous brick furnace at its center. Using two hands, Grove pried open the giant cast-iron doors, revealing two half-burned bodies. The eyeholes in one skull faced straight my way, and I flinched at the sight. In front of the oven was a huge butcher block, which some of the interrogated guards had admitted was used to crush the gold fillings from the teeth of the dead.

But death had come too swiftly of late for far too many in Balingen to dispose of them in one furnace. Everywhere—between the huts, along the camp's roads, around every corner we turned—were the bodies, ghastly grayish-white mounds of dead human beings in various states of decomposition, every body stripped naked and pitted by the appetites of vermin. The piles here were nothing, Grove said. At the edge of the camp, there was a giant pit full of human remains that the inmates still standing had been forced to drag there in the last few days. Someone from G-3, trying to find a way to communicate the scene to superiors, had begun counting the corpses heaped about the camp and had quit after reaching 8,000. For me, again and again, as I stared at these hills of human beings, so pathetic in their nudity, with their stick-figure limbs and exposed genitalia, I experienced the same panic, because I could not tell where one person began and ended in the pile.

Several times I noticed that the uppermost bodies in these mounds were marked with bloody gashes in their abdomens.

"Why?" I asked Grove. "What was in their stomachs that anyone wanted?"

The Lieutenant looked at me. "Food," he said.

My war without tears ended at Balingen. A moment after entering the only hut I visited, I rushed behind the building and vomited. Afterward, I found I was weeping. I tried for several minutes to gain control and eventually gave up and continued walking beside the Lieutenant, crying silently, which made my eyes ache in the strong sun. "Cried like a babe myself," he said at one point. "And I don't know if it's worse that I've stopped."

But it was not simply the suffering that had brought me to tears, or the staggering magnitude of the cruelty. It was a single thought that came to me after my first few minutes in the camp, another of those phrases that cycled maddeningly in my brain. The words were "There was no choice."

I had been on the Continent now for six months, half a year, not much longer than a semester in school, but it was impossible to recall the person I had been before. I had fought in terror, and I had learned to despise war. There was no glory in the savagery I saw. No reason. And surely no law. It was only brutality, scientifically perfected on both sides, in which great ingenuity had been deployed in the creation of giant killing machines. There was nothing to be loyal to in any of this and surely no cause for pride. But there in Balingen I cried for mankind. Because there had been no choice. Because knowing everything now, I saw this terrible war had to happen, with all its gore and witless destruction, and might well happen again. If human beings could do this, it seemed unfathomable how we could ever save ourselves. In Balingen, it was incontestable that cruelty was the law of the universe.

Amid all of this, I had lost any recollection of why I was there. When Grove walked into one of the yellow buildings near the gate, I expected him to expose another horror. Instead he led me down a cool stone stairway, into a rock cellar where an MP guarded an iron door. I could not imagine what the Germans had needed with a jail in a place like this, until I remembered that the camp had originally been a military post. This, apparently, was the stockade. There were eight cells here, each with stone walls and a barred front. Josef Kandel, the former camp commandant, today known as the Beast of Balingen, sat in one, erect in a spotless uniform but wearing no shoes, his legs chained. There were two SS officers in adjoining cells who'd been through rough questioning. One was in a heap on the floor; the other was largely toothless, with fresh blood still running down his chin. And in the farthermost cell, on a small stool sat United States Army Major Robert Martin of the Office of Strategic Services. The lousy clothes which he'd stripped from one of the corpses as a disguise had been burned following his capture and replaced with a fresh officer's uniform, a russet shirt, under a sleeveless wool sweater, his oak leaves still on the right point of his collar.

Confronting him, I knew my features were swollen by weeping, but he was surely more changed than I. On the left side of his face, the skin shone, pink as sunrise, and his ear was a gnarly remnant melted to the side of his head, above which no hair grew for several inches. The end of his left sleeve was empty.

"Major," I said, "by the order of General Roland Teedle, you are arrested and will appear before a general court-martial as soon as it may be convened."

He smiled in response and waved the one good hand he had.

"Oh, come off it, Dubin. Get in here and talk to me."

His power of attraction was durable enough that I nearly did it before thinking. Even with one hand, Martin probably could subdue me and engineer yet another escape.

"I think not."

He laughed, shaking his head at length. "Then pull up a chair out there, if you must. But we should have a word."

I looked at Lieutenant Grove, who asked to brief me. As we walked down the dim hall, he whispered about what had transpired with the detail that had locked up Martin yesterday. While they were escorting him to the cell, he had informed his jailers about a mountain two hundred miles from here, where he claimed the Germans had stored all the stolen treasures of Europe. Thousands of gold bars and jewels were hoarded in the caverns, including American ten- and twenty-dollar gold pieces. A U.S. Army detachment, he said, could fake its way in and out just by saying they had come to take custody of the American tender and head home with every man a millionaire. Martin had offered to lead the way. Informed of this story, Grove had regarded it as preposterous. Instead, when he'd contacted OSS, Winters had confirmed that only a few days ago the 358th Infantry Regiment had taken a salt mine at Kaiseroda in the Harz Mountains, where they discovered a vast booty stored in the underground channels. Paintings, gems, rooms full of currency and coins. Billions' worth. Grove's theory was that Kaiseroda had been Martin's objective all along.

"What does OSS think?"

"Those fellows never say what they think."

I weighed the possibility. It remained appealing to believe that Martin hadn't ever been intent on spying. Rather, he would resign from war and make himself rich forever. Perhaps. But I'd become reconciled to the fact that I'd never really understand Martin's motives. Only he could explain them, and no one could accept a word he said.

A few minutes later, at Grove's order, an MP lugged a heavy oak chair down the stone hall for me. I sat outside Martin's cell, and he brought his small stool close to the bars. He still appeared chipper, even though his steps were mincing in his leg irons.

"So," said Martin. "As you've long wanted. You have me in chains. I knew that was poppycock about house arrest."

"You are far better off than any other prisoner here, Major."

He accepted my rebuke with a buttoned-up smile. "Even down here, there's the smell." He was right, although it was remote enough that I could also detect the familiar rot bred by cellar moisture. "I had no idea what I was headed to. But your dogs were on my heels, Dubin. And with the camp about to be surrendered, I thought I'd mingle and depart. Once I was here, of course, it was plain that I'd have trouble passing as an inmate, even with my injuries. But I couldn't stand to leave. In three nights, Dubin, I killed four SS. They were easy pickings, trying to skulk out the back gate in the middle of the night. I just laid a trip wire." He gave a kind of disbelieving snort. "There won't be any killings that lie easier on my conscience."

As ever, I had no idea whether to believe him.

"And what about your plan to make yourself the new Croesus?" I asked. "Were you going to abandon that?"

"You don't believe that, do you, Dubin? It was a ploy, I admit. I was happy to make those boys think I could make them each into a Rockefeller. But we're two hundred miles away. If I was heading for Kaiseroda, I'd have been there by now."

"So where *were* you heading, Martin?"

"You want to know my plan? Is that why you're sitting here? Well, I shall tell you, Dubin. Gita knows, she'll tell you anyway when you find her. You do want to find her, don't you?" His hostility about Gita got the better of him, and he showed a quick vulpine grin. I was surprised and somewhat relieved by Martin's pettiness—it was a crack in his perfect edifice—but I felt little other reaction when he mentioned her name. Not today. "You can tell my friends in OSS what I was up to and save them some time. I'd rather talk to you anyway."

I gave him nothing by way of response.

"You know, Dubin, you needn't be so peeved with me. I'd have kept my word to you in Savy. About surrendering? I had every intention. You don't think I prefer this, do you?" He lifted his handless arm, so that the bright red stump, a distorted knobby shape, crept out of the sleeve. I could have debated with him about dropping me off when he knew I wouldn't find Algar at his headquarters, or the last two and a half months that Martin had spent on the run since Gita helped him flee from Oflag XII-D. But I discovered that I had one enduring gripe with Robert Martin over and above all the others.

"You took advantage of my regard for you, Major. You made me think you were a bright shining hero and used my admiration as the means to escape."

"All for the right reasons, Dubin."

"Which are?"

"I was doing a good thing, Dubin. You'll understand that. The Nazis, Dubin, have been working on a secret weapon that can destroy the world—"

I erupted in laughter. It was a starkly inappropriate sound given where we were and the noise ripped along the rock corridor.

"Laugh if you like, Dubin. But it's the truth. It's the one way the Germans could have won the war, even now may still hope to. The Allies have long known this. The Germans have had their best physicists laboring feverishly. Gerlach. Diebner. Heisenberg. In the last several months, their principal workplace has been at a town called Hechingen, only a few miles down the road. Their efforts are rooted in the theorems of Einstein and others. They want to build a weapon, Dubin, that will break apart an atom. There's enough power there to blow an entire city off the map."

As usual, Martin seemed in complete thrall of his own entertaining nonsense. I was not much of a scientist, but I knew what an atom was and understood its infinitesimal size. Nothing of such minute dimension could conceivably be the killer force Martin was pretending.

"There is a race taking place now, Dubin. Between American intelligence and the Soviets. They each want to find the German scientists, their papers, and their matériel. Because whoever holds this weapon, Dubin, will rule the world. Ask your chums at OSS. Ask if this isn't true. Ask if there is not a group of physicists in Germany right now, working hand in glove with OSS. The code name is Alsos. Ask. They'll tell you they're going after these physicists even while we speak."

"This is where you were headed? Hechingen?"

"Yes. Yes."

I leaned back against the hard chair. Martin's dark hair was tousled over his brow and he had an eager boyish look, despite the relative immobility of the features on the florid side of his face. I was amazed at the magnitude of what he was confessing, probably unwittingly.

"If what you're saying is so, if all this Buck Rogers talk about a secret weapon bears any speck of truth, they'll hang you, Major. And well they should."

"Hang me?"

"Surely, you aren't working for OSS. Of that I'm certain. So it's quite obvious you were going to Hechingen to capture these scientists for the Soviets and spirit them off to the Russians."

"That's false, Dubin. Entirely false! I want neither side to prevail. I want neither Communists nor capitalists to stand astride the globe."

"And how then is it that you know all this, Major? The plans of the Americans? And the Soviets? If you are not at work for the Russians, how do you know their intentions?"

"Please, Dubin. I was informed of all of these matters by OSS last September. When I returned to London. But certainly not by the Soviets. I've told you, Dubin. I belong now to neither side."

"Would the Soviets say that?"

"I have no idea what they'd say. But listen to me. Listen. I was going to Hechingen, Dubin. But not for any country. My goal was destruction. Of the whole lot. The matériel. The papers. And the men. Let their dreadful secret die with them. Don't you see? This is a second chance to contain all the grief in Pandora's box. If this weapon survives, no matter who has it, there will be constant struggle, the victor will lord it over the vanquished, the vanquished will plot to obtain it, and in the end it is no matter which side has it, because if it exists, it will be used. There has never been a weapon yet invented that hasn't been deployed. Men can call that whatever they care to, even curiosity, but this device will be released on the globe. Let the world be safe, Dubin."

He was clever. But I'd long known that. No one—not Teedle, not me—would ever be able to prove he was working for the Soviets rather than for the sake of world peace. He and Wendell Willkie. It was, as I would have predicted, a perfect cover story.

"Dubin, find Gita. Find Gita. She will tell you that what I am saying is true. These are my plans. And there is still time to carry them out. No more than a few days. American forces will reach Hechingen shortly, depending on how the fighting goes. It's only a few miles up the road. Find Gita, Dubin."

How artful it was. How inevitable. Find Gita. She will persuade you to join my cause. And open the door to yet one more escape.

"She is here, Dubin. In the Polish sub-camp. There are Jews there from her town. She is nursing them. Go to the Polish camp. You'll find her. She will tell you this is true."

"No." I stood. "No more lies. No more fantasies. No more running away. We're going to Frankfurt. As soon as the armored vehicle arrives. Tell your story there, Martin. You must think I'm a child."

"I speak the truth to you, Dubin. Every word. Every word. Ask Gita. Please."

I turned my back on him while he was still assailing me with her name.

31. GITA LODZ, OF COURSE

This woman, Gita Lodz, is, of course, my mother.

I have no slick excuse for the months it took me to catch on, or for the elaborate tales I told myself during that period to hold the truth at bay. I guess people will inevitably cling to the world they know. Bear Leach's eventual explanation was more generous: "We are always our parents' children."

But sitting in the Tri-Cities Airport, reading the last of what my father had written, I had understood the conclusion of his account this way: Deceived yet again by Gita Lodz, Dad had proceeded to his final ruin and let Martin go. And then somehow, even while my father was absorbing the desolation of his most catastrophic mistake, he must have met this other woman at Balingen, Gella Rosner, and been transformed. It was love on the rebound, a lifeline to the man drowning.

In retrospect, all of that seems laughable. But for months I accepted it, and was frustrated and confused by only one omission: Dad never mentioned the courageous young Polish Jewess I'd been brought up to believe he instantly fell in love with in the camp.

As for Barrington Leach, from the time I asked him what had become of Gita Lodz, he had realized how misled I was. Yet he made no effort to correct me, although I often visited with him, trying to glean every detail he recalled about my father's story. Bear was a person of gentleness and wisdom, and, given all his caveats at the start, clearly had promised himself that he would tell me only as much as I seemed willing to know. He presented me with the recorded facts. It was up to me to reach the obvious conclusions. Bear kept his mouth shut, not so much for my parents' sake as for mine.

One day in April 2004, my sister phoned me at home to discuss our mother's health, which was declining. Sarah wanted my views on whether she should accelerate her plans to visit in June around the time of my parents' anniversary, which had been an especially hard period for Mom in 2003 in the wake of Dad's death. I knew my parents' marriage had lasted almost fifty-eight years. They'd made no secret of their wedding date, June 16, 1945. Yet until that moment, I'd never connected the dots. I stood with the telephone in my hand, jaw agape, while Sarah shouted my name and asked if I was still there.

By then, it had become my habit to see Barrington Leach once a month. I went mostly for the pleasure of his company, but my excuse to write off the expenses was that Bear was helping me edit Dad's typescript for publication. (Because of the scam I'd run on my mother and sister, my plan, at that point, was to tell them Dad's account was actually my work, based on my lengthy research.) When I saw Bear, I'd hand over the most recent pages and receive his comments about what I'd done the previous month. Not long after he was wheeled into the front room for our visit in late April, I told him what had occurred to me while I was on the phone with my sister the week before.

"I just realized a few days ago that my parents got married right before Dad's court-martial. Did you know that?"

"I should say so," answered Bear. "I'm the one who arranged it."

"Arranged the wedding?"

"Not their meeting," said Bear. "But getting the military authorities to allow them to wed, yes, that was my doing. Your father was concerned, quite rightly, that when he was convicted, as was inevitable, he would be transferred immediately to a military prison in the U.S. He was therefore desperate to marry before the proceedings, so that your mother, as a

war bride, would have the right to immigrate to the States. She had remained an inmate in a displaced persons camp that had been erected
after burning down the Balingen huts. The conditions were far better, of
course, but she was anything but free. It required countless petitions to
the Army and the Occupation Authorities, but eventually your mother
and a rabbi, also held at Balingen, were allowed to visit your father for
half an hour at Regensburg Castle for their wedding. I was the best man.
In spite of the circumstances, it was quite touching. They appeared very
much in love."

Bear said only that and glanced down to the pages I'd handed him,
allowing me to work my way through this information in relative privacy.
Despite the horrors of the camp, or Mom's unfamiliarity with the military,
or even her limited English at the time, someone as innately canny as she
was couldn't possibly have failed to grasp the essentials of Dad's situation. She knew he was under arrest, and as such, had to be gravely concerned for her new husband. Clearly, then, Mom recalled a great deal
more about Dad's court-martial than she'd been willing to acknowledge
to me. Yet even at that moment, my first impulse was to accept her reluc-
tance as a way of honoring Dad's desire for silence.

But somehow my mind wandered back to the question that had per-
plexed me for half a year now. Why did Dad say he desperately hoped
his children would never hear his story? Out the paned windows of
Northumberland Manor's sitting room, there was perfect light on the red
maple buds just showing the first sign of ripening, and beholding them
with the intense museum attention Dad wrote of, a moment of concentrated sight, I found the truth hanging out there, too. It was simple. My father's remark about keeping this from his children was not philosophical.
It was practical. Dad had not wanted the truth to emerge at his trial, or
to survive it, because it would have imperiled his wife and the lie she was
to be obliged to live. That is why it would have been a disaster to call
Gita Lodz as a witness. That is why he hoped we never heard the story—
because that silence would have meant they had made a life as husband
and wife.

Bear's head was wilted in his wheelchair while he read, and I reached
out to softly clutch his spotted hand and the fingers crooked with disease.

"She's my mother. Right? Gita Lodz?"

Bear started, as if I'd woken him. His cloudy eyes that still reflected the depth of the ages settled on me, and his lower jaw slid sideways in his odd lopsided smile. Then he deliberated, an instant of lawyerly cool.

"As I have said, Stewart, I was not there when you were born."

"But the woman you saw my father marry—that was Gita Lodz?"

"Your father never said that to me," he answered. "Anything but. It would have compromised me severely to know that, inasmuch as I had spent months begging the military authorities for permission to allow David to marry a concentration camp survivor of another name. I would have been obliged to correct the fraud being perpetrated. I believe that was why he never contacted me once we were back in the U.S.A.—so that I didn't have to deal with any second thoughts about that."

Despite failing on the uptake for months, I now bounced rapidly along the path of obvious conclusions. I instantly comprehended why Gita Lodz, hero of the French underground, came here pretending to be the former Gella Rosner (whose name was Americanized as Gilda), David Dubin's war bride, allegedly saved from the Nazi hell called Balingen. In the spring of 1945, my parents had every reason to believe that OSS would never have permitted the sidekick of Robert Martin, suspected Soviet spy, to enter the United States. Indeed, as someone who had repeatedly abetted Martin's escapes, Gita stood a good chance of being prosecuted if OSS and Teedle had gotten their hands on her. A new identity was the only safe course. One that could never be disproved amid that ocean of corpses. One more role to add to the many the would-be Bernhardt had already played flawlessly. And one that guaranteed that Gilda would be welcome in David's family. A Jewish bride. As his parents wished. And as Gita herself, when she was younger, had once wanted to be.

And, probably not insignificantly, it was also a weighty declaration for my father. When I had changed my last name in 1970, Dad had never really responded to my implication that I was reversing an act of renunciation from decades before. There was only one thing he cared to be clear about.

"Do not doubt, Stewart," he said to me once, "that Balingen made me a Jew." Since I knew he would never describe what he'd witnessed there, I did not pursue the remark. On reflection, I took it as one more way of telling me how devoted he was to my mother. And even now I'm not completely certain of the precise nature of the transformation he was alluding to. I don't know if he meant that he had realized, as had been true for so many in Germany, that there was no escape from that identity, or, rather, as I tend to suspect, that he owed the thousands annihilated there the reverence of not shirking the heritage that had condemned them. Certainly, there was a touching homage in Gita's new persona, which allowed one of the millions who perished to be not only remembered, but revived. But I see that Dad was also making an emphatic statement about himself, about what an individual could stand for, or hope for, against the forces of history.

I, on the other hand, who had proudly reclaimed Dubinsky, who sent my daughters to Hebrew school and insisted we have shabbas dinner every Friday night, I now reposed in the nouveau-Federal sitting room of a Connecticut nursing home realizing that by the strict traditions of a religion that has always determined a child's faith by that of his mother, I am not really Jewish.

These are the last pages of my father's account:

I emerged again from the dungeon darkness into the brilliant day and terrible reek of Balingen. I suppose that humans recoil on instinct from the rankness of decaying flesh and I had to spend a moment fighting down my sickness again.

Grove was waiting for me. I thought he wanted to know how it had gone with Martin, but he had other news.

"Roosevelt is dead," he said. "Truman is President."

"Don't be a card."

"It's just on Armed Services Radio. They say FDR had a stroke. I kid you not." I had been raised to worship Roosevelt. My mother, who regarded the President as if he were a close relation, would be devastated. And then I looked to the nearest mound of broken corpses. At every one of these instants of paradox, I reflexively expected my understanding of life to become deeper, only to find myself more confused.

I asked the MP who'd accompanied me if we had an estimated arrival time on the half-track that would carry Martin back, but the news about Roosevelt's death seemed to have brought everything to a halt for a while. Nonetheless, I wouldn't countenance the idea of spending the night within Balingen. Whatever hour the convoy arrived, I said, I wanted Martin transferred. We could bivouac with the 406th Armored Cavalry a mile or two away, nearer Hechingen.

An hour or so later, vehicles reached the camp, but not the ones I awaited. They carried the first Red Cross workers. I watched with a certain veteran distance as these men and women, accustomed to working tirelessly to save lives, began to absorb the enormity of what they were confronting. A young French doctor passed out when he saw the first hill of bodies. Inexplicably, one of the wraiths moving vacantly through the camp, an elderly man who had somehow lived to liberation, fell dead only a few feet from the unconscious doctor. As with everything else, we all seemed bereft of the power to react. If the sky fell, as Henny Penny feared, we might have had more to say.

Many of the American infantrymen were standing in little groups, speculating about what the President's death might mean with regard to the Nazis' final surrender and the war in the Pacific. I could see that the shock of the news was welcome in its way, a chance to put where they were out of their minds for a while.

The half-track I awaited, a captured German 251 that had been repainted, finally appeared at 2:30 in the afternoon. Only a minute or so after that, Grove came to find me. We were preparing to load Martin. He would be in leg irons with at least two guns trained on him at all times.

"There's an inmate looking for you," Grove said. "She asked for you by name."

I knew who it was. A shamed and exhausted fantasy that Gita might appear had circulated through my mind, in just the way it had for months, even as I'd tried to banish it.

"Polish?" I asked.

"Yes, from the Polish camp. She looks quite well," he added, "but there are several young women here who look all right." He made no further comment on how these girls might have managed.

She was in the regimental office that had been established in the largest of the yellow buildings the SS had abandoned earlier in the week. The room was empty, paneled to half height in shellacked tongue-and-groove, with a broken schoolhouse fixture hanging overhead from a frayed wire. Beneath it, Gita Lodz sat on a single wooden chair, the only furnishing in the room. She sprang to her feet as soon as she saw me. She was still in the gray uniform the nuns had given her in Bastogne, although it was frayed at both sleeves and soiled, and bore a yellow star pinned above the breast.

"Doo-bean," she said, and with the name, more than the sight of her, my poor heart felt as if it might explode. I had no need to ask how she knew I was here. She would have maintained her own surveillance on the building where Martin was jailed.

I dragged another wooden chair in from the hall, taking a seat at least a dozen feet from her. We faced each other like that, with no barrier between us but distance, both of us with our feet flat on the worn floor. I was too proud to lose my composure, and waited with my face trembling, until I could drag out a few words.

"So we meet again in hell," I said to her in French. I felt my heart and mind pirouetting again with the unaccountable extremes in life. Here I was with this gallant, deceitful woman, full of wrath and anguish, while I was still reeling from the reek of atrocity, sitting where some of history's greatest monsters had been in charge only a week ago. Roosevelt was dead. I was alive.

Although I did not ask, she told me about the last several days. Martin and she had snuck in through the same breach in the rear fence the SS guards were using to slip away. After only a matter of hours, she recognized four people she had known in Pilzkoba and last seen on the trucks the Nazis had loaded for deportation to Lublin. One of them was a girl a year younger than Gita, a playmate, who was the last of a family of six. Two younger siblings, a brother and a sister, had been snatched from her parents' arms and promptly gassed when they arrived at a camp called Buchenwald. There the next year her father had been beaten to death by a kapo right in front of her, only a few weeks after her mother had succumbed to pneumonia. But still this girl from Pilzkoba had survived. She had marched here hundreds of miles with no food, her feet wrapped in rags, a journey on which another of her brothers had perished. Yet she had arrived at Balingen in relative health. And then yesterday she had died of one of the plagues raging through the camp.

"In Normandy, Dubin, when we helped to direct the Allied troops through the hedgerows, I saw battlefields so thick with corpses that one could not cross without walking on the bodies. I told myself I would never see anything worse, and now I see this. And there are souls here, Dubin, who say the Germans have created places worse yet. Is that possible? *N'y a-t-il jamais un fond, même dans les océans les plus profonds?"* Is there no bottom even to the darkest ocean?

With that, she cried, and her tears, of course, unleashed my own. Seated a dozen feet apart, we both wept, I with my face in my hands.

"There is so much I do not understand," I finally said, "and will never understand. Here looking at you, I ask myself how it can seem possible, amid this suffering, that the worst pain of all is heartbreak?"

"Do you criticize me, Dubin?"

"Need I?" I answered with one of those French sayings she loved to quote. *"Conscience coupable n'a pas besoin d'accusateur."* A guilty conscience needs no accuser. "But I am sure you feel no shame."

She tossed her bronze curls. She was thin and sallow. Yet unimaginably, she remained beautiful. How was that possible either?

"You are bitter with me," she said.

"You decimated me with your lies."

"I never lied to you, Dubin."

"Call it what you like. I told you secrets and you used them against me, against my country. All for Martin."

"Entre l'arbre et l'écorce il faut ne pas mettre le doigt." One shouldn't put a finger between the bark and the tree. In our parlance, she was caught between a rock and a hard place. "This is not justice. What you were about to do—what you will do now. Martin placed in chains by his nation? He has risked his life for America, for the Allies, for freedom, a thousand times. He is the bravest man in Europe."

"The Americans believe he is a spy for the Soviets."

She wrenched her eyes shut in anguish.

"The things they have asked you to accept," she murmured. *"C'est impossible.* Martin despises Stalin. He was never a Stalinist, and after Stalin's pact with Hitler, Martin regarded him as the worse of the two. He calls Stalin and Hitler the spawn of the same devil."

"And what then is it he has been doing all these months, defying his orders, running from OSS, from Teedle, and from me? Has he told you his goal?"

"Now? Lately, he has, yes. Up to the time of the Ardennes, I believed what he told you—that he was on assignment for OSS, as he has always been. He would not say where he was to go, but that was not unusual."

"And do you believe him now?"

"I think what he says is what he believes."

When I asked her to say what that was, she looked down to her small hands folded in her lap, clearly reluctant even now to disclose Martin's secrets. And still, I cautioned myself that the reaction I saw might be another pose.

"Since I took him from the hospital at Saint-Vith," she finally said, "he has maintained the same thing. Martin says that the Nazis are making a machine that can destroy the world. He wants to kill all who understand its workings and bury their secret with them forever. It is madness, but it is madness in Martin's style. It is glorious. He claims this is his destiny. For the most part, I have felt like, what is his name, the little one who walks beside Don Quixote?"

"Sancho Panza."

"Yes, I am Sancho Panza. There is no telling Martin this is lunacy. And I have stopped trying, Dubin. The scientists are at Hechingen. Martin has established that much. But a single device that could reduce London to cinders? It is fantasy, like so much that Martin tells himself. But it will surely be the last."

"Because?"

"Because he will die trying to do this. A man with one hand? His left leg is still barely of any use. The pain is so severe at night from the nerves that were burned that he sheds tears in his sleep. And he has no one to help him."

"Except you."

"Not I. I will have no part of this, Dubin. He does not ask it. And I would not go. I have been a member of the resistance, not a vigilante. He has no allies in this, no organization. But it is paramount to him nonetheless."

"But not because of the Soviets?"

"Dubin, it is how he wishes to die. Whether or not he admits as much to himself, death is clearly his goal. He is maimed and in unending pain. But now when he dies, as he surely will, he will believe he was doing no less than assuring the safety of the world. It is a glory as great as the one he has always wished for. That is what you would deny him. He says that the Americans will hang him instead, if he is caught. True?"

I had told Martin as much a few hours earlier, and with time to calculate, I had decided it was no exaggeration. The story Martin had told me would be enough to send him to the gallows. Whether he was working for the Soviets, as most of his superiors would believe, or as the new Flash Gordon, he had admitted that he was an American soldier trying to undermine American forces and deny them a weapon regarded as essential to the security of the United States. That would, at a minimum, make him a traitor and a mutineer. The law would need to sift no finer.

"And is that just, Dubin?" she asked, once I'd nodded.

"Just? Compared to anything that has happened in this place, it is just. Martin disobeyed orders. He brought this on himself."

"But is that what you wish to see, Dubin? Martin trembling at the end of a rope?"

"That is not my choice, Gita. I must do my duty."

"So the guards are claiming here. They did as ordered."

"Please."

"I ask again if that is what you would choose for him."

"I dare not choose a destiny for Martin, Gita. The law does not allow it. It would say I am hopelessly biased by jealousy. And in that, the law is surely wise."

"Jealousy?" She looked at me blankly until my meaning reached her. "Dubin, I have told you many times, you have no need to be jealous of Martin."

"And that proved to be another lie. You slept with me to learn what I would find out about Martin and then deserted me to rescue him. Jealousy is the least of it."

She had drawn herself straight. The black eyes were a doll's now, hard as glass.

"You think that is why I slept with you?"

"I do."

She looked askance and made as if to spit on the floor. "I misjudged you, Dubin."

"Because you thought I was more gullible?"

She actually lifted a hand toward her heart, not far from where the star was pinned.

"What do you believe, Dubin? That I am a statue and cannot be hurt? I value your esteem, Dubin. More, apparently, than you can understand. I cannot tolerate your scorn."

"I admire your strength, Gita. I still admire that."

She closed her eyes for a time.

"Be angry, Dubin. Be hurt. Think I was too casual with your feelings. But please do not believe I would make love to you with such ugly intentions. Do you see me as a harlot? Because I am a harlot's daughter?"

"I see you as you are, Gita. As someone who knows how to do what she has to." I repeated Winters' story about the German officer in Marseilles to whom she'd succumbed in order to win details of the London bombing. And even as I recounted the OSS's sniggering about her sleeping with the enemy, I realized I had awaited this moment for months so that she would tell me it was untrue. She did not.

"*Qui n'entend qu'une cloche n'entend qu'un son.*" He who hears one bell hears only one sound. There were, she meant, two sides of the story. "Something like that, Dubin, is so easy to judge from a distance."

I mocked her with another proverb. "*Qui veut la fin veut les moyens?*" He who wants the ends wants the means.

"Is that not true? In this place, Dubin, there are thousands who have done far worse to save just their own lives, let alone hundreds of others. Thousands probably were spared because of what I did. There are many mistakes I have made, Dubin, for which I forgive myself less freely. I was young. It was a poor idea only because I did not understand that even when the soul wears armor, it remains fragile. I thought, a cock is just another thing, Dubin. And Martin, by the way, knew nothing of this in advance and begged me never to consider such an act again, for my own sake as much as for his. But let me tell you, Dubin, what was the most confounding part. This man, this Nazi, this officer, he was kind to me. He was a man with some goodness in him. And to learn that about him on false pretenses—that was the most difficult part."

"As I am sure you have said the same of me."

"It is not the same, Dubin! I will not leave this place with you believing that." She continued to sit tall, her face folded in fury. "I care for you, Dubin. Greatly. You know that. Look at me here. You cannot tell me that even four meters away from me, you cannot feel that? I know you can."

"And that is why you crushed my heart. Because you cared for me?"

"My only excuse is one you must acknowledge as true. I left you before you left me."

"As you say. That is an excuse. I believed I loved you."

"You never spoke to me of love."

"You were gone before I could. But please do not pretend that would have made any difference. What I felt and what I showed could not have been clearer with a name applied. You rewarded my love with lies. Until I came here, I thought that was the cruelest thing in life."

"Yes," she said. "Such a thing is unkind. But understand, Dubin, please understand. Could I have stayed and loved you and watched as you took Martin off in chains to be hanged? He gave me back my life, Dubin. Should I have quietly condemned him for the sake of my own happiness?"

"I do not believe that is how you thought of it."

"How I thought of it, Dubin, is that a man like you, a proper bourgeois gentleman, would never make your life with a Polish peasant with no schooling. That is how I thought of it. You would return to your America, to your law books, to your intended. That is how I thought of it. I dream of children, as you dream. I dream of being as far from war as a happy home is. For me that is a dream that will probably never come true."

"These are excuses."

"This is the truth, Dubin!" She shook her small hands at me in rage, again in tears. "You say I would not forsake Martin for you. But you surely have your own idols. If I had stayed and begged you not to do your duty with Martin, would you have refused?"

"I would like to believe that my answer is 'Yes.' But I doubt it. I am afraid, Gita, I would have done anything for you."

"And who would you be after that, Dubin, without your precious principles?"

"I do not know. But it would be who I had chosen to become. I could tell myself that. I could tell myself I had chosen love and that in a life as harsh as ours, it must come first."

She was motionless, staring at me in that way she had, a look so intense I thought it might turn me to flame. Then she asked if I had a cloth, meaning a handkerchief. She took it from me and returned to her chair to clear her nose. Finally, she sat forward and clasped her hands.

"Do you mean this? What you have just said? Do you speak from the heart, Dubin, or is this merely a lawyer's argument?"

"It is the truth, Gita. Or was. It is in the past."

"Must it be? We have our moment, Dubin. Here. Now. It can all be as you would like. As I would like. We will have love. We will have each other. But let him go, Dubin. Let Martin go and I will stay with you. I will tend your hearth and cook your meals and bear your brats, Dubin. I will. I want to. But let him go."

"'Let him go'?"

"Let him go."

"I cannot even imagine how I could do that."

"Oh, Dubin, you are far too clever to say that. You would not need an hour's reflection to concoct a scheme that would work. Dubin, please. Please." She walked to my chair and then put one knee on the floor. "Please, Dubin. Dubin, choose this. Choose love. Choose me. If you send Robert to the hangman, it will stand between us forever. Here in hell, Dubin, you can choose this one good thing. Let Quixote fight his windmill. Do not make him die in disgrace. He has lived to be a hero. It would be worse than torture for him to die known as a traitor."

"You would do anything for him, wouldn't you?"

"He saved my life, Dubin. He has shown me the way to every good thing I believe in. Even my love for you, Dubin."

"Would you pledge your love to me, give up your life, just to see him die one way rather than another?"

"Dubin, please. Please. This is my life, too. You are precious to me. Dubin. Please, Dubin." Slowly she reached for my hand. My entire body surged at her touch and even so, I thought: Once more, she will engineer his escape. But I loved her. As Biddy had said, it was pointless to try to reason about that.

With my hand in hers, she wept. "Please, Dubin," she said. "Please."

"You have the personality of a tyrant, Gita. You wish to turn me into a supplicant so you will think better of yourself."

Despite the tears, she managed a smile. "So now you know my secret, Dubin."

"You will mock me for being bourgeois."

"I shall," she said. "I promise to. But I will be thrilled, in spite of myself." She lifted her face to me. "Take me to America, Dubin. Make me your wife. Let Martin go. Let Martin be the past. Let me be the future. Please." She kissed my hand now, a hundred times, clutching it between hers and embracing every knuckle. What she proposed was mad, of course. But no madder than what I had watched men do routinely for months now. No madder than parachuting into a town under siege. No madder than combat, where soldiers gave up their lives for inches of ground and the grudges of generals and dictators. In this place, love, even the remotest chance of it, was the only sane choice. I pulled her hands to my mouth and kissed them once. Then I stood, looking down on her.

"When you betray me, Gita, as I know you will, I will have nothing. I will have turned my back on my country, and you will be gone. I will have no honor. I will believe in nothing. I will be nothing."

"You will have me, Dubin. I swear. You will have love. I swear, Dubin. You will not be betrayed. I swear. I swear."

Gita Lodz is my mother.

32. BEAR: END

When I first read Dad's account, the end had seemed disappointingly abrupt. Not only did I think there was no mention of my mother, there was also no recounting of what had happened with Martin. Supposedly writing to explain things to his lawyer, Dad was silent about whether Martin fled, as Dad claimed, or had been murdered, as Bear feared.

According to the testimony at the court-martial, late on April 12, 1945, Martin had been loaded at gunpoint into the armored vehicle Dad had awaited. In convoy with the MPs, they traveled only a mile or two beyond the perimeter of Balingen toward Hechingen, to the bivouac of the 406th Armored Cavalry. There Martin was chained to a fence post before a tent was erected around him. At roughly 3:00 a.m., my father appeared and told the two MPs guarding the Major that Dad could not sleep and would spell them for two hours. When they returned Dad was there and Martin was gone. My father told the guards, without further explanation, he had let Martin go. A day later he was back in Frankfurt to admit the same thing to Teedle.

The first time I came back to visit Leach in Hartford, in November 2003, I got right to the point.

"What Dad wrote doesn't answer your question."

"My 'question'?"

"Whether my father murdered Martin once he freed him."

"Oh, that." Bear gave his dry, gasping laugh. "Well, what do you think, Stewart?"

Before I'd read the pages Bear gave me, his suspicions were astonishing, but once I understood that Dad had abandoned everything for Gita Lodz, I comprehended Leach's logic. As my father had told her, if she betrayed him again, he would have had nothing. With Martin dead, on the other hand, she could never rejoin him. Certainly, Dad had no need to fear discovery if he murdered Martin. There was virtually no chance one more body would ever be identified among the thousands decomposing in the massive pit at the edge of Balingen. Dad was armed, of course. And after combat, he was sadly experienced in killing.

In other words, Dad had motive and opportunity, which I'd listened to prosecutors for years label as the calling cards of a strong circumstantial murder case. But my faith in my father's decency, which even now seemed as tangible to me as his body, remained unchanged. Realizing everything I hadn't known about his life, murder still seemed beyond him, and I told Leach that. Bear was very pleased to hear it, favoring me with his funny sideways smile.

"Good for you, Stewart."

"But am I right?"

"Of course. It became critical for me to determine the answer to my own question, especially after the verdict and sentence. Quite frankly, Stewart, if there was a worse crime to be discovered, I might have thought twice about pressing ahead with appeals. Five years for the murder of another officer, even a wanted one, was not a disappointing result, if that's what had actually occurred."

"But it turned out Martin was alive?"

"When your father last saw him? Without doubt. Where are my papers?" The Redweld folder, Bear's treasure chest, as I thought of it, rested against the chrome spokes of his wheelchair, and I handed it up. Leach's bent fingers stumbled through the pages. He would touch a paper several times before he could grab it and then bring it almost to his nose to read. "No," he'd say, and the process would begin again, with his apologies to me for the agonizing pace. "Here!" he said at last.

LABORATORY

60TH EVACUATION HOSPITAL

APO #758, U.S. ARMY

APO

May 16, 1945

REPORT OF AUTOPSY

C-1145

NAME: (Name, Rank, Unit & Organization Unknown)
AGE: Approx. 42   RACE: White   SEX: Male   NATIVITY: Unknown
ADMITTED: Not admitted to this hospital
DIED: Approx. May 9, 1945
AUTOPSY: 1230, May 13, 1945

CLINICAL DIAGNOSIS

1. Malnutrition, dehydration, severe

PATHOLOGICAL DIAGNOSES

MISCELLANEOUS: Malnutrition, dehydration, severe burns, third degree, partially healed

PRESENT ILLNESS: This patient was found dead sitting on a divan in the Hochshaus Hotel in Berlin, Germany (Grid Q-333690), upon the arrival of U.S. troops in that sector on or about May 11, 1945. He was dressed in the uniform of a United States Army Officer, with oak leaf cluster on his right shirt collar, but otherwise without insignia or identity tags. He evidently had been held as a prisoner for a period of time and had starved to death.

PHYSICAL EXAMINATION: Examination at the cemetery revealed no fresh external wounds. Patient appeared to be recovering from third-degree burns several months old; his left hand is missing.

AUTOPSY FINDINGS

The body is that of a well-developed but markedly emaciated
male, about 40 years of age, measuring 70 inches long and
weighing approximately 105 pounds. Rigor and liver are
absent. The head is covered with long black hair, except
for an area of scarring above the left ear, upon which most
of the helix has been lost, apparently due to burning. The
anterior portion of his deeply sunken eyes is below the
lateral portion of the orbital margin. A beard, several
weeks' growth, covers his face and contains some gray
hairs in front of each ear. All of his teeth are present.
The rib markings are very prominent and the thin
anterior abdominal wall rests only slightly above
his spine.

Evidence of recent third-degree burns also appears on the
distal portion of the leg and thorax; scar tissue remains
livid and taut, and appears abraded in several places. The
left hand is absent below the wrist. The uneven stump reveals
similar burn scarring, suggesting the hand may have been lost
in an explosion or amputated thereafter. Suture scars
indicate recent surgical reparation.

PRIMARY INCISION: The usual incision reveals one
millimeter of subcutaneous adipose tissues, thinning muscles,
normally placed organs in the smooth abdominal cavity, and
normal pericardial and pleural cavities.

GASTROINTESTINAL TRACT: The stomach contains only a
slight amount of light mucus, the bowel is empty, and a
minimal amount of fecal material is in the colon. All the
mesenteric vessels are prominent on the colon.

NOTE: Nearly all of the adipose tissue throughout the body
has disappeared, and is diminished even around the kidneys
and heart. The tissues display lack of turgor indicative of
severe dehydration. The absence of recent external trauma

and only mucus in the gastrointestinal tract would seem
to indicate that this man died of malnutrition and
dehydration.

> s/ Nelson C. Kell
> Captain,
> Medical Corps
> Laboratory Officer

"I received that in June 1945," Bear said, "from your father's doctor friend, Cal Echols, only a few days after the court-martial concluded. Cal had been transferred to headquarters hospital in Regensburg and visited your father often before and after the trial. Since I had been on the look-out for Martin from the start, I had asked Cal to inform me discreetly if he ever heard reports of a one-handed burn victim. My thought was that Martin might seek medical treatment. Instead, this autopsy had come across Cal's desk as the object of considerable curiosity.

"When U.S. troops entered Berlin on May 11, the Soviets had directed the Americans to this body, citing it as another German atrocity. But you'll note the pathologist's conclusion that death had occurred within the last seventy-two hours. The Germans had surrendered Berlin to the Russians on May 2. This man didn't die until a week later. The American doctors suspected that the Russians, not the Germans, had had custody of him."

"The Russians killed Martin?"

"Well, that certainly was how it appeared. After several weeks Graves Registration still had had no success in identifying the remains. But the circumstances of the death, particularly the involvement of the Soviets, spurred continuing interest and finally had led the autopsy to be passed up the line in the Medical Corps. After a good deal of thought, I decided to report this development to General Teedle."

"Teedle?"

"I'd had contact with him now and then. We did not get off on a particularly good foot. I thought he was going to get out of his chair and throttle me during his cross-examination. But Teedle had remained preoccupied with your father's case, regarding it as totally enigmatic. He had let me know that he would always hear me out if I came up with any extenuating evidence. And I'll give Teedle credit. He recognized the prime significance of the autopsy at once."

"Which was?"

"Well, it was hard to believe that the Soviets would have killed a loyal agent, especially by starving him to death. There were many alternatives—perhaps Martin had fallen out with his Soviet masters—but with your father now under a prison sentence, Teedle recognized that the autopsy raised plausible doubts that Martin was a spy. After he turned it over to the OSS, they dispatched a team to identify the body. As usual, OSS wanted to keep the results of its subsequent investigation to themselves, but Teedle would not stand for that.

"As it developed, everything Martin had said to your father about the Alsos Mission was essentially true. OSS had recruited teams of physicists who were racing across Germany, hoping to reach the German atomic scientists before the Soviets. And Hechingen, where the top German physicists had been sent from Berlin, was indeed Alsos' foremost target. There's been a good deal of writing about it."

Out of his folder, Bear handed me photocopied sections from several histories explaining the Alsos Mission, which I scanned. Hechingen was in the sector of Germany where the Free French were leading the combat effort, but because of the atomic secrets that rested with the German scientists, a large American force cut in front of the French without permission and entered Hechingen on April 24, 1945. They seized Werner Heisenberg's laboratory, secreted in a former wool mill on Haigerlocherstrasse above the town center, where they found several of Germany's foremost physicists, including Otto Hahn, Carl von Weizsäcker, and Max von Laue, along with two tons of uranium, two tons of heavy water, and ten tons of carbon. Hunting around, the Americans also located the records of the scientists' research secreted in a cesspool behind Weizsäcker's home.

"Heisenberg," Bear said, "the foremost physicist in the group, and Gerlach, were missing. Under OSS interrogation, their colleagues soon explained that Heisenberg and Gerlach had fled about ten days earlier, in the wake of a strange incident. A lone one-handed man had been apprehended about to detonate an enormous explosive charge, which would have brought down the brick mill building, killing everyone inside it. The would-be bomber had discarded his dog tags and claimed at first to be French, but when the SS arrived, they identified his uniform, which bore no insignia, except for an oak leaf cluster, as that of an American officer. Given his mission, and the fact that he had slipped into town well in advance of American forces, the SS concluded he could only be OSS.

"The German scientists at Hechingen had foreseen that the Allies, including the Soviets, would want to capture them to learn about their research. This was disheartening on one level, because they knew they were doomed to a lengthy captivity, but they had assumed that whoever caught them—and they much preferred the Americans or the British— was bound to keep them alive in order to absorb their knowledge. The implication of this attempted bombing was far more distressing, since it suggested that the Americans instead were intent on killing them all. Hahn and Weizsäcker and Laue decided to remain with their families and accept their fate. But Heisenberg and Gerlach and one or two others literally ran for their lives, only to be tracked down by the Americans within ten days."

Bear's photocopies described Heisenberg's apprehension. Naturally none of the scientists were killed. Instead, as they'd originally anticipated, all were removed to the British intelligence facility at Farm Hall in England, where a lengthy debriefing established that Heisenberg's team was far behind the Manhattan Project.

"And did OSS realize this one-handed soldier was Martin?" I asked.

"Immediately."

"So that was late April, right? Before the court-martial hearing. And did they tell you about this attempted explosion?"

"Not one word. Bear in mind, Stewart, the A-bomb remained America's deepest secret. OSS wouldn't say anything concerning that or Alsos—not to Teedle, the trial judge advocate, or least of all me. But their mania to suppress all knowledge about anything to do with the bomb worked to our advantage. The prosecuting TJA on David's case was a lawyer named Meyer Brillstein, who seemed far angrier at your father than Teedle. One may suppose why. But early on—I'm sure at the insistence of OSS—Brillstein offered to dismiss the capital charge against your father in exchange for David's guilty plea and a mutual agreement not to seek discovery or offer proof of any of Martin's OSS-related activities, aside from those David had witnessed firsthand. Both your father and I saw this offer as the proverbial gift horse, since it meant that the court-martial panel would never know that David deliberately released a suspected Soviet spy. If they had, there's no telling how much longer your father's prison sentence would have been.

"Of course, we can see now that Martin knew much less than he thought he did. He had been briefed for Alsos in London in September 1944, with the idea that he would lead the team of American physicists into Germany. Although Martin necessarily was informed about the German atomic program, in that need-to-know world, no one told him about the Manhattan Project. He had no inkling that the U.S.A. was close to perfecting the bomb on its own, and thus no foresight that in less than four months, Pandora's box, as he called it, would be opened over Hiroshima and Nagasaki. Of course, Martin's superiors at OSS became even more determined to keep him in the dark once he began openly expressing doubts about whether a weapon like the Bomb should be in the hands of any nation. By October 1944 he'd passed one comment too many. London decided to pull him in. And Martin decided to defy them.

"At OSS, when they learned in April 1945 about Martin's attempt at Hechingen, the meaning was regarded as patent: the Soviets had recognized that they would not get to Hechingen first and had dispatched Martin to destroy the facility to prevent the scientists and their research from falling into American hands. Game, set, and match on the issue of whether Martin was a spy. Within the agency, a small faction led by Colonel Winters maintained that it was dubious to believe the Soviets would have supported such an improbable effort. According to the physicists at Hechingen, Martin had assembled a jerry-rigged device made of unexploded artillery shells, was traveling in an American jeep with a short-circuited ignition, had no visible collaborators, and was done in because he'd not yet mastered the striking of a match with one hand.

"When the autopsy turned up in June, showing that Martin had suffered a cruel death in Soviet custody, it renewed the controversy within OSS concerning Martin's loyalty. Winters began to theorize that Martin might have been on a solitary crusade to enforce his expressed belief that this new weapon ought to belong to no nation. As a result, the agency redoubled its search for the SS officers who'd taken custody of Martin at Hechingen. Early in July, two of them were located in their hometowns on opposite sides of Germany, both with their uniforms burned and lengthy cock-and-bull stories about how they'd never served in the German Army. The Americans quickly loosened their tongues, and the two officers told roughly parallel tales.

"The SS installation which had been guarding Hechingen had been delighted to lay hands on Martin, but not for his intelligence value. By mid-April, they knew the war was over. However, an American OSS officer figured to make a valuable bargaining chip in securing the SS men's freedom, once the Americans got there.

"For that reason, they claimed they did not interrogate Martin. Rations were short and at first when he refused food or water, they thought nothing of it. He claimed to have a severe intestinal infection and they took that at face value, because it made no sense to think the man would prefer starvation to being returned to his army."

"But Martin knew we'd hang him, right?" I asked.

"Certainly that's what your father had told him. At any rate, the SS abandoned Hechingen a day before the Americans entered, and carried Martin off with them. German forces were falling back from the Oder in hopes of breaking the Soviet siege of Berlin which had begun. The SS men followed, and once they were surrounded by the Soviets, decided to see if they could buy their freedom with the same prize they were going to offer the Americans: a U.S. OSS officer.

"Many historians have puzzled about why Stalin was willing to lose the thousands and thousands of troops he did in besieging and conquering Berlin without the assistance of the Allies, especially since he eventually honored his promise to share the city after it fell. Some speculate that the Soviets wanted the unfettered right to wreak vengeance on the Germans, which they surely took. One hundred thousand German women were raped during the Russians' first week in Berlin, Stewart." Bear took a second to wobble his old head over one more of the war's disgraceful facts.

"But the foremost theory today, bolstered by documents found in KGB archives, is that Stalin wanted to reach Berlin alone because the Kaiser Wilhelm Institute there held the only pieces of the German nuclear program that the Americans had not already laid hands on. Indeed, the Soviets discovered stores of uranium oxide at the Institute with which they ultimately revived their flagging atomic program.

"Once the SS officers made contact with the Soviets, and revealed the circumstances under which they had captured Martin, they found Soviet Army intelligence quite willing to let the SS men go in exchange for telling all they knew about Hechingen and turning over the American. Upon learning he was being handed off to the Soviets, Martin, who was now very weak, asked the Germans, as gentlemen, to shoot him. When they refused, he attempted to escape, despite his condition. He never got through the door. That was the last the SS officers saw of Martin. In the custody of the Soviets, sixty miles outside Berlin."

"And why would Martin prefer to die in German rather than Soviet hands?"

"One can only assume. Given what he'd said to your father, it's clear that Martin realized the Soviets would be desperate to learn whatever they could about American knowledge and suspicions concerning the A-bomb. For Martin, it would not be an appealing prospect to die while having every American secret he knew extracted by torture." Bear and I both were silenced for a second, contemplating that.

The other thing that puzzled me at that moment was how Bear had learned all this. Some, he answered, had come through Teedle. More of what he knew was the product of his lingering curiosity about my father's case. He had read the histories as they emerged over the years. But he had also stayed in touch with Colonel Winters, Martin's OSS commander, who eventually became a senior intelligence officer at the CIA.

"After Bryant retired from the Agency in the early 1970s, I saw him for a drink at the Mayflower. Winters told me he'd had an intriguing exchange a few years earlier with a Soviet counterpart who said he'd been involved in Martin's interrogation in Berlin, an event which the Russians officially deny to this day.

"Martin had refused to talk, of course. This Soviet officer acknowledged that they would have tortured him, but Martin was so weak from his hunger strike that they suspected his heart would stop. The only way they found to pry more than Martin's name, rank, and serial number from him was purely accidental, when they called in a doctor, who proposed putting Martin on intravenous. At that point, the Major agreed to answer questions, if they would allow him to die. They interrogated Martin for an entire afternoon. Two days later he was gone. And, of course, it turned out that every word Martin had spoken, while compelling, proved an absolute lie."

Bear stopped to wipe his lips. I thought this might have been too much talking for him, but he insisted on continuing. He'd worked too long to learn all of this not to pass it on.

"Over the years," he said, "I've thought often of Martin at the end. He was disfigured and in great pain from his burns, while the nation in whose service he had suffered these wounds was intent on hanging him. Yet he would not betray us. Instead, he accepted death as his only honorable option. Dying in the hands of the Soviets, ironically, ended up reestablishing his bona fides at OSS, especially once they'd heard from the SS officers. They now saw Martin as lost on a frolic and detour, but not a Soviet spy, one of many men who'd broken under the strain of war rather than a true turncoat determined to aid America's enemies."

I sat awhile digesting what Bear had told me. It was interesting as far as it went, but I had a hard time connecting any of this to my principal remaining curiosity, namely how my father had escaped his prison sentence. I said as much to Bear, who responded with his abbreviated off-kilter nod.

"I understand that it's far from obvious, but these events in fact paved the way for your father's release. OSS had learned of all of this—the autopsy and the SS account of Martin being handed over to the Soviets—by July 1945, only a few days before Truman, Stalin, Churchill, and Attlee met to discuss postwar arrangements at Potsdam. Robert Martin ended up figuring in those discussions, because our diplomats had realized they could use his fate to our advantage. It was an incendiary notion that our Soviet allies would hold an American OSS officer and, rather than repatriate him, interrogate him about our secrets and starve him to death. It showed that Stalin was not an ally at all, but was in fact preparing for war with us. The Russians continued to officially deny that Martin had died in their hands, but the medical evidence was clear and the circumstances of the Major's death kept the Soviets on the defensive. Furthermore, the proof of their desire to acquire the A-bomb pointed the way for the ultimate revelation of Potsdam, Truman's announcement to Stalin that America had in fact perfected the weapon. I don't want to exaggerate the importance of Martin's death, but it was a clear note in an

Allied chorus aimed at forcing Stalin to observe the agreements of Yalta about national boundaries and troop demarcations—and thus, ironically, in avoiding another war.

"However, in order to engage in a diplomatic dance in which the tune was our indignation over Martin's fate, it was essential that Robert Martin be portrayed as a great American hero, and certainly not a rogue agent. The inconvenient details about Martin's insubordination, the order for his arrest, and his many escapes from American hands had to be quickly blotted from community memory, which necessarily meant that the court-martial of David Dubin was required to swiftly become a historical nonevent.

"On July 26, 1945, I was called to Third Army Headquarters by Teedle, who informed me that the case was being dropped. He was forthcoming with the little he knew, but the General himself had been given only spare details. He was, however, all for anything that provided an advantage versus the Soviets. And from his perspective, the case against your father was far less meaningful now that OSS was saying that Martin had not been working for the Russians. Teedle was, frankly, quite chagrined by the about-face, and seemed to feel he'd been seriously misled.

"In court, I had learned never to question a favorable ruling. I thanked Teedle heartily and prepared to leave with the papers recalling the charges in my hand, but Teedle would not dismiss me. Instead, he came around his desk and bore down on me.

"'Why the hell did he do this, Leach?' he asked, referring to your father. There was a tremendous animal ferocity in Teedle. He was not an enormous man, but when the General became intent, it was frightening because you felt he was on the verge of assault. It made for an uncomfortable moment when I had to outline the bounds of lawyer-client confidentiality. But it turned out the General had a theory.

"'I think Dubin was convinced Martin was not a Soviet spy, and was afraid that between OSS and me, the man would hang for it anyway. Is that close?'

"I knew I wasn't leaving without telling the General something, and what he had posited was true, as far as it went. I thought I'd satisfy him by saying his guess was accurate, but instead he grew solemn.

"'I've long suspected this whole damn thing with Dubin was my fault,' he said. He was a very sad man, Roland Teedle, fierce and thoughtful, but morose at the core and full of a sense of his own short-comings, which he felt had led him to eagerly accept a false view of Martin. I don't know if you realize this, Stewart, but after the war Teedle went on to get a degree in theology and achieved quite a bit of renown in those circles. He published several books. His main theory, as much as I understand these things, was that faith was the point of existence, even while sin was life's overwhelming reality. Society's goal was to lower the barriers to faith, since faith was all that could redeem us. Very complex. As a warrior theologian, Teedle even attracted two biographers after his death. One book was completely unsparing—alcoholism, wife-beating, bar fights into his seventies, but not a whiff of the kind of scandal your father had heard about from Billy Bonner. I wouldn't be surprised if you checked your father's bookshelves and found one or two of Teedle's works there." In fact, when I looked, every book written by or about Teedle was in Dad's library, each, from the feel of the pages, well-read.

"There was not much I could say to Teedle," Bear said, "when he claimed the whole episode was his fault. It was consummately Teedle. The willingness to accept responsibility was admirable, while the egotism that made him think he was the motive force for everything that had occurred was ironic, at best. But on the other hand, the fundamental quarrel between your father and Teedle had always been about Martin's core intentions, whether Martin, in a few words, was a good man or a bad one. In the end, the General seemed willing to grant the point to your father, and with that finally let me go to bring this news to my client."

"Who was delighted, I assume?" I asked.

"Very much so. There'd been so much intense scurrying about once the autopsy had turned up that we'd known some change was in the wind, but neither your father nor I ever dared to hope the entire case would be revoked. David responded appropriately. He jumped to his feet and pumped my hand, he read the discharge paper for himself several times, and once he realized that his house arrest was over, he insisted on buying me a drink. I expected him to ask about his manuscript, which I had yet to return, but he never did. Perhaps, at some level, he was willing to see me do what I'd urged, namely preserve it for his children. That, at least, is the excuse I have given myself, Stewart, in sharing all of this with you.

"Your father enjoyed the summer air on the way over to the café, but by the time two glasses of champagne were placed before us he had grown quite somber. I was sure it was remorse for the many losses he'd suffered in chasing Martin, but that was not what preoccupied him at the moment.

"'I drink to you, Bear,' he said, 'and you should drink to me. Wish me luck.'

"Naturally, I did, but he let me know I had missed his point.

"'I must go to Balingen,' he said, 'to see how my wife reacts when I tell her I am free to be her husband.'"

33. ORDINARY HEROES

If you asked my mother, as I did now and then during my childhood, she would describe my father as the love of her life, the hero who, like Orpheus, had retrieved her from Hades and whose passion brought her back to the realm of the living. That was her story, as they say, and she was sticking to it. And I think, at heart, it was true. Despite the doubts my father expressed to Leach when he was freed, my mother remained loyal to him always, and he to her. There were the usual daily frictions, but my parents treated each other with appreciation and kindness. Whatever the other improvisations in their histories, the intensity of their bond remains an enduring reality for me. It was like the mystical forces that unite atoms and was the very center of the household in which I was raised. They always had each other.

My inch-by-inch discovery of the wartime travails of young David Dubin, so resolute, high-minded, and frequently unwise, eventually made some of my father's shortcomings as a parent easier to bear. Tenderness came hard to Dad, like so many other men in his generation, but I understand now that, very simply, he'd exhausted his capacity for daring in Europe. He'd bet everything on my mother and, having won, never put all his chips down anywhere else. The terror of the battlefield, the cruelty he'd witnessed, and the damage to his proudest beliefs were a weight always holding him a step back from life. Yet I grant him the one grace we can ask as humans: he had done his very best.

But the revelation of my mother's identity shook me to the core. How could she have done this? How could she have deceived my sister and me about our heritage? How could she have denied her own past? I barely slept for weeks. The world, as I knew it, seemed as dramatically changed as if I'd found out I was the offspring of an amphibian.

I had always accepted that there was an element of mild deceit in my mother's character. She was essentially a straightforward person, but she could lie like a champ when required. I was quite a bit older when I realized my parakeet, whose cage I had constantly failed to clean, did not simply fly away when I was seven. And she was very good at sticking up for utter implausibilities that she thought were good for us—like the alleged bout of childhood pneumonia she'd contracted because she had gone outside without a jacket.

But the autobiography she'd passed off was no little white lie, especially laying claim to the hallowed status of a survivor. How could she have done this? The words were buzzing through my mind at unexpected moments for months.

But time slowly began to leach away my anger. All parents keep secrets from their children. I eventually realized that neither she nor my father could have anticipated the abiding reverence the Jewish community ended up paying to those who had suffered in their names. True, that purported legacy allowed my mother at times to exert considerable emotional leverage over my sister and me, as well as my father's family, but she explicitly rejected any effort to celebrate her for what she had supposedly endured, always insisting without elaboration that she had been far, far luckier than most.

More important, I accept now that my parents really had no choice. They had started down this road before the revelations of Martin's death in Soviet hands and were stuck with it when Dad was released. Admitting they'd falsified Gita's identity would have been foolhardy; he'd risk renewed prosecution, and she, in all likelihood, would never have been admitted to the U.S. Once here, the legal perils remained real, both for him, as a licensed attorney, and for her. Ironically, every time our government pounced on a former Nazi and tossed him out of the country for lying his way in, I'm sure their fears were reinforced. Certainly no one would choose to reveal a secret so dangerous to loose-tongued creatures like small children. The years passed. And their joint refusal to speak about the war stiffened their resolve not to tell Sarah or me. The anguish and disorientation I felt when I discovered the truth was, oddly, testimony to the fact that they had been sparing us pain.

Nor do I think they made anything easier for themselves. Everyone who has so much as nodded toward therapy knows that the turmoil of the past is never wholly forgotten. Unresolved, it seeps through even the strongest foundation. My mother was warm, strong, and courageous. She was a venerated champion of the needy, who could count hundreds of persons rescued through the Haven, the relief agency she ran. But I never had the illusion she was happy. As the past receded, she grew more brittle and dwelled closer to her anger. Some of that fury, I think now, might have been easier to set aside if she'd been free to acknowledge the shame of being the town bastard, instead of pretending to come from a tragic but loving Jewish family. Yet my parents had taken to heart the lesson of Orpheus and could return to the world of light only by never looking back.

I do not judge. I still cannot fathom enduring or witnessing what they and millions of others had. My mother referred so frequently to the "darkest time humanity has ever known" that the phrase lost any power for me—she might as well have been saying, "Things go better with Coke." But my excavations finally brought me nose to nose with the staggering truth she had been trying to impart. More human beings were killed in Europe from 1937 to 1945 than in any epoch before or since. Yes, six million Jews. And also twenty million Russians. Another three million Poles. A million and a quarter in Yugoslavia. Three hundred and fifty thousand Brits. Two hundred thousand Americans. And, may a merciful God remember them, too, more than six million Germans. Forty million people in all. Mom had called it right. Not merely dark. Black.

In June 2004, my sister made her intended trip home to look in on Mom, who was declining. Caged by my own lies, I had debated for months what I would tell Sarah. By rights, our parents' story was as much hers as mine. I just didn't think I'd get much credit for sharing it. Still, the day she was leaving, I buttoned up my courage and gave her a copy of Dad's typescript, and a handwritten summary of what Leach had added. She read that letter in my presence and, despite the labored apology it contained, responded in the spirit of our era.

"I'm going to sue you," my sister said.

"And what good will that do?"

"Hire a lawyer, Stewart."

I did, my high-school pal Hobie Tuttle, but no papers were served. Sarah called two weeks later. She was still boiling—I could literally hear her panting in the phone—yet she admitted that she'd been moved reading Dad's account.

"But the rest of it, Stewart? About Mom being this other woman? You're making it up. The way you've always made things up. Reality has never been good enough for you. Dad didn't write one word saying that."

I reasoned with her for just a moment. Leave Leach aside, whom she dismissed as an addlepated ninety-six-year-old. Why else would Dad have let Martin go? What other woman could Dad have married, given the fact that Teedle had him in custody a day or two after freeing Robert Martin? By then, I'd sorted through dozens of Gideon Bidwell's two-by-twos, copies of photos which Dad had kept after sending everything else to Biddy's family. I found one showing my father in uniform, conversing with a woman who is indubitably my mother. They stand in a courtyard in front of a small château constructed around a medieval turret, a "little castle" if ever there was one. Sarah had a duplicate of the picture, but she claimed it might have been taken at another time and place.

"Believe what you want," I said.

"I will," she answered. "I will. But here's my bottom line. Leave Mom in peace. If you show her one page of this, I'll never speak to you again. And if you so much as talk to anyone else about this while she's alive, I swear to God, I really will sue you."

Mom, by then, was suffering. Within a year of my father's death, in an eerie reprise, she began to develop symptoms of most of the diseases that had killed him. There was a spot on her lung and serious vessel damage around her heart. The body contains its own brutal mysteries. How could an organic illness be aggravated, as it clearly was, by Dad's absence? The surgeons took a lobe from her left lung. Cancer showed up on the scans again within two months. We'd been down this path with my father. She was brave and philosophical—as he had been. But her time was dwindling. She had good days and bad. But having watched Dad slide over the cliff, I knew that if I was ever going to say anything to her, it had better be soon.

I checked on her every day, bringing groceries and other necessities. She resisted a caretaker, but we had someone coming in for a few hours each afternoon. One morning, when Mom and I were alone in the kitchen, having our usual daily discussion, which wandered between family gossip and global affairs, I brought up my book about my father.

"I've decided to put it aside for a while," I told her.

She was next to the white stove, where she'd been making tea, and faced me slowly.

"Oh, yes?"

"I think I've gotten what I wanted to. Maybe I'll go back to it some-day. But I'm doing a lot of freelance stuff now and I don't really have time to get to the end."

"This, I think, is wise, Stewart."

"Probably so. There's just one thing I'm curious about. You may not remember."

She was already shaking her gray curls, the same stark refusal to be quizzed I'd dealt with for nearly two years now.

"Well, just listen, Mom. This might be something you want to know."

Sighing, she seated herself at the old oak kitchen table, where the his-tory of our family was written in the stains and scratches. She was shrink-ing away inside her skin, a small person now reduced to the minuscule. I recited the one paragraph my sister, after months of my begging, had given me clearance to utter, my prepared statement as it were.

"There was a woman Dad knew," I said, "named Gita Lodz. She was amazing, Mom. Brilliant, beautiful, a commando who worked under-ground with the OSS. She'd been orphaned in Poland and made her way to Marseilles. She was like Wonder Woman. She was ten times braver than most of the soldiers who won medals. I think she was prob-ably the most remarkable person I learned about."

Mom peered across the table, the same obsidian eyes my father of-ten described.

"Yes?" she asked. "What is your question?"

"I just wondered if Dad ever talked about her?"

"She must have been someone he knew before he came to Balingen. I never heard her name from him once we were together there."

Disowning herself, she remained utterly serene, the same would-be Bernhardt who had saved Martin a hundred times. But the truth, as I'd recognized, was that the life she'd claimed was the life she'd lived. Who are we, she'd once asked, but the stories we tell about ourselves and believe? She had been Gilda Dubin now since 1945, nearly sixty years, far longer than she had been Gita Lodz, the firebrand and ingénue who'd cast her spell over my father. Gita, like millions of others, had been incinerated in Europe. As Mrs. David Dubin, she had raised me and loved me. She'd been to hundreds of Holocaust remembrances and synagogue services, had worked tirelessly at the Haven to aid Jews in need, most of them survivors or Russian immigrants. Her identity was assumed as a matter of necessity, but she was loyal to it, just as she had been to my father.

True to what Sarah and I had resolved in advance, following that brief excursion I let the subject go. I'd said what I meant to. I checked her pill counter to be certain she'd taken her medications, and prepared to leave. As usual, she asked me about Nona, whose past-tense status Mom refused to accept, even though I'd begun seeing someone else.

When I moved toward the door, she spoke up behind me again.

"Stewart," my mother said. "You know Emma Lazar?"

"Naturally, Ma." Emma was my mother's closest friend, a survivor of Dachau.

"Emma remembers every day. Every day she recounts something. She walks down the street, she is remembering—someone who was raped by a guard, a man who died from eating a scrap of rotten meat he'd found, the moment she last touched her father's hand as they were pulled apart. This is what she lives. She must, of course. I do not blame her. But that is a crippled life. To go no farther. That is the brutal scar the Nazis laid upon her.

"When I came here, I promised myself a new life. A life that would not look back. This is life." She touched the wood of the table and then reached for a perfect orange atop the mounded fruit bowl that was always there. "Right now. This is life. You know the philosophers? The present never stops. There is only the present. You cheat life to live in the past. Isn't that so?"

"Of course."

"The past is beyond change. Good or bad. I am your mother, Stewart. That is the present and the truth. And your father was your father. That, too, is the truth. Whom he knew, or didn't know, I never dwelled upon. He saved me. He chose to love me when that was the bravest possible choice. From there, we both vowed to go forward. For me he was a hero."

"To me, too, Mom. More today than ever. I see him as a hero. But you were a hero, too, Ma. An amazing hero. You are both my heroes. I just want you to know that."

When the word 'hero' was applied to my mother as a camp survivor, she rigidly refused to hear it, citing the greater bravery of millions. And she rejected the title again today.

"I knew people, Stewart, who aspired to be heroes, to live beyond human limits because they found routine life a misery, and who were therefore doomed to disappointment. But I am an ordinary person, Stewart, who was fortunate enough to realize she wanted an ordinary life. Your father, too. In unusual circumstances, we did what we had to in order to preserve our chances to return and live normally. We all have much more courage than is commonly imagined. Every day, Stewart, as I get older, I marvel at how much bravery it takes to go on, to bear the blows existence so often delivers. I bore mine and was lucky enough to survive to have the ordinary life I desired with your father and Sarah and you, a life that means far more to me than anything that went before. Does that," she asked, in a way that made me think she actually expected an answer, "does that make me a hero?"

They are both gone now. To quote a favorite author, "Death deepens the wonder."

As I have acknowledged, over many months I edited, reshaped, and occasionally rewrote many of the passages in Dad's account for the sake of publication. At this stage, with the manuscript having been put aside while I waited for my mother to make her rocky passage from this world, I frequently cannot remember whose lines are whose when I turn the pages.

I could go back to my father's original manuscript to sort that out, but, frankly, I don't care to. I've done my best. This is as real as I can make my parents, as fully as I can imagine them, as honest as I can stand to be with others, or myself. There are inevitably limits. When our parents talk about their lives, they relay what they think is best, for their sake or ours. And as their children, we hear what we want, believe what we can, and, as time lengthens, pry and judge and question as our needs demand. We understand them in that light. And when we tell our parents' tales to the world, or even to ourselves, the story is always our own.

A NOTE ON SOURCES

This book is a work of imagination, inspired by the historical record, but seldom fully faithful to it. Although I began from reported events, the action throughout the novel is my embroidery, undertaken by characters who, except for the largest historical figures, are entirely fictitious.

My principal imaginative starting point was stories about World War II, which I heard from my father when I was a boy, before he put away those experiences and retreated into silence. My dad, Dr. David D. Turow, trod much of David Dubin's path through Europe as commanding officer of the 413th Medical Collecting Company, which was attached to the Third Army after October 1944. From my father, who was a field surgeon at the Army hospital established in the Sisters of Notre Dame convent at Bastogne, I heard many tales that stayed with me: about that loose-sphinctered parachute jump into Bastogne; being taken captive by German troops who needlessly executed his driver; the horror experienced by the initial medical teams to enter Dachau and Bergen-Belsen.

My father's stories are grossly transmogrified in *Ordinary Heroes*; they provided only a point of departure. David Dubin is in no way a portrait of my dad. For those who might wonder, my mother, Rita Pastron Turow, was a schoolteacher in Chicago during World War II. I owe profound thanks to her for lending me my father's files and photographs and letters (from which I borrowed several lines appearing in the letters in the novel), since they inevitably revealed many things a child would never otherwise know, including the depth of Dad's devotion to my mother as a young husband. To Peggy Davis, who added the photos and memories of her father, Technical Sergeant Donald Nutt, my dad's clerk, I owe special thanks.

After a television appearance in which I said that my next novel would concern World War II, Mr. Robert Freeman of Tequesta, Florida, contacted me at the urging of his wife, Julie Freeman, to offer me free use of a variety of materials he had retained relating to his cousin Carl Cohen, an infantryman who was found starved to death in a Paris hotel room at the war's end. I am grateful to Mr. and Mrs. Freeman, and to Carl Cohen's sister, Dottie Bernstein of Bennington, Vermont, for sharing these materials with me, even though I have contributed nothing to solving the mystery of how Cohen fell into Nazi hands, or why his death was misreported by comrades who said they saw him die on the battlefield.

On slender historical footings like these, the novel was then imagined. All of Robert Martin's activities, for example, are invented, although they occasionally hark back to reported operations of the OSS. There was no ammunition dump at La Saline Royale, which is actually situated a few miles from the site I describe. A team of U.S. soldiers made unsuccessful efforts around December 22, 1944, to rescue a stranded ammunition train outside Bastogne, but not in the precise manner set forth in the novel. Heisenberg did run from Hechingen, but not because anyone had attempted to blow up the secret location of the Kaiser Wilhelm Institute on Haigerlocherstrasse. FDR's death was announced near midnight overseas, not in the afternoon of April 12, 1945. Und so weiter. A concentration camp was situated at Balingen, but it was much smaller and not as heartless as what I have portrayed, which is drawn instead from accounts of Bergen-Belsen.

With all of that said, I have tried to be mindful of the larger historical record, especially the chronology of the war, and the movement of forces, and to accurately reflect the individual experiences of American soldiers. A bibliography of the sources I consulted is posted at www.ScottTurow.com.

My research was enormously aided by several persons whom I must thank. Colonel Robert Gonzales, U.S. Army, Ret., a former Army JAG officer now employed at Fort Sam Houston, Texas, shared with me the manuscript of his excellent history of the JAG Department during World War II, which incorporates interviews of numerous JAG Department members of that period. I reached Colonel Gonzales at the end of a lengthy bucket brigade of helpful hands that began with Carolyn Alison, Public Affairs Officer for the Office of the Judge Advocate General of the Department of the Navy. With the grace of her boss, Rear Admiral Michael F. Lohr, the Navy's Judge Advocate General, Ms. Alison put me in contact with a number of able Army historians, starting with Colonel William R. Hagan, U.S. Army, Ret., another former Army JAG Corps member, who is now a civilian employee at Camp Shelby in Mississippi and who was of continuing aid. Bill Hagan went far out of his way to acquaint me with a number of his colleagues, to whom I am indebted, including Mitch Yockelson of the National Archives and Records Administration. Dan Lavering, the Librarian at the Army's JAG School Library in Charlottesville, Virginia, was particularly generous in providing me with materials, including copies of The Judge Advocate Journal, the JAG Department's newsletter during World War II, and the 1943 revision of A Manual for Courts-Martial, U.S. Army.

Mary B. Dennis, Deputy Clerk of Court for the Army Judiciary, responded to my requests to obtain a court-martial record as an exemplar. Alan Kramer, Director at the Washington National Records Center at Suitland, Maryland, was a kind host and guide when I visited. I also must acknowledge research assistance from my friends at the Glencoe (Illinois) Public Library and the Western New England College of Law. Great thanks to Henri Rogister and Roger Marquet of the Center of Research and Information on the Battle of the Bulge (CRIBA) for responding to my questions. And to Michel Baert, formerly of the Belgian Tourist Office, who guided me on a trip in 2004 along David Dubin's route, I am especially grateful. He was both remarkably well informed and a congenial traveling companion.

Several veterans of the European campaign offered comments on the initial drafts of this novel that kept me from making even more mistakes: my law partner Martin Rosen of New York; Sam L. Resnick of Bayside, New York, President of the 100th Infantry Division Association; and Harold Tauss of Wilmette, Illinois. Thanks, too, to Bill Rooney and the other members of the World War II Round Table, as well as the librarians at the Wilmette Public Library.

I had incisive literary comments from several early readers: Rachel Turow, Jim McManus, Howard Rigsby, Leigh Bienen, Jack Fuller. Dr. Carl Boyar answered medical questions, as he has often before. My assistants, Kathy Conway, Margaret Figueroa, and Ellie Lucas, kept me on my feet, with Kathy making a number of special contributions, ranging from proofreading to compiling the posted bibliography. My agent at CAA, Bob Bookman; my law partner Julius Lewis; Violaine Huisman; and my French publisher, Isabelle Laffont, each contributed many corrections to my ersatz French, for which I'm sure I still owe apologies to French speakers around the world. Thanks to Sabine Ibach for correcting the tattered remains of my high school German. Robert Marcus was chief consultant on Things Jewish. Eve Turow was a valued sounding board about many questions connected to the book's presentation. And of course the edifice stands only with my three pillars—my editor, Jonathan Galassi; my agent, Gail Hochman; and, at the center, my wife, Annette.

I will not even begin the mea culpas for the errors I must have made, notwithstanding my substantial efforts to avoid them. I hope none of these mistakes are taken to diminish my admiration for the men and women who fought that horrible and necessary war. I can only paraphrase the remark of my old mentor, Tillie Olsen, which is quoted at the novel's end: Time deepens the wonder.

S.T.